Shades of Blue

Black & Blue #1

Shades of Blue (Black & Blue #1)
By
Melyssa Winchester

Copyright © 2016 Melyssa Winchester

This is a work of fiction. Names; characters; places and incidents are the products of the author's imagination or are used fictitiously. Any resemblance to actual events, locales or persons living or dead is entirely coincidental.

Cover Image Copyright © Suns27 @ Dreamstime
Cover Image Design by Joey Winchester

To the woman that inspired Emery and has done nothing but treat me like her Avery from the moment I met her. This one's for you, darlin'. Mordiase Forever.

"I love her and that is the beginning and end of everything."
– F. Scott Fitzgerald

Prologue

Avery

Avery,

This is a hard letter for me to write. I must have written it a dozen times already and each time, I stop and discard it before I have the chance to finish and send it.

This should have come a long time ago and for that, I'm sorry. I fear that I have waited too long, but it's my hope that as you read, you'll forgive me for the timing.

My name is Rebecca Davis...and I am your mother.

I'm not sure how much Richard has told you about me—if anything at all, but the time has come for you to know the truth.

Twenty-five years ago, you were taken from me. I will not speak of everything that happened in a letter as I believe it would be much better handled in person, but just know that I did not give you away and I most definitely didn't turn my back on you.

I've spent the last twenty-five years searching for you around every corner, hoping to find the smile that mirrors my Emery's so perfectly, but it has never materialized. After years of searching on my own, I finally employed someone much more qualified to help. Which is how I am about to sit and write you this letter.

I'm sending it now because the truth of the matter is, I don't know how much time I have left, and I need to make right all that has gone wrong.

Now that I've finally been able to locate you, I can't let things continue on the way they have.

You have a twin sister. I'm not sure if your father ever told you that, but she's here with me and she knows everything. When we were given your location, we sat down and debated what the right move would be. Whether to keep letting you live your life the way you have been or to tell you the truth.

We are both in agreement that this is the right thing to do, but more than that, we also believe that before any more time has the chance to pass, we put an end to the distance that the last twenty-five years has created and we all meet.

It's up to you, of course, as I would never dream of taking your choice away, but Avery, I miss you. I've missed you every minute of every day for the past twenty-five years. I want nothing more than to spend what's left of my time surrounded by you. Loving you while you're near instead of just settling for doing it from afar. Your sister Emery wants and feels the same.

All of this must be a lot to take in, so please take as long as you need responding, but there is one thing that I want you to remember once you close this letter and put it away.

I have loved you from the moment I first heard your heart beat inside of me and it hasn't lessened at all in our time apart. My final request is just to see you one more time, so I can leave this world knowing both of my daughters are okay.

You will find all of my contact information, as well as Emery's attached. Whether you choose to speak with us, meet with us, or walk away from this entirely; at the very least you have it. I hope that once this has had a chance to sink in, I'll be hearing from you, but if not, never forget.

I love you.
Mom

✳✳✳✳✳

When I got up this morning, making my coffee to go, because as usual, I ignored my alarm for far too long, the last thing I expected to be met with the minute I sat down at my desk was this letter.

I'm the lifestyles editor at the City Voice, so receiving mail every morning is standard procedure. It's the days where there's nothing waiting for me that are most surprising. A lot of the time, they're letters to the editor; or pieces that I need to go over, but this morning, while I had plenty of the other mail I'm used to, I also had this.

Rebecca Davis.

It seems that even after my dad did as she said and took off, she'd never thought to change her last name since it mirrors my own. It's seeing my last name written beside her first that first leads me to believe in the words I'm reading.

Where I may have thrown this letter away and thought of it as some kind of cruel joke before, I can't this time.

My father, *the* Richard Davis spoken of in the letter, was a well-known and respected entertainment lawyer before his sudden passing from a stroke two years ago. One so respected that when it came time to bury him, everyone from famous actors to musicians turned out in support. So while anyone could have pulled his name from the tabloids or even from the news and written this letter easily, especially with him no longer here to dispute it, there are just too many other details within it that make what she's claiming all too real.

For instance, the experiences I've had over the years that I haven't been able to make sense of. Sensations, I guess you could say. Things I can't explain.

I can be driving home from work or even to an assignment and out of nowhere, I'll feel a pain in my chest or tears will just fall from my eyes. No rhyme or reason for them.

For a while I thought I was losing my mind, but when that proved untrue, I came to recognize the signs and adapted until they became second nature.

Now, though. Now I have an explanation.

It's because I'm a twin.

The pain in my chest, the unexplained tears, and the up and down of my mood at the most unexpected times. It all happened because out there in the world somewhere is another me.

There's another girl, Emery; that looks just like me.

So as much as I want to deny everything about this letter, I know that I can't. It's all true.

Every single word of it.

I've been home for well over an hour now. I've read the letter a total of six times throughout the day, but no matter how many times I do it, nothing ever changes. I should feel more put out by this. Angry even that this woman seems to want to bring my father's name through the dirt, but I don't.

There's no confusion, no upset, no real show of anything that one would expect when getting a letter like this.

Rebecca Davis might not realize this, but in writing the way she did, finally able to track me down after all of these years of us being apart, she's given me something that after my father passed, I never thought I would experience again firsthand until I settled down and created one of my own.

A family.

The right thing to do here may be sitting down and really thinking this through before jumping the gun, but that's not what I'm going to do.

What's right for everyone else, well, it's not for me.

Like she said in the letter, it's been too long.

I'm sure she would be content with a phone call, or even an email if Emery is staying with her, but I don't want to do things that impersonally.

No. If I'm going to respond to this letter, I've got to do it in the way that means the most. I need to give this woman—my mother—her final request. Looking over the address on the accompanying page, what I've got to do now has never been so clear.

I need to go to Delaware and meet my mom and twin sister.

Rebecca was right.

Twenty-five years is long enough.

It's time for a family reunion.

Chapter One

Emery

Standing in the mirror and taking in my reflection, everything just seems wrong. I've always looked this way. Nothing's really changed, but the way I've always been, how I look at myself now, there's nothing right about it.

And I know what's causing me to act like this.

It's because Avery's on her way here.

I'm going to meet my sister for the first time since our father stole her from us when we were babies.

My *twin* sister.

The girl my mother has talked about every year since I was old enough to talk back. We're identical twins, which means the way I look, in a few hours is going to be reflected back at me. So in picking myself apart, I'm also managing to imply that she's wrong too.

Stop it Em. She's just a girl.

I've been doing this since my mom got word earlier that Avery would be making the trip down. Finding fault in myself. Worried that when she does get here, I won't be what she's expecting and she'll leave us in her rearview once we've all met.

I guess that's what happens when your life gets turned upside down. Everything becomes so displaced you don't know which end is up.

Turning my back on the mirror, determined not to let my mind run away from me, I exit the bathroom and begin the trek down the stairs. After making it about halfway down, I hear the door open, signaling someone's arrival. My breath catches until I realize there's no way it could be Avery. She only let my mom know a few hours ago. A plane, not to mention the drive, is going to take way longer than that from where she's coming from.

Canada.

All this time my sister has been living in one of the largest cities with absolutely no knowledge about her family a whole country away.

What was life like for her growing up in the city? I've always wondered what living in one as big as Toronto would be like, considering the slower pace here in Brandywine. Not enough to travel and find out, though. This place and the familiarity that comes with it not something I'm chomping at the bit to give up.

As I finally hit the floor, I'm met by the smiling face of the one person that has no issue walking in and making himself at home.

Michael Wallace.

The boy that literally lives next door. Also the one who my mom has been telling me for years would one day give her beautiful looking grandbabies.

The guy otherwise known as my best friend.

"I thought you'd be upstairs, so I let myself in. Hope that's alright."

Bridging the gap between us, I wrap my arms around him and as he responds, bringing my body even closer into his, I sigh contentedly. It doesn't matter how much time passes. Being held by him always manages to keep me grounded, which with everything that's happened since my mother reached out to Avery, I need.

"Of course it's okay. You know you've got full reign of the house. I'm just glad it was you. For a second when I heard the lock, I thought it might have been her."

Mike's known about Avery almost as long as I have. That's how close we are. When you live where we do, the friends you have, you make them early on, and you've got them forever. If there's anyone that understands what this whole thing is doing to me, it's him.

"You're really freaked about this, huh?" he asks, releasing me from his embrace.

"You know me. I don't usually get worked up about anything, but a twin? I know it's probably worse for her because at least I knew about her all these years, but there's no way this wouldn't freak someone out."

He smiles knowingly and motions to the stairs. "You up there staring a hole in the mirror again?"

I blush as he lays his hand softly across mine. "You look great, ya know? It's not like staring a hole in the mirror is gonna change the fact that you're twins. She's going to get here, look just like you, and the reunion is going to be great."

Sighing, hating that my insecurities are being exposed, I stare down at my fingers and try not to let my fears get the better of me. Even with as well as Mike knows me, I don't make a habit of putting the way I feel out there. Especially when it's over something like this. All this is doing is making me feel more awkward.

"I get that she's my identical twin, but what if she's rich or something? She could come here, see the way we live, and think we're just backwoods hicks. How does someone prepare for what's about to happen?"

"They don't. I really don't think there is a way to be prepared for this kind of thing, Em. You just suck it up and get it over with the same way you've always done. If it helps, I got the entire day off so I can be here with you."

Something about the sincerity in his voice, how willing he is to see me through this, touches me and before I know it, I feel the lone tear sliding down my cheek and his hand coming up in an effort to stop it.

"Is it wrong that there's a part of me that wants her to come here, think we're no good and leave us behind?"

"No." he answers easily. "It's a natural response to an unbelievable situation. Rebecca never hid her existence from you, but the same can't be said for your father. She could come here, want nothing to do with either of you, and leave or it could go the opposite way. She could get here, meet you and realize that she needs you just as much as you need her. We'll never know until it happens. When is this supposed to happen by the way?"

"A few hours according to the call Mom got earlier."

"Well, let's find something to do for the next few hours then. You need to take your mind off this, otherwise you're gonna be a mess when she does get here. We can worry about the meeting and exactly what's gonna happen when it actually does happen. How does that sound?"

Unable to hide my smile, I beam it brightly at him. This is exactly why I love that Mike is the one here. He knows exactly what I need.

"What do you got in mind?"

Avery

When I stepped off the plane an hour ago, I couldn't believe my luck.

Making the plan to come here, I didn't know what to expect, but breathing in the fresh air, the type that living in Toronto doesn't afford very often, was like a dream come true.

I didn't think it could get any better, but as I picked up my rental car and started the hour long drive from the airport, that's exactly what it did.

This was more than just coming into a different country.

It was like experiencing another planet all together.

The way the breeze felt as it made its way through the half open window was amazing, not to mention relaxing. There was no rush to get anywhere. No crazy people speeding from one point to the next and not paying attention to what was going on around them. The calm and slow way the world moved made me thankful I left Toronto behind.

Casting a look at the gas gauge and realizing that sooner rather than later I was going to have to stop and fill up, I keep my eyes peeled for a sign. Using it as my new excuse not to focus on the reason I'm even taking the drive to begin with.

The letter sitting folded underneath my purse in the passenger seat doing as it did when I came across it days ago. Calling to me.

Reminding me of a secret kept by who I thought at the time was the only parent I had. How long it was kept, and all of the awful things I had heard over the years about the woman that wrote it. But more than all of that, the other person involved. The twin sister I didn't even know existed.

Emery.

So wrapped up in thoughts of her and what her life had been like without me in it; I almost miss the turn off leading to the station. Catching the sign partially hidden in the trees at the last second before the turn off hits.

Pulling off and then into the station, I pull the car up but instead of stepping out right away, I give into the overflow of thoughts that have been accompanying me the entire ride. Words from the letter that stand out more than the initial revelation and based on the lack of information actually given within it, leave me with more questions than anything else that was said.

I have loved you from the moment I first heard your heart beat inside of me and it hasn't lessened in our time apart. My final request is just to see you one more time, so I can leave this world knowing both of my daughters are okay.

Rebecca isn't well and based on her own words about wanting to make things right before she passes, whatever is going on, is deadly. But how bad is it? Does she have days? A week or two? Hours? Is coming here and doing this, even knowing it's what I want and the right thing to do, only going to end in heartbreak later?

Am I going to get her only to lose her?

Focusing on what I'm here to do, I shove the questions down and finally get out of the car. Turning my attention to the pump, I focus on the climbing numbers as they continue to grow, until the sound of gravel crunching and flying from behind me pulls my attention away.

Another vehicle that with as dead as the road had been when I turned off the highway onto it, I'm actually surprised to see. Also one that based on the way they'd swerved and sped in, has the miniature rocks flying everywhere before they finally pull to a stop and the dust settles.

What a car like that, a newer model Porsche no less, is doing in a small town like this is beyond me, but it definitely doesn't fit in with the picture I've been shown of Delaware since I stepped off the plane.

Eyes locked on the car as the driver cuts the ignition, I watch as two guys step out and studying them as they both seem to stop and take in everything around them, I can't help smiling.

Looks like I'm not the only one that's out of sorts in a place like this.

"Holy shit, Brady! Looks like there are actual people in this town after all."

Using the chance once the driver turns to the person I can only assume is Brady, I take him in. His dark brown hair catching my attention first. The length of it reminding me of a lot of the indie rockers I interviewed when I first started writing for the magazine. Only after I've had my fill of that do I let my eyes fall next to the sheer size of his body.

The way the sharp and defined muscles in his arms threaten the very fabric they're contained by. The shirt he's wearing clinging to every contour, almost as though it had been sculpted for him alone.

God, he's beautiful. I think before snapping my eyes back up to his face when I hear the sound of boots on the gravel.

Moving my eyes to the guy known as Brady, the one that after leaving me to ogle his friend finally steps away from the car, I do the same to him. Brady seeming to be the drivers complete opposite in every way.

Where the taller guys' hair had been brown, Brady's is dusty blonde, cropped short and framed to his face. His body, muscular for certain, but smaller than his friends. It's his eyes that capture and hold me though.

Crystal blue. Almost see through.

Whoever these guys are, it's obvious they mean business.

Before I can turn back to the pump, reminded of the rising numbers and my limited cash flow, Brady steps toward me, immediately making the fine hairs on the back of my neck rise.

I'm from the city. A city where if you met two strangers the way I am now, you'd be smart to be wary of them. Especially with how much bigger they are in size. I get that this isn't Toronto, but two against one still isn't great odds.

These two may look harmless but the reality is, they could be anything but. A thought process that doesn't seem to do me a lick of good as my heart starts to pick up in speed.

All thoughts of my earlier perusal of them out the window and fear replacing it.

Avery, chill. They're just two random guys.

What might have been a fantastic pep talk if Brady didn't choose that exact moment to take yet another step in my direction.

"Don't worry, darlin'. We're not gonna hurt you. We just stopped for gas, since speed freak over there," he pauses, nodding toward the other man with a smirk. "Decided to waste all of ours doing tricks in his new ride."

Focusing on the accent when he calls me darling and not on the growing lump of distress building in my stomach, I just nod nervously. My eyes filtering toward the door of the station and the quick escape I need to make.

A move that once he catches it has Brady speaking up again.

"My name's Brady as I'm sure you heard, and well, the speed freak is Jax. We're on our way to a show."

"Uhh," I stammer. "It's n-nice to meet you. I'm Avery and I'm—" I break off, not sure how much I really should say. Sure, the blonde guy seems decent enough, but it doesn't change the fact that I don't know them. So starting again, this time clearer, I say the only thing I can.

"I'm heading home."

Chapter Two

Jax

"Speed freak? You're kidding, right?" I ask the second her car turns out of the station and back onto the road.

"Come on, man! You have to admit you were showing off a little too much in that ride of yours." Brady says pointing to the car. "I was attempting a little small talk. If you didn't notice, she seemed pretty scared of us."

Shaking my head, not even dignifying it with a response, I pull the door open and slide inside, slamming the door on him and the conversation altogether.

The last thing I wanna do is get into it with him about Avery. I mean, he's right. It's obvious she was freaked, but it wasn't something that needed to be dragged out and made into something big for his amusement.

I also don't wanna admit he's right, and it was my bonehead moves that killed the tank to begin with.

"She did seem pretty freaked, huh?" I ask after Brady finally takes the hint, gets in and we've pulled out of the station. Bringing her frightened face easily to the forefront of my mind and going against my earlier words entirely. When no response comes, I reach over and slug him in the arm. "Earth to Brady!"

"She reminds me of home. Except the girls at home don't usually get quite that spooked. So if I had to lay bets, I'd say she's from a big city." He muses. "It's gonna sound so fucked up, but when she smiled, it was like coming home to Kelly in the beginning."

Nodding in understanding, I turn my attention back to the road and think about what he just admitted.

Kelly Raines is his soon to be ex-wife, and before everything blew up, to hear him tell it, they'd been inseparable. It's all different now though and as he turns toward the window again, completely silent and lost in thought, I have no doubt just where he's letting his mind go.

About six months ago, she served him with divorce papers, and given the way I know Brady still feels about the entire thing, it's been a pretty heinous process.

Divorce is never easy, but considering the way Brady was when he first showed up in CPW years ago, and the way he is now, it's easy to see the cause.

We just started riding together not that long ago, but even a blind man would be able to see that he hasn't exactly been himself.

"Yeah, she was freaked, Jax." He says, seeming to recall my earlier comment. "It's why I did what I did back there. We might not come here more than two or three times a year, but the last thing we need to do is scare people. We already get enough shit as it is for what we do."

"But did you have to throw me under the bus to do it? I mean, you called me a speed freak. If she's a city girl like you think, she probably thought I was some kind of addict or something."

"You're overthinking it. You were behind the wheel of a car for Christ's sakes. Gotta figure she's smart enough to put two and two together."

He's right, but I still grunt my disapproval anyway.

"Are you telling me the *Mojo Master* is a druggie?" he grins, balling up his fist and shoving it under my chin like a microphone.

Shaking my head, I focus my attention on the road ahead, trying to ignore the nasally sound of his laugh and failing. Since leaving the station, I've been taking it easier on the gas, but right now in order to end this drive, I'm about ready to push it again.

"Tell me something, Jax."

This isn't going to be good.

"What?"

"You've done nothing but complain about this entire trip. So why would the opinion of some random girl at a gas station matter?"

He's got me by the balls with that question and we both know it.

"Could it be that the guy who hasn't so much as looked sideways at a woman since Melinda, actually finds a woman attractive again?"

I haven't been in a relationship, much less even thought of getting laid since everything went down with my ex, Melinda. For two years we were up and down. Running hot and cold. From one week to the next, I never knew what we were. All I knew was that I cared despite it. The last thing I want in my life now that it's finally been resolved, is for it to happen all over again with someone new.

Avery, though. There's no denying she got my attention.

Just not enough to actually do something about it.

"Geez, Brady. Don't you have enough shit of your own to deal with? You really wanna throw yourself into mine?"

It's a little below the belt, but there's no way I can admit there's any truth to what he said. That's only going to make his ribbing now even worse.

"She was just some girl getting gas in the middle of nowhere. Nothing more, nothing less."

"You keep telling yourself that, buddy. Maybe if you do it enough, you'll actually start believing it." He laughs. "I saw you back there and I'm seeing you now. You don't get an attitude like the one you've got unless—"

"Unless what?" I ask as he cuts off.

"Unless you've been bitten."

"Bitten?" I ask unable to hold back my own laughter at the insanity he's spouting off.

Where does he come up with this shit?

"Yeah. You were attracted to her."

Sighing, I turn away again, realizing too late that in reacting at all, I've given him even more reason to continue to ride me. I need to just man up and admit what he's trying so hard to get me to.

Tell him the cute little brunette with the soft hazel eyes and painfully awkward smile was beautiful. Mesmerizing.

"She was hot. Is that what you wanna hear?" When he nods, I give him what he's after. "Yes, Brady. The random chick at the gas station in the middle of nowhere was a hottie. Mission accomplished."

"Jax, the mission is far from accomplished. Your Mojo gimmick prevents that on its own. I do have one more question though."

Sighing again, while resisting the urge to let my frustration out on the steering wheel, I motion with my hand for him to continue.

The sooner we get this over with, the better.

"What?"

"Why didn't you get her number?"

Not even dignifying that with an answer, I turn back to the road and focus all my attention back into getting us where we need to be without stopping along the way and killing my road partner.

This is going to be longest drive in history.

Chapter Three

Avery

I've been sitting here doing this exact thing since I pulled up over fifteen minutes ago. After the weird encounter at the gas station, I turned the radio up as far as it could go and lost myself in the music, all the while drumming my fingers on the wheel. I drove up and in, put the car in park and I'm still doing the same repeated motion.

It's my nerves of course. I'm doing this because I know what's gonna happen the minute I get out of the car. I'm going to have to suck up as much strength as I can muster, make my way to the door and greet whoever is waiting for me on the other side.

Drumming my fingers on the wheel with the music blasting so loud I'm sure the entire town can hear it, seems like a much easier option. One I plan on sticking to if the shaking in my legs is an indicator of my readiness to do this.

With the way I've always operated, having this proof and knowing the facts, should make me happy, but all it's really doing is turning me inside out. My life until the day the letter landed on my desk had been fine the way it was. I didn't want or need for anything. I seemingly had it all. At least to anyone that looked at it from the outside.

Now though, it's as if I'm seeing for the first time in twenty-five years that maybe everything isn't so perfect. I don't have everything I could want and need. I didn't have the one thing that people the world over crave more than material possessions.

A family.

My father made sure of that before he up and died on me.

Get a grip, Avery. You got this.

Shoving down my fears and willing my leg to stop shaking, I rest my hand on the door and just as I'm about to push it open and finally do what I came here to do, there's a tapping on the window. Looking up and seeing the guy standing on the other side, not expecting anyone, I jolt back across the seat as my breath jams in my throat.

Shit just got real.

As he backs away, I push it open and slide out slowly, every move I make as deliberate as his next words.

"You must be Avery. Your sister sent me out when she saw you slamming your hands on the wheel."

"I was air drumming. Haven't you ever done that?"

"Um, ya, but air drumming usually has more air. From where we were standing it looked like you were unloading on the car."

"And you are who exactly?"

"I'm Michael, but most people round here just call me Mike."

Deciding to check him out while he rambled on, I notice that not only did he have the greenest eyes I've ever seen, but his hair looks almost sun kissed in color. A light shade of brown with blonde mixed throughout. Tall too. Definitely a couple of inches more than me.

"It really is uncanny how similar the two of you are. I mean, I've heard of identical twins before, but never this up close and personal." Flushing a shade of pink I'm familiar with as often as I do it, he attempts to cover it up with his hand before speaking again. "I just rambled, didn't I?"

"A little." I admit. "It's nice to meet you, Mike. I guess you know I'm Avery, and what you caught me doing is what I do when I'm nervous. Sorry if it freaked anyone out. I'm not crazy, I promise."

"Wanna know a secret?" he asks and the way he's grinning, it's hard for me to say no.

"Sure."

"I listen to music and do air guitar when no one's around to see. It's all good. Considering how nervous Em is, I think it would be weirder if you weren't reacting at all."

"Thanks."

"So, you ready to meet her?"

This is where the twisted flutter in my stomach from earlier comes back. As much as I do want to walk up those stairs and head inside, meeting them, there's no escaping just how freaked I still am by the mere thought of it.

"Um, sure. Lead the way."

Nodding, Mike turns toward the house and motions for me to walk ahead of him before trailing behind the minute I start moving.

As we walk up the drive to the house in virtual silence, and taking in as much as I can of the large amount of land my sister and mother seem to own, I decide there's no better time to get answers than now. With as forthcoming as he's been already, I can only hope it carries over to the people I'm about to meet.

"How well do you know my sister?"

Mike, slowing his pace when he realizes I've stopped, pauses beside me.

"I've known her my entire life. She's my best friend. I know her better than she knows herself sometimes, but good luck getting her to admit that." He chuckles to himself. "And since I know you asked that because you've got questions, ask away. I'll tell you as much as I can before I let her to do the rest."

"Honestly, there are so many questions that my head is practically overflowing with them. I'm pretty sure if I start, I'll end up keeping you out here all night. So as much as I want to pick your brain before I meet her, I think I should probably wait and get it all from Emery."

Nodding in understanding, he smiles again, motioning to the house.

"Emery is the kindest person I know. It gets her burned a lot more than she's willing to admit, but she never changes. It's one of the things I love most about her. She's secure with who she is and what she believes in. When she loves, she does it with her whole heart. I honestly think she's got more to fear from you than you do from her."

His words sting. I know he's saying this because he's spent a lifetime with her and I'm an outsider, but it bothers me. I'm the last person on the planet that anyone has to fear.

"That just means we're a lot more alike than I thought, Mike. Which only makes me want to meet her more. So, thanks for that."

Nodding, he turns and heads up the stairs with me closely on his heels.

Alright, Avery. I tell myself when he pushes down on the doorbell. *It's time to meet your sister.*

Emery

I hear the doorbell, followed by the squeaking of the screen door, until finally the heavy knock of knuckles comes and my stomach somersaults. The reality of what's about to happen when I finally open the door hitting me like a tidal wave.

I think I'm gonna be sick.

Which is an absolutely fantastic way to meet your sister for the first time.

'Oh, hey there, Avery. I'm Emery. Excuse me while I puke all over your expensive shoes'.

It's dramatic, I know. I mean, I have no idea if she's got expensive shoes, or even if she's got shoes at all. All I know is, the security I felt a few minutes ago when Mike was with me is all flipped around now. I'm feeling awkward and out of place again. The way I did when I was standing in front of the mirror this morning.

I watched them while they were talking by her car. I really tried not to do it, but the curiosity being so strong, I hid behind the curtain and studied them. The first thing I noticed, after the beating I saw her giving her steering wheel, being how different her hair is from mine. Avery's being wavier and lighter in shade. Down, where until Mike showed up and I'd pulled my own out of the ponytail, mine had been combed back and lifted. Darker in color thanks to all the product I'd put it in over the years.

Running my hand over my head self-consciously, secure that its resting flat and not standing on end, I make my way over, resting my hand on the knob while I take one final breath.

Content that at least for the moment, I've got my nerves under control, I open it. My eyes falling first to Mike and his familiar smile before turning to the person standing to the right of him. Sure as I do it that I'm prepared for what I'm about to see, but as I really take her in, I realize I don't even come close to feeling.

From her hazel eyes to the heart shaped face and even the length of her hair even though it was colored and styled differently, it's like the last few hours have been a dream and I didn't actually leave the bathroom earlier. My reflection is standing on my porch looking back at me. Making all the plans I had to reach out, introduce myself and maybe even chancing it and embracing her, fly right out the window. An awkward silence setting in the longer we stand staring in utter silence.

What Mike clearly picks up on when after another minute or two of nothing but looks passing between us, he speaks up.

Thank God.

"Hey, Em. You gonna let us in or what?"

Gaining some control over my body, I nod slowly and motion for them to come in. Waiting until they both step over the threshold into the house and following behind them when Mike leads her straight into the living room.

Which, when we've all made our way in and taken our seats, sets in motion the reunion twenty-five years in the making.

"Emery, this is Avery." Mike says before breaking off and turning toward Avery, this time the smile not quite the same. "Avery, meet your twin sister, Emery."

Chapter Four

Jax

Exiting the gym after putting my body through one of the most grueling workouts in recent history, I make quick work of the parking lot and throw myself into the front seat of my car, making sure as the roar of the engine hits my ears that I turn the stereo on.

The music doing what nothing else has been able to since we started this trip and blocking out everything Brady's earlier ribbing dredged up. What with the mood I'm currently in, doesn't do much to help, since it's got me thinking about everything else too.

Take how all of this started for instance.

When I was younger, other than the short period of time where I was hell bent and determined to be a professional surfer, all I could see myself doing was wrestling. It started watching it on television, and transformed into something bigger where for a period of a few years, I actually believed I could do it. Not only could I, but I *needed* to do it. It was like I became a man obsessed, and this was long before I even stepped inside the squared circle in order to make it a reality. Which only feeds into what Brady said yesterday. Making it true, even if he was talking about a girl at the time.

With me and wrestling, I was bitten by it at eight years old and nothing else has made a whole lot of sense for me since.

After training as much as humanly possible and then hitching myself onto a bunch of smaller promotions based out of my hometown in California, I finally found a home.

CPW—otherwise known as Combat Pro Wrestling—saw something in me at twenty and from that moment on, everything else has been in my rearview. I haven't looked back. Wrestling, well, it became my life.

Flash forward almost eight years and here I am in a new flashy car that saving in that time has been able to afford me, and I'm on my way to a signing for a DVD marking every major event in my career since signing with them.

Glancing over at the empty seat before pulling out of the lot, I don't know whether to feel depressed or elated. For the past six years, there hasn't been a time that I've been without a road partner. In the beginning, it was Melinda Richardson, my on and off girlfriend. When that imploded three years ago, it became a different guy every couple of months until Brady.

Doing this drive alone, with him miles away back at the hotel, with only my thoughts and memories as company, well, I'm not sure how much I like it. Hence the music. Being alone in a quiet place like this with just the mess of my own mind isn't the least bit appealing.

As much as I hate admitting it because it means I'm focusing on it when I swore I wasn't going to, I haven't been able to get what Brady said earlier out of my head.

Since the final straw with Melinda, coming up on three years ago, I haven't let anyone close. After what happened with her, I thought keeping everyone at arm's length was the way to stay safe. As long as I didn't let anyone get close, I wouldn't get hurt. I had more than enough of that over the years and wasn't looking to invite in more.

With CPW getting popular, fans travelling hours out of their way to shows, along with these DVD signings and fan meet & greets, I put on a mask. Going through the motions, I fulfilled obligations and I never let any of it penetrate my fortress.

It's worked pretty well up until this point because I compartmentalized everything. There were the fans, the people I worked with, the ones I rode with and then my family. Even the occasional friend apart from the business. Every one of these groups packed neatly into their own little box.

That is, until the damn gas station.

Until Avery penetrated my fortress. With a single look, managing to throw all of my safe little boxes into complete disarray, while at the same time, driving me crazy with my inability to figure out just how she did it.

Slamming my hand off the wheel, pissed that I let this get the better of me again, I force all thoughts of her and what Brady said down, determined to just drive and not go down this road anymore.

Reaching forward, I flip the knob for the volume up as high as it can go and after a few seconds of one of the radio hosts talking, the music hits and just like that, my mood plummets even further down into the toilet.

Of course they would have to play a song that reminds me of the past.

Of her.

And what in the end, had been one of the worst moments of my life.

The day I stopped feeling.

*****

"Jax, you have to believe me! This isn't what I wanted to happen."

"Sure." I mutter bitterly.

"I mean it. I never meant to do this to you. To us. But I have and it's time I was honest about it."

I want to tell her to shut up. Curse the words coming out of her mouth and burn them from my mind altogether, but I know I can't.

The woman that up until fifteen minutes ago I would have given up my life in exchange for, who I love more than I've ever loved anything in my life—including wrestling—is admitting to everything, and as easy as it would be to close myself off from it, I can't.

I won't.

I'm not blind or deaf. I've seen and heard the rumblings from the guys in the locker room. Read the stories in dirt sheets and listened to them as they were repeated back in every new town we ended up in. I knew there had to be something going on, but love, well shit. It blinded me to it.

Nothing anyone said stuck because I trusted her. Had faith in her.

All the while ignoring the very real signs that things weren't right.

Fuck.

Hitting something or even smashing it to bits would be great right now. Even better, smashing the guys' face that's to blame for all of this in the first place.

"Be honest?" I shout, shaking my head at how ludicrous it sounds. "You've been fucking him for at least six months and now you wanna be honest? If you wanted to be with him all this time, why not just tell me that?"

She's driven into silence and I'm thankful for the reprieve of sound. What would most likely only be more lies if she spoke.

The man in question, the one she's been letting hold her, touch her, and with this latest bombshell, fuck her, is none other than the current main attraction, Gavin Fortune.

The man that holds the championship and that for the time being, CPW has put all of their money into. A man capable of using that advantage to crush the hopes and dreams of all the guys who got him where he is.

Also the man I want to smash the living shit out of.

"I didn't tell you—I couldn't *tell you, because it just happened. I got caught up in the whirlwind. Things have changed. You deserve to know the truth.*"

You're damn right I deserve to know the truth. I deserved it a hell of a lot sooner than now.

Turning away, unable to look her in the eye after everything she's just admitted, I focus on the walls, getting lost in the dull lifeless color of the wallpaper. What, given the way I feel right now, mirrors me so completely.

"It didn't just happen, Mel." I offer up in weak argument, all of my earlier fight slipping away. "You had every chance to tell me you weren't happy. Break up with me. You didn't. You chose to do it this way and now you've got to live with it."

"When he leaves you," I summon up every ounce of strength I've got, turning and letting her see the damage she's caused in my eyes. "And he will leave you. I want you to remember this moment. Remember giving up the best damn thing that ever happened to you. The one person that despite everything he knows and has *heard over the last two years, would have loved you until his very last breath."*

Turning to go and making it all the way to the door without breaking, I throw one final look her way. What she says when she catches me looking serving only to pour more salt into my very open wound and make me regret not stomping out when I had the chance.

"I won't ever forget Jax and neither will you."

*****

Rousing myself from the memory that even three years later seems to hold me captive despite my every attempt not to let it, I pull over to the side of the road. I've got a few minutes before the signing and right now with the road my thoughts are on, I'm going to use it.

I need to exorcize the demon that is Melinda and my memories of her, because until I do, I won't be fit to meet with anyone or sign anything.

Slamming my hands and then my head down onto the steering wheel the second the car is safely roadside, I linger on what she said that day before I turned my back on her and finally walked out.

If she right? Will it always be this way? Never being able to let go of her and what we shared. Will she always own me even though it's been years since we've been together?

Will I ever move on and better yet, even if I could, would she let me?

Chapter Five

Avery

"Just a thought here, but are either of you actually going to speak or should I set myself up to do all the talking?" Mike asks and I watch as Emery shoots him a look.

There is so much tenderness behind it even though she's trying to look annoyed that I feel my heart tighten. It's obvious they've known each other for a long time and are just that comfortable with one another, a feeling that since my—*our*—dad died, I haven't been able to experience with anyone. Just when I think I'm starting to feel comfortable being here, one look and it's all falling down again.

"So, Avery, how was the trip down?"

Looking up from my lap when I realize it wasn't Mike that asked, I'm struck again by just how alike we are. If it wasn't for her hair, there would be no real way to tell us apart. Paperwork can easily be forged, but this, there's no doubt about it.

We're definitely sisters.

"I can't really say much for the plane, I was in and out for most of it, but the drive was amazing. You don't see trees and land like this in the city much anymore. It's pretty great."

Hearing my voice, I feel sick. My nerves getting the best of me are making me sound robotic and that's the last thing I want. This situation can't be easy for anyone, so I need to do better the next time they ask me a question. The last thing I want is Emery thinking I'm blowing her off or not interested.

"I've never been, but from what I've heard about Toronto, it's the place to be when visiting Canada. It must be pretty awesome to live there."

"You'd be surprised. I've never been much of a city girl. Give me something like what you have here and I'm in Heaven."

The look I get from Emery; it's one I'm used to seeing. She thinks I'm crazy. Our dad used to be the same way. He thought I lost my mind the first time I admitted that if I had the choice, I'd move far out in the country and never look back. The few friends I made over the years weren't much better. It was like being born and raised in a city meant I had to love everything about it.

I had to be the complete opposite of who I am.

"Maybe one of these days we can switch places for a while." Emery laughs. "I've been dying to live in the city!"

Mike looks between us and shakes his head and when Emery scowls, I laugh.

"I'm sorry, guys." I blurt out as the laughter falls away and the unease seems to set back in. "I know I'm making things awkward with how nervous I am. Being here is just a lot to take in and I'm still trying to adapt."

Emery nods in understanding and the simple motion causes the tightness around my heart to ease. Maybe I'm not as alone in this insanity as I first thought.

"What was Toronto like for you growing up?" she asks, her voice low, speculative.

"Cold in the winter, real hot in the summer. People constantly in a rush to get somewhere, even if they didn't know where somewhere was at the time. It's so fast paced that if you want to survive there, you have to move with it. After a while it becomes tiring, keeping up with the constant motion. I assume it's the complete opposite of living here."

Emery laughs and shoots another look at Mike who is still smiling.

"Never a dull moment here, but that's got a lot to do with my choice of friends." she smiles, pointing to Mike. "You're right though. It *is* a slower pace here. The weather, well, it's about the same as where you're from, though right now it's gorgeous."

She fades off, her face pensive and I'm curious to why that is. What is she thinking about that could change her expression so easily?

Thankfully it doesn't take long for me to find out.

"I know this must be a pretty big mind-fuck for you, Avery; and I really don't want to make it any harder than it already is, but I want you to know that I'm really glad we found you and that you're here now."

I can tell from the way she's dragging the words out slowly that she's worried about how I'm going to react to her admission. This is such a monumental experience for both of us. Every step we take akin to walking on eggshells because now that we're here, neither one of us wants to screw it up.

"I feel the same way. I've always wondered what it would be like to have a sibling. I wanted one for a long time, but when Dad didn't remarry, I gave up on ever having it. He always said it was better just being us, but living and dying alone, I don't see how any of that is better."

Emery's eyes raise at the mention of our father and I begin to think I've said too much.

"I'm starting to see now why he thought it was better."

"Why do you say that?" she asks, and my answer, it comes out easily because it's something I haven't been able to put out of my mind since I read Rebecca's letter days ago.

"Who keeps their family a secret? I mean, who makes the decision to take one child and walk away from the other one, keeping them apart for twenty-five years without one mention of it? He died alone because it was the position he put himself in. Even in death, he held onto this persona he spent twenty-five years building and perfecting. He kept me away from the only family I have left and he did it without a second thought."

Emery just nods when I'm done, turning her attention to Mike before flicking her hand toward the door.

"Mike, do you think you can give Avery and me a few minutes alone? As much as I appreciate you being here and everything you've done, I think it's time that we take this up on our own."

"Of course." He says, getting to his feet and heading for the door. Calling out again when after watching what appeared to be him leaving, his voice filters over to us again from his place at the entryway.

"Avery, I know it hasn't been said yet because everything's awkward, but welcome home."

Emery

"I know this must be hard, but how much were you told by your—I mean, our father?"

The second she brought up the man I only know as Richard, I knew this was going to be my first question. I needed to know if he had let anything slip since he walked out all those years ago, even if it wasn't anything huge. I had to know if he thought about me at all.

"He said absolutely nothing. It was just the two of us against the world. At least, that's what he led me to believe. There were some family members on his side, but I haven't seen any of them since I was a little kid."

"Rebecca...Mom, she made sure really early on that I knew what happened between them. She said Richard got cold feet at the thought of twins and one night, after insisting she go to bed early, he put whatever his plan was in motion. He packed up as much as he could carry, grabbed you and that was the last she saw of you."

"That was him, alright. He always did like to travel light. I know it's not the same thing and I don't want to make light of it, but it's nice to see he's always been that way. That there was one thing about him that wasn't a complete lie."

"How was he with you growing up?"

I want to know as much as she's willing to tell me, not just about the man who raised her, but about the way she was raised without us.

"He was an attentive father. Well, as much as he could be with how much he worked. I never wanted for anything. Between the time with me and working, I don't remember one instance where he brought anyone home or even went on so much as one date. I should have questioned it more I guess, but I just chalked it up to him being a workaholic."

I nod, understanding completely what she's trying to say. It's not her job to question his actions, especially when she was just a kid. As long as he did what was needed for her, that's all that mattered.

It gave me a little comfort knowing the man hadn't been a complete asshole and she'd grown up okay, even if she had the option of doing it together stripped away.

"When I got the letter and the detective contacted me, it was hard to believe there was anything about this that was real. It seemed like the kind of thing you see on television. Even on the trip down, I still couldn't let myself believe it all the way. Now though, sitting here with you, my mind is full of questions and I'm not even sure where to start."

"What kind of questions?" I ask, prompting her. She's not the only one with questions and the sooner we start getting them out, the sooner the awkwardness we've been feeling can hopefully begin to dissipate.

"Our mother. What's she like? Did she really miss me? Why would our dad want to hide this from me? Then there's you and me. Are we as similar in personality as we are in looks? Do I look like Rebecca or more like him? You see what I mean?" she asks after taking a quick breath. "My mind is running wild with this stuff."

I chuckle to myself, seeing more of myself in her now than I have since she showed up on my doorstep. "I can answer some of that for you, but there's a lot that I don't think either of us will ever know as it pertains to our dad."

Avery's eyes sink in, growing sad and my heart hurts for her. Our dad passing away before we could confront him has left a hole for the both of us moving forward. His motivations behind keeping this a secret, and the lengths he went to in order to keep her hidden, they would never be answered and no matter how much we hated it, we were just going to have to accept that.

"Our mom," I begin with a soft laugh. "Is a grown up version of me. She leads with her heart always. At least until good sense kicks in. She jokes around a lot because she wants to make anyone she comes in contact with as comfortable as possible. She's just a really good person and her energy is good to be around. At least that's how it was before she got sick. She's still the same person; just not as full of life as before."

"To answer your question about whether or not she missed you. Not a day went by when I was younger where she didn't find some way to bring you up. You were constantly on her mind, which meant you were on mine too. She would pull out the album of pictures she had of us and share them with me, telling me how much she loved you and wished that she could see you again."

Avery, seeming to take in my answers, nods her head at the appropriate times, her eyes even lighting up at certain points, but never says a word to indicate how any of it is making her feel. Leaving me unsure of where to go from here, or what exactly is right to say next. After waiting her out for an extra few seconds, where again nothing comes, I just keep going.

"I can't answer to what Richard was thinking, you know that. Neither of us can. We just have to deal with the hand we've been dealt."

She nods again but this time, she follows it up with words.

"All I know is that when he was with me, away from work, he was a good father. Not the best, but I mean, who determines what the best is?"

I shrug and offer up the barest of smiles. There's not a whole lot more I can say about our father, and even if I could, I'm not sure I want to. I never knew the man and speaking ill of the dead just seems wrong.

"So, aside from being my mirror image, what else do you think we have in common?"

Avery laughs and for just a quick moment, I allow the uncomfortable nature of the conversation to take a backseat and I just sit back and revel in the sound.

For so long, it's just been my mom and me, and despite her illness taking a lot out of her, she's still always tried to maintain normalcy, especially in finding ways to laugh with me. But this is different. Fitting even.

"Well, I sort of cheated. Mike described you a bit before we came in. I was so nervous that I picked his brain. I'm sorry for that...or maybe I'm not." She laughs again. "The things he said, it makes me think that not only do we look identical, but we might also have identical personalities. Do you think that's possible?"

"Honestly, I have no idea what's possible. Where Mike's concerned, I think he has his blinders on, so I'm not sure how much truth there is in what he told you. I'm glad you were able to see parts of yourself in what he did say though."

"Well, either way, I think it's pretty great. But now that the haze has kind of lifted, I've got a question."

She's not kidding about the haze lifting with the way she appears now. Where Avery was nervous and standoffish at first, now she seems to be coming into her own. The first sign of the change being the way she finally allows her body to mold into the sofa and her body to go lax.

"What's the question?"

"With me having all this city experience and zero when it comes to what to do in a place like this, do you think you can share some of the things you do for fun around here?" Before I can process what she's asking, she takes a breath and continues. "I know I just got here and we've just met, but the stress of the last few days has had me tied up in some serious knots. So I was thinking that doing something together might help break some of that up."

She has no clue, but I'm right there with her. This meeting and all of the tension and worry that lead up to it, well, there was nothing fun about it and with as great as everything seems to be going now; getting out and doing something fun, especially together, seems like the best idea I've heard all day.

"Promise you won't laugh when I tell you?"

"Scouts honor." She says, placing her fingers in the air and making me laugh from the determined look on her face as she tries to master it.

"It's not for everyone, but I like to go to wrestling shows when they come to town. Ask Mike. I think I've been to so many, I can classify it as a religion now. We've got a few local ones that come through a few times a month and then a few of the larger independents. So if you're looking for my kind of fun, that's it."

"Wrestling, huh?" She mulls over. "Like the high school kind or the professional stuff on TV?"

"The professional kind."

"And you go all the time?"

"Yeah. Well, Mike and I do. If I told you there was a show tonight and Mike scored a bunch of tickets, would that be something you'd wanna do together?"

"Well, since I haven't been to a show like that in years, I think it sounds like the perfect way to take the edge off. But are you sure you're going to be okay with the sheer amount of questions I'm going to have for you about it?"

"I can't wait!" I say, and it's the truth. I really can't.

For the first time since Mom got word that we found Avery, I'm happy.

Things can't possibly get any better.

I'm sure of it.

Chapter Six

Brady

Staring at the phone for what has to be the hundredth time, I struggle with the need to dial the familiar number. A numeric sequence so engrained in my head that I know it as easily as I do my own name.

Punching in the digits would be so incredibly easy, but I can't bring myself to see it through.

Every time I try, I get halfway through them and stop, clearing the screen and putting the phone down again. The urge may be getting the better of me, but not enough that it changes the cold hard reality of the way things are.

Kelly told me it was the job. She couldn't be with someone who was on the road as much as I was or working with women, both inside and out of the ring. She freely admitted to her paranoia about it early on, which meant at the time I couldn't be mad at her. It's only when that paranoia got the better of her, along with a few voices nipping in her ear where everything went to shit.

We were married for nine years and never once in that time did I even think of straying. When I met her at seventeen, she was it. I was hers forever. She'd been the one to show me what true love was, and now, staring at the phone this way; wanting to call her so damn bad, she's also the one showing me what heartbreak is.

No matter how badly I wish we could go back and do things over, we can't. Too much has happened since we got married and it's marred us. Her paranoia over me cheating was always going to win out over the obvious truth that I was as loyal as a dog, and I couldn't walk away from what I know I was born to do.

So when the hammer came down months ago and she delivered her ultimatum, the decision was an easy one. At least it seemed that way at the time. Problem is, it's anything but easy now that I'm living with the result of it.

Kelly filing for divorce not long after the last fight and me being frozen in a pause position ever since.

Pulled from the minefield that is my mind at the sound of my phone ringing, I push all thoughts of my soon to be ex-wife to the back of my mind and answer.

"Raines." I mutter, inwardly groaning when I hear the voice on the other end.

Cameron Wilson.

Great.

"Hey man, we're heading to the gym. You wanna come with?"

"Didn't we just do that a couple of hours ago, Cam? Even the champ's got a limit on how much he pushes himself." I respond, unable to resist the chuckle that falls just thinking about Cameron overdoing himself at anything.

I've known Cameron since we were kids. He's new to the CPW roster though, and desperate to prove himself. Which apparently for him means spending every waking moment at the gym.

"Gotta get myself in top shape, man. I want a shot at the middle weight belt and this time around, actually wear it."

I can't exactly fault him for that. We started out working together when he came in, but over the last few months have been phased apart and even switched so we're not even working the same shows anymore. This one being the first in weeks.

"No amount of working out in the world is gonna guarantee that, Cam. You know how it works. The more you talk, the more you sell. It doesn't matter how much ability and drive we've got physically. If we can't talk, we're gonna get shafted and screwed out of show time. Focus on the promos for now. The rest can come later."

It's too bad I can't take my own advice. Not in the ring and definitely not in my personal life. What with one taking me on the ride of my life, while the other was dangerously close to a flat line and there not being a damn thing I could do to change it.

"Dude! Are you even listening to a word I'm saying?"

Shit. I heard him start talking but like always, zoned out and am now getting nailed for it. Looks like it's time to sling some bullshit. *Again.*

"Trying, but this phone is giving me fits. What was the last thing you said?"

"I asked how the ride with Merrick went. You and him have been together a lot lately and since he's been a prick before, I'm wondering how he is now that our gimmick is done."

Our gimmick. *Right.* The one where Cam and I go around acting like two entitled spoiled brats who thinks the world owes us something. The very gimmick that I'm secretly glad ran its course because it was a little too close to home with who my old man is.

Jax being a prick, though. That had nothing to do with the gimmick and everything to do with Cameron. There was just something about my old friend that set Jax off and most days, I'm the same way. It's not like I'm up for telling him that, though.

"He's been fine with me. He knows what we did was just business."

"Yeah, well, I'll believe that when I see it. He still treats me like shit when we're in the locker room."

As much as I'm enjoying this conversation and the break it's giving me from dealing with my personal problems, I've had about as much as I can take. I'm gonna need a little more than Cam's lame comments about Jax to get over this crap with Kelly.

"Look man, I've got another call coming through. Can we catch up after the show or something?"

Hearing Cam's muddled reply, I hit end and toss the phone back down on the bed, resisting the urge as I do to pick it back up and attempt to dial the familiar number again.

If I'm gonna enjoy what's left of my free time before the show later, I'm gonna have to do it out of the room and away from my phone, seeing as just being this close to it is making me do something I know I shouldn't.

For six months straight I've had to listen to everyone and their mother tell me that I need to get back on the horse. Accept the fact that my marriage is over, move on and enjoy the single life for a while.

It's the dream of a lot of the guys I work with really, being single and on the road the way I am now. It means hooking up with random women in whatever town we happen to land in and forgetting them again when we ride out in the morning.

Doing things like that isn't exactly my style, but there is some truth in what they all want me to do. What's been working for a lot of them for years. So even though I'm not exactly feeling it, maybe it's time to do what I've been avoiding since it all went down.

Maybe it's time to move on.

Grabbing my jacket off the chair by the door and slipping my phone into the back pocket of my jeans despite my earlier thought of leaving it behind, I head out.

It's time to get back on the horse.

Jax

The lights are on and the stage is set for another show in a six week string of them. Everywhere you look, you see superstars. Some big—behemoths really. Others small. All solid guys that I've worked alongside since I started here eight years ago.

It's a scene I've lived so many times over the years that it's as familiar as breathing. And tonight, after staying out longer than I wanted after the signing in an effort to get my head clear, one I'm thankful for as I head toward what will be our locker room for the night.

When I'm out there under the ebb and flow of the lights, executing a match with a partner I trust implicitly, nothing can reach me. It's like I come alive with each new match, fueled even more by the crowd, no matter how big, chanting or booing me. It solidifies the decision I made so many years ago, and I know there's no other place I'd ever fit. Let alone want to be.

Reaching my destination and pushing my way through the door, I make my way across the room and toss my travel bag down onto the bench. Stripping my shirt off first before making quick work of my pants. More than ready for the relaxation that's sure to come once I'm in the shower and under the warm spray of the jets.

A task I'm sidetracked from when after wrapping a towel around my waist, Brady steps up announcing his presence and boxing me in.

"Jacky boy! I wondered when you were gonna grace us with your presence."

Meeting him head on, I roll my eyes before attempting to shove my way past him.

"It's a real shame you didn't get the hottie's number. You could be going on your first real date in months tonight instead of spending it drinking with me."

Yeah, I definitely gotta do something about this.

"If the only other alternative is partying with you, then you're right. It's a *crying* shame I didn't get her number. Now, don't you have a match to prep for?"

Nodding, his grin never wavering, he slaps me on the shoulder and heads for the door and releasing a sigh of relief, thankful that it looks like he's gonna finally let up about Avery and whatever affect she had on me, I turn back to my bag. Grabbing the travel bottles of shampoo and body wash out, I head for the shower but not before I catch Brady leaning against the now open door.

"What the hell are you doing?"

"I wasn't gonna say anything man, but one of these days you're gonna have to face facts."

"Oh yeah? And what facts would those be?"

"The fans and those lights out there that you say drive you. There's going to come a time when they're not gonna be able to get you through anymore. I just hope you realize that sooner rather than later. There's more to love than wrestling, Jax."

Before I can respond, he pulls himself off the door and heads out, bringing the door securely closed behind him. Obviously having said what he needed to and staring at the closed door he just exited through, it's not annoyance at what he's said that gets me the way I expect.

It's a question. One I'm pretty positive he was hoping for, saying what he did.

What if he's right?

Chapter Seven

Avery

Surveying the place we just walked into, some banquet hall that's been stripped and flipped into a makeshift arena for the night, I swallow the huge lump of nervousness threatening to rise in my chest.

There aren't many places where I feel out of place, but this is definitely one of them. Chairs are set up all around the room, a metallic fence running all the way around in a square formation and ending with a ring that looks a lot bigger than the ones I've caught on TV slapped right in the middle.

People are already here and seated, some drinking beer and smoking cigarettes—the law obviously having no bearing here—talking amongst themselves. Paying no attention to the two people decked out in gear that makes them appear to belong and the girl just coming along for the ride.

What the hell have I gotten myself into?

The only experience I've had with anything remotely like this was the few times I did write-ups on events for the WWE. Their set up nothing at all like what I'm a part of here. The WWE's production taking on more of an entertainment feel and this one, well, this one whatever its polar opposite is.

When Emery explained CPW to me on the way here, attempting to enlighten me to what she called the top independent promotion apart from one called Ring of Honor, I had actually expected a grungier atmosphere. I just hadn't been expecting it to be this cramped, or worse, humid.

If the rate at which this place is heating up is any indication of what's to come, it's not going to be long before I was joining in with a few of the guys sitting around and giving the people a show as I strip down to my undies.

I'm not claustrophobic by nature, but with the amount of times I've brushed against another body just in the few minutes since we got here, I'm thinking I'm going to be after tonight.

Looking up at the sound of laughter, I find myself face to face with the smiling and laughing faces of both Mike and Emery. Both of them obviously amused by my very real reaction to everything I'm now experiencing.

"First time at something like this, huh?" Mike asks.

"Is it that obvious?"

He nods before motioning with his hand toward the seats we've stopped in front of.

"Don't worry. Emery was the exact same way when I dragged her with me the first time. It passes after you go through it enough times."

Slipping my hand into his now outstretched one and letting him guide me to our seats, I give the room another once over as more people begin filing into their seats.

Yep. This is definitely the craziest thing I've ever agreed to.

"Don't worry about anything. This is as natural as breathing to me and Em. Soon you're gonna be surrounded by a bunch of wrestling junkies, and as Em calls them," He air quotes "Hot, sweaty men."

Reaching over me, Emery slaps at him playfully, the smile I swear she's had since we left the house only seeming to grow bigger. A pang of jealousy hitting me when again, I'm privy to the easy going way they are with each other.

Another painful reminder of what I don't have.

As the two of them lean back in their seats and begin a conversation, I tune them out, taking in just how close we are to the actual ring. Another surprise sprung on me since when Emery explained how this was all going to go down, she'd said nothing about the seats being quite this close to the action.

Remembering what little I did about my experience with wrestling shows, I shudder. The last show I had to report on had been bloody. So much so that a few of the people in the first couple of rows had been hit with the spray of it as the performers were broken open.

What I later learned was something called gigging, but that to this day I'm still unable to wrap my mind around. Why anyone would willingly cut themselves open and spill their blood onto a sea of unsuspecting people far out of the scope of my understanding.

Also what I hope that with as close as we are, doesn't end up repeating itself tonight.

"So when does this start again?"

"Eight." Emery answers with a quick glance down to her watch. "So, five minutes?"

Turning to Mike, I watch as she motions with her head toward the door we just came through. "You mind staying with her for a bit? I wanna head out and grab her some stuff to take home."

"Yeah, of course. Just don't take too long. Wouldn't want you to miss your boyfriend." He winks, bringing his finger into his mouth and gagging loudly.

"Her boyfriend?"

"I'll explain everything later." Emery sighs. "Until then, don't believe anything he says."

Before I can respond, she's off and racing toward the door.

"So, I know Emery mentioned a lot of people on the ride over, but who's the person to beat?" I ask, still wanting to know what he meant by his boyfriend comment.

"The champion is Gavin Fortune. He's a pretty big deal. Tonight he's in the main event with Jackson Merrick. It'll be the last match of the night. For me and Em though, it's about the other guys. Mid carders. The ones that should be at the top and holding the titles, but that the promoter won't push."

"And they are?"

"Raines, Thomas, Ortiz and Kemper."

"So those guys are your favorites?"

"Pretty much. For you though, I'd say just watch the show and see who gets your blood pumping. By the end of the night, I guarantee you'll have at least one that does it for you."

I'm not quite sure a wrestler is going to be what does it for me, but with the lights choosing that moment to go low, I just acknowledge what he said with a shrug and turn my attention to the other end of the room where a curtain hanging above a set of double doors and the mats leading all the way to the ring await.

Smiling weakly at Mike when he nudges me and points to where I can now make out the curtain opening, I turn my attention to the body now stepping through and the music blaring through the speakers as the man seems to make quick work of the distance and gets closer to the ring.

Someone that once he's close enough for me to really make him out and the lights come back up, I realize I know.

At least in the vaguest sense of the word.

My mouth drops in surprise as he makes his way up the steel steps to the right of me and Mike chooses that moment to lean in and explain just who it is I'm seeing.

Who I don't have the stomach to tell him I already know.

"That's one of the guys I mentioned. Brady Raines. He's the resident rich boy for CPW, and Emery's boyfriend." Gagging again, I just smile uncomfortably.

He might be the resident rich boy to Mike, and he might just be some wrestler to the rest of the people here, but he's something else entirely to me.

The guy from the gas station.

Shaking off the surprise at seeing him, I force feed Mike another weak smile while pretending to focus on what's about to happen as *Paradise City* by Guns N' Roses stops playing and another song starts. The signal that his opponent for the night is about to step through the curtain. All the while caught up in thinking only one thing.

I'm definitely not in Kansas anymore.

Jax

What I should be doing is focusing on my upcoming match, but no matter what I do in order to distract myself and get my head in the game, all I'm able to actually do is sit here replaying Brady's words.

"One of these days you're gonna have to face facts. The fans, those lights out there that you say drive you, there's gonna come a

time where they're not going to be able to get you through anymore. I just hope you realize it sooner rather than later. There's more to life than wrestling, Jax."

Melinda had been my life for so long, the main thing I focused on when I should have been more interested in my career; that with her gone it seems like I'm moving at the speed of light in an effort to make up for lost time. Not bothering to take in the sights and sounds around me. Trying to be the person I was before she barreled her way into my life was hard, so I was choosing instead to become another version. One that was almost robotic.

Brady's words tonight driving the point home.

I know what I want and deserve. I want there to be more to my life than the fans, the lights, and the rush I get from putting on a show in the ring. I want more than what wrestling gives me.

I want love. A real life away from the ring. A family.

The whole package.

Being on the road though, it's become second nature. It's gotten to the point where those other things I want have been deemed completely unattainable until I give up the crazy life I signed up for when I said I wanted to be a wrestler.

You can have it all. I've seen it happen with other guys, especially when you look at the bigger promotions. Wrestlers that I grew up idolizing in Shawn Michaels and Triple H. They got everything they could ever want, all while still doing what they love. But for me, some random guy trying to carve out his own path in this crazy life, it's not the same. I don't see how I can have it all like they did.

Taking a risk and dating after Melinda, I could possibly end up with a girl like Brady's ex, who in the end doesn't trust me and is just looking for any reason to give me shit for cheating when that's not at all what's happening when we're apart.

I don't want that.

I had a future mapped out with Mel. I saw marrying her and settling down in a few years when we'd saved enough and were able to get a nice place somewhere. It's just too bad that while I could see all of that long term stuff, all she could see was screwing around with the very guy I'm supposed to go out and face off against tonight.

Leaving me to pick up the pieces of that broken picture in my head on my own.

Shit. I really hate thinking about this. Damn Brady for putting it all there to begin with.

Brady's realities, I don't know if I'm where I need to be in order to really hear them.

I don't think I'll ever be there.

Looking up at the sound of the door opening, I see Brady enter with Ron, the both of them worn, sweaty, and like every other night, smelling like absolute garbage.

Any hope I had that Brady would have forgotten about his earlier ribbing trashed the minute he locks eyes with me.

"There's a surprise waiting out there for ya, Jax. About three rows back from ringside on the right side. You can thank me later."

Not saying another word, he struts his way toward the shower, grabbing a towel from his bag on the way and disappearing around the corner, leaving me alone with Ron, who looks even more confused than I'm sure I do.

Just what kind of game is Brady trying to play?

"You know what the hell he's talking about?"

He shrugs and I sigh. *So much for that idea.*

"He locked eyes with some chick out there while he was picking his chin up off the floor. It might have something to do with that."

"Thanks man. At least now I know what I'm walking into."

This night really can't get any worse. Not only have I spent the entire time I've been in here attempting to mentally prepare for my match with a guy I can't even stand, thinking about what the asshole told me before he walked out of here earlier, but now I'm about to walk into something he set up.

It's definitely time for a new road partner.

Avery

Once the match started, I followed along with what everyone around me seemed to be doing and let myself get caught up in the action. Watching as the match progressed and Brady being declared the winner after taking a whole lot of fists to the face that I didn't think could be legal in any kind of real sanctioned fight. In the time it takes to blink once he's been declared the winner, he's hopping back out of the ring and making his way down the steps toward me.

And that's when it happens.

His eyes, they lock dead on mine. But before I can stand or even so much as acknowledge that I remember him, he's turning and sauntering back the way the way he came. Taking himself completely out of my view. Sadly, it's not the only look I've gotten since he came out and started wrestling either. There's been a few of them. All ones that despite my need to jump up or say something, the action prevented me from acting on.

The first, when he landed on the mats directly in front of where we were seated, I rose to my feet and our eyes met. His were pained at the time, but there was recognition shining there. Recognition that at the time sent shivers down my spine and forced me back into my seat. The second coming when after rolling over on the mat after his opponent landed a move from the top rope, he found me again.

Such a random meeting earlier that I didn't even give much thought to after it happened and now here we are, here he is, proving that it's not so random after all.

"Where the hell is Emery? She's gonna be pissed when she realizes she missed her boy toy!" Mike yells over after nudging me in the side to get my attention.

"I'm not sure, but I need a break. Maybe I'll take it now and go look for her."

"Yeah. Okay. But if you see her, be sure to break the news gently."

Believing he's just screwing with me, but not about to call him on it, I play along. Anything to get me out of the stifling heat and the looks from Brady that are still lingering.

"Sure. Let me know what I miss when I get back."

Throwing him one final smile, I turn, and after excusing myself past the other people in our row, make my way out the same way I'd seen Emery before.

Finding the nearest wall once I've made my escape and leaning against it, inhaling and exhaling, sucking in as much air as possible as I attempt to shake off whatever the hell that was with Brady inside. The surprise at seeing him and the way I seemed to respond every damn time he looked my way definitely not a reaction I'm used to having.

I've heard of small worlds before, even encountered a few situations that felt that way, but this feels different.

What are the odds that some random meeting at a gas station would lead me here to this banquet hall? This specific wrestling event? And what, if anything, does it mean?

But most important...

What the hell am I going to do with it now that it's happened?

Chapter Eight

Brady

I always like this time of night best.

The majority of the guys have grabbed up their stuff and made their way out of the building. Leaving the locker room, which is in complete disarray for the few hours we're here, empty and completely devoid of sound. The only thing you can hear when it's like this, the sound of your own heart as it steadily beats away.

Gavin and Jackson's match is next, and there are a couple of people standing around outside the locker room watching on the monitors, while everyone else hightailed it out of here so they could go get their drink on at the nearest bar.

I'm not like them. I like the solitude of being in here, even if all the quiet does is bring things to the surface much better left not thought about.

Storylines are wrapped up, promos for the next set of shows are in the record books and there's not much to do but sit and reflect on the last couple of days while I wait for my road partner to get done with losing his match.

Yeah, I know he's losing. Everyone knows he's losing.

There's no way in hell Gavin would let him win, even if it wasn't already decided by the promoter Radley Smith.

It's just not in his nature, egotistical prick that he is.

The shit I pulled with Jax earlier, it was a joke. I'm the last person in the world to say anything about the way anyone lives their life, but I do know that he needs more fun in it. Especially with who he's out there in the ring with right now. What that match, whether it's business or not, means. I also know it because I need it and I've been noticing lately just how similar we actually are.

Coming out and partying with me was the biggest joke of all. It's actually one of the things I respect most about Jackson Merrick. He doesn't do that shit. He drinks—we all do—but he does it in moderation. I swear the guy really does buy into the whole *my body is my temple* bullshit. I'm the same way, but while Jax does it naturally, mine is from years of having it hardwired in my brain by my overbearing father.

I could always rebel against the voice of Bill Raines, but the truth is, the real reason I don't join in with the boys is because there's a part of me, even knowing I'm facing divorce, still hopes Kelly will come to her senses and call me to come home. I know it's a bullshit hope, but just on the off chance it does magically happen, I don't want to be plastered off my ass at the time.

I don't go home much these days. I don't like the emptiness that's there waiting when I walk in the door. So I take on as many shows, travelling the road as often as I can with Jax, working my body to the bone because it beats the alternative. I moved out of the house a couple of days after she asked for the divorce, settling into some crappy one bedroom apartment across town and I swear I've only been there a total of three or four times since. There being absolutely nothing about that hole in the wall apartment that feels remotely like home.

So in an effort to distance myself from that feeling and the memories of our life together that always seem to hit when I crawl back into town, I threw myself into work.

As long as I was wrestling and keeping busy, it made everything easier to escape from.

The problem with throwing your all into work and forcing yourself to ignore your shit though, is that it always has a way of catching up to you, and when it does, hitting you even harder than it would have if you had just squared off with it in the first place.

You can never truly escape the bad things that happen, no matter how fast you run and no one knows that better than I do.

My payment for running and attempting to escape my problems coming in the form of our last fight playing on an endless loop in my mind.

✳✳✳✳✳

"No beer this time, baby?" I ask, a smirk playing at the corners of my face as soon as I'm inside and she comes into view.

It wasn't completely unheard of for her to be caught up in work when I'm on the road, and this is my standard response when it happens. It's always been a running joke between us.

Only this time it seems she's forgotten her lines.

"Brady, can we not do this now? I've got to get this finished."

It's hard not to freeze from the icy coolness in her voice, and it also hasn't slipped past me that she hasn't so much as looked me in the eye since I walked in.

This is definitely not the way things are supposed to go.

"Can I help with anything?"

"How could you possibly help me, Brady? You don't have the first clue about this. Pretending doesn't just make it happen, ya know."

She's done this before. Thrown these shards of ice my way, attempting to cut me with them, but usually she apologizes right away.

It's been happening more often lately, and the apologies? Well they're few and far between.

"You wanna tell me what I did this time?"

Finally looking up, she levels me with a look that stops my heart. This isn't the look of a woman in love with her husband. Not even one that is annoyed with him. This is wrong. There's a finality in her eyes, almost as if she's done with this. Done with me. I don't like it.

"You never do anything, Brady."

"What the hell is that supposed to mean?"

She doesn't speak at first, but there's no doubt she's thinking a whole hell of a lot about what she's going to say and that just makes the blood in my veins that had been running hot a few seconds ago, turn ice cold.

"I can't do this anymore, Brady. As much as I love you; I can't in good conscience keep up this charade we call our lives."

It's a miracle I'm as strong as I am, because right now, if I didn't have that to rely on, she would have knocked me over right where I stand. As it is, I'm standing here now trying not to break. Other than my mother, Kelly is the only woman on the planet I've *ever cared about and given everything I have to. Hearing her say she can't do this, it's threatening to rip me in two.*

"Kel, I don't get it. What do you mean you can't do this anymore?"

"Us. I can't do us anymore, Brady. You need to make a choice. It's me or your job."

I didn't want to admit it before, but I've known for a while she was reaching this point. That it was only a matter of time before she forced me to choose. She's never been happy with what I do for a living, what helps keep this roof over our heads, but she's been downright incensed lately.

"You're asking me to choose between you and wrestling? What kind of question is that? Wrestling is what allows us to have all that we have!"

"It's more than that and you know it. You're on the road for weeks at a time, except the random times you request days off to come home to be with me. You even work holidays! I mean, when's the last time we actually spent a holiday together since you started working for CPW, huh? Can you even tell me that?"

This is where I know she's got me because I can't give her an answer she's going to like. I do work holidays, and I am *on the road a lot throughout the year, but it's only because I enjoy what I do and the guaranteed money I've been making.*

"You knew this when you married me! I didn't hide it from you. So what is this really about, huh? Because it sure as shit isn't about me wrestling."

"My mom called the other day. She said she caught the show when you were in town. You weren't alone, Brady! You had two fucking women on your arm and you didn't even acknowledge your mother-in-law's existence. So you tell me. We're married, you supposedly love me, yet you're fucking off around town with other girls!"

I'm trying to remember something like that happening. I've had girls on my arm when they're part of the show and we're doing things in the ring, but that's always storyline related and I always tell her about it when I come home. Being out on the town with them?

I know I've never done that.

"Your mother." I scoff. "The one that hates wrestlers and has never liked me? That's your source? You can't really believe this shit. I've never walked around this town or any other one with another woman on my arm. You know this!"

"I don't know what I know anymore, but what I am sure of is that my life has become a joke right before my eyes and I can't deal with it anymore. I don't want to. You can have your so called career and all those whores on the road, but I'm done. You can't have me anymore."

"Will you please stop for a second and think about this? You know I can't give up my career. But you also have to know I love you and would never do anything to jeopardize what we have!"

She takes a few steps away and with each one I swear the strings holding my heart together snap a little more. No matter what I say, I'm not getting through.

"I've had months, years even, to think about this, Brady. No matter how many times I see and hear things about you, it always comes back to this. What's happening right now. I can't do this anymore. I need to get out."

"Get out how?" I ask, my voice coming out strangled and as broken as I feel inside. "Take a break? Move in with your mother for a while? What?"

She shakes her head, effectively blowing off every suggestion I've made and with her final words, cuts me so deep I'm not sure I'll ever recover.

"I want a divorce. I'm done."

Chapter Nine

Emery

Having done this so much, I've become a master at weaving in and around the people that come out with the same idea as me. It's always the same, whether you're at a bigger show or a smaller venue one like this.

It's been awhile since anyone used Timothy's Banquet Hall for an event, but having been here a lot as a kid and then with Mike for random shows, I know my way around better than anyone.

When you first walk in, there's a wide open space where coat checkers and valet parking guys usually stand while waiting for people to make their entrance. For a wrestling show like this one, it's where the merchandise is being sold. You climb a few stairs after that and it brings you into where the show takes place.

The place where my sister and Mike are waiting for me to get back, and after being out here long enough to miss not one, but three of my favorite guys wrestle, I want to get back to before I end up missing the entire show.

I'm pretty good about keeping my temper in check. There's always the fan girls who stand in line and gush over superstar merchandise, wanting it all but unable to afford it. Wasting time as they make up their minds. It's not different tonight, though my patience was definitely tried with the Gavin Fortune fan in front of me. Hearing her go on about needing to own everything and how amazing he was, it was enough to make even the strongest stomach sick.

Grabbing a hat, shirt, and some other random things I want Avery to have, finally having waited out the Fortune fangirl, I pull open the door and step back in. Noticing the match going on around me, I make my way quickly across the room and through the sea of other people until I'm back where I need to be beside Mike.

Looking over and noticing me, Mike squeezes my hand before leaning in. "Did she find you?"

"Did who find me?"

"Avery. She said she needed a break and was gonna look for you. I figured you two would have connected by now considering she's been gone for three matches. What the hell took you so long?"

Rolling my eyes, the mere thought of the Gavin fangirl enough to make my skin crawl, I fill him on everything he missed while I'd been off trying to get my sister mementos to remember the night.

"Gavin fangirl. Remind me never to turn into one of those please."

"Of course. Like the world needs any more of those anyway. So you never saw her?"

"No. I probably just missed her if she ducked into the bathroom though."

"Do you think she got lost?"

Thinking about the likelihood of that happening, I shake my head. Her being from Toronto and the sheer amount of arenas and sporting events that took place there, getting lost didn't seem likely, even if it was in a place she'd never been before.

'She's from the city, not the back woods, Mike. She'll be back when she gets through the crowd of people I just had to maneuver through."

Mike shakes his head, obviously not agreeing with my assessment but remaining silent as he turns his attention back to the ring. The match that had been going on when I came back ending and the lights going low, setting up for what the second *Rock You Like A Hurricane* by the Scorpions hits, signals the main event.

The *Mojo Master,* Jackson Merrick versus the guy the girl outside went absolutely bat-shit over in CPW Champion, Gavin Fortune.

Damn. I was gone a lot longer than I thought.

Brady Raines might be the reason I'm here tonight, along with seeing the returning Remy Ortiz, another match I seemed to have missed being trapped outside, but getting to see Merrick in action was a definite bonus.

From the first event Matt ever brought me to, I've been following him. His run in CPW, unlike a lot of the others. The one guy on the roster that seemed to fit in whatever place you put him. Matches where he would job to another star on the rise, mid card matches, and now the run for the championship. To say I was fascinated by him is an understatement.

Faster than a lot of the other guys, bringing high flying moves to the table that not a lot of others even dared to try. Along with the way he seemed to have no fear for his safety, taking risks at every turn whether they paid off or not, well, he pulled me in the way I'm sure the bosses in the back wanted him to.

Making Jackson Merrick a guy worth watching, and one that if the bigger promotions ever caught sight of the smaller shows, would end with him being picked up. I'm sure of it.

There's something different about him tonight, though. Normally, when he makes his entrance, he's all over his fans. Stopping and shaking hands, even leaning in for half hugs and a couple pictures before finally getting into the ring. He always wears a smile. What I always thought meant he was happy to be there and even happier to be doing what he was.

It's one of the reasons I like him. He was personable.

Tonight though, he looks distracted. He isn't wearing his normal smile and even his stride to the ring is different. He's not as into it, and if that wasn't enough, he hasn't reached out to touch a fan once since he walked through the curtain. Which only seems to get worse when he gets to the ring steps and looks around. His eyes dejected as he takes everyone in. At least until he reaches our side of the room and he lands on me.

Gone is the vacant expression and in its place, surprise. His eyes going wide and his eyebrows lifting before his head dips to the side, his gaze lingering as he studies me.

Why is he looking at me like that?

Feeling a light tap on my arm, I blink and breaking eye contact with Jackson, lean in toward Mike.

"Why is Merrick looking at you like you're dinner?"

Shrugging, I look down to my lap. Determined not to look up again until Gavin is out and the match has gotten underway.

"You can look up now. It looks like he finally got the meal he really wanted."

Looking up, I see he's right. Jackson's in the ring leaning back on the ropes behind him, watching Gavin as he practically glides his way to the ring.

The crowd of people around us is in a frenzy now. An equal sounding chorus of booing and cheering happening and reminding me of the last time I was here. Back when there had been a lot more cheering for Fortune, but what had obviously tapered off with as long as he'd been holding the belt.

Gavin Fortune finally wearing out his welcome.

Thank God.

As the bell sounds signaling the start of the match, I'm reminded again of Avery, especially now with her missing out on one of the reasons I really wanted her to come tonight. Brady, Ortiz and a few others aside, there was just something about Jackson that I knew she would like. After the conversation we had on the way here, a lot of it having to do with music and the type of stuff she liked when we weren't talking about what she could expect at the show, I just knew based on his look, it would be someone she could get into.

Who I hope she could get into so we could have something else to share.

"I can't believe she's not back yet." Mike yells over as Jackson climbs to the top rope. "Should I go look for her?"

"I'm sure she's fine. You know they always have something lined up after the match is over, so if she's not back by then, I'll go find her."

Accepting my answer as good enough he turns back to the ring and I follow him. Our attention turning just in time to see the match turn again. Gavin catching Jackson coming off the top rope, executing what has to be one of the highest super kicks I've ever seen, effectively putting him back on top. Capitalizing on the moment by rolling Merrick up, my breath catches as I silently pray for Jackson to kick out. Have this match end differently than every other one has, as the ref starts his count on the mat.

One—two—three.

Just like that, it's over. The hope I had that this one match would be different than all the others dashed as Fortune pulls out another damn win he doesn't need and putting a bad taste in my mouth.

One time. That's all I want. One time for things to be different. For it to not be so fucking predictable. But of course, with Fortune running around with the belt, it'll never happen and having hope that it ever would just makes me a sucker.

Keeping my word to Mike as soon as I see movement from the curtain and Matthias Kemper making his way through, I stand and smacking him on the arm, point to the door when he looks my way. Turning to go once he acknowledges what I'm gonna do, I slip out to the end of the row about to take a step when a hand brushing against my arm, pulls me to a full stop. Twisting around, fully prepared to shove Mike and tell him to knock off his shit so I can find Avery, I freeze when I look up and it's not his familiar eyes I'm met with.

Holy shit.

Jackson Merrick is standing in front of me, holding onto my wrist wearing the same look I caught when he looked at me earlier. Acting like he knows me, yet other than watching him wrestle here for the last couple of years, we've never met.

This is creepy and Mike; strong, loyal Mike, is utterly useless as he seems to be as frozen in place as I am.

"I can't believe you're here!"

Excuse me? Say what?

"I think you're confused. I have no idea what you're talking about."

I'm trying to be as nice as possible here, but this entire thing is freaking me out. Is there a chance I've met him somewhere before and forgot about it?

Doubtful. Wouldn't forget him or those eyes for a second.

He looks wounded, like my answer hurt him, but for the life of me I can't understand why.

What the hell is going on here?

"You don't remember me?"

"Well, when you put it that way, I could never forget CPW's rising star. But since I'm pretty sure that's not what you're getting at...no. I don't remember you."

I've had more than enough of this now. Turning from him and attempting to take the steps that will lead me out the doors so I can find my missing sister, again there's a hand on my arm, but this time, his grip is lighter and where before I had whipped around pretty quickly, this time I go slower.

"It's fate. Kismet. Call it whatever you want, but we've met before and this time I'm not letting you go without getting your number."

If this was any other time or place and I wasn't irked by the way it all started, his words would get to me. I'd be putty in his beautifully crafted hands. As it stands though, there are still a few people standing around watching us and the attention is making me nervous.

I'm not big on being the center of attention and I hate that Jackson is making it happen.

"You want my number?"

He smiles and I can feel my annoyance at this happening starting to crack.

God damnit! What the hell is wrong with me? What girl in their right mind wouldn't want this guy smiling and asking for their number?

Me. That's who.

This is not my thing at all.

"I can't, I'm sorry. You're like one of my favorite people, but I think you've got me confused with someone else. I've never met you before. Now if you'll excuse me, I need to go."

Jax

Slamming my way into the locker room, I'm like a man possessed.

I need to shove my shit in my bag and get the hell out of here. Put this town—this place—in my rearview as fast as humanly possible.

I've never been so embarrassed in my life.

How long have I been doing this? How many times have I been told that you don't go into the crowd unless you've worked it into your match or you're working an angle that requires it? Apparently not enough for it to sink in because what I just did out there went against every damn rule Smith laid down when he brought me in.

A boneheaded move that was going to end up costing me, but no more than my already bruised ego was paying.

Stripping off my shirt and throwing it across the room, thankful it's cleared out and I'm alone, I exhale heavily as I throw my body down onto the bench.

"I like you, Jax, I do, and if wrestling doesn't pan out for ya, you could definitely be a stripper, but please spare me the show."

Looks like I'm not alone after all.

I want to laugh at the obvious joke, but I can't. I'm still mentally beating the hell out of myself for the way I acted out there. Still dealing with the fact that the girl from the gas station, the one Brady has been ripping on me about and the one I'd been unable to get out of my head, didn't even register me on her radar.

"Not in the mood, Brady. I just pulled the stupidest move ever and it's your fault it happened."

"You wanna tell me what it is you think I did?"

"*Oh, Jax,*" I mock, copying his voice from earlier. "*There's a surprise three rows back from ringside for you.*"

"What did you do?"

"The match was over, Kemper came out to set up their feud and seeing the surprise you were talking about, I walked right up and asked for her number. She acted like she'd never seen me before. I said some other stupid crap too, but again, shot down. She ran from me."

"Okay, let me get this straight. You actually asked for her number? Were there other people around when you did it? Shit,

Jax. Please tell me you were smart enough to wait until no one else could see it."

Covering my face with my hands and sighing again, I pray my reaction is enough for him. Yeah, I'd done it when other people were there to see, which means if any of them had their phones and had taken video, it wasn't gonna take long for my stupidity to go viral.

Ugh. This shit is giving me a migraine.

"You see how this is your fault? You and all your stupid talk about me taking chances and not letting this business take over my entire life. Going on about that girl at the station like I missed out on something. Look where it got me. She doesn't remember me and even worse, she ran off with a guy. For all I know he was probably her boyfriend."

"Jax, I don't get it."

"What's not to get?"

"I was out there! She looked right at me and smiled. She remembered me. There's no getting around that. It makes no sense that she would remember me and not you."

"Maybe you're the memorable one." I answer, defeated.

"It's not like that and you know it. I was nice to her because she was scared shitless. That's it. You're the one that went anal because I called you a speed freak. I knew right off you liked her, at least aesthetically speaking. Besides, we only talked to her for like two minutes. Not long enough for her remember one and forget the other."

Done with this conversation, not wanting to focus any more on the idiocy of my stunt, I shake my head, not willing to hear any more of his explanations.

"Screw this. I was gonna take a shower, but I'll just do it when I get back to the hotel. It's like a damn ghost town. You ready to get out of here?"

Brady nods, hoisting his bag off the seat and tossing it around his neck, giving me all the answer I need.

"Look, I know it's probably the last thing you want to do with what happened out there, but when you get your shit squared away, what do you say about meeting me in the bar and having a few drinks?"

I'm not much of a drinker, but after everything that happened, what he's suggesting has never sounded better.

"You're on."

Emery

"This is unbelievable!" I shout behind me as I weave through the sea of people searching every face I pass, looking for my reflection and becoming increasingly more frustrated when she doesn't appear.

We've been doing this for what feels like hours and there's no sign of her anywhere.

It's starting to freak me out even more than the altercation with Jackson did. The worry I had earlier about her getting up and leaving me behind is back again and despite my best attempt at not letting it, I'm failing. I really don't want to think she left me hanging like that, but there's no other real explanation for us being unable to find her.

This is what you get for not letting Mike go look for her earlier.

About to turn around and head back inside, thinking that maybe she was sticking around there to make it easier to be found, my eyes lock on the wavy hair first and as the woman turns, even from this distance, I make out my eyes staring back.

"Avery! Over here!" I call out, waving my hands frantically as my sister's eyes finally lock on mine and starts making her way toward us.

"Is everything okay? You were gone a really long time!"

"I got out, went looking around for you and then couldn't get back in. They locked the doors or something. I'm fine."

Not wanting to move until I was positive she really was fine, I give her a once over and content that not one hair is out of place on her head, allow Mike to slide himself in between us, taking our hands and leading us through the throng of people toward the car.

"Relax, Em." Mike whispers when after a consistent stop and go, I groan. "I'll get you out of here as fast as I can. Just breathe."

I see Avery throw Mike a look, one that proves she never got back before Jackson had come up to me. She's confused and she has every right to be.

"You okay?"

"No, she's not okay, Avery. Jackson Merrick practically jumped her when the show was over."

"Mike, you know I hate when you do that. I can answer for myself." I snap, my patience for dealing with any of this at an all-time low. "It's pretty much what he said, but a lot creepier than he's letting on. It was like he thought I should know him or something. I feel kinda bad that he seems so mixed up. I guess Gavin hit him a little harder than he should have."

Coming up on the car, Avery leans in when Mike turns his attention to unlocking the door and after giving me a sympathetic look, asks what she really wants to know.

"He just came at you?"

"No. Mike's blowing it out of proportion. He came up and asked if I remembered him. Said he didn't want to lose the chance again and asked for my number. It was weird and it freaked me out, but whatever. It's over."

Hearing what I swear is Mike cursing under his breath, I roll my eyes and give him the finger when he turns his attention back to us.

"I just wanna go home, soak in a bath and forget all about this crazy night. You think you can handle that Mike?"

Before he can answer, Avery interrupts. "If Emery wants to go home, do you mind dropping me off at the hotel? I brought some work with me and if I don't at least attempt to get it done, when I get home, my boss is going to kill me. Since I'm planning on making this trip again, I've gotta make sure that doesn't happen."

She says the last bit with a smile and it's one that despite the night I've had I can't help returning. With everything that's happened since she arrived, it didn't even occur to me what she was leaving behind coming down here.

"Hotel it is. Then I have to get Jackson's girlfriend home to bed." Mike counters and despite the tension of the moment, we all break out in laughter. All thoughts of what happened in there beginning to fade and everything settling back into normalcy again.

Just as Mike's about to slide into the car though, I reach out and slap him. He might have thought because I laughed at his remark that he'd gotten away with it, but he had another thing coming.

Jackson Merrick's dream girl I'm definitely not.

Chapter Ten

Avery

Hugging Emery one more time, with a promise of calling her in the morning so we can set up a time for me to come by to meet our mother and securing Mike's promise to drive my rental back when he's done dropping Emery off, I wave as they pull away. Only turning and heading up the steps of the hotel when they've completely pulled out and driven off into the night.

Pausing as I pass by the hotel lounge, I debate whether to stop in for a drink or head up to the room to get started on the very real work I have waiting. The need to celebrate everything I conquered today winning out in the end as I step in and make a beeline past the tables straight to the bar.

Smiling at the bartender as I slide up onto the stool, I mouth my drink order and shifting in my seat once I'm sure he's gotten it, turn my attention to the rest of the people around me. Doing what I'd attempted to do at the show earlier and people watch.

When I first started out as a writer with the City Voice, I found out quickly just how much information could be gleaned just from studying people when they weren't aware anyone was watching. Mannerisms, body language and other tells on full display and no one being the wiser as I did it. What has become every day after a welcomed pastime.

Also the perfect way to celebrate meeting my sister and surviving to tell the tale.

As the bartender places the napkin down on the bar, my drink quickly coming to rest on top of it, I smile and lifting the glass bring it to my lips in celebration, making quick work of downing the shot of amber liquid before motioning to the bartender for another.

Turning back to the room, I let my eyes fall on a couple at a table about four feet away. Eavesdropping on their conversation, what sounds more like a transaction than a love connection, I flick my eyes away just in time to see two men making their way up to the bar near me. My breath catching when after a few seconds of staring, the reality of just who it is I'm gawking at hits.

Looks like show isn't going to be last I see of him after all.

Brady, leaning against the bar, does the same thing I did when I got here and looks out over the bar, taking it all in for a few seconds before turning his attention to his buddy and hopping up onto the stool. What his partner seems to copy a few seconds later as they both motion to the bartender.

Powerless against the pull to watch them, I do my best to hide my inner stalker, making sure that my hair is doing what I need it to and keeping me hidden as Brady's eyes flick down the bar toward me, before turning his attention back to his companion.

A chance I use to take him in the same way I'd done earlier. Surprised by just how average he looks now that he's away from the ring and the outfit he'd come out in.

Dressed in loose fitting jeans and a shirt emblazoned with the name of a rock band I don't recognize, he completes the look with a pair of black combat boots. He looks clean. Polished. Normal. A definite step up from the way he'd been only a couple of hours ago.

If I didn't already know he was a wrestler, there's no way that looking at him now I'd be able to tell it's what he did for a living. He blended in with everyone else here nicely.

Mentally chiding myself for staring, thankful his attention seems to be elsewhere, I switch my attention to his companion, the other guy from the station, whose name is on the tip of my tongue, but for the life of me, I can't place.

Where Brady looks relaxed, this guy looks anything but. His body language awkward, like this is the last place on earth he wants to be and is ready to bolt. His hair, like mine, down and shielding the rest of him from me as much as I'm sure I'm doing for them. What despite not being able to see, I have no problem recalling from the way he looked at the station. Sapphire blue eyes, softer than I expected them to be when he finally pulled his shades up and lips that despite him being a total stranger, I'd wanted to reach out and touch to see if they would be as soft as they appeared from the distance between us.

He's dressed in jeans and black boots like Brady, but that's where the similarities between them end. His shirt is a button down, dark blue in color and even though I can't make out his eyes, I have no doubt that the clothing choice would only make what I remember of them, more hypnotic.

Letting my gaze fall lower, I bite my lip when I see how form fitting his jeans are. Clinging to his legs in a way that from this angle, make them appear as though they're painted on. Pants that leave *absolutely nothing* to the imagination.

Enough, Ave. He's not a piece of meat.

Shifting my attention back to the bar and running my fingers over the empty shot glass, it doesn't take long for their conversation to filter its way down.

"I told you, Jax. I have no idea how she recognized me and not you."

My ears perk up at Brady's words. Eavesdropping on them, as bad as it is, actually working in my favor as it gives me information I didn't even know I was after.

Jax.

That's the speed freaks name.

"Well, she didn't. I told you. I asked for her number and she ran. She probably thought I was messed up in the head, and looking back, maybe I was. I mean, I did something based on advice from you. That's pretty fucked."

The room begins to spin as I put together everything I'm hearing. What are the odds that this happened more than once in the same night with these two? It didn't take a genius to figure out they were talking about me and my sister.

"Jax, it's not that big of a deal. So the girl turned you down flat. It happens all the time."

"Has it happened to you?"

Brady goes silent and it takes everything in me not to laugh. It's obvious that for all the support he's trying to give his friend, he doesn't have the experience to back it up.

Somehow I find it hard to believe anyone would run from these two.

"See?" Jax moans. "It was humiliating."

"You really let what I said get under your skin, huh?" When Jax doesn't bother responding one way or the other, he continues. "Dude, I'm going through the divorce from hell. My wife thinks I've spent our entire marriage cheating on her because I wrestle and her mother is filling her head with so much garbage she's turned my entire world upside down. I'm the last person that should be telling anyone how to live their life. I was just screwing with you."

"You think you could have told me that *before* I went and made a jackass of myself?"

"How was I supposed to know you were gonna head into the crowd and ask some random chick out?"

Jax goes silent again, this time using the silence to take a long swig from the beer resting on the bar.

"Are you sure it was even the same girl? I was there. She remembered me."

"You were the one that told me I had a thing for her. That I found her hot, which I already said I wasn't going to deny. Do you really think I would have talked to the wrong person?"

Just as things start picking up, and I lean across to hear a little better, another body steps forward, effectively blocking me off completely from Brady and Jax and whatever the two of them were about to say next. Looking up, annoyed that he chose now to come stand in the way, I'm met by a smirk that despite it probably being his go-to move, I don't find the least bit appealing.

I've been around long enough, interacted with enough people to know how this is going to play out now that I've been caught in his net.

Any second, he's going to offer to buy me a drink, hit on me a few times and then after I shoot him down, he's going to become even more belligerent and make an even bigger ass of himself.

Suddenly, getting a drink before heading to my room for the night seeming like the worst idea in the world.

I'm definitely not in the mood for this.

"Buy you a drink, darlin?"

Can I call it or what?

"No thank you. I'm good with the one I've got."

"Oh, come on! Pretty girl like you sitting in a bar all alone, you gotta be here for the free drinks. Let me buy you a beer."

Great. I think. *This one is gonna be an attention getter. Just what I wanted to deal with tonight.*

"No thank you." I repeat, this time more forcefully, adding a shake of my head to emphasize my point. "I would also appreciate you removing your hand from mine. Despite what you think, I prefer to drink alone."

When after a few seconds, the guys hand is still on top of mine, completely ignoring everything I just wasted my breath saying, I feel my anger starting to rise.

"I said," I hiss, lifting my free hand in order to remove his hand myself. "Move your hand."

What happens next happens so quickly I barely have time to register it. Seats scrape across the floor almost right after the words have left my lips, and in the time it takes to blink the two wrestlers from the end of the bar are flanking us. Towering over the guy beside me and honestly, scaring the living hell out of me. Their hardened faces the complete opposite of the way I'd originally seen them when we met earlier in the day.

Jax's hand slamming down hard onto the bar and when that doesn't get the response he's after, lifting until it's coming down hard around the douchebag's arm and yanking it off.

"The lady asked you to move your hand." Jax says, his words controlled but his face giving away his true feelings. "You didn't listen, so it looks like I'm gonna have to do it for you. Take your beer and get the fuck out of here. *Now.*"

Looking up and meeting Brady's smirking face, when after taking the hint, the guy slinks off with his drink, I laugh before turning my attention to the real white knight. The second our eyes connect, the face from the shirt Emery bought and I'd left in her car earlier, flashes through my head, along with the recognition of just who it is I'm looking at.

Jax isn't just Jax. He's not just the guy from the station that was with Brady.

He's Jackson Merrick.

"T-thank y-you." I manage to choke out, completely mesmerized by his eyes. I was right. His eyes and that shirt really are an explosive combination. One that despite how inappropriate it is considering the situation he just rescued me from, has my body reacting in ways I was almost positive with as long as it had been since it happened, it had forgotten how to do.

"It's you."

"It's me." I confirm as I adjust myself on the stool, turning my body into his and giving him my full attention. "So...run over anything in that new car of yours lately?"

Jax

As I get a view of her now, taking her in as she stands here thanking me for making the pushy guy leave, I can't believe the way the world is working against me.

She'd been sitting here the entire time and neither of us noticed because we'd been too damn caught up talking about her. I can't help wondering just how much she heard considering her stool is only about four or five down from where Brady and I were.

When I realized it was her, the iconic line from Casablanca popped into my head and as cheesy as it sounds, it's pretty damn accurate.

"Of all the gin joints, in all the towns, in all the world, she walks into mine."

Agreeing with Bogart, I remember the question she asked and just where it originated from. Looking past her to where Brady is flanking her other side, I roll my eyes when he smirks.

Realizing I've gotta say something before she clues in and starts thinking I'm crazy, or worse yet, decides to run again, I say the first thing that comes to mind and instantly feel like punching myself.

"Not recently no."

Nice one, Jackson. Way to use your words.

As I mentally berate myself over the stupidity that keeps coming out of my mouth whenever I'm within a few feet of this girl, I see Brady bridge the gap and come close enough to extend his hand in her direction, his smirk now a full on smile.

"I thought that was you at the show earlier. Nice to see you again."

Watching them shake hands, my blood boils and my head rages.

This is bullshit. Why does everything with Brady have to come so easily? He never stammers or trips over himself, especially not where women are concerned. So why am I struggling to do the same?

Why can't I summon the charisma I have when I'm in character?

The answer to that is easy. It's because I'm not the fucking Mojo Master. I'm just plain old Jackson Merrick. Loser extraordinaire.

"It's nice to see you too. Thank you for what you did. I was starting to think he would never take the hint."

Brady laughs and my chest tightens. I know I need to get in on this conversation before my road partner walks out with the very girl I can't seem to get out of my head, but I don't have the first clue how. Especially since all I can see is red with how close he is to her.

"Most of us, as much as I hate admitting it, don't get the hint right away. We're a bunch of filthy animals."

She laughs again and I'm captivated by the sound. I remember her laughing at the station this morning at something Brady had thrown out, but this time is different. This morning she was skittish and now she's at ease. Relaxed. It's like night and day.

"Well, the women of the world are thanking two of you animals tonight. I am, anyway. I'm sorry I interrupted your night. I'll let you two get back to it."

"Don't go." I choke out, not exactly trusting my voice, but knowing I can't let her leave. Now that she's here again, it's like the universe is giving me some kind of do over. I need to make things right. Something I can't do if she disappears again.

Brady, obviously sensing the importance of having her here picks up where I left off and despite how twisted him being so close to her is making me, I'm thankful.

"You don't have to take off. Stay and join us. There's always room for one more."

"You sure you don't mind?" she asks, her eyes skirting between us, but seeming to linger longer on me. As if my approval of her staying is what's holding her back.

Unable to find my voice and unsure of whether or not I would make sense even if I could, I just nod and offer the barest trace of a smile, which when its returned, gives me what I really want.

Instead of using our words, we both nod and smile and it's in that moment, when she sees our reaction that her decision is made.

She's staying.

Brady, motioning to the end of the bar, heads down and takes his seat first, signaling to the bartender for another round and following suit, I make my way back to the seat I vacated just as Avery slips into the one beside me. Turning her body into mine once she's comfortable and throwing my attention at relaxing straight out the window when shifting due to her closeness, my leg brushes against hers and a bolt of electricity shoots straight through me.

"So you came to the show?" Brady asks, the sound of his voice snapping me away from the sensation and back to reality.

"I did."

"What did you think?"

I want to hit him so hard right now. The last thing I want to talk about is what she thought about the show. There are more important questions that need to be asked and given our earlier conversation, I would have assumed he thought so too.

"What I was actually there to see, I thought was pretty solid."

"Solid, huh?" Brady laughs and again I'm swallowing down the urge to reach out and punch him.

"What I mean is, I left after I saw you wrestle and ended up getting lost, then locked out. I didn't get to see as much as I would have liked, but what I did catch was entertaining."

"You're not a wrestling fan are you?"

She blushes and the damn shock I felt when I touched her is back again, only this time stronger.

Is everything about this girl gonna cause me to lose my mind?

"Not really, no. I'm also not from around here, so I haven't quite mastered the art of not getting lost yet. Was it that obvious?"

Not wasting a second, Brady and I answer at the same time. "Yes."

She laughs and the minute she does, with both me and Brady joining in, it's like all of the tension is gone and we're getting the chance to start over.

"I was invited to go. I wasn't a fan, but after tonight, I could be."

"We're that good, huh?" Brady asks and she blushes.

"In your dreams maybe."

Well, shit. Maybe I don't need to be jealous of Brady after all.

"Alright, you convinced me."

"Convinced you of what?" she asks, bringing the glass to her lips and finishing it off, signaling to the bartender as she pushes the glass across the bar that she's done.

"That I'm in the wrong line of work." Brady pouts, causing Avery to laugh again, and where I should be joining in, has me doing the opposite as my mouth with a mind of its own pops open and before I can stop myself, lets the stupidest question in the world fall out. Affectively killing the mood.

"Why did you pretend you didn't know me earlier?"

Avery

After eavesdropping on them, I knew it was only a matter of time before one of them brought up what happened with Emery.

Expecting it didn't make me any more prepared for it though.

"I have no idea what you're talking about. I didn't run from you. I wasn't even there when you had your match. The doors were locked and I was stuck outside."

"See! I was right. I said you talked to the wrong girl." Brady picks up, shooting his friend a look.

"I *did not* talk to the wrong girl." Jax snaps back and seeing the strain all of this is taking staring back at me through his eyes, I end the torture.

"He's right *and* wrong. He didn't talk to me at the show, but he did talk to someone close to me. Jackson…" Reaching my hand out and running it over his, I lean in as close as I can and say what I've been dying to since I sat down beside them. "You spoke to my sister."

"Your sister." He repeats slowly, mulling my words over as if trying to make sense of them.

"I still don't get it, so you mind filling in the blanks?" Brady interjects.

"When we met at the station and you told me where you were going, I said I was going home. I wasn't telling the truth."

Brady starts laughing and he slaps the bar as if everything I've said confirms what he already knew.

"I told you she was lying to us. She's got city girl written all over her!"

"Yeah, I'm from Toronto. So now that I've cleared that up, here's the rest. I came down here to meet my sister. A sister that until a couple days ago, I had no idea even existed. She lives in Brandywine and I was coming here to get to the bottom of it all." Taking a deep breath, I give them the rest. What I hope will clear this entire thing up. "Emery…she isn't just my sister. She's my twin."

"You mean to tell me, there are two of you?" Brady asks, slapping his hand down on the table and roaring in laughter when I nod.

Turning my attention back to Jax and being met with his perplexed expression, I explain what I know.

"You asked *Emery* for her number."

"I met her and not you." He repeats, letting the truth settle in.

"Yes."

"So the person I saw when I came out was you?" Brady asks and I nod again.

"Yes. Both times you've come across me, it's been me. Jax is the only one that met Emery."

"I'm sorry. I know you gotta feel like shit, Jackson, but this is fucking hilarious!"

Brady isn't wrong. It is funny, but for Jax, not so much. It had to have been extremely uncomfortable for him doing what he did and then finding out it wasn't even the same girl. Where all I had with Brady was a few looks, he had taken everything a step further.

"Jax, can I ask you something?"

"Go ahead. I don't think I can say or do anything quite that embarrassing twice in one night."

"Why did you want my number?"

The way he looks at me, the softness in his eyes making them appear even lighter than they are, it pulls me in. I've never reacted to a guy like this before. So drawn to them that even the sliver of space between us seems like way too much and all I want is to come up with a way to get even closer.

He hasn't even spoken and I'm practically hanging on every unsaid word.

"According to that idiot," he motions to Brady. "I don't take enough chances. So this was my way of proving him wrong."

"Hey, speed freak! Watch who you're calling an idiot!" Brady scowls, attempting to appear offended but failing as his smirk gives him away. "So, Avery...about this twin of yours. Is she anything like you?"

"She's exactly like me. We *are* twins, Brady. Why?"

"Well, since Jacky boy here had the balls to take a chance, I think it's my turn to do the same. You think your sister would be interested in hanging out?"

Chapter Eleven

Emery

Turning over and coming in direct contact with the stream of sunlight now breaking through the half open window, I bring my hand up in an effort to block it and with a groan turn over to my other side. Opening my eyes just enough to be able to make out the alarm clock and the hour flashing back at me.

Flinging myself up in the bed, I throw my legs over the side, pissed at myself for oversleeping.

Leaning over, I grab my phone and waking it up from its own slumber, stare at the screen full of notifications waiting for me. Messages. A lot of them from the looks of it. Avery's name along with Mike's staring back at me and causing me to groan again.

It's going to have to wait. I've already overslept and made her wait long enough. I'm not wasting any more time.

After coming up yesterday afternoon and telling her that I was going to take Avery out and show her around, successfully stalling their first meeting, my plan was to wake up before the shift change in nurses and fill her in on everything she'd missed. Everything I'd learned in the short amount of time I'd spent with my sister.

Giving her the full report that she deserves before Avery comes over later and they officially meet.

Slipping from the bed and deciding against changing out of my oversized nightshirt sleepwear, I tiptoe across the room and down the hall until I get to her door, knocking lightly.

"Come in, Emery." She calls, louder than she's been the last few days. Giving me hope for the way the rest of the day will turn out. If she's this alert today, it means it's going to be one of the good ones.

Entering the bedroom, I walk over to where she's seated in her favorite chair by the window. Sitting on the bed and waiting patiently as she attempts to shift her weight around to face me.

A light in her eyes the second our eyes meet that I haven't see in months. One that her illness stole and that no matter what I did to try and stop it, never seemed to make more than the odd appearance these days.

"So tell me. What's she like?"

"There's still a lot I don't know, but she's real, Mom. There's also no doubt she's a Davis. You can't tell us apart."

"What about Richard?"

I knew this was coming. My mom can try and pretend she doesn't care about her ex-husband all she wants, but I don't think she's ever gotten over him or the way they left things.

"He passed away, Mom, but something tells me you already knew that."

I watch as she attempts to nod and fails. Her body so frail these days that most movements cause her excruciating amounts of pain.

"Did he tell her about us?"

I shake my head, not wanting to say the words out loud and be the reason my mother feels even more pain, even if it is the emotional kind this time.

"She knew nothing about us before she got my letter a few days ago, then." She says, and again I nod.

I'm the same way she is. I was hoping that when Avery showed up, she would say that near the end, he came clean with her. Told her everything. But just like she is now, I was forced to live with the reality that given everything Avery said, he'd taken the truth to his grave.

"How did she seem? Has she been able to come to terms with the truth?"

"She's strong, Mom. Just the way you raised me, it seems Richard did with her. She's emotional, but guarded about it. I'm not sure if that's just because this is all new or she's that way normally, but she's taking everything she's learned well. Better than I expected, honestly. You should be proud of her."

"When do you see her again?"

There's more behind this question. I can tell by the crack in her voice that has nothing to do with her physical pain. It's an ache in her heart from wanting to meet her daughter.

"We made a plan for her to come over today, but when I'm done checking in, I'll give her a call and see when for sure. I'm assuming in a few hours."

She nods and when I stand, prepared to head out and let her rest, she reaches out, her frail hand brushing against my arm, pausing me.

"Bring my girl to me the minute she gets here and not a second later."

"I will, I promise. Rest for now. You're going to need your strength for when she gets here."

Resting back in her chair, her attention again turning toward the window, I back myself out of the room quietly, hearing the vibration of my phone on the table the minute I'm safely back in my room.

Scooping it up, fully expecting another message from Mike since he hadn't heard back from the first one, I'm shocked instead to find another one from Avery.

The message tally once I go in, reaching four.

Emery! When you get this text me. Big news!

Last night makes sense. Would you text already?

Well, if you won't answer the other messages, try ignoring this. WRESTLING NEWS!

If you don't call or text in the next fifteen minutes, I'm coming over. XOXO. See you soon.

Scrolling through and reading each one over a few times, I'm lost. As far as I knew, last night was her first time at a wrestling show, so how she could have news I don't makes absolutely no sense.

Not bothering to wait for her to show up, I open a new message window and start texting her back. Before I can get dressed and head downstairs to make breakfast, I need to make sense of the big boulder of confusion Avery's messages has created.

Keep your pants on. I overslept. I'm awake now. What the hell is going on?

Tapping my phone and waiting a minute or two for a response that doesn't come, I toss the phone back on the bed and head to the closet. Resigning myself to the fact that if I want answers, there's only one way I'm going to get them.

Waiting it is.

Jax

Bang—Bang—Bang.

Turning over in bed, I grab one of the pillows and slam it down over my head, making sure to smother myself in an attempt to block out the horrendously loud knocking coming from the door.

Bang—Bang—Bang.

Fuck. Whoever it is, it's obvious they're not going to let up.

Throwing back the covers and sliding my legs over carefully, I get to my feet and buckle down for the sway I know is coming.

It may have been a long ass time since I drank that much, but there are some things you don't forget and this is definitely one of them, though as it happens and I reach out to the nightstand in order to steady myself, I really wish I could forget it.

Bang—Bang.

"I don't fucking think so, jackass." I curse under my breath the second my hand lands on the door handle and I'm met with another knock.

Swinging the door open, not even caring that I'm answering the door in nothing but a pair of ratty boxers, I come face to face with the person I should have punched last night when I had the chance. The one responsible for the way I'm feeling by asking me to join him in the first place.

"Well, good morning to you too, sunshine! You ready?"

"Ready for what exactly?" I ask, moving away from the door and stalking back over to the bed. Grabbing my jeans from their place on the floor and sliding into them as he throws himself down onto the bed and makes himself comfortable.

"Got a call from Smith. He said the show tomorrow night is cancelled because of some storm coming through. Which means, no driving and a day off. I was thinking we could take the day and check this place out."

"You're banging my door down at seven in the morning because you wanna hang out?" I ask in equal parts disbelief and annoyance. There is no way with the amount of shit we drank last night that he should be here now looking this damn perky.

"Well, yeah. Did you hear anything I just said? I'm supposed to hear back from Avery about her sister, so I thought while I wait we could grab some breakfast."

That clears everything up. I know what this little unexpected visit is about now. He's eager to meet the twin sister of the girl we met in the bar last night and wants to drag me along for the ride. As miserable as I feel right now, it's the last damn thing I want to be doing today.

Misery might love company, but definitely not Brady and his kind.

I want to be left alone.

"Jesus, Brady. I thought I was the one that had it bad. If you keep twitching like that, I'm pretty sure you're gonna pass out. Did you even sleep?"

He tells me all I need to know when he scowls.

"Yeah, I slept, but man, you don't get it. This is the answer to our prayers."

"I'm gonna regret asking this, I know it, but what do you think is the answer to our prayers?"

"You haven't had a date since Melinda ripped your heart out and stomped on it three years ago, and with Kelly filing for divorce, I need a freaking distraction. It's a win-win, brother."

This is a switch. Brady admitting he needs a change when for the last two days he's done nothing but ride me about mine. Shit, if I wasn't hearing it with my own ears, I'd think I was dreaming it.

He's obviously lost his fucking mind.

"This might be a win for you, but not for me. In case you forget what happened last night, let me refresh your memory. Avery was more interested in you than she was me. So it looks like you get double the fun."

"You're a fucking idiot."

"Excuse me?"

"You heard me. You're a fucking idiot. I was there last night, you're right. She did seem to respond more to me, but that's because I actually spoke to her. I mean, seriously man. What the hell was up with you? I know you were pretty screwed up over what happened with her sister, but I didn't figure you for oblivious."

"What the hell is that supposed to mean?"

"Chill, dude. I just...you really didn't see the way she was looking at you all night? The way she was more interested in making you feel better than she was telling me about her sister?"

Blowing off everything he just said, I flip him the bird. He's earned that and more. He's full of shit. I was there watching the two of them talking back and forth easily. Hell, I tried joining in a few times and felt left out because it just didn't seem to work.

"The girl was all over you and you know it, so spare me."

"Whatever, Jax. Even if you didn't see the way she was with you, I'm not letting you screw this up for me. With the shit I've been dealing with lately, I need this. You need it too, even if it's more brutal than a root canal getting your dumbass to admit it. What's the harm in spending a few hours with the girl?"

"You're not gonna stop until I agree, are you?"

"Nope." He smirks and I swallow down the urge to slug him. "You might as well just submit now. I got all day to go round with you."

He's right. There really isn't any harm in hanging out with Avery. I might not be in the best headspace right now, but he's also right about that. We do deserve to have some fun, especially since out of the four people involved in our personal lives, we're the only ones that seem to be stuck and unable to move on.

"If I agree to do this with you, you've gotta promise me something."

"Name it."

"You're on your own with this girl and you do your own driving."

Living down that stupid speed freak comment is bad enough. The last thing I need is to spend the day with Brady and the twins and have it get drawn out or worse, turned into something equally damning.

"Meet me downstairs in twenty and you've got yourself a deal." He says, hopping back off the bed and heading for the door. "And Jax? Make sure you shower first. You smell like a fucking brewery."

Chapter Twelve

Emery

It's been an hour since the last text from Avery and I'm driving myself crazy wondering what her earlier messages were about. Especially since she hasn't responded to the one I sent.

In an effort to distract myself, I had this bright idea to make breakfast so that when she finally did get here, we could have our first real breakfast together, but as evidenced by the way the scrambled eggs look in the pan right now, it didn't work the way I hoped. There being a lot of brown on them than the yellow coloring I'm used to.

Exhaling and blowing the loose strands of hair falling in my face, I grab my phone off the table. In my preoccupation with Avery's texts and the insanity that ensued, I'd forgotten all about texting Mike back. What I now attempt to rectify as my fingers move quickly across the screen in what has to be the lamest text I've ever sent.

Sorry I didn't text you sooner. Getting together with Avery for breakfast. Will message you when I can - Ems

Ugh. See?

Tossing my phone on the table, I head to the fridge and grabbing the pitcher of orange juice out, place it on the table at the exact moment the doorbell sounds.

Wiping my hands quickly, I head for the door. Pulling it back and being met not by Mike the way I expect, but my sister.

"I come bearing gifts." She says, handing a coffee over and stepping inside. Breezing her way straight into the kitchen once I've taken the cup from her hands and making herself at home at the table as she pulls a chair out and throws her body down into it.

"So this is cozy, huh?" she asks, taking in the display of food on the table in front of her.

"Yeah. I was thinking we could start making for lost time and have breakfast together. Maybe, hopefully, even getting to do it more often."

Reaching across the table, she rests her hand down gently over mine and wrapping her fingers around, squeezes. My words obviously giving away more of my feelings than I thought.

"You know where I live now, Em. It's not like I'm going to leave and forget you exist. I'll come down as often as I can and make sure we do this again. Make sure we do it a lot."

That's the thing. I know she'll visit and I'll find time and go there and see her too, but it doesn't exactly make her leaving any easier. I just found her. The thought of losing her, even in a day or two, isn't something I'm ready to face. It might only be losing her to a border this time, but it's still a loss and one that with as sick as our mother is, hurts to think about.

I really wish she could stay.

"How much longer do you have before you have to get back?"

"I talked to my boss this morning before I came over, which is actually why I took so long. He's giving me a couple of days. So knowing him, I need to be on a flight out of here in two days." Pulling her hand back and picking up the fork from the table, she settles into the silence from my lack of anything to say and starts digging into the breakfast. Taking three bites in quick succession before looking up and leveling me with a soft smile. "How much fun do you think you can cram into that time frame?"

"As much as you can handle." I laugh, wondering again what her kind of fun is. "But before we get into all of that, you mind telling me what all those texts were about?"

Avery grins again, but this time there's something more to it. A mischievous dance taking place, like she knows something I don't.

"You will never guess who is staying at my hotel."

This is one of those statements that can never have a proper follow-up unless you know all the info beforehand, so instead of saying anything, I just motion with my hand for her to spill.

"Brady Raines and Jackson Merrick."

Say what?

I'm pretty sure I've stopped breathing. I can feel my heart beating so I know I'm still alive and haven't died of shock, but my throat is sealed up tight. Depending on how you look at it, she's either the luckiest girl in the world or the unluckiest with what happened to me last night.

"And this has to do with me, how?"

"I may have met up with them at the hotel bar last night." She winks and the reason for the dance in her eyes becomes all too obvious. "As it turns out, I also learned a couple of things."

"Like?"

"Like...Jax wasn't being weird with you. He thought you were me and when he saw you, he acted on some half assed advice from Brady and came after you."

I've digested everything she's said, but I'm stuck on how Jackson even knows who Avery is. Was last night not her first experience with CPW?

"Why would Jax want your number?"

"I stopped for gas on the drive from the airport and they pulled in after me. I had no clue who they were at the time and still didn't until we got to the show last night and saw Brady in the ring."

"So you knew of them before we went there, Brady saw you and probably told Jackson and that's what caused the awkward crowd thing. Am I getting this right?"

Avery nods and I breathe a sigh of relief. All of her messages were starting to make sense now and it made me feel a whole lot better knowing that what happened with Jackson wasn't as crazy as it seemed. The last thing I wanted was to believe one of my favorite wrestlers was actually a creep.

"There's more."

"Of course there is." I laugh, catching her excitement with the bounce she does in her chair.

"I explained the situation to the guys last night. Told them why I came here and after a few hours and a lot of drinks, Brady suggested maybe getting together later and doing something."

"Brady wants to go out with you?" This just keeps getting more and more surreal the more she says. Is this for real?

"No. He wants the four of us to get together. You and him, Jax and me."

No way.

Everything else might have been true, but this, it's gotta be some sort of sick joke. *What the hell would two wrestlers want with the likes of me and Avery?*

"So, Em. What do you say? You wanna go on a double date with me and a couple of not so bad looking wrestlers?"

"Not so bad looking?"

"Okay fine, they're hot, but come on. I'm pretty sure they hear that a million times a day. I wanted to be different."

Laughing, I let the offer sink in. Could I really spend the day doing this considering everything that's going on here? With the shift change with the nurses a little over an hour ago, I knew leaving was possible, but that didn't make actually doing it any easier. My fear over leaving and coming back to something happening while I was away driving me to stay firmly planted in the chair. The same fear that's been driving everything I do, including work, since the hospital discharged her and set up home care.

"I don't know if I should..."

"Why?" Avery inquires and instead of beating around it, I just lay it all out there. Coming here and wanting to meet us, she's in this now. She needs to know how worried I am about our mother.

"It's Mom. I don't feel right leaving her. Not now. I mean, she seems to be having a good start to the day, but after watching her have days start off like this and then dive straight downhill, I'm not sure how comfortable I am leaving."

"I get it. I'll call Brady and let him know we can't do it."

Something about how easily she would give up her own end of the plans for me—for our mother—stops me cold. Since she's here now and once we're done with breakfast, I was going to bring her upstairs anyway, maybe we can do this after. Maybe I can swallow my fears of leaving and do something for myself. Lord knows with as often as she's always telling me to do it, I know our mother would be fine with it.

"No, you know, don't do that. I'll go with you. There's just something pretty important we need to do first."

Looking from me to the table and back around again, she reads my mind.

"It's time isn't it?"

"Yeah, Avery, it is. It's time to meet your mom."

Avery

It doesn't matter how sympathetic you are after learning of someone's diagnosis or how much research you do on it after the fact so that you can understand more and help. Unless you're going through it yourself, you're never truly going to understand what the person living with it is going through.

There is no greater representation of that then what is going on with Rebecca Davis.

When I quietly enter the bedroom after knocking, Emery by my side, all of the research I'd done after receiving her letter was for nothing. Coming face to face with a woman that had not only lost her breasts to the disease, but also their hair because of the chemotherapy, her body frail and almost lifeless. No amount of research in the world could have prepared me for that.

Her bedroom, right from the second we slip in, is made up to be almost a duplicate of what she would have if she had wanted to spend her remaining time in the hospital. Her bed surrounded by machines, all of them keeping an electronic and paper record of various different stats and her bedside tables just off to the side of the machines, littered with medication bottles, among other medical supplies.

"Mom, there's someone here to see you."

Moving a hand across the arm of her wheelchair and pushing a button, she begins to turn and it's in the moment when my eyes meet hers that all of the pep talks I've given myself since I learned about her and Emery, fall away and I became the crumbling mess that deep down I was trying really hard not to be.

I don't care if it's been twenty-five years and I don't know her. No one should ever have to go through this. Definitely not someone who looks as serene as she does as we stare at each other in deafening silence. The faintest trace of a smile guiding not only her lips up, but her cheeks too. Her eyes, full to the brim with tears she's probably been waiting years to shed.

Happy ones.

"Oh, Avery. My sweet, beautiful baby girl. It's..." she breaks off, slowly lifting her hand and wiping away a stray tear. "It's so good to see you again."

So good to see you again. Not, so good to meet you. Not a cold hello, but words that mean so much more. Making me feel as though we've just been separated momentarily instead of the years it has been. Also words that make the water works I'd been attempting to hold back, begin to fall freely down my face as a broken and garbled sounding sob escapes.

There has to be some proper etiquette when it comes to meeting your mother for the first time. You shouldn't want to dive across the room and fall into her arms, but even knowing that, it's exactly what I do.

For years, especially in the times when just having a man around the house wouldn't do, I wanted nothing more than to have my mother there with me. To reach out to on the day I officially became a woman or when a boy showed interest and I had no idea how to deal with it. Even more so when said boy ended up breaking my heart. All I ever wanted during all of those moments was my mother, and now here she is.

I have never missed someone I never knew so much in my life.

"I missed you, sweet girl. I am so happy you're here now." She whispers against my hair before pulling her body back from mine and studying me. Her eyes beginning at the top of my head, pausing at my face and the smile that's somehow plastered there even through my tears, before finally lowering to my feet before coming back and meeting my stare again.

"You're the most beautiful vision I have ever seen. Welcome home."

"I-I...I really have no idea what to say right now. I'm sorry." I stammer, following her earlier move and wiping the tears from my eyes in an effort to see her more clearly. "I spent so long believing I didn't have anything to miss; that standing here now and seeing you, how real you are, it's like a wave of twenty-five years of needing and missing you has slammed straight into my chest."

Eyes deviating away from me over to the person standing close to the door, the very person that is making this moment right now possible, I watch as her lips part and she mouths a thank you before turning back and pulling me to her again. Both of us suspended in time. The only sound around us that of all three of us breathing and the sound of our combined tears.

"I'm going to step out and give you guys some time. I'll be downstairs when you're done, Avery." Emery says softly and before I can turn to thank her, I hear the click of the door closing as she lets herself out.

"You really are a combination of the very best parts of us." Rebecca shares quietly after we pull away from each other and I've gotten comfortable at the end of the bed.

Us. *Her and my dad.* Richard. Dick.

A name that considering the little bit I've learned since I've been here, has never been more fitting. If he'd just fixed this before he passed away, told the truth years ago instead of making us wait this long, I might have gotten the chance to know the woman sitting before me before the cancer hit.

I could have been here to help Emery when it did.

Instead, other than Mike, she'd gone through it alone.

I've never wanted to make someone hurt for causing this much pain before. I don't operate that way, but when it comes to what is happening now and what could have been avoided had my father just spoken up one damn time when I was younger, all I can see is digging the cold hearted bastard up and making him pay for what he put us all through.

Catching sight of a picture on the dresser across from where we're sitting, a picture of who I know beyond all doubt is Emery and her, I wipe at my eyes again and attempt to smile through the pang of regret I feel at not getting to be a part of it.

"How old were you there?" I point over, and when she follows my hand, her lips curve up into the most wistful smile, making my heart pang again. I look like her. So much like her. From the shape of my body, to the contours of my face, right up to the color and waviness of my hair. I'm all her.

"Well, I was young when I had both of you, just barely nineteen, and since Emery was six in that picture, that would put me at the same age as you are now. Twenty-five."

Other than a few subtle differences, it was like looking in a mirror instead of a picture. It's uncanny.

"We look a lot alike."

"We do. Your sister did at one time as well, but then she was introduced to hair dye and well, I haven't seen her natural shade in years."

Laughing at the way she explains Emery's hair, even though I happen to like that it's different from mine, I reach out and squeeze her hand, finally able to get the words out that I should have the second we walked in.

"I'm so sorry that I didn't know sooner. That I wasn't here for you the way I should have been."

"You have nothing to be sorry for, sweet girl. Decisions were made on both sides that caused this. Not a bit of it was your doing."

Doesn't she get it? I should have known that what my father told me was wrong. I should have felt she was alive and looking for me. Missing me. She's trying to make me feel better but the truth is, I could have figured this out a whole lot sooner if I'd just given it the attention it deserved.

"But it was. If I had just pushed more when I was younger, maybe this wouldn't have taken so long."

"With Emery not being here, I can say this and know that you'll understand it. Richard wasn't the type of man to give anything away, even to the people he cared about most. I believe you encountered that growing up, so you have to realize that no amount of pushing and prodding would have gotten the answers we have now. We're back together. That's what matters. There is no sense dwelling on the things we can't change."

She has a point. My dad wasn't exactly the most forthcoming man in any aspect of his life, especially with something as personal as this would have been to him.

"What happened between the two of you? What made him do this?"

"I can only tell you what I witnessed before he took off. I can't speak to his motivations after the fact. I wasn't privy to any of that, but your father, he wasn't ready for this." She answers, motioning between us. "Something inside him broke shortly after you girls were born and even though I saw it happening, I didn't do everything I could have to stop it."

"I'm pretty sure that if I'm not supposed to blame myself for what he did, you can't blame yourself either. Before or after."

"Fair enough, but I do hold some accountability. When I told him I was pregnant, when we believed that it was just the one child, he seemed prepared. More than ready to begin our lives together. If I'd just paid a bit more attention, I might have been able to see that just like the lies he told you about me were a façade, his readiness was as well."

Remembering what I was doing with my life at the age she had us, I can sympathize with the fear that must have been present for both of them. What I can't seem to get past though is how differently I would have responded to it than my father did. Where he made the decision to take me away and leave Emery behind, I never would have left. I would have fought, even if I was scared out of my mind because that's what a parent is supposed to do.

No matter how much Rebecca wants to take responsibility for the mistakes my father made, it doesn't change the facts. He stole me away from her. It wasn't right and I'm not going to let her take the blame for it anymore.

"How old were you when you married?" I change the subject and her answer is almost immediate, even though it takes a few heavy breaths to get the words out.

"I had just turned eighteen. It was right after graduation."

"Were you pregnant with us at the time?"

"If you're asking if we married because I found out I was pregnant, it's a no, Avery. I was pregnant when we got married, but our decision was based on what we believed at the time to be the greatest love story ever told. We were deeply in love when we conceived you and your sister. If you take nothing else from our conversation, take that."

"You don't hate him." I surmise after listening to her explanation.

"I don't. As strange as it may be, I lost two things the day he walked out with you. I lost the chance to watch you grow into the beautiful woman you've become," she pauses, smiling as she gently strokes my hair. "And I lost the man that I'd given everything to. Heart and soul. One loss was no worse than the other. They both left a void in my heart."

"Is it wrong that despite hearing the way you're talking about him, I hate him for causing this?"

"No. You were lied to and betrayed as much, if not more, than the rest of us were. It would be strange if you didn't feel anger toward him. Toward me as well. Just as you say you could have figured it out if you'd just tried and pushed, the same could be said for me. I could have searched for you sooner than I did."

"But you still did it. Reb—Mom," I catch myself. "I don't care how long it took you to start searching. I'm just glad that you did. That even though it may have taken time, you didn't give up."

"I never planned on giving up. Even if you hadn't written back or called, and just let the letter fall away, I never would have given up on you, Avery. You're my child and you don't give up on your children."

You don't give up on your children.

The very thing Richard had done and now, with him being gone, would never get to rectify. I don't care how much she loves him, he's still a bastard.

How do you forgive someone and look at them the same when they take away the one thing you've always wanted and never even knew you had?

You can't.

I can't.

"Why did he take me and not Emery? What was it about me that made him decide I was the one?"

"I can't be certain, but I can say that from the moment we brought you both home from the hospital, you were with him almost every second. Even when he was buried away in his office under a mound of paperwork as he attempted to get his business off the ground, you were there. So I have to assume that it was you he chose because it was you that bonded most with him. Emery, for as much as I believe she would have grown into a daddy's girl, favored me in the weeks and months leading into when he took you away."

I don't want to hear that. It makes my head hurt and my heart ache.

She didn't deserve to be left behind any more than I deserved to be taken away.

All of this just hurts.

"There is so much I want to know, things I want to ask you, especially as it pertains to your life in Toronto, but these days, it takes everything I have to sit for this long. I fear that I can't push it anymore."

I'm not ready for this to be over! I silently scream and then immediately feel a rush of guilt over.

As much as I want to prolong this visit and learn all that I can about her, I can't push her any more than I already have. It's not right.

We might not have much time together, but we did have at least another day. Whatever else we want to say could wait.

Almost as if they've heard her words, there's a light knock at the door and two women stepping through, breaking up our moment and bringing the reality of the situation to the forefront even more than her earlier words did.

It's time for me to go.

Standing from the bed, but making no move toward the door, I turn instead to her, my mother. Leaning over until my entire upper body is encompassing her chair and my arms are wrapped securely around her body, pulling her into a warm embrace. One that now that I've done it, I don't ever want to be released from.

Wiping a tear from my eye as I feel it begin to fall, I do what she'd done to me earlier and kiss the top of her shaven bald head, letting my lips linger a few extra seconds, wanting to keep the scent of her, along with the feel of her being this close tightly wrapped around me for as long as possible.

"I know it's been a long time, and it might even be too soon to say out loud, but I love you, Mom."

Feeling her grip tightening around me as the first of many strangled cries escapes, her tears falling like rain and saturating my shirt, I meet her halfway. Allowing my heart to believe in things I'd long since given up on, and accepting what I know to be the truth. I missed her, I love her, and I'm going to spend the rest of my remaining days with her letting her know just how much.

"I love you too, Avery Marie Davis. I always will."

Chapter Thirteen

Brady

I can't believe I'm here and about to go through with this.

For months now I've been trying to make Kelly see I'm not the person she thinks I am. That whatever we were going through, it could be fixed and that we belong together. I'd fought to have her in my life in high school when we met and that same drive inside me, needing to prove how well we fit together, it never really left.

I ached for her now, needing to have her near me even though it had been six months since we imploded and our divorce was one pen stroke away from being finalized.

Hooking up with Avery's sister. This insane idea I came up with on a whim. It was more about doing right by Jackson than it was attempting to move on. It was more than a little obvious he had more than a casual fascination with the woman, and I wanted to do something to help him out even though he saw me as nothing more than a nuisance.

It also helped that I wanted to meet the woman that had taken Jackson's best and managed to not slap the fuck out of him. What he did, I'm not sure I could have done even though it's been proven I'm the more outgoing of us. It took real balls to step of the box and talk to some random woman, and I was curious to meet the person on the receiving end of it.

Staring at the phone as I wait for the call that would signal the twins arrival, I swallow the lump in my throat and try to ignore the nausea growing in my stomach that always seems to appear whenever I so much as think about moving on.

Think about her.

This, the first morning in the last six months where I didn't pick up the phone first thing to call. Instead, taking a step back and trying to come to terms with the fact that she wasn't coming back and it was over. That despite my need to have it go down differently, I would have to move on without her. Something that until Jax's little dilemma, I didn't even believe I was capable of doing.

Avery and Emery offering the perfect opportunity without even realizing it.

Considering what I do for a living, picking up random girls for a quick suck and fuck is the easy part. At least, it's easy for most. Problem is, I'm not that guy and I definitely don't like things easy. The character I portray comes off that way, sure, but the last thing I want is to screw some random girl in a random place and forget all about her when the sun comes up.

This double date—hangout or whatever, it has to be about more than that. Even if it's more for Jax than myself, I want it to mean something. I want to show Emery a good time, especially knowing she's a fan of what I do. I'm just not sure given my track record as of late, that I'll be able to do it.

I tried for years to make sure Kelly knew she walked on water and look where it got me.

Looking down at the phone in an attempt to distract myself, and finding nothing, I head straight into my contacts. My finger hovering over the number I know by heart, I take a deep breath and press down, bringing the phone to my ear and keeping it there despite the urge to hang up right as the rings start going in.

"Brady, you need to stop doing this."

"Hello to you too."

"What do you want?"

"I had to hear your voice, Kel. My life is hell. Everything is going to shit and for some stupid reason, I needed you to know."

"I don't *want* to know that, Brady. We're going through a divorce, remember? We shouldn't even be talking, so why don't you just hang up now and save us both the heartache?"

Her words cut like a knife. Making me realize that despite my hope to the contrary, it really is as over as everyone believes it to be.

"Why does it have to be like this? When I said those vows on the beach, I meant them. I never stopped meaning them."

"Look, Brady, I didn't want to tell you this, especially not over the phone, but there's someone else. I'm sorry. I can't do this with you anymore. See you in court."

As the click of her hanging up rings in my ears, her final words play back on a loop in my head, preventing me from pulling the phone away, even after it follows suit and my phone goes dark.

She's moved on.

It's over.

Emery

Avery hasn't said a word since she came out of our mother's room and back downstairs.

There had been the weak smile she gifted me when we got in her rental car, so I know whatever was said couldn't have been all bad, but with the silence that follows it, all I want to do is pull the car to a stop as force her to tell me what happened. Force her to talk to me. A situation made even more dire given where we're heading. A double date of sorts with two virtual strangers.

Maybe that's it.

I can just bring up meeting Brady and Jax and lead into what happened with Mom after.

"So, this whole thing is pretty crazy, right?" I start, realizing almost immediately that the question could be about our family issues and not about the men we're about to see.

"Which part?"

"Jackson and Brady. I mean, how insane is that?"

"Pretty insane." She replies with a tight smile.

"Do you wanna talk about it?" I ask lightly, not wanting to push, but also not wanting to sit for the entire drive in more of this same uncomfortable silence.

"What's to talk about?"

"Well gee, I don't know, Avery. Maybe we can talk about how you just met your mother for the first time."

"I don't need the reminder, Emery. I was there."

She's tense and her response is clipped. Despite not wanting it to get to me, it does. I don't want her to ever talk to me that way. We're sisters who were both dealt the same shitty hand, just in reverse ways. I want her to see that and feel safe opening up.

"I didn't mean it like that. I just meant, what you did was pretty big. If you want to talk about it, I'm here."

Her eyes soften and my heart slows. *Maybe I haven't totally ruined this after all.*

"What she told me in her letter is pretty much what we talked about. I'm not bothered by anything she said. I'm just not having very nice thoughts about our dad right now."

Our dad.

"I'm sure he had his reasons." I say, even though I don't believe it.

"Reasons I'm never gonna know. *We're* never gonna know." She sighs. "Twenty-five years, Emery."

"I know."

"Maybe I should just call Brady and cancel. I don't think I'm going to be the best company right now."

"I know you feel that way, but maybe this is *exactly* what you need. I mean, think about it. What better way to take a breather than to spend time with two delicious looking guys that also happen to enjoy getting hot and sweaty on the regular?"

"Sorry to disappoint you, but I'm pretty sure they're gonna be showing up with their clothes on, Em."

"Doesn't mean a girl can't dream." I laugh and when after a second or two she joins in, I know I've gotten us back on track.

I just hope that Brady and Jax know what they're getting themselves into.

Chapter Fourteen

Jax

"And there he is! Man, with as long as you took getting down here, we were starting to think you weren't gonna show." Brady calls out the minute I step off the elevator.

Swallowing down what's left of the nervousness I feel, I look up and see both women standing beside Brady and the minute I take them both in, I know I'm in big trouble.

The view from where I am, I can see both of them easily, but I can't tell them apart. They aren't dressed the same or anything else that might be used to confuse us, but their expressions right now were the same, even the way they stood on either side of Brady was identical and it left me at a loss.

I don't know if it's a result of all the alcohol I ingested last night or if there's really no way of telling them apart, but I can actually see this entire thing imploding before it even begins if I walk up and stand beside the wrong girl.

Shit. There has to be something about Avery last night I can remember that makes her stick out from her sister. I can't blow this.

Willing my legs to move, I walk over to where the three of them are standing, all the while hoping that they won't be offended when I stop near Brady until they clear it up.

Brady, seeming to pick up on my unease wastes no time turning it into a joke.

"You alright, buddy? You wouldn't be having trouble telling them apart would ya?"

Apparently lack of sleep doesn't slow him down any. I think as I plaster my best 'I have no idea what you're talking about' expression on. While they all stand around waiting for me to make a move, I take each of the girls in separately.

The girl to Brady's right is dressed in jeans, as is her mirror image on the opposite side. The same shade of dark blue, similar to the one's I'm wearing. The one difference I can spot after staring at them for what feels longer than the few minutes it's been, being the girl on the right wearing a local band t-shirt while the other is decked out in a baby blue cashmere sweater.

Their hair, just running past their shoulders styled the same, dangling loosely down their backs. The one on the left wavy and brown to the other's straight and auburn colored.

It's then that it hits me. The hair has been the answer all along.

Making my way over until I stood directly in front of Brady, I shift in beside him on the left, turning to who I hope is Avery and studying her for some sort of clue that I'm right. When she smiles shyly, I know I've picked correctly. The same electric shock when she brushed against me last night reappearing when she leans in close and our bodies connect again.

"Thank you." I mouth, Emery and Brady none the wiser. Her eyes twinkling as her lips tug up higher, giving me all the answer I need.

"Glad you could tell them apart. I sure as hell couldn't. This one here," Brady laughs, motioning to Emery. "Enjoyed screwing with my head."

"Oh, come on!" she exclaims. "What's the point of being a twin if you can't have a little fun with it? And really, that's just payback for what happened to me last night."

I want to bury my head in the marble floor the minute she speaks of the night before. Not exactly one of my finer moments and one I'm gonna make sure I apologize for now.

"About that. I'm sorry. I don't usually do things quite that crazy."

"Don't even stress about it. From what I hear from Avery, it was all this guy's fault anyway." She says, flicking her eyes to Brady.

"I'm innocent! I told him about the girl at ringside. How the hell was I supposed to know the girl I saw wasn't the one he did?"

Brady throws a look in Avery's direction and she blushes, which despite my every attempt not to, affects me in a way I'm not expecting. I thought after last night it was only her smile that could get to me, but apparently her blush does the same. Just the sight of her cheeks changing shades making my body hum in a way I'm not familiar with.

"Yeah, imagine that. The girl that's never been here before, much less to a wrestling show, getting lost."

"Well, for what it's worth, I think it worked out pretty well that you did get lost." Brady jokes.

"You might be right about that." Avery agrees, smiling. "Now, I hate to break this up but has anyone figured out what we're going to do now that we're all here?"

Catching my expression, she leans a little more into me, and even though I probably should have stepped away in an effort to keep things casual, I don't so much as blink, much less move.

I can't.

I like having her this close.

Completely unaware that in focusing so intently on just how close Avery is, I've completely tuned everything else out, I'm jolted back to reality when after slugging me in the arm, Brady clears his throat.

"Earth to Jax. You hear anything I just said?"

Catching Avery's blush, I shoot him a look. Warning him with the not so hidden glare not to call attention to what he caught me doing.

It's one thing for him to ride me the way he does when we're riding together, but I'm not gonna have him doing it to Avery.

"Obviously not so why don't you go ahead and repeat it."

"Well, before you two went off into your own world, I was saying that even though we said originally we'd double, I was thinking it might be better to split up and do our own thing."

I chance a look between Avery and Emery, knowing that it was really up to them. A decision that in the end, Emery makes for all of us.

"If you guys don't mind, I think I want to have Brady to myself for a while. He keeps calling this town *slow* and I need to prove him wrong. You okay with that, Ave?"

"Yeah, that's fine. After listening to the two of you arguing about it for the last fifteen minutes, I have to agree. Brady needs to be taught a lesson."

"I don't need to be taught. If anything, Jax does. He's the one that grew up in LA." Brady scoffs, his attempt to throw me under the bus after what he started, failing when Emery, not missing a beat throws in her two cents.

"You're right, but he hasn't said one word about this place since he came down to meet us. You've done nothing but." She had him and everyone, including him, knew it. "So now that we know Jax and Avery are cool being on their own, what do you say I get to showing you what Wilmington has to offer?"

Brady nods, pretending to sulk and after another round of laughter, they break off from us and say their goodbyes.

"So," Avery says once we're left to our own devices. "Now that my car has been commandeered, what do you say you show me what you can do in that ride of yours, speed freak?"

Brady

"So, you really think you can change my mind about this town?"

Emery had insisted on driving and I didn't feel like putting up a fight over it. With her wanting to take the lead, it gave me the chance to learn about the woman I had agreed to spend the day with. So while she drove, I intended to keep her good and occupied with constant conversation.

It was the least I could do.

"Are you kidding me? You seriously need to be schooled for your comments back there."

It was impossible not to notice her smile and the way it seemed to eclipse her entire face when she did it. The first of many things that I see she shared with Avery, having that very same smile shone in my direction on more than one occasion the night before.

"Consider yourself warned. I don't change my mind very often. I find my original impression is usually the right one."

"Your daddy teach you that in the back woods of Mississippi?"

If I didn't know she was joking, I would have been pretty pissed off with the flippant way she just said that. Emery, in just the few minutes we were together before Jackson came down, seemed like someone that gave as good as she got and knew exactly which buttons to push that would get a rise out of me.

Something she has no problem taking full advantage of.

"Yeah, right. My *daddy* didn't teach me anything about small towns like this one, unless you count the learning I did about how to get the hell out of one when the show was over."

"Yet, here you are. Still here. I guess all that schoolin' didn't work too well, did it?"

I couldn't help it. I laughed. She's unbelievable, but I wasn't about to let her know it.

"Worked better than you think. In this case, I was given a bonus incentive to stick around."

Emery, still driving to a location unknown to me, raises her eyebrows in mock surprise. "And the bonus incentive would be what exactly, Mr. Raines?"

With how easy the conversation seemed to flow between us, I found I could have given her any smart assed answer and it wouldn't have mattered, but for some reason, I felt the need to at least be halfway serious with my response.

"It's always a bonus when a pretty lady agrees to date you."

"A date? Is that what this is?"

"You know what I mean." I say before realizing she might not have the first clue what I'm getting at. "You do know what I mean, right?"

Slugging me in the shoulder lightly, she laughs. "Of course I know what you mean, but I have to admit I didn't expect something like that to come from you."

This is where things were about to get real interesting.

"What do you mean by that? What did you expect to hear?"

Sucking in a breath, she taps her fingers on the steering wheel before letting it out and skirting her eyes in my direction.

"I just mean, I know what I see on television and that guy never would have said something like you did. You called a date with me a bonus incentive, and if I'm not mistaken, it sounded like you actually meant it."

I nod, now understanding and not faulting her one bit for it. What she knew had nothing to do with the real me. Well, except the money part. That was unfortunately something I couldn't turn my back on or deny so there was no point in even trying.

"Emery, if we're going to spend the rest of the day enjoying each other's company, I think it's best you forget everything you think you know and we start over. I know what you see on TV and at shows, but that's not me. Not even close. So let me show you the real me."

It was the most impassioned speech I've ever done and judging from the way she's now pinching her brow with the hand not on the wheel, she was affected by it as well.

"Well, if you want me to take you as you are and not as you were, then you need to do something for me first."

Thankful to be back on more playful ground, I stare her down with a smirk. "And what would that be?"

"Let me prove to you how wrong you are about this town. Agree to not make up your mind until I'm completely done with you."

It's an easy enough request to agree to, but I wasn't about to give in easily. I was going to let her stew in it for a bit. Just the thought of keeping her off kilter brought a smile to my face. One that not even distracting myself by taking her in could wipe away.

"What are you smiling about, rich boy?"

"Just wondering when the car ride ends and you finally show me what this town has to offer. So tell me, Emery. When do we start?

Pulling the car off the road and down into what looks like an underbrush of trees and shrubs, she shoves it into park and pulls the key from the ignition with a quick point outside.

"It begins now, Mr. Big Shot."

Before I can respond, she's got her seatbelt off and the door open, exiting the car. Grinning at me and giving me the finger after slamming the door and making her way around to my side. Saving the best for last and jutting her tongue out when I return the favor.

Emery Davis is clearly insane.

Consider me officially intrigued. Hooked even.

Following her lead and slipping off the belt, I exit the car. Making sure before I head over to where she's waiting that the door is locked up tight. Already knowing that despite her need to get me to see otherwise, there's no way in hell with where she's brought us that I'm going to change my mind on this town anytime soon.

Unless her plan is not to use the place we're at to change my mind, but instead going with the company I'm with to do it.

That's something that with just the short back and forth in the car, she's already got me swaying my opinion on.

Game on.

Chapter Fifteen

Avery

I've been in this car for at least fifteen minutes and I'm still pinching myself every couple of seconds, wondering when I'm going to wake up from this obvious dream I'm starring in.

If someone had asked me a few hours ago if I pictured myself riding around in one of the best looking cars on the planet, not to mention the fastest, I would have laughed them out of the room.

Yet, here I am and I'm still trying to figure out just what I did to get here.

"You're awfully quiet. You okay?" Jax breaks the silence, softly asking.

Things were different before we left the hotel. I was still pretty quiet, but at the same time I was upbeat. It's only the last few minutes where things have turned awkward.

Tucking the stray pieces of my unruly hair behind my ear, I look over to him at the exact moment he seems to have the same idea, pulling his attention from the road in front of us to study me before looking back.

"I'm fine, Jackson."

"In that case, do me a favor?"

"Sure."

"Call me Jax."

Nodding, I try again. "I'm fine, Jax. Really. I'm just…"

"You're just what?"

"The car." I admit with a sigh. "It's like nothing I've ever seen before. I feel kind of awkward sitting in it. Like I don't belong."

Looking down to my lap, embarrassed by my admission, I flick at some imaginary speck of dust until his voice clearing the air pulls my attention back.

"Are you sure it's the car and not me?"

"What's that supposed to mean?" I ask, my body tensing up defensively.

"When I get around you," he explains. "I seem to become completely unglued. I can't really explain it any better than that. I've noticed that you kind of do the same unless it's Brady you're talking to. I mean, he's not here and we haven't said so much as one word to each other past what we're saying now about the car. I guess I'm just wondering if you'd rather just go back to the hotel."

Crap. Crap. Crap.

I guess it's true what they say about there being a first time for everything. I've managed to drive this off into a ditch in ten minutes or less.

Maybe splitting up wasn't such a good idea after all.

Jax

I really wasn't planning on admitting everything I did, but I can't deny it feels better knowing I did and it's out there.

Tired of trying to have a conversation where I could only look at her for a second before putting my focus back on the road, I push down on the brakes, slowing down before pulling over.

Putting the car in park and cutting the ignition, I lean back in the seat, twisting over until I'm facing her down, finally able to give her the attention I've been wanting to since we decided to go for the drive earlier.

"You've got the wrong impression here, Jax. When I said what I did about your car, I meant it. I have drooled over a car like this since I was sixteen years old and living minutes from the dealership. But drooling was all I could ever do because the only people that could afford a car like this were people with money. More than I ever made growing up, even though I wasn't exactly living the hard life. Sitting in one, it's a little uncomfortable, that's all."

"It's really just about the car?"

Opening her eyes again, having closed them after she spilled her guts, she turns toward me and with a sheepish grin, nods.

Shit. If I wasn't so hyper sensitive to every single move she makes and paid more attention to what she actually says and the way she looks while she's saying it, I would have seen that she's telling the truth. I remember her eyes when we pulled in behind her yesterday and they're the same way now. It's too much for her. The fucking car I insisted on buying myself with all the money I'd managed to save over the last few years is too flashy.

"Why would you think I wanted to be here with Brady?"

"It's stupid," I release an embarrassed laugh. "But last night, things just seemed easy between you two. The conversation seemed to move. When it came to me, other than a few glances and heavy looks, we didn't seem to share much of anything."

"You haven't exactly been the most talkative, Jax. The reason it was so easy to talk to Brady is because he doesn't show emotion the way you do. You exude what you're feeling. They do call it body language for a reason."

My cheeks start to burn with embarrassment at being called out again for the way I acted the previous night. First Brady and now her.

Fantastic.

"Was I really that bad?"

"It was noticeable, but it wasn't bad. That's not the right choice of words."

"You really want to be here with me?"

The way she looks at me after I ask, it's like she can see right through me. Like she can see that I'm insecure because of all the shit I went through with Melinda. That I'm nothing like the person I was before she walked into my life and turned it upside down.

I'm not sure how I feel about that. *It's too close.*

"Yes, Jax." she smiles. "In fact, right here in the middle of nowhere, in a town I barely know, is *exactly* where I wanna be."

The feeling that erupts as she said that has the power to blow me completely off my feet. My heart seeming to expand to three times its normal size.

"Will you do something for me?"

Catching her eye as she asks the question, I hold us in place with an intense return of my own.

"Anything."

"Walk with me. I think I've had enough of the car for a little while."

Such a simple request and one that earns my immediate agreement as I slide myself back up, open the door and slip out. Making my way around to the passenger side and opening her door for her before extending my hand and helping her out.

My proximity to the door as she slips out having her body brushing against mine and just like every other time we've come into contact, leaving a mixture of electricity and heat in its wake.

"Where would you like to walk?"

Watching as she points to the left of the car where the trees aren't as heavy, I start to move but her hand falling to her side and brushing innocently against mine halts me.

Steadying myself from the jolt of electricity that seems to shoot from hand straight up through mine as our fingers find their way together, I catch and pull her close as her own reaction has her skirting and starting to stumble on a rock jutting up from the ground.

"Thank you." She whispers, and taking a chance with as close as we are, I brush my fingers across her cheek, reveling in the feel of her before leaning in with a whisper of my own.

"You're welcome."

Chapter Sixteen

Brady

Unbelievable.

What could she possibly want to show me here that would change my perception of this town? If I wanted trees, land as far as the eye can see, and picture perfect scenery I could have easily gone to visit my old man.

There's a part of me that wants to tell her that, but like my dad never misses a chance to tell me, I lack the gumption to follow through. As quick as Emery is with comebacks, I'm kind of afraid she might take me out into the trees and chuck me down an embankment and no one would be the wiser.

"You wanna tell me what could possibly be down in this wilderness that would make me change my mind?" I call out, surprised she made her way so far from me in the short time since she'd gotten out of the car.

"Something I bet you've never done!"

It's only when she stops a few seconds later, and I follow her eyes as they fall to the ground that I catch the first problem with her plan.

My shoes.

Pretty sure with whatever she has planned, I'm not dressed right. An expensive pair of loafers definitely not suitable for this trek. Something I was going to pay for when we got back to the hotel.

"We can go back if you want." She says, her eyes never once lifting off my shoes. "I assumed that you'd be able to handle this, but I didn't give much thought to what you were wearing."

"Tell me where to go and I'm good. I can always replace my shoes."

I know how it sounds the minute it comes out, but sneaking a glance at Emery, I have no idea how she's taken it. Her face is a blank slate.

"I'm sorry. That was a stupid thing to say."

Her eyes lift and she studies me, still not saying a word, and as her eyes move up and down, I can only imagine what she's thinking. I'm in an outfit that probably costs more than what she can make in six months, and my cologne, a unique blend that was personally made for me, another thing she probably wouldn't be able to afford.

I've seen the look before, and just like I loathed it then, I do again now. She's judging me and who can blame her. I make it pretty easy with off-handed comments like the one I just let slip.

"I'm sorry." She says.

"For what?"

"You asked me not to judge you, but I did it just now. I feel horrible."

Moving forward, I stop directly in front of her and lean in. Pressing my lips as close to her ear as I can get.

"I'm the one that casually threw out the stupid comment about my shoes. I know better, but sometimes, that loafer covered foot of mine becomes attached to my mouth and there's no getting it out."

I'm rewarded when she laughs and despite how mixed up I've been feeling, my heart swells hearing it.

With as often as I was exposed to girls growing up, family friends and then some of the girls at school before I met Kelly, I'm amazed at how comfortable it is standing here with a normal girl. Not one that's interested in what I can buy them or do for them, but one content in her own skin. Doing things her way. The kind of girl that apologizes for making a judgment that is more spot on than not.

"Foot in mouth happens to me a lot too. I really am sorry."

Reaching out, I press my finger to her lips, the only way I can think of to quiet her. Let her see that I'm not upset by her assumptions. It's not the first time I've heard it, been judged by it and it definitely won't be the last. Her feeling bad about it is pointless.

"You have nothing to be sorry for, Emery."

Stepping back, I pull my finger away, shoving my hand into the pocket of my pants and flash her my trademark grin.

"Now that we got that resolved; where exactly are you taking me?"

She starts walking again, this time even faster than before and as I follow along, paying more attention to the ground in front of me instead of the girl, I look up after a few minutes and realize she's nowhere to be found. Sliding my way slowly down the embankment, assuming that's where she went, I'm faced with her reason for bringing me here the second my feet hit solid ground. A cliff overlooking what has to be the clearest body of water I've ever seen.

Moving closer, parking myself beside where Emery is standing, I follow the direction of her gaze and leaning over, catch the water crashing into the rocks about thirty feet or more below us.

The view is breathtaking.

"Are my eyes deceiving me? Have I really made the rich boy speechless?"

With the amount of time I spend on the road, I've had the pleasure of seeing some of the most beautiful places, but this is by far the most serene. My mind slowing for the first time in weeks as I just stand in awe of what I'm seeing.

I've never had a place I could call mine. Somewhere I could just be and not worry about anything or anyone disturbing it. My job prevents it. But here, I feel like this could be my place.

Nothing can get to me here.

"Not speechless. Just surprised. I don't think I've seen anything like this before and I've been around and seen a lot."

"Well, there's still time to make you speechless, since you don't know the best part yet."

"Somehow I doubt that'll happen, but go for it. Humor me."

Grinning, possibly even brighter than she had before, she accepts my challenge and runs with it.

"Do you wanna know what people do on this cliff?"

I can definitely think of a few things I would do up here, but I'm pretty damn sure that's not what she's getting at.

"Growing up, my friends would come down here and one day, while we were all just sitting around, one of them jumped off. Then after they did it, someone else followed until pretty much all of us were doing it."

Hearing Emery talk so casually about jumping off a cliff has me backing up and away from the edge. The idea of standing there talking with her about taking that kind of risk was enough to scare me off mountains, water, and cliffs for the foreseeable future.

I might be a wrestler, and it might be a risk going against guys double my size, but nothing near the level that jumping off a cliff is.

"People actually jump off here?"

She nods and continues with her story. "It's called cliff diving. They've made a joke of it in movies and shows, but this is where it originated for a lot of the people that live here."

"Are you all crazy? Don't you realize that all it would take is one slip and you could end up dead?"

Emery laughs lightly, before joining me a few steps back from the edge.

"We're aware of it. We just don't care. So, Raines. You wanna take a risk and experience one of the best things this town has to offer?"

Taking stock of what she's asking and prepared to answer her with a hearty *no fucking way in hell I'm doing that*, she puts her fingers to my lips and smiles.

"Don't answer yet. I want you to think about it as I take you to the next town highlight. If you really want to enjoy this town though, you'll come cliff diving with me just once before you hit the road."

Jax

Walking for what feels like hours, Avery finally comes to a stop, lifting our hands up and over to a collection of rocks, motioning to them in earnest.

"Had enough walking finally?" I joke, following her over and taking the rock next to her when she sits.

"I did." She admits with a soft chuckle. Looking from her out in the direction we just came from, realizing how far we've walked when I can't even so much as make out the car anymore, I settle back onto the rock, breathing in the air before shifting my body and attention to her.

"So what was it like, meeting Emery for the first time?"

"Pretty much what you would expect really. She had the advantage, knowing about me. So it was basically just me sitting there scared out of my mind and forcing her to deal with it."

"Are you glad you did it?"

"You know, if you asked me a month ago if I wanted to have a sister, I probably would have laughed at you, because the idea of it was just so preposterous. Now, I can't imagine going back. I'm glad I saw it through."

"It had to be surreal though, right? Like being awake in a dream?"

She nods almost instantly, my words fitting her initial reaction perfectly.

"What about you? Do you have any brothers or sisters?"

"Two younger sisters. Denise and Jennifer. We don't get to see each other as much these days, but we try to talk at least a couple of times a week and get together at least once every few months."

"Were you all close growing up?"

"Growing up they idolized me, but I never really understood why. I mean, I was just me. They hung on everything I did, though. I didn't have the heart to tell them that their brother just wasn't all that cool."

"Jackson Merrick not cool? Please tell me you're joking!" Avery calls out, slapping a hand over her mouth in mock surprise.

"I know it's hard to believe, but I wasn't the guy I am now. I was shy and awkward. But now you, I'm betting you were the opposite."

Laughing when she snorts, her obvious attempt to call bullshit on my attempt to turn things around her, I ask again.

"What were you like growing up?"

Falling silent, she stares out away from us, bringing her hand down to her lap and tapping her fingers against her leg.

"Truthfully, I was a book worm. And before you ask, it hasn't changed much since. I didn't have many friends, but the few I did have never let me down. I guess you could say I was a gigantic nerd by todays standards."

There is certainly nothing nerdy about you now.

"You don't seem so nerdy to me, but even if you are or were, it doesn't really matter. We're all a little nerdy."

She blushes and attempting to hide it, shifts on her rock, burying her face into my side.

Rendered incapable of speaking, I surrender to the way it feels having her this close. Not wanting to over think what's happening, but unable to deny my mind and hearts need for more, I slide my arm out from under her as smoothly as I can and bring it up and around until I'm resting it around her shoulders and bringing her in closer.

"Is this okay?" I ask when after a few seconds, she doesn't pull away or attempt to right her position.

Murmuring out a reply that with the force of the wind makes it impossible to make out, I ask again only this time she doesn't respond with words. Instead snuggling herself even more into the embrace.

"Why did you agree to this whole thing, Jax?"

The answer to that is easy. Between my own need to finally move on from Melinda, along with Brady's constant pushing, it's a no brainer why I'm sitting here.

"It's been almost three years since I've been out with anyone that wasn't a co-worker. I was never ready. There's a small part of me that feels that maybe I'm still not ready, but I had to take the chance to be sure. Does that make sense?"

"It does."

"Why did you agree to do this? Was it really to help Brady out the way you claimed last night?"

"No. There was more to it than helping Brady, Jax."

Speaking so softly that I have to struggle to hear her, I piece together what I've heard and push for more.

"Then what was it?"

Shifting in my arms, she begins to sit back up and I'm immediately affected by the loss of her. The cozy place she's carved out in my arms, no longer warm, but deathly cold.

"I knew Brady would want me to hook him up with Emery the second the word twin came out of my mouth. Even though having a twin was still new to me, I do have some experience with guys. It's a standard response for most. So when he did it, I just used it as a means to get what I wanted at the same time."

What she wanted?

"Jackson," she pauses, taking a breath. "Last night, I got the feeling there was something between us. Something that might have been mutual. So despite having no experience with anything like it before, I did what I had to do."

The electricity and gravitational pull to her I've had, she's explained it. Felt it too.

The first woman in years I've felt it with.

"You wanted to go out with me?" I ask to be sure. "Even after I made a fool of myself more than once in the same night?"

She nods before swallowing hard, obviously not trusting her voice to speak. A sentiment I can sympathize with as I'm in the same predicament.

But now, armed with the answer I'd secretly been hoping to hear, there's no way I can continue on like I haven't heard it.

Been moved by it.

As comfortable as it's been sitting here and talking with her, the time for talking is over. I need more.

Shifting closer and bringing her tighter into me, needing to recreate the warmth we were wrapped in before I let her pull away, I lift her chin up until our eyes are solely trained on each other. Lowering my lips to hers, I do what I've been wanting to do since I came down from my room earlier and saw her again. and holding onto her tighter, needing to recreate the warmth we were wrapped in before I'd let her pull away, I lift her chin up until our eyes are trained solely on each other. And lowering my lips to hers, do what I think I've been wanting to do since I came down from my room earlier and saw her.

As my lips brush against hers and she responds, her lips parting and giving me what I need in order to deepen it, I say everything with it that I couldn't find the words to tell her before.

Making Avery understand that even though this is moving at warp speed, I want it.

I want her.

Chapter Seventeen

Avery

Long after the kiss ended, Jackson stayed close. His lips lingering on mine in a way that spoke of the same deep seeded desire I have to keep them near. As if in staying close it could erase everything we'd gone through in our pasts before this moment. At least, that's what my heart wants to believe, because it's what I feel having him this close.

A spell wound around us both, our eyes lingering on each other, as unable to look away as our bodies are to create distance.

I can't even remember the last time I'd been kissed so tenderly and felt so much.

I know why I can't remember. It's because it's never happened before. Not like this. Which means, I've experienced a first with Jackson Merrick.

"I'm sorry." he finally says, breaking the silence. Effectively bringing to an end the spell we've spent the last few minutes under, slamming us full force back into reality.

"W—what for?" I stammer, struggling to catch my breath and slow my racing heart.

"I shouldn't have done that."

Feeling my heartbeat slow to a crawl, I inhale a deep breath of air and swallow down the urge to cry that's clawing its way to the surface at his apology.

Who kisses a girl and says sorry? Was the kiss really that bad?

"You're kidding, right?"

As swept up in the moment as I'd become, and as amazing as the kiss itself had felt, I'm struggling to understand where it all went wrong.

Wasn't he the one that made the first move? The moan I heard escape from somewhere deep inside him when I kissed him back, did I imagine it?

No, of course I didn't. So why is he sorry?

"No, Avery. I'm not joking. I feel bad for taking advantage of you. It wasn't right and I'm sorry."

If I wasn't still locked in his embrace, tangible proof I'm still very much in the moment, I would believe this had been a dream. He can't possibly be sitting here apologizing because he thinks he overstepped when the reality is he gave me what I wanted.

"You have nothing to be sorry about, Jackson." I tell him, reverting back to his full name as I attempt to assuage some of his guilt. "I was in that kiss as much as you were, if not more. So please stop apologizing."

With the spell broken and what I believed to be a pretty life altering moment ruined, I feel the awkwardness beginning to set in and before it can get any worse, I shift and move away from him entirely. Being so close with what's happening now, far too intimate.

"Why are you pulling away?"

Having put enough distance between us, I push myself up off the rock and begin to pace. My mind replaying the last few minutes, trying to figure out where it all went wrong. Where we went from kissing to riding off into a ditch. Unable to shake with each pace back and forth that I make, the feeling that in some way, the kiss didn't live up to his expectations, leaving only one person at fault.

Me.

"Avery, please stop and tell me why you pulled away." He pleads, reaching out and attempting to bring me to a stop.

"Don't you get it, Jax? I know you haven't dated in a while, but Jesus. It's pretty obvious."

My heart plummets when I see him flinch. Making me wish in the moment I could magically teleport myself out of here. This space. The hotel. Maybe even the state altogether.

Finding out my mother was alive and learning that not only did I have a sister, but a twin, may have brought me here, but how quickly things turned south between me and Jax was making me wish I'd never learned the truth at all. At the very least, making me wish I learned it on a day when he wouldn't be crossing my path.

No, Avery. Coming here and meeting Emery, connecting with her and your mom was a good thing. The best thing. Jackson Merrick doesn't get to ruin that.

"You know what," Jax interrupts my internal pep talk. "I don't get it. And contrary to what you said, it has nothing to do with my limited dating experience. But thank you for throwing that in my face. I managed to go almost five whole minutes without the reminder of how much of a loser I am when it comes to the opposite sex."

"Jacks—" Cutting me off before I can even finish getting his name out, he continues.

"Why don't you tell me why apologizing to you is such a horrible thing?"

I know that bringing his past—or lack of it—into this was a bad idea. That I'd hurt him in doing it, but with the way everything has played out since the kiss, it can't be helped.

My head is a mess.

When he kissed me, it was almost as if the world stopped moving and it was just the two of us. The force of the wind had changed and slowed to a crawl, the trees rustling, which the entire time we'd been talking had been loud, had fallen away until it was barely there at all. Every conceivable distraction was obliterated for the short period of time his lips were on mine.

And then he had to pull away, apologize for kissing me and make me think that everything we shared was all in my head. It had to be because the only reason for someone to say sorry after sharing a kiss like we did is because they regretted it.

"It's not horrible, but think about it. We kiss, I experience something I've never felt before and before I can even process it, you speak and the first thing out of your mouth is *'I'm sorry'*. You made it sound like you wish it hadn't happened at all."

Content that I'd gotten the point I wanted to make across, I finally stop pacing and sit back down on the rock, making sure as

I do to keep my distance. The magnetic pull between us still very much alive the second my butt is planted, but one I need to fight.

"Is that really what you think? That I regret kissing you?"

"You tell me. What did you feel?" I mumble through the cracks in the hands now covering my face, determined to shield myself from him and whatever he's about to say next. Words I'm sure my head and heart aren't ready to hear.

He's not the only one with limited experience when it comes to dating. I've only had two boyfriends in the last ten years and neither of them made me feel even a fraction of the things I am being with him.

Sensing his movement before hearing the tread of his boots scraping across the ground, I lower my hands at the exact moment he drops to his knees in front of me. His hands coming out and resting on my legs, his eyes trained on mine even though I have yet to meet them head on. A gaze so penetrating it's impossible not to respond to.

Hearing him sigh at the exact moment I look up, he runs his hand roughly through his hair in what appears to be frustration, but who it's directed to, me or him, I can't be sure.

"God, Avery. The last time I kissed a woman, I thought it was the one I was going to marry. She was cheating on me. Deceiving me. When I think about the last kiss I shared with her, and the one we just shared, they don't even compare. That scares the shit out of me. I don't know what to do with it."

"What do you mean they don't compare?"

"I mean," he says, his voice worn. "The last time I kissed Melinda, all I felt was hurt. I was just empty. Completely devoid of any kind of feeling remotely pure and good. The way it should feel when you kiss someone."

"And kissing me?"

"The only word that comes to mind for what I felt kissing you is...calm. Absolute tranquility. The purest peace I have *ever* felt. So, no. I didn't regret kissing you. If anything, it was probably the first right thing I've done in years."

Not wanting to take away from the conversation but still needing answers, I forge ahead with what I really want to know.

"Was it really that bad with your ex?"

He seems to weigh the options as his teeth grind deeply into his lips. His eyes lifting to the sky and closing as he releases a heavy sigh before lowering them back down to mine.

"In the beginning it wasn't. That's what everyone says I think, but honestly, it felt like the two of us were a force to be reckoned with. I was happy. Near the end, when I found out where she was really spending her nights and just how long it had been going on, yes. It *was* that bad."

Wetting my lips and parting them, more than ready to apologize for what had obviously been a severe overreaction, he stops me in my tracks.

"This isn't the way I imagined the day going. A little too heavy for a first date, huh?"

"You think this is a date?"

"I realize we only officially met yesterday and that a lot of the reason we've been thrown together like this has to do with my friend and his need to go out with a twin, but yes, Avery. For me, this is a date. One I'm pretty sure I've blown."

Alright, I've let this go on long enough. It's definitely time for me to apologize. I can't let him believe, now that I know what is really going on, that any of this is his fault. The fault here, it's mine.

"I'm sorry, Jackson. I overreacted when you apologized. I know what I felt and when I heard the word sorry, it scared me."

Finally lifting from his crouched position on the ground, he lowers his body down onto the rock beside me and even though each movement he makes as he inches his way closer is calculated and slow, when his arm finally does come around me again, I waste no time melting into him.

"You have to believe me, Avery. This is all new to me. We've barely made it into our first date and I'm already addicted to the way it feels being around you. The way it felt when you kissed me back. I can't explain it, and I'm not even entirely sure I want to, but what I do know and can explain is that I don't want to lose it or worse. Do something that could possibly send it and you running."

"Like the way my sister ran from you at the show?"

"Yeah, just like that." He laughs and the sound mixed with the feel of it against my face as it resonates all the way through his body has me burrowing even closer. "Do you understand now where I'm coming from?"

Nodding my head against his chest, his body freezes and no longer thinking, instead allowing myself to just feel, I bring my hand up and let it rest just over his heart. Feeling the strong but steady beat before bringing my head back down in order to feel it. Allowing myself the chance to really feel him.

"I understand now, Jax. This scares me too. I mean, can meeting someone and spending time with them over the course of twenty-four hours really lead anywhere?"

His next words come so quickly it's as though he said them without thinking, his question probative.

"Where do you want this to go? Or is it too soon to ask that?"

I desperately want to answer his question, but am unsure of just what the right answer is. Despite my need to dive into this headfirst without thinking, the very real situation we've found ourselves in can't be denied.

We've known each other less than a day. Spending a couple of hours in between sleep and the show the night before together does not a love story make. We know next to nothing about each other. Things that most people learn before diving into something infinitely more serious than a one night fling together.

Admitting that based on those couple of instances alone that I want more, or that I want to explore exactly what is taking place between us seems wrong. Fast. Like maybe we need to take a step back from one another, swallow down the pull we seem to have and go about this a different way.

A way that would prevent this from crashing and burning.

Just do the right thing and tell him what you feel.

"I want you to kiss me again, Jax. Only this time, with no apologies attached. I want to enjoy the way I feel when you're holding me and not question it or overthink it. Can we do that?"

Not leaving another second to chance, he gives me his answer as he leans down, this time cupping my face in both of his hands before bringing his lips down on mine. Rougher than the last time, deeper even, yet somehow, even with the level of force he's using, still coming across as tender as he did the first time. Giving me his answer and effectively making all voices, inner or otherwise, go silent.

He wants to do this.

Chapter Eighteen

Brady

"So what could you possibly show me that would top the cliff?" I ask once we're settled back in the car and well on our way to what she called the busy part of town.

What I don't have to heart to tell her with how spaced out everything seems to be and the sheer amount of green still surrounding us, looks about as dead as every other part I've seen so far.

"You'll see soon enough. I'm not giving away my plans, otherwise this would be for nothing." She motions between us. "Have you given any more thought about jumping off the cliff?"

Jesus. She doesn't even try to hide her smirk. Catching on quickly to the unease I feel and running with it.

"I know we don't exactly know each other, but you gotta know by now that I'm never going to do that."

Eyebrows lifting, she continues driving, but her smirk raises into a full blown smile.

"You don't seem like a 'fraidy cat to me, Brady Raines. In fact, if I had to guess, I would peg you as more of a risk taker given what your job entails. So why is it that you're scared shitless to do something that aside from being exhilarating, is also incredibly easy?"

"Jumping off a cliff is your idea of easy, huh? All this time I thought the definition of easy when it came to a woman was a chick that put out on a first date. My bad. Thanks for clearing that up."

With how stupid I sound even to my own ears, I'm completely unprepared for the boisterous laugh that escapes. In fact, with the way I shifted closer to the door right after I said it, it's safe to say I was prepared for a punch. Definitely not a laugh.

Emery really is in a class all her own.

"I bet you've met a lot of easy girls in your line of work, so you'd know the real definition better than me."

Despite knowing she's joking, I can't control the eye roll that follows her statement. That line and others like it having been said so many times over the years that it's as familiar as breathing to me now. Also another way I'm not like the others.

The guys I work with; the ones I consider my brothers, have no problem indulging in the women that come to our shows. Not all of them do it, but when faced with willing partners ready to give them what they want, a lot of them will succumb and take what they want.

Groupies. Hangers on. Or what the guys I work with like to call them—ring rats. They're everywhere. Women that despite knowing better and on an average day, even command better from people they encounter, seem to leave their self-respect at the door the second they get to a show and do everything in their power to get as close as possible to the performers they love. Even taking it so far as to sleep with the guys on our crew, hoping it gets them one step closer to the real prize.

Having the wrestler they love buried balls deep in them at the end of the night.

Maybe it's because Kelly and I were together straight out of high school that I didn't fall victim to it, but the idea of sleeping with another woman when I had a beautiful one waiting at home, just never appealed to me. I do get why it happens with a lot of the other guys though.

Weeks on the road without companionship, other than the guy you're sharing the road with, can get rough. It can tear apart even the strongest relationships. So picking up some willing girl at the end of the night and getting off, it makes sense.

Wrong? Sure, but we're guys, and everyone knows, guys can be pigs. Me included. I just choose to be a pig in a different way than most.

"Hey, rich boy! We're here."

"Your big plan to get me to change my mind about this town is to take me bowling?" I ask in disbelief, when after sitting up a little straighter in my seat, I take in where here is.

She laughs again, the same infectious one from earlier, her eyes practically glowing with the evil grin now plastered on her face and like before, I can't look away.

"Did you have something better in mind? Maybe you'd rather I drive you across town to the gym so you can teach me how to wrestle?"

Filing that idea away for another time because it's definitely something I wouldn't mind doing if she was game, I focus on the issue at hand.

"That's actually not a bad idea since I've never wrestled a girl before, but this isn't about what I want. It's about you changing my mind about this place." I remind her. "You really think bowling is the way to do it?"

"Why not? You got something against getting beat by a girl?"

"I guess that means you bowl a lot?" I laugh, and Emery just shrugs before slipping off her seatbelt and shoving her door open. Jumping from the car the same way she'd done earlier when we arrived at the cliff.

Well, shit. That didn't go the way I was expecting.

This all started out as a joke. Learning that Avery had a twin, it was just supposed to be about getting to live out some stupid teenage porno style fantasy. It quickly turned into an experiment of sorts, because I wanted to use this experience as a test to see how ready I was to move on from Kelly. Now, though, even with as up and down as its appearing to be, I'm actually in it.

I want to do it with her.

Even if in the end it means swallowing my fear and jumping off the damn cliff.

So wearing what I'm positive has to be the stupidest grin, I spot her heading across the parking lot and make quick work of following suit. Shoving my way out of the car and picking up the pace until I'm pulling her to a stop right after she steps through the door.

"Why don't you get the shoes and I'll pick the lane." she points in the direction of the shoes, completely ignoring the brush of my hands across hers. "Mine are a 10."

Ignoring the rush I experienced when we touched and swallowing down the awkwardness at how quickly she chooses to ignore it, I do what she asked. Jogging over to the counter and picking up the two sets of shoes. Thanking the guy behind the counter before making my way over to where she stands in the right of the alley, standing between two lanes with a look of indecision written all over her face.

"You need a hand picking what lane to play in?" I joke before tossing the shoes on the floor beside the seats and heading over to where she's standing, eyes flitting between the two lanes.

"Nope. We can use this one." She points to the one closest to the wall. "I just wanted to pick the best one to beat your ass in."

This girl. Damn.

"Are you sure you're not a wrestler? I don't think I've ever come across that level of cockiness outside of the ring before."

"Jealous?"

"Yeah, that's it exactly. Pick a ball, champ. It's time to put your money where your mouth is." I motion toward the balls, and with a soft laugh she taps what has got to be the ugliest looking ball in the place before picking it up and making her way over to the seat to slip into her shoes.

"Care to make a friendly wager?" she asks once I've slipped off my boots in favor of the shit brown and off white bowling shoes.

"Sure. What'd you have in mind?"

With the way her eyes seem to spark and come alive, I can easily see it's not going to be something I like.

"If I win, you've got to cliff dive before you head out of town."

Damnit.

"You've got a deal. But just in case I happen to suddenly remember how to bowl and beat you, you've got to do something for me."

Questioning me silently, her brows raising and her eyes going wide, obviously wondering what it is I could possibly want from her, I laugh. Other than countering her wager by pulling out of the cliff diving, she really can't imagine what else I might want from her and just like her indecision over the lanes was cute, this is downright adorable.

And it makes me want to see how far I can take it.

"Well, you looking at me like that makes me want to barter for two things. Do you think you'd be up for two if I win?"

"How much is two worth to you? Will you make it *'rain'*, Brady?"

If my father were here and got a load of the way Emery is acting, he'd say he couldn't believe the gumption she had. Even with me throwing her off by asking for two things, her level of cockiness is still as strong as ever. Not only making fun of my name but my signature move in the same breath.

Is nothing sacred to her?

"It's worth a lot, believe me, but not enough for me to make it rain. So what do you say? Can I have two things or not?"

"Sure, why not. It's not like you're gonna beat me anyway." She goads me. "Hit me with your best shot, rich boy."

Answering her confidant grin with one of my own, I tell her what I'm after.

"I win, you agree to go out with me again before I leave town."

Watching when after I've told her the first thing I want, her face doesn't so much as twitch in response, I let her have the rest. Enjoying the way her jaw drops the second the second part of my plan comes to fruition.

"And you owe me a kiss."

Emery

After playing four frames and readying for the fifth, I had a pretty significant lead on Brady. What, if the sweat beads pouring down over his face and down to his neck is any indication, was obviously starting to get to him.

I'd been expecting him to get competitive once the game started, it worked the same way with Mike whenever the two of us hit the lanes, but this level of concentration, how serious he is as he sets up for his turn, it's a whole other beast. Like the idea of cliff diving has freaked him out so much that he's putting everything he's got into this game. One that if I keep going on the roll I am, I will win. His reaction now making me doubt the entire wager altogether.

Watching as he takes another step forward, I focus on the rigid stance of his body as he prepares to take his shot. The entire mood changing as he lets go and it travels straight down the middle of the lane, impacting with the pins and knocking them all down. His rigidness quickly turning into a body hanging loose, completely with a smirk to completely the package.

"Yeah, baby! Strike!"

"Your first strike of the night and you're getting that excited? Rich boy, let me take you to school. You need to be taught."

"Is that your way of saying you're willing to be my teacher?"

"Only if you're willing to be my student." I shoot back, causing his mouth to drop open, but standing and heading past him to take my turn instead of calling him on it. Laughing all the way down the lane, I set up and release the ball, not paying a lick of attention to what I'm actually doing and being slammed with the reality that his little display and the banter after it had thrown me off my game.

The ball that at first had been running a straight line down the middle, now veering off to the side at the last second and sliding easily into the gutter.

Shit. So much for my plan to school him.

"Looks like someone is losing their edge." He jokes, when after releasing a defeated breath, I turn and face him down. My entire body reacting to what's happened as my shoulders slump in defeat.

"In your dreams, pal." I counter quickly, before he can realize just how rattled I am and attempt to exploit it.

I might not know much about him yet, but I do know my way around guys. Mike teaching me all I need to know.

We're at a pivotal point in this competitive dance we're doing. One slipup, where I show even the tiniest bit of weakness, and he'll be all over it.

Brady can't get that here. Call it me being one of the guys or wanting to attempt to be as confident as I was earlier, but if he's taking this seriously, so am I.

The rounds pass quickly after his first strike and despite every attempt at shaking his effect on me off, I continue to lose a little bit more of my edge with each passing frame, until we're running straight into the final round. With him surpassing my lead and actually coming out ahead.

Could he really be one of the top performers in the ring *and* some kind of bowling champion too?

Given that he's the son of one of the biggest names in the wrestling business in Bill Raines, I suppose it shouldn't come as a shock. With Bill as his dad, he's probably proficient in every damn thing he does.

And that, with as serious as I'm now taking this, is something I'm not happy about.

"You were holding out on me." I state evenly, still trying to piece together how he could be in the lead when not four rounds before, I had basically been handing him his ass.

"Not on your life, darlin'. I just seem to have found my groove where you seem to have lost yours."

Stalking down the lane after picking up his ball, all I can do is pray that he didn't hit another strike this time around. If he does I'm guaranteed to lose.

Screw changing the conditions of our bet. I need to get him on that cliff.

Brady Raines may think he's been living his dream wrestling all over the world the way he does, but he hasn't lived at all and I'm determined to make him see that.

Closing my eyes as he releases the ball and it begins its slow descent down the lane, I do something I haven't done since my mom got sick. I pray that his ball swerves at the last second and ends up the gutter.

As the ball hits and the pins all seem to fall down simultaneously, my heart seizes in my chest. Meeting his eyes when he turns back to me with his face lifted in the same smile he's been wearing for the majority of our time playing, my breath hitches and I ready myself for the inevitable bragging about to commence.

Bragging that with the shitty way I played, is deserved.

But he doesn't do that. Instead he makes his way over slowly, stopping completely when he's directly in front of me, his body lingering closely to mine as he brushes his fingers across my face before leaning in and whispering.

"Let's get out of here. I'm starved, and after that game, you've officially worked up my appetite."

Oh, he's hungry alright, but with the weight of his words and the look in his eyes now—one that looks suspiciously like I'm the real meal he's after—I somehow doubt it's for whatever fast food joint I would end up directing us to.

Backing up quickly and breaking the contact his hand made with my face, I plant my butt on the seat and immediately bend over, setting to work on my shoes. Ignoring the tingling sensation flooding me when less than a minute later, I feel him doing the same next to me. Determined as I slip back into my boots, not to give into it. More than willing in the moment to sit here all day staring at the floor rather than admit that a shift has taken place.

"Pass them over, Davis." He says, and when my eyes dart up long enough to see what he means, I catch his hands motioning to the shoes. "The sooner I hand them in, the sooner we can gorge ourselves on garbage."

Laughing despite myself, I hand over the shoes and watch as he grabs his own and heads back over to hand them in. Moving naturally, as if the shift between us hadn't happened at all. That we hadn't just played the most competitive game of bowling because of the wager we made beforehand and everything is right as rain.

Slowly making my way toward him, but pausing a few feet back and watching him interact with the guy behind the counter, I bite down hard on my lip when turning and gesturing in my direction, he smiles. My breath catching as his eyes lower and begin their descent down over my body as he shamelessly takes me in.

Damn. What is happening right now?

When did things change from an innocent bowling match to the two of us being unable to take our eyes off each other? And when did they turn the damn temperature up in here.

"You look like a deer caught in headlights, darlin'." He says, nudging me in the arm and making me realize just how long I stood gawking. "You alright?"

If I wasn't so aware of what I know with his win is going to happen later, I might have even been touched by his concern. As it is, the nervousness I felt when he touched me before is rearing its ugly head and feeding into my need to know just how long he's going to keep me guessing.

Does he want to kiss me now and get it over with? Or is this something he's going to enjoy hanging over my head for the rest of the day and eventually taking when I least expect it?

"I'm fine, Brady. Let's just get something to eat. I still need to do something big in order to show you how great this place really is. Something I can't do if I've gotta listen to your stomach rumbling."

"Then show me the way, tour guide."

Pointing to the other end of the alley, where groups of other people are all sitting around tables and eating, figuring this to be as good a place as any to eat, he follows my lead when I start walking.

Feeling his eyes on me as I head to the counter and order as he steps in and grabs us the one free table left, I turn around and meet his light smile with one of my own.

Turning back to the man behind the counter when he clears his throat and mutters how much I owe, I toss a twenty down onto the counter, accepting my change before heading back to the table to wait. Brady wasting no time calling me on what I was hoping was only obvious to me when I finally take my seat.

"Me winning changes things, doesn't it?"

"Don't know what you're talking about. Like I said before, everything's fine."

"No, Emery, it's not. It hasn't been since I won the damn game. Admit it. My winning makes you nervous."

"What you want doesn't make me nervous, Brady." I tell him truthfully.

It's you that makes me nervous.

"Really? Because I'm the one that suggested it and I'm nervous as hell. Probably even more than I would have been if you had won and I had to jump off a cliff."

Raw honesty. *How often does that happen?* I definitely didn't expect to get it with a guy that by design has to live a fake existence every damn place he goes.

"Can I ask you something, Emery?"

"Sure."

"Would you like to hang out again?"

Here's my out. He's giving me the chance to back out. One I should probably take with as nervous as he make me, but that deep down I know I won't. It's not the date I'm worried about. I could easily see myself going out with him again. I mean, even though we didn't talk a whole lot while we were playing, I was having a good time.

What really worries me is the kiss.

Letting a man I barely know put his lips on mine, and worse, dealing with how much I want him to. It's turning me socially inept.

"Of course. I agreed when we made the wager, didn't I?"

"So it's the kiss that changed everything."

Feeling the heat rising in my cheeks despite my very best attempt at stopping it, I attempt to turn away before it hits the surface and he sees, but before I can, he runs his hand over my cheek gently, freezing me in place and making it impossible to look anywhere but at him.

"Do you not want to kiss me, Emery?"

Giving a great deal of consideration to his very loaded question, I realize quickly that there's really no collection of words I can put together that can explain what I'm really and truly afraid of. So doing the only thing I can with his hand still brushing across my face soothingly, I move in and press my lips to his. Gently at first and when the initial shock passes, going all in and deepening it.

It's in the instant when my lips meet his I feel it happening.

All thoughts of what I'm afraid of draining away.

Filled with the soft feel of his lips, his musky scent and the hunger the combination brings out of me, I give in and live in the moment. Giving in completely to the drug that is Brady Raines.

Chapter Nineteen

Emery

You need to get a grip, Em. It was one kiss.

I've been trying to make myself believe that's all it was for the past half hour as we made our way from the bowling alley to parts unknown.

A ride that besides trying to talk myself into it just being a kiss, I was also mentally berating myself for letting happen in the first place. Overwhelmed by a sense of guilt I've never felt before. It seems like every second after the kiss happened has become my own personal hell and I don't have the faintest idea how to get myself out.

For all the awkwardness my behavior is creating though, Brady seems none the wiser to my readiness to explode from the inside out. Still going on as though nothing had really changed. Casual. Nonchalant.

The very way I wish I could be.

Sure, it was an innocent kiss and something not worth making a big deal over. It only happened because I lost a bet. But for as long as I've been aware of the right and wrong way to handle things, I've never once done something I would consider wrong or deceitful.

Kissing Brady though, that changes things.

Despite not being together in a romantic sense, Mike and I have never actually sat down and defined our relationship. Never labeled it. With as close as we've become, especially since my mom got sick though, to anyone looking at us, we read more like a couple than the best friends I know we are.

I shouldn't feel like I've cheated when we're not together, but that's exactly what this feels like right now. Like I cheated on Mike and no amount of talking myself around it, shakes the stench of it off me.

I'm not that girl. I'm not a cheater. At least I wasn't until I got the bright idea to end the torture and put my lips on Brady's. Now I feel like I am her. Like I've just done something that is going to change things forever.

"You know for someone with such witty comebacks, you sure have been silent." Brady breaks the silence.

Pushing the guilt I'm feeling as deep down as I can, I flash him the faintest of smiles and turn back to the road again.

"Sorry. I guess I just have a lot on my mind."

"Anything you feel like sharing?"

Shaking my head, but another round of guilt proving otherwise and making me feel like I owe him more, I offer up a few pointless words. The sound of my voice, even to my own ears making me sick.

"Not really, Brady, but thanks for the offer."

The only saving grace about this entire thing, what gives me a sliver of hope that this is all going to work itself out, is that come tomorrow night, he'll be gone and I won't have to worry about seeing him again for a long time. If ever. It wasn't much consolation, but it sure made it easier to keep my mouth firmly shut instead of taking him up on his offer and spilling my guts the way I really wanted to.

"You're welcome. So what's on the agenda next? Any more surprises or should we just call it a night?"

"There's nothing else planned. I just assumed you'd want to head back to the hotel."

Throwing me a look but thankfully remaining silent, he focuses his attention back on the road. Him stealing the keys to Avery's rental at the alley, given the misplaced way my head is right now, one of the only things left to be thankful for.

"Is that really what you wanna do, Emery? Drop me at the hotel and call it a night?"

Wincing at the way it sounds when he puts a voice to my copout, I collapse further into the seat and pout.

Dropping him at the hotel and ending this is the last damn thing I want.

Despite my earlier reservations about doing this, it's the first time in a long time where I can actually say I had fun. Where I didn't spend the entire day worried about my mom and whether she was okay at home. It's the first day in a long string of them where I actually feel like myself again.

If you would just be honest with him, maybe it could end the way you want.

"Would you mind just going to the hotel? I mean, I know I promised you a day you'd never forget, but I'm beat."

I can tell by the way he sits up straighter in his seat and grip the wheel tighter, that he's easily seeing through my bullshit. I've never been the best at doing it, Mike telling me once that I had a nonexistent poker face and could be read too easily, but I'd been hoping since Brady really didn't have the background that my best friend did, I'd be able to get one past him.

So much for that.

"Does this have to do with the kiss? Because if it does, I—"

"No." I quickly cut him off. "It has nothing to do with that. I enjoyed every part of today, and I do mean every part. I just need some time."

Bullshit. Bullshit. Bullshit.

My mind is screaming at me, even as he nods in understanding and leaves it alone instead of pressing, despite the twitch of his jaw that tells me he's not happy with my answer.

I don't blame him. I'm not happy with it either.

Looking at my watch as the car begins to slow when he pulls into the hotel, realizing quickly that we somehow just spent ten minutes without so much as a look or word spoken between us, I steel myself for the inevitable kiss off that's coming.

Pulling to a stop in the circular drive, he doesn't waste any time getting out, being sure to slam the door behind him before making his way over to the passenger side while I contemplate what happens now.

Do I get out or just slide over into the driver's seat? Should I roll down the damn window and explain myself a little better or just leave things the way they are?

God. Why does everything have to be so damn complicated?

Knocking on the window, I turn and noticing the pained expression on his face, roll it down, willing myself not to react. No matter how badly I want to seeing as I'm the cause.

"So, I guess we'll talk tomorrow?" he asks as he rests his arms across the window.

"We will, I promise." I offer with a soft smile. "And Brady, I'm really sorry about this. My heads just spinning and I don't want to put you through that."

With a quick nod, he slides his head through the exposed space and gently grazes the side of my face with his lips.

Before I can react, turn the way my body is begging me to, so it's not just my cheek he's kissing but my lips, he's pulling back out and turning away. The only thing left to remind me that his lips were anywhere on me, the raw burn his stubble leaves behind.

Taking his turning away as a sign that we're done, I roll the window back up and move myself over into the driver's seat. Revving the engine a couple of times, but making no move to leave. Instead watching as his body retreats up the stairs leading to the hotel doors. Only making good on my need for escape and pulling away when I see him finally duck inside,

The dejected look on his face after he knocked on the window haunting me the further I drive away from him and this day. Making me think that Brady and the day we had wasn't the only thing I left back at the hotel.

I'm pretty sure with the tremendous ache in my chest and the throbbing pain that feels as though it's coming straight from my very soul, I left something far bigger than both of us behind when he walked into the hotel.

My heart.

Brady

Entering the lobby and looking around, trying to see around the people making their way back and forth for any sign of Jackson and coming up empty, I head for the hotel bar. The need to drink away the sting of being left behind winning out over the more logical one of heading to my room and really calling it a night.

It's only when I make my way in and hit up the bartender for whatever beer he's got on tap, turning around while I wait and taking in the room that I catch them.

Seated at one of the tables in the corner, two drinks in front of them, looking like two people that just had the world's most successful date are Jax and the spitting image of the girl that after kissing her, I'd run off. Even looking at them from this distance, it's easy to see how they only had eyes for each other.

Grabbing the glass the second it's placed down on the bar, I take the world's longest swallow, continuing to watch them and question just what the hell they have that I don't. How their day could have turned out this way when mine ran straight off into the gutter faster than Emery's balls did when we were bowling.

Bringing the glass up again, this time polishing it before placing it back down, I swallow the pang of jealousy that I'm hit with watching them together and just the way a third wheel should, saunter slowly over to where they're sitting, the scraping of the chair I grab from the table adjacent to them, successfully pulling them apart and signaling them to my arrival.

"Hey guys. Fancy meeting you here." I announce, forcing a laugh I most definitely don't feel before throwing my body down onto the seat.

"Brady." Jax acknowledges. "We were wondering when you were gonna get back. Where's your date?"

"She said she wasn't feeling well on the ride back so we called it a night. She went home. We're supposed to hook up tomorrow."

"Is that what she told you?" Avery uses that moment to interject, the slight raise to her voice giving away her surprise at my response.

Not wanting to get into it with her, I turn my attention to the bar and with a quick signal to the bartender, order another round. If I've gotta sit here and talk about Emery, I'm damn sure getting drunk to do it.

The burn of her kiss still evident on my lips and the smile that I swear is seared into the deepest recesses of my mind a little more than I can handle now that I'm being confronted by her twin.

"She took to me to a couple of places and we made a plan to get together before Jax and I get back on the road. It sucks since I was having a pretty good time, but I guess with everything we did, it took a lot out of her and she needed to get home."

"You don't sound so sure about that, Brady. What's really going on?" Jax asks, seeing straight through my bullshit. Damn all of those weeks on the road. He's figured me out.

"When we left you guys, she took me to see the most amazing view. I mean, I grew up around nature and you know my old man. He was big on us being out in it even when all we were doing was training and working out. He wanted me out walking the trails, hunting and fishing. But this was different. We were on top of this cliff overlooking a lake or an ocean and it wasn't like anything I'd grown up around. It was better."

"She tried to talk me into jumping off because apparently that's what people from around here do, but when it didn't work, we went to the bowling alley. Not really sure how the hell that was supposed to sell me on this place, but it was fun. We were getting along great."

"That all sounds good, man. So why are you sitting here looking like someone died?"

"We made a bet when we got to the alley. A friendly one and by some stroke of luck I still don't get seeing as I haven't bowled in years, I won. The bet was, if I won, she'd agree to see me again before we head out, and well, that she owed me a kiss. It was stupid. I really didn't think she'd agree, but she did."

"You kissed her?" Avery asks as my stomach recoils remembering just how quickly everything shifted after she did.

"Yes—well, no. She kissed me."

"Okay, I'm missing something here." Jax speaks up. "If you kissed, why the hell are you here alone?"

"That's where shit gets weird. Screwed up even. I have no idea why or what I did wrong, but she was completely different after it happened. I could actually see the light drain out of her eyes. I mean, if the last thing she wanted to do was kiss me, why did she? And I know I haven't kissed anyone since Kel, but was it really so bad that she had to completely shut down after? Who the hell does that?"

Jax, leaning back in his chair, exhales heavily when I finish my diatribe and it's not hard to see why. It's because with as long as we've been riding together, I've never spoken this much in one sitting. I'm usually a man of few words, making the ones that I do say count. The complete opposite of the way I am now.

Emery and her reaction obviously hitting a large enough nerve to change it.

Change me.

"Brady, I don't think it was the kiss." Avery muses before focusing her attention on taking a drink of her own.

"What else could it be?"

"I've seen a few things since I got here and I think it might have something to do with that."

If she's not sick the way she claimed, and it wasn't my kissing ability that sent her running, just what the hell was it?

"Do you remember when you saw me at ringside and there was a guy with me?"

Jax answers before I can even process what she's asking.

"Brady might not have, but I did. When I asked your sister for her number there was a guy. I assumed it was *your* boyfriend and that's why you took off so fast."

"Right. Now that you know it wasn't me, but Emery that you met, I suppose it's time you know the rest. The guy with her was Mike, her best friend."

Jumping back into the conversation, questions firing away in my head, I waste no time getting right to them.

"I don't get what her being at the show with her best friend has to do with this. What would Emery and I kissing have to do with him?"

Avery sighs and my heart plummets. If she's reacting like this then it means that this Mike guy is a whole lot more than a friend.

"There's more to it. They've been best friends for years. They're close. Emery mentioned something about it in passing when I met her yesterday, but nothing specific about them dating. I didn't press for details because honestly, it was none of my business. But it's pretty obvious when you see the two of them together that there's something more going on there."

I slump back further in my seat and run my hand down hard over my face.

It all makes sense now.

Emery wanting to put distance between us after the kiss wasn't because of something I'd done, but because of something she had. There was someone else, whether she looked at him as a friend or not. If it was guilt over our kiss that caused the change, it means her heart looked at him differently.

Which only makes me feel worse than I did when I walked in a few minutes ago.

I felt something when we kissed, even though I hadn't told her or even put a name on what the feeling was. Knowing what I do now though, it makes that feeling seem dirty.

Wrong.

"I'm sorry, Brady. I should have said something last night. I guess I figured that if there was something you needed to know, Emery would have told you herself."

"It's not your fault, Avery. This was supposed to be a one off, so I shouldn't even care."

But you do. You care a lot.

"Look, since it's pretty obvious you guys aren't ready for the night to end and I'm more than a little tired of talking, I'm gonna head up to the room and leave you to it."

"You don't have to do that." Jax attempts to stop me and despite how much I appreciate him being so willing to sacrifice his night, I can't let him.

"It's cool. I'll get all the dirty details from you later. You two have a good night."

Pushing the chair back from the table, I lean over and whisper goodnight to Avery, hightailing it out of there as fast as my legs can make it happen. Not realizing the effect that sitting there with Emery's mirror image had on me until I feel the weight become significantly lighter on my shoulders the more distance I put between us.

Stepping into the elevator as soon as the doors open, the last thought I have as they start to close being just how thankful I am to be heading out tomorrow night.

Because once I did, two things would happen.

I wouldn't have to see this town or Emery Davis ever again.

Chapter Twenty

Emery

Pacing back and forth in the living room, wearing a line into the carpet with as many times as I've done it, I stop long enough to peek through the curtain again before looking down at my watch.

I called Mike almost the second I walked through the door a little over thirty minutes ago, and despite knowing he was at work, asked him to come over when he was done. Every second after he agreed and we ended the call spent startling at every noise while I pace back and forth all over the house waiting for him to arrive.

Sweet, kind, dependable Mike.

That's always been how I've looked at him since we became friends as kids and it's something that even as we grew up, never changed.

When my mom decided to look into finding Avery and the stress level in the house seemed to go through the roof, especially during the time where we waited to see if anything would come of it, it hadn't been my mom or any other friends and family I'd leaned on. It had been Mike.

My very best friend and the one person that if Brady hadn't come along today and thrown his own hat in, I probably would have ended settling down with.

Settling for.

Something that according to my mom, no one should ever have to do and that until earlier, we didn't see eye to eye on.

I may have ended up with Mike because it was safe and given the disarray in my life, safe actually appealed, but I never would have believed I was settling.

My best friend is one of most beautiful human beings on the planet. Anyone lucky enough to spend their life with him wouldn't want or need for anything, especially not love. He would give them that because he has a never ending supply.

He's impossible to settle for.

Considering the way I reacted when Brady kissed me though, him being the first person to make me feel something in years, I know now that settling is exactly what I would have done.

The conversation I'm gearing up to have with him when he gets here should have happened years ago. Deep down I know that whatever comes of this, I earned, because instead of nipping what looking back, I could clearly see happening between us, I'd gone along for the ride instead. I fostered what I knew were his growing feelings for me, never doing a damn thing to stop it.

Bringing us to now. The moment where I have to take the heart I knew wanted to beat alongside mine and smash it to bits.

I lied to him. It wasn't a big lie, but in not telling him this morning that I was going to be doing a whole lot more than just hanging out with Avery, I'd lied and there was nothing I could say to take it back.

The more I think about it, I've been lying to him for years.

Every time I said he was the best thing that ever happened to me and I wouldn't know what to do without him. That I was blessed and lucky that he was a part of my life. I meant every word, but they were still lies because all those words had done was feed something that would never happen.

I wasn't in the same place and I don't think I ever would be. I was selfish, keeping him so close, and all it took was what happened between me and Brady and the resulting guilt and shame I felt to see it.

Selfishness that ends tonight.

Peeking out the window when I hear the sound of tires across the gravel leading in from the road, I make my way from the living room over to the door. Opening it at the exact moment his boots hit the porch.

"Hey, beautiful." He says, leaning in to kiss my cheek. My stomach recoiling right before he connects, forcing me to take a step back and no doubt leaving him confused.

"Come in." I say, making my way inside quickly. "Thanks for coming over. I know you're probably dying to get home."

Not dignifying my thanks with a response, he follows blindly behind me as I dart back into the living room, throwing himself down onto the sofa as I take the recliner across from him.

"So, how was the day with Avery?"

"That's actually what I wanted to talk to you about..."

"All ears, Em."

"There was a change in plans. What was supposed to be me and Avery spending the day together turned into something else."

"Like what?"

"Brady Raines and Jackson Merrick."

"You and Avery hung out with Brady and Jackson? For real?"

Finally meeting my eyes, the name dropping obviously enough for him to finally give me his attention, I'm struck by the innocent smile he's wearing.

Little does he know that what I'm about to say isn't something to be happy about.

"Apparently, Brady and Jackson are staying at the same hotel as Avery and after we dropped her off last night, she met up with them. After making plans to hang out today, she texted me and brought me along for the ride." I explain, swallowing the growing lump in my throat before spitting out the rest of it. "Only, that's not how it ended up going."

"What do you mean?"

"We split up. Avery and Jackson went and did their own thing and I hung out with Brady."

I'm totally making light of it, I know, but I can't just drop what happened on him. None of it feels right, but if I do it all at once, it feels worse somehow.

"And?" There's no missing the large intake of breath and the hard swallow that follows. I've been around him long enough to know that he has some idea of where this is heading, though I'm positive he doesn't know it all.

"*And*...I agreed to it because the way Avery explained it, Brady pretty much got a hot nut over the idea of going out with twins. At the time, we had no idea they'd wanna split off and once we did, it didn't seem right to say no."

Lie. Lie. Lie.

"When we got there, he made a crack about how dull the town was and it bothered me. I wanted to prove him wrong. Show him how fun it could be if he just gave it a shot."

"You went on a date alone with Brady Raines? Am I hearing you right?"

"Yes," I start to answer but stop myself. There's still so much I need to make him understand. Answering yes is too final. "It was innocent. I took him to the cliff and then bowling."

There's a split second when I see the smile he's still sporting that I think maybe I've read into things between us and he doesn't feel about me the way I assume. That maybe this isn't going to be so bad. But it only takes me bringing up the bet for the real truth to come out.

"To keep things fun, we made a bet."

His jaw twitches as his eyes lower away from mine and it's in that moment the reality I know, the one I'd been so sure of before he smiled, makes its presence known.

"For what?"

"If he won, I owed him a kiss and if he won, he would have to cliff dive."

Shaking his head once I admit what Brady would have to do if I won, he laughs and despite knowing I can't, there's nothing more I want to do in the moment but freeze time. Keep that soft laugh in place because I can't imagine being the one that takes it away.

"Who won?"

"He did."

Waves of emotion flood his face after I've answered. Hurt and pain. Anger and upset. Confusion and shock. One after the other until it all seems to start again and he just looks lost.

"You kissed Brady Raines." He says, his tone even. His voice unwilling to betray him the way his eyes are.

"Yes."

"Then what does that mean for us? I know we haven't exactly talked about it, but I was pretty sure with the way you let me be with you that something was happening between us. What exactly are you trying to say here, Em? Did you feel something when you kissed him? Do I need to be worried?"

Question after question. All ones I can answer with a simple yes or no answer, but that Mike deserves better than me doing it that way.

"Mikey...that's just it," *Cue the heartbreak in 3...2...1.* "There is no us. I've known that you wanted there to be for a while now, and I know it was wrong of me not saying something sooner. I just didn't want to hurt you. Honestly, I also didn't say anything because up until now, I didn't think it was going to be an issue."

Rendered speechless, I wait for him to say something. Anything that will let me know he's heard what I've said. Instead, he just motions with his hand for me to keep talking.

"What happened today with Brady was a wakeup call. It made me really think about things. We've spent pretty much every waking second together since we were kids. Other than those few weeks with Neil when we were in high school, you've been the only guy I've ever allowed myself to get close to. I selfishly kept you to myself and it wasn't fair."

"I get it, Em. You don't feel the same and you have a thing for Brady. You don't need to spell it out."

"That's not what I'm doing. At least, not what I'm trying to do. This has nothing to do with Brady, honestly. It's me doing what I should have done a long time ago."

"Bullshit, Ems. Bull. Fucking. Shit. This has everything to do with Raines. If you hadn't met up with him today, we wouldn't even be having this conversation right now."

"Maybe not, but we would have eventually, Mike. I let everything go on for so long because it was the one sure and easy thing. That wasn't right or fair."

"I don't believe you."

"This is not happening because of Brady." I argue. "Did I feel something when I kissed him? Yes. Do I want to explore what that means? Maybe a little. Does that mean I want to throw away years of friendship on the off chance I might be able to date him? No. This is about me, Mike. What happened today was my wakeup call."

"And what exactly you do think you need to be woken up about?"

"How I treat you. What you really are to me. I needed to see how selfish I was with you. Keeping you to myself when I knew I would never be able to give you what you deserve. I needed to see it all."

For the first time since he walked in, I'm not lying. I'm not holding back and keeping things a secret. For the first time in a long time, I'm being honest with him *and* with myself.

"I need to start living my life independently, Mike. I love you. You're always going to be important to me, but we're never going to be more than friends. I can't spend another minute, hour or day letting you believe we can. It's not fair and I'm so damn sick of being unfair to you. I'm sorry."

The tears begin falling after I've said my peace and there's not a damn thing I can do to stop them. Just like the kiss with Brady had been an eye opener, this is too.

It doesn't matter how right this is, me finally stepping up and doing the right thing by myself and by my best friend, it doesn't change the fact that I'm going to lose my best friend.

"I understand where you're coming from, Emery, I do, but I've gotta be honest. I don't agree. I think this is about more than you needing to do right by me. I think it has everything to do with Raines and the attention he paid you today. Attention that I'm sure he's given a ton of other girls before. Making you one of a million."

About to interrupt and tell him how wrong he is, that despite knowing about their reputations, that's not the vibe I got from Brady today, he forces my silence when he picks up again.

"I am *in love* with you and I've known that for a long time. Maybe if I just said something sooner, this wouldn't be happening. But it doesn't change the fact that it is. Emery, to me, you would never be one of *a* million. You are my one *in* a million. You're right though. My feelings for you, they're never going to change as long as we keep doing things the way we have been. The more I stay, the stronger they'll be. I can't force you to feel the same way and even if I could, I wouldn't. So I guess that leaves us at a crossroads."

There's no crossroad here. His own words prove it. His mind is already made up.

Pressing his hand down onto the arm of the sofa and pulling himself up, he begins to make his way back over to the door, but before I can call out to stop him, put together a string of magical words that will somehow make my best friend stay, he turns back around.

"I love you, Emery Davis. I always will. But I don't think I can be just your friend anymore. Not when my heart is telling me that we have the ability to be more."

Making those his final words, he turns his back and leaves. From my vantage point still frozen on the sofa, his legs picking up speed until he's out the front door and I can barely make out the sound of his boots as they race down the porch steps.

His actions along with everything he said giving me exactly what I was after when I got home earlier.

Leaving me alone.

A fact that with the way my heart feels after what I've just done, is him giving me exactly what I deserve.

And I have no one to blame for it but myself.

Chapter Twenty-One

Jax

After watching Brady leave and the way Avery seemed to follow him, even after he went out of our view, I see the night I imagined spending with her going up in flames.

You don't need to have a degree in reading people to know she's taking the way Brady's night with Emery played out, on herself.

Further evidenced when she finally turns back to the table and her attention immediately goes to her glass, running her fingers over the condensation on the rim instead of looking to me and engaging in conversation the way we've done since we got back earlier.

If we're taking blame for everything that went down between those two, I'm just as guilty as she believes she is. I knew about Mike last night when I jumped the barricade and made an ass out of myself. I hadn't spoken up and considering I saw more of Brady than anyone, I could have.

Making me even guiltier than Avery.

"So, I guess this means we're left to our own devices for dinner."

Pulling her attention from the glass and meeting my eyes, she gifts me with a soft smile.

"It looks that way. So, Mr. Merrick, what exactly did you have in mind?"

Given the way she's been acting since Brady showed up and laid his day on us, I resigned myself to the fact that I wouldn't be getting to spend the night with her. So having her ask, still showing interest despite the pull I'm sure she's feeling to check in with her sister, is surprising.

"Promise you won't laugh?"

"Food is no laughing matter." She tells me seriously before breaking and laughing when like a chump I buy into it by going silent. "That was entirely too easy, Jax."

"Or maybe you've just mastered the art of being serious."

"Could be. Now, are you gonna tell me what you had in mind or am I gonna have to come up with something?"

"It's gonna sound so cheap."

"I happen to like cheap, so spill."

"I was thinking we could head down to the boardwalk and maybe grab a hot dog from one of the vendors."

The idea sounded so much better when it was just in my head. It's not only cheap, but pretty damn lame too. Surely with as much time as I've had to think about it, I could have come up with something better.

"It doesn't sound cheap. It sounds great, actually. The perfect way to end the night and get our minds off what happened with Brady and Emery."

"It's really getting to you isn't it? What happened with them."

I'm asking questions I already know the answers to. Just in the way she acted after Brady left and how quiet she'd been even when she turned back to me, it's easy to see she's a person that takes a lot on herself. Even things that have nothing to do with her.

She cares, and if I didn't already like her, that would seal it.

"Yeah, I guess it is. I hate that I knew something and didn't think to mention it. Maybe if I had, I could have spared them both what happened tonight. At the very least, I could have talked to Emery about it before we all met up."

"I get it." I sympathize, knowing exactly where she's coming from. "I feel the same way."

"I'm sorry."

Huh? She's what?

"You don't have anything to apologize for, Avery."

"But I do." She says with a shake of her head. "Tonight was supposed to be about us and I'm more focused on Brady and my sister."

"I still say you have nothing be sorry for, but if you really want to make it up to me, you can start by doing something small."

"Like what?"

"For the next few hours, focus on us. You heard Brady. If he knew that what happened with him ruined our night, he'd never forgive himself. I don't know Emery, but I get the feeling she's the same way. They'd want us to enjoy ourselves. So what do you say? Will you stay with me or am I letting you go so you can be with Emery?"

Sliding her hand across the table and resting it on mine, she smiles and even though she hasn't exactly voiced her agreement to what I'm proposing, something tells me she will.

Our night is not over yet.

Avery

Until Jax brought up letting me go so I could be with Emery, the way I wanted to spend the night was clear.

I wanted nothing more than to spend it on the boardwalk with him.

Now though, thinking about Emery at home alone after having taken off from Brady, I'm starting to think my place isn't here with Jax, but back at the house with my family.

What would Emery think if I went to her instead of staying with Jax? Would she be like Brady and blame herself or would she welcome the company? Not knowing her as well as I wish I did, makes that question impossible to answer. I have no clue, but imagining what it would be like if our roles were reversed, I have to believe Jax is right.

"I think you're right. If I went to Emery and she found out that I gave up the chance to be here with you, especially with how I know she feels about you guys, I don't think she'd ever forgive herself, much less me. So you've got a deal. Let's enjoy the time we have."

With a smile so big it etches itself into the very fabric of his skin, he slips his hand out from under mine and squeezes it.

"Sounds like the second best idea I've heard all day."

"Second best?" I ask, curious.

"Yeah, the second. The first happened when you and Brady set this whole thing up in the first place."

Shielding my face as I feel the warmth beginning to rise and flood my cheeks, he chuckles before reaching over and pulling my hand away.

"It's been awhile since I made someone react like that, but one thing hasn't changed since then. I like seeing it, so please don't hide it. Pink looks good on you."

If it was possible to flush a darker color than the one I'm already wearing, this would be the moment it happened. Every word he's saying sweet, but more importantly, refreshingly honest. His sincerity not only easy to see in the way he says things, but the look in his eyes as he does as well.

Releasing his hand from mine once he's made his way around the table and pulled me to my feet, he heads to the bar, and after slapping down a few bills for our drinks, makes his way back to my side. His hand finding and slipping into mine effortlessly, as though we were never separated at all.

"A perfect fit." I hear him whisper under his breath before he looks to me and with widened eyes, smiles shyly before looking down to the ground.

Knowing he's been caught.

"So where's this boardwalk you were talking about?"

"Just behind the hotel."

Guiding us out of the bar and toward the door, pausing long enough to hold it open for me before falling in line and taking my hand in his again, I grin like an idiot. The feel of his hand in mine and how true his earlier statement was, all I can think about as we head down the stairs and around through a gate leading us to the back and the boardwalk that awaits.

"Here we are." He whispers softly, pulling us to a stop before lifting our hands and pointing to the lengthy walkway laid out in front of us.

"It's breathtaking."

Looking from our hands swinging together as we start walking and back up to him, seeing my own smile reflected on his face as he maneuvers his way down the small embankment to the beach, I'm struck again by just how right this is.

Especially with the stars that seem to be exploding in the sky the closer we get to our destination. Stars that I haven't gotten to see this way in years.

It's like in the moment, everything is aligning to make what was already a pretty great day that much better.

"You see it?" he whispers, leaning in after bringing us to a stop and motioning to the very sky I'd just been so caught up in. A burst of light that at first glance looks like just another star among many, now standing out as it streaks its way across the sky.

Wow.

"Yes, I see it." I tell him softly, the sight of the shooting star now making its way across the darkened sky enough to steal my breath.

It's only when his hand shifts in mine that my focus on the sky breaks and I turn into him. Following his gaze out to what looks to be a never ending walkway stretched out in front of us.

"It goes on forever." I blurt out, falling into the softness in his eyes when they shift back to me.

"It would be really nice if everything in life could go on forever the way this boardwalk seems to."

"Jax..." I sigh, positive he's talking about us, but also seeing my mother in them. Overwhelmed with a flood of emotion so strong I find it impossible to say anything more.

He has no idea what he's done.

Taking a hold of my free hand with his own before I have the chance to bring it to my face in an effort to hide my reaction, he brings it to his lips and kisses it.

"I want to walk the way we planned, but before we do, there's something else I need to do first."

"And that is?"

Lowering our hands, he leans in, covering my lips with his. Capturing them. My body responding by melting deeper into him, like a moth to a flame.

With the moon beginning to light up the sky, the sound of the water moving in tandem with the twinkling of the stars in the sky and his lips on mine, I fall into the spell that is Jax and what might possibly be the most romantic moment of my life.

What I hope is the first of many to come.

Jax

I'd been unable to get it out of my head since she agreed to walk the boardwalk, and now that we're here and it's happening, I can't get enough.

I'm hungry for the taste of her cherry lip gloss. A devilish elixir I'm sure she wore just to drive me crazier than I already feel in her presence. Making it impossible to think of anything but the lips coated in it.

Lip gloss that I devour as I deepen our kiss and slip my tongue over her lips before slipping it deeper into her mouth. Her own hunger for more seeming to match mine as she pushes back, our tongues and lips caught up in the slowest but most passionate dance. One that we both seem to give into as all thought seems to fade away and we let feeling and emotion take over.

With my body radiating a heat that I can in no way control, a beast is awoken as my dick hardens, pressing uncomfortably against my jeans. The steady pulse flooding me as it makes its own demand to be freed. A sensation so unfamiliar, it pulls me back from the edge before I can give in completely and do something I know neither of us is ready for.

Feeling something this soon and wanting to act is fine. But actually acting?

If we do that, it's something we won't ever be able to come back from. As much as I want to experience what it would feel like to be buried deep inside this woman, feeling her moving beneath me while I make love to her, I don't want it going down this way.

A quick fuck. Her sweat laden body slick and hot underneath me while I took her repeatedly. It's not enough. I want more.

So pushing back, I attempt to catch my breath, not at all prepared for her to collect herself so quickly or for the words that follow.

"You aren't going to say sorry again, are you?"

"Not on your life." I assure her. "Never even crossed my mind."

"Good." She smiles, slipping herself easily back into my arms. Filling the space so perfectly I begin to question if she was made to fit. If my arms were made only for her.

Her innocent move also reigniting the need I felt when we kissed, as her scent mixing with the soft feel of her body against mine is enough to make want to say fuck it to doing things right and taking her right where we stand.

The desire for her and the aching need for release one I haven't experienced in well over three years, but that feels so damn right despite it.

"So before I pick up where we just left off and kiss you again, what do you say we grab that hotdog now?"

Shaking off my own need to recreate the kiss and this time, not pull away, I nod and slip my arm tighter around her, pulling her to me and start to walk what seems like the longest boardwalk I've ever come across. Wanting to look down to her when just like before, I'm hit with the spark when our bodies connect, wanting to know if she feels it too, but resisting, I I keep my eyes trained on the other people moving around us, pausing only when my eyes catch movement across the sky.

"Avery, look!"

Pointing up to what I can see now is another large flash of light making its way across, I hold my breath in anticipation of her response as her eyes flick up and catch what's happening.

"Wow. It's another one."

"Must be our lucky night."

Turning her attention from the sky, she smiles.

"You know what we have to do now right?"

"What's that?"

"Jackson! Seriously? You're telling me you've never wished on a shooting star before?"

"I haven't. You don't see this too often where I'm from."

"In that case, allow me to impart some wisdom. When you see a shooting star, you make a wish. So think fast. We already missed one shot tonight."

It doesn't take me but a second, and when I see her look back up to the sky before shutting her eyes, I waste no time doing the same.

Closing my eyes and focusing on the feel of her in my arms, the scent of her perfume and the lingering taste of her lip gloss, I make the only wish in the moment I want to come true.

I wish to know what Avery wished for, because I want to be the one to make it come true.

Right here on this boardwalk with this beautiful woman in my arms, it hits me.

I want to make all of Avery's dreams come true.

Chapter Twenty-Two

Emery

"Was that Michael I heard downstairs?"

After everything was said and Mike left, I wandered around aimlessly downstairs. Knowing I needed to head up and see my mom, but needing to get a handle on my emotions first.

Back and forth from the kitchen to the living room and back to the front porch, I'd done it all. Now I'm upstairs and of course, my mom has to say the one thing designed to make the waterworks start again.

Even before she got sick and Mike started coming around more, she adored him. Everyone did. He was just that kind of guy. Inherently nice. Almost to a fault it would seem.

Especially when it came to me.

I don't know many times over the years she voiced her opinion on our relationship. What she wanted for me and what she hoped would happen between us.

"Yeah, he was here. He came over after work."

"And is it Michael that caused those tear stains I can see on your cheeks?"

When I came up here, it was my plan to keep the focus on her. Definitely not getting into what happened downstairs. But as I've come to learn over the years, what you want is never what you get when it comes to Rebecca Davis.

"He didn't cause them. I did."

Patting the empty spot on the bed to the left of where she's resting, I sit, only moving when I see her struggling to sit up and failing. Gripping her tight and pulling her up into a sitting position, I move back when I'm sure she's comfortable and wait for what I know will be her next question.

Why.

"How did you manage that and better yet, why would you want to cause yourself pain?"

Biting my lip, I look from the bed back to her. The last thing I want is her wasting what little energy she has worrying about me.

"Emery, if there's one thing I know about you, it's that despite how big your heart is and how much you care about people, you don't spend a lot of time crying unless you're given a good reason. So tell me. Did you and Mike have a fight?"

"No, Mama. We didn't fight."

"Then what happened?"

"Mike's in love with me, Mom. He's been in love with me for a long time."

Nodding her head but not offering up any further insight, I just keep going.

"I don't feel the same and for the last few years, even though I knew he was, I led him to believe there was a chance of more. That one day, he would be more than my best friend."

"I see."

"Yeah."

"So I'm guessing that tonight was the night you put an end to that hope."

"Yes."

"Why now, Emery? What changed?"

Brady Raines happened.

His self-satisfied smirk, playfulness and his honesty. Hell, even his nervousness, and until him I had no idea something like that could be appealing.

"Something happened today that put a lot of things in perspective."

"Like what?"

"I met someone."

Shifting on the bed, I move my attention away from the duvet I've spent the last few minutes staring a hole into and put it on her. A soft smile now beginning to form on her face as she leans forward and slips a frail hand over the top of mine.

"Why are you smiling?"

"Because I was waiting for the day this would happen."

Say what?

"I don't follow."

"Of course you don't. Let me explain." She shifts again, her hand tightening around mine. "I've known for quite some time that Michael was in love with you. I've also known the feelings were not reciprocated. I figured this would have happened long before now, but considering all that is going on with me, I can't say I'm complaining that it's happening while I'm still here."

I still don't follow.

"Michael was never meant to be the one, Emery. As much as I enjoy having him around, the two of you were never meant to be more than what you are to each other."

Could have fooled me. She did everything in her power for years to make sure we were together as much as possible. Since when did that all change?

"This doesn't make any sense. Did you forget I've lived with you my entire life? I saw the way you were with Mike. How you felt about him. The way you put us together any chance you got. Am I supposed to believe I just imagined that?"

Releasing a shaky breath, she shakes her head.

"No, you didn't imagine it. I fostered the two of you getting close because I saw the good it did for you. Your confidence level was already high, but with Mike by your side it seemed to take on a life of its own. But just because I wanted the two of you to spend time together doesn't mean I believed the two of you to be anything more than the friends you were."

Alright. I'm glad that's cleared up. Still doesn't explain anything else though.

"The reason I know Mike isn't the one for you, and why I believe that the person you met tonight holds more significance is because not that long ago, I was in a similar situation."

Wait. Hold the phone.

"What do you mean similar situation? Was your best friend in love with you too?"

"As a matter of fact, yes. Well, I don't want to say it was love, because we were so young at the time, but I did have a best friend that had feelings for me."

Wow. Maybe coming up here tonight wasn't such a bad idea after all.

"What happened?"

"I met your father." She pauses, her hand losing some of its grip as she takes in what I'm sure is the disgusted scowl on my face. She's brought him up a lot over the years and every time she does it, my reaction is the same. I don't want to hear about the man that stole my sister in the dead of night and kept her away from us.

"Now, Emery. I know how you feel about him, but in order for me to explain things, I have to bring him up."

"Fine. As long as you know that no matter what you say, it won't ever change my feelings."

"Fair enough." She concedes, taking and releasing another shaky breath. "As you know, Richard and I met in high school. I became taken with him quite quickly and luckily for me, he did the same. It wasn't the way things are now, where things are more drawn out. We rushed into things."

"What does this have to do with Mike and me?"

"William was my best friend from the time he moved in across the street in second grade. We grew close and became fast friends. We were inseparable really. At least we were until the day he met Richard. I didn't understand it at the time, Emery, but the way Richard and I reacted to one another, it was visible to everyone. Especially William. He saw what was happening and it didn't take long after their first meeting for his true feelings to come out. True feelings that I knew I couldn't reciprocate."

"He was in love with you?"

"Yes. I've given it a lot of thought over the years. Even though I didn't know what love was at the time, I do believe that what he thought he felt for me was in fact love. It saddens me that I couldn't give him what he deserved in that way."

We're a lot more alike than I realized.

"So what happened after he told you how he felt?"

"I suppose the same thing that just took place between you and Michael downstairs. I couldn't give him what he wanted so we parted ways."

She nailed that spot on, but what she hasn't hit on is how it feels knowing I've lost my best friend. The gaping hole it seems to have opened up inside me that even replacing him won't fix.

"Did it hurt this bad for you too?"

"Yes. Maybe worse. But considering the alternative, it had to be done."

The alternative being continuing to lead Mike on. Something I won't do. Not anymore.

"Tell me about the young man you met today. What took place during your time with him that seemed to change things? Awaken you to the reality of your relationship with Michael?"

"It wasn't just one thing, Mama. It was an entire days' worth of things."

"Like?"

I know it's going backwards, but if I'm going to be honest, it's where I need to start.

"We kissed, or rather, he won a bet where a kiss was on the table and I decided to put an end to things and take the lead by kissing him first."

"And how did he respond?"

"He kissed me back. It wasn't one sided."

"How did it feel?"

"I don't know what you mean."

Patting my hand, her smile returns. "You know exactly what I mean, Emery. How did it feel when you kissed this young man?"

Kissing Brady had been exhilarating. I'd kissed people in the past, I mean, it's pretty hard to find a person in their twenties who hasn't kissed at least one person, but those hadn't compared to what I felt when I placed my lips on Brady's. I came alive. There was a hunger, a burning there that I have never experienced before.

When I kissed Brady, everything seemed to align. It just felt right.

There's just no way I can explain all of that to my mom. It's weird enough admitting to her that I kissed someone. I mean, I'm not exactly a teenager anymore.

"It felt right." I admit, summing it up in the best way I know how.

"That's how it felt with your father. Which is why I know what I'm about to say next is the truth. For all of the times I've told you to keep your wits about you and to never lose sight of your goals or let anyone steer you away from them, I think in this one instance, you need to leave that at the door and follow your heart."

Following her heart is what landed my mother where she is. She had fallen hard for Richard Davis and in the end all it had gotten her was sick and alone.

Except it also gave her you and Avery.

"What happens if I act on what I felt kissing Brady and it turns out he's no better than Dad? What then, Mom? Maybe keeping my wits and following my head on this one, *is* the right thing to do. I've seen what losing Richard did to you. I don't want to live through that again."

"Then don't. Demand more from this Brady than I did from your father. Just because our situations are similar doesn't mean they have to have the same ending. You can create a much better ending for yourself, Emery, but only if you allow yourself the chance to begin."

"And if he doesn't feel the same way?"

"Then at the very least you've gained some valuable knowledge for when the right person does come along. But something tells me, if you felt anything remotely close to what I felt for your father when we were kids, he feels the same way and is just waiting for you to admit the same."

"What about Mike? He's gone and I'm pretty damn sure he's not going to come back."

"Give Michael time. Mark my words. When enough time has passed, you two will be together again in the way it's meant to be. If anyone can do this, take this chance, it's you."

Her faith in my ability to stand on my own two feet is a hell of a lot stronger than mine. I'm not sure I'll ever have that level of faith in myself.

"Emery, stop overthinking things. The situation with Mike will work itself out. What won't is the sense of loss you'll feel if you don't take the chances afforded to you."

Chances afforded to me.

Brady Raines.

What she wants me to do and what I have to do, are the same damn thing. I need to make things right with Brady. I won't be able to move on until I do.

Brady

She had a boyfriend and kissed me anyway.

Letting that sink in, I can't help comparing it to the very thing I was accused of by Kelly. The only difference between the situations being, I wasn't screwing around and Emery kissing me the way she did, meant she definitely was.

What could have possessed this woman to keep this kind of secret? It's not as though either of us had gone into this expecting the earth to move. But despite that, something had moved and Emery was there as much as I was. Which meant I deserved to know the truth.

Better yet, she never should have gone out with me to begin with. I already had enough shit trying to dispel the rumors that I'm screwing around on Kel. I don't need to be a part of someone else doing it.

If it hadn't been for Avery's confession downstairs, I never would have known why she pulled away. Even if in doing so, she's pulling the same damn stunt I am in putting distance between us. Forgetting it even happened at all.

Except, I'm not exactly forgetting about it or pushing her out of my head.

I'm making myself sick over something that shouldn't even matter.

Why does everything have to be so goddamned complicated?

A knock on the door pulls me away from my thoughts and thankful for the reprieve, I jump from the bed and practically run to the door. Swinging it back, expecting to find Jax on the other side, it's not him I get.

It's Emery.

Dressed differently this time with her auburn red hair wet and straight and her face completely wiped clean of the makeup she'd worn earlier, she looks younger. More natural.

"Emery? What are you doing here?"

Looking up and meeting my eyes, her lips tight and expression grim, she grimaces before lowering her head back down.

"Can I come in?"

"Sure."

Closing the door once she steps in and makes her way over to the other side of the room, not missing the distance she's putting between us, I lean against it and ready myself to get some answers.

"I'm sorry about earlier." She says, beating me to the punch. "I'm pretty sure you don't wanna hear it, but there's some things you should know."

"If you're going to tell me that the reason you took off is because you had to get home to your boyfriend, don't bother. I already know."

If she's surprised I know her secret, she doesn't let on. At least not in any way I'm able to pick up on. Well, other than the sharp intake of breath that comes before she takes a few steps toward me.

"You know a version of the truth, but it's not the right one. I have," she pauses, closing her eyes and shaking her head with a sigh. "*Had* a best friend. He was at the show last night with me and Avery."

"That didn't seem so hard." I say and she just stares at me blankly.

"What didn't?"

"Telling me the truth. Now that you have though, you wanna go for two for two and tell me why you couldn't just tell me that earlier when I asked if there was anything you wanted to talk about?"

She shrugs and as upset as I am, all I want to do after hearing the way she changed up her words and how she seems ready to fall apart any second, is pull her to me and hold her. Making whatever craziness that's happened since we parted ways vanish altogether.

"I should have just told you the truth after we kissed, and honestly, I don't really have a good reason for why I didn't. Well, other than not wanting to bring you into the mess I created."

"You didn't want to bring me *any more* into the mess you created, you mean. I was brought into it the second you agreed to spend the day with me."

"I guess you're right, but it really wasn't my intention to do that."

"So if there was someone waiting at home for you, why even agree to this at all?"

"There's two reasons I agreed. Well, three, but one of them was only a small factor."

"I'm all ears."

"At first I said yes for Avery. When she came over this morning and explained about the mistaken identity with Jackson, it just seemed like the right thing to do."

"And the other reason?"

"You." She admits easily, almost like it should be a no brainer that wanting to spend time with me was a motivator. "I don't go to these shows hoping to one day catch the eye of one of the performers. I mean, I find some of your attractive, sure. I am human after all. For me though, it's more about the show you put on. The action. When Avery told me Brady Raines wanted to hang out, well, the wrestling fangirl in me sort of went off the reservation. I'd been following you, Jackson, Matthias and Ron for so long, there was no way I was going to miss the chance to spend time with you when it was presented to me."

That explains a lot and also manages to answer one of the questions I've yet to ask her. The situation we've found ourselves in isn't exactly one I've come across before, but women attempting to get close in hopes of being thrown a scrap of interest from us, I have been. Knowing that Emery wasn't one of them made me feel a whole lot better about the chance I'd taken on her earlier today.

It's not exactly like I'm guilt free in this whole thing. I mean, I originally set the entire thing up because I was curious what it would be like to hang with twins. She may have held back some info from me, info that wasn't really any of my business, but I'd been far worse with my objectifying of her and her sister.

"So what was the third reason? The one you said wasn't a huge motivator?"

"My mother. She's sick, Brady. Really sick. For the last couple of years, it's been up to me to take care of her when the nurses can't. Day in and day out, other than when I've gotta go to work so I can make money to pay the bills, I'm there with her. She'd been telling me for a while to do something for myself. That she didn't want this to be my life, I ignored her. So when Avery gave me the chance, I didn't want to let it pass me by."

Damn.

Where I expected her honesty, I hadn't been expecting quite that much of it. Hearing about her mother, it stripped away everything that happened earlier and actually made me feel bad for the way I reacted.

"I figured I would do this for my sister and to settle the fan girl in me. We'd have a bit of fun and it would be done. You guys would leave town and things would go back to normal. I never imagined that things would turn out the way they did."

She brings up a good point.

I was leaving tomorrow night and I had no idea when, if ever, I'd be returning. I never did right away. It's one of the ways that working with CPW when my real goal was to eventually make it to the WWE, sucked. We're also in agreement on our first reason for wanting to do this. Her for Avery and me for Jackson.

"Seems in a way we both had the same idea. So what changed?"

"You changed, Brady." She pauses, looking down at her hands awkwardly before shifting her eyes back up. "I had so much fun with you and when we kissed it was like the most natural thing in the world, despite how nervous I was before I did it. I knew I should have told you even then, but I couldn't. Not when it was going to cause exactly what I saw when you opened the door a few minutes ago. I hurt you and that's the last thing I wanted to do."

"You should have told me before the date happened, or if things are that complicated with your best friend, just not gone along with it. I appreciate you being honest about it." I tell her, making sure to leave the part out where I've already forgiven her. "There is something I'm curious about, though."

"What's that?"

"Now that you've come here and apologized, what else is there? What's the real reason you're here, Emery?"

I might not have a whole lot of experience in the dating arena seeing as I spent the better part of my teens and now adulthood married to the same girl, but I do know a little bit about women from having to work alongside them over the years.

She can claim the only reason she's here is to apologize all she wants, but with the glances she keeps giving me when she thinks I'm not looking, to the way her voice softens whenever she explains something to me and her body leans more toward me, there's obviously more to it.

"Brady, after I dropped you off I drove home and on the ride there, I did some serious thinking. When I was done thinking, I did what I should have done years ago and I called Mike. I laid everything that happened today out for him, minus some feelings that like with you, I was attempting to shield him from. I told him the truth and did the best thing for both of us. Then, I talked to my mom."

She told her mom about me?

"I needed advice. For the first time, I needed to just unload everything to someone. Someone that wouldn't be hurt by the things I've done. I needed to get some clarity. Direction. Something only an outsider could provide."

"And that was?" I ask, finally finding my voice again.

"I wanted to know if I should take a chance on something new or stick with the sure thing. The safer option."

"What does that have to do with me and why you're here?"

"The realizations I came to on the drive home, she gave them credibility. Proving that when I told Mike we could never be anything more than friends, it was the right decision, even if it was the one that caused the most pain. What I felt when I kissed you, no matter what it means in the grand scheme of things, it showed me that. I want something more than Mike can give, maybe even more than someone like you can. I deserve the chance to do that. Find it. So I blew up our friendship, broke his heart, and here I am."

"Emery…" God, I don't even know what to do with this. Less than twelve hours ago, before I had a chance to experience the day the way I did with her, I was still wrapped up tight in the past. Trying to get my soon to be ex-wife to change her mind even though deep down I knew she never would.

To stand here and judge Emery for ending things with her best friend over something we did together was wrong.

I'm not better than she is. If anything, with my inability to let go, I'm worse.

I can't believe what a complete jerk I've been.

"Here's where you tell me why, right?"

Again she's quick with her response.

"I'm here because despite everything I've done to you and to Mike, I had to know something."

"And that is?"

"If it will feel as good the second time around."

Smiling playfully, all traces of the earlier somber atmosphere erased, she moves toward me. Wrapping her arm around my neck and pressing her body into mine, she exhales softly before pressing her lips to mine. The taste of her instantly invading my senses and making it impossible to process anything but her.

The way she smells, the way her lips taste and the way her body feels pressed to tightly to mine. It's all her.

All Emery.

The time for talking is over.

For the first time since I split from Kelly, I don't want to think through every action.

All I want to do is feel.

Chapter Twenty-Three

Jax

Ring—Ring—Ring

Shifting in the bed at the sound of the shrill call of the phone and slamming my hand down onto the table next to it, greeted by nothing but hard wood, I roll over and sit up, hating the loss of the warmth from the blankets the second they fall down around my chest.

Spotting the phone about a foot away on the table from where I slammed down my hand, I reach out and grab the receiver, groaning as my muscles pull from the stretching. Bringing it to my ear, I prepare to chew out the person on the other end.

"Yes?"

"Mr. Merrick, this is the wakeup call you requested."

"Thanks." I politely spit out, dropping the phone back into its cradle before falling back onto the now cool mattress.

So much for enjoying a couple hours of extra sleep.

Turning over and catching the time on the alarm clock beside the bed—the one that despite being set, hadn't bothered going off—I groan again.

It wasn't bad enough that I'd barely gotten two hours of sleep after spending the day with Avery and being unable to do anything but toss and turn after we'd said goodnight, but now with this wakeup call, I'm reminded of just how long it's going to be until I see her again.

Booked solid for shows over the next two months, with only a day or two off in between—not nearly enough time to fly out to see Avery with the way the night before went—my mood only plummets more.

After the walk on the boardwalk, where we'd stopped and had the vendor dogs I told her about, we walked along the water's edge for a while before slipping off our shoes and making our way out into it.

Cooling down definitely needed with the way the heat seemed to rise whenever we so much as brushed against one another.

What stays with me more than just how we spent the night together is the smaller things I noticed during our time together. Small things that I know when I leave here later and am not surrounded by, are going to be the death of me.

The sound of her squeal when after running into the water, the cold hit her or the orgasm inducing low throaty moan she'd let escape when she took the first bite and swallow of the hot dog on the boardwalk. The smile that tugged at her face every time I caught her looking at me and the blush that quickly followed.

Everything Avery did last night seemed to spark something in me and even though I didn't understand it and still don't, it only seemed to make me even more determined to have her repeat it.

Somewhere between hitting the boardwalk last night and waking up this morning, Avery stopped being a want. She's a need now. One that I won't be able to shake until I get my fill.

Laying back on the bed and looking up at the ceiling, studying the pattern, I'm reminded again that in a few hours, I'm going to have to walk away from that need. One that even after just one day together, I know I'm never going to get my fill of.

This is why you don't get involved with random women on the road, jackass. You can't promise them anything and all you're going to do in the end is lead them on and hurt them.

The last thing I want to do is hurt Avery. Though, with as hollow as it feels thinking about leaving later and heading back on the road, I have a feeling that of the two of us, Avery would be the one left unscathed.

Especially after everything I learned about her.

✳✳✳✳✳

"Will you try something with me?" she asks and willing to do anything she wants if it means keeping her here, I agree.

"Sure. What'd you have in mind?"

We've been out of the water and laying back on the sand for a few minutes and as comfortable as the silence has been, I'm thankful she was the one to break it.

"Since we talked about some of the heavier aspects of our lives earlier, I was thinking we could play twenty questions or something similar. Learn random facts about each other, but in a less stressful way. Maybe see how much we have in common."

"Sounds like fun. Who's gonna start?"

"I can start unless you want to."

Motioning with my hand for her to go ahead, I flip from my position on my back looking up at the stars, to the side where I can get a better view of her smiling as she starts.

"Where were you born?"

"Arcadia, but we moved to Los Angeles when I was three. Your turn. Same question."

"According to my birth certificate, I was born in Wilmington, Delaware, but I only remember ever living in Toronto, so I'm going with that."

It's been awhile since we got into her reason for being in town, so her answer surprises me, but not because of what she said. It's how casual she sounds saying it. Not wanting to get into anything heavy, I would have expected this to be off limits. Not said with the ease it is.

"So born and raised in Toronto, huh?"

"Until about a week ago, yeah." She smiles softly. "Your turn. If you could choose to live anywhere in the world, where would it be?"

"Honestly, I'd choose to stay where I am. I'm a city guy and I'm comfortable in LA. What about you?"

"I don't have any specific place, just anywhere that's like this."

"Come on, Avery. Don't be cheap with your answers. You're the one that asked the question so I think you have a place."

"Asheville, North Carolina." She admits, shutting my teasing down, but proving just how easily I read her. "I went there once to cover an event back when I was still writing and fell in love."

There it is again. The blush from before. The one that transformed her face every time I stopped us during the walk and kissed her. The blush I can't seem to get enough of.

"One visit was all it took for you to fall in love, huh?"

Turning and looking out toward the water with a smile, her hand starts to come up to her face but thinking better of it, she lowers it back down before turning her attention back to me. Her flushed cheeks on full display.

"I know you're an editor now, but was that always your dream or did you want to do something else when you were a kid?" *I ask, keeping the game going.*

"I wanted to be a lot of things, but an editor for a magazine wasn't one of them."

"So what did you want to be when you grew up?"

"I wanted to be a counsellor for a long time. The few friends I had in school always seemed to use me as their sounding board, always asking for my advice. So for a long time, it seemed like that's what I would end up doing. At least until I started writing. After that, nothing else would do. What about you? Did you always want to be a wrestler?"

"No. I had it in my head for a long time that I was going to be a professional boarder."

"A what?"

"I love to surf. When I'm back home and got a good chunk of time to myself, I'm out on the water. I was pretty positive that when I got old enough, I would do it professionally."

"Okay, I gotta know. How did you go from that to wrestling?"

It having been so long since I gave it a lot of thought, I just shrug. It also helps that I can't nail down one specific instance when it comes to me and wrestling that made me know it was something I would do for the rest of my life.

"I watched it a lot and I guess after a while, I was bit by it."

"Can I ask you something a bit more serious?"

"Sure."

"Travelling as much as you do, does it ever get to be too much?"

As often as I'm interviewed, I don't think I've ever had anyone ask me that question before. It's a good one and even though she doesn't know, it's one I've thought a lot about over the last few years.

"I love being on the road and seeing all of the different places and people, I do. It's the best part of doing what I do, aside from getting to create a story in the ring. A show, really. But yeah, sometimes, it does get to be a lot."

"Has it always been that way?"

"Not really. When you're first starting out, you eat, sleep, and breathe what you're doing. Every move, every match, it's all you can see and you throw everything you have into it. You're so determined to prove yourself, be the best in the world at what you do that you'll do whatever it takes. When you're where I am now though, doing the same thing day in and day out, it's different." Reaching across and picking her hand up out of the sand and slipping my fingers down through hers, I change gears. "How did you and Emery get separated?"

Lips drawing up and into a straight line with her eyes falling away from mine and to the sand, I feel like kicking my own ass. Curiosity got the better of me and with her own questions changing and delving deeper, I thought I was safe to do the same.

Shit.

"Ave—"

"My dad bailed on his family and instead of just leaving me like he left everyone else, decided to take me with him."

"I'm sorry. I shouldn't have asked that."

"No, Jax. I'm glad you did. I can't process and deal with what happened if I don't talk about it. It's just a sore subject."

"Considering what happened, I think it would be weird if it wasn't."

"Mhmm." She murmurs and silence envelopes us again, one that is definitely not as comfortable as the one that was there when we sat down.

A silence I need to put an end to.

"Mac and Cheese or Pizza?"

Caught by the sound of her laughter as it falls softly between us, I'm warmed by the knowledge that me asking something so random caused it.

"Both?"

"Really? You don't have a favorite?"

"I grew up on Macaroni and Cheese. With my dad working so much, and it being the one meal I didn't burn to a crisp, it's a clear favorite. But pizza is just...sooo good."

Swallowing down the lump in my throat that appears as she moans over the thought of pizza, willing my body not to react to the sound the way it wants to, I throw another random choice her way.

"Jeans or sweats?"

"Sweats. Hands down. If I have to go out somewhere important but casual, jeans are my go-to, but any other time, I'm the sweat pants and ponytail girl."

An image of me coming home from the road to our apartment and having her lounging on the sofa looking exactly as she explains floods my brain and it takes everything I've got not to give into the rightness of it.

"What about you?"

"The same." I offer up and when she meets my eyes and smiles, I know I'm done for. The hammering of my heart, the sweat I can feel building on my palms, along with the incessant need I have to rake my hands through my hair so I can get it to behave and stop obstructing my view of her. She's causing all of it with just the sound of her voice and her smile.

I'm a goner.

A little over thirty-six hours since we met and I'm pretty damn sure she owns me.

Needing to move or say something to get us back on track and away from the crazy road my thoughts seem to be taking me down, I'm given the perfect opportunity when she shivers and pulls her hand out of mine in favor of wrapping both of them around her body.

This is the out I need.

"You're cold."

"I wasn't going to say anything, but yeah. I'm getting pretty cold. I guess I wasn't strong enough for the water after all."

Shifting to my knees and standing, I move toward her and hold out my hand, pulling her to her feet. Wrapping my arm around her and bringing her close, I rub my hands over her back. When it *doesn't seem to help and I feel her next shiver hard against me, I settle for pulling back and shrugging out of my windbreaker. Hanging it over and watching as she slips it on effortlessly.*

Like she's done it before.

"You didn't have to do that, but thank you."

"It was my stupid idea to walk into the water. The least I can do is give you my jacket."

"Even if it means you're the one freezing?"

"Even then, but I'm fine."

Slipping into place beside me, our hands meet and like every other time we've been this close, I slip my hand through hers, locking our fingers together before turning us in the direction of the boardwalk and the hotel in the distance.

All the while, with every step we take, wishing I could tell her the truth.

That her hand in mine is better than any jacket and that when we do get back to the hotel and we have to go our separate ways, I'm not going to want to lose it.

I'm not ready to give Avery up.

*****

I'm still not ready to let go.

Leaning over the bed, rifling through my bag and finding what I'm after, I pull my cell out and scan through the numbers. Another move I'd made last night before we parted ways and one that right now, I'm extremely thankful that I did.

Having her number, even if I never planned on using it again after she went back to Toronto and I went back out on the road was a smart move. It gave me the chance to capitalize on what little time I did have left.

And not have to say goodbye quite yet.

Hitting send and waiting as the rings go in, my breath hitches when I hear her voice say hello. But before I can get a word in edgewise, I realize it's not her, but her machine. Hanging up, not wanting to leave this on a voicemail she might never get,

I maneuver into my messages and pulling up her contact info, shoot a quick one off.

Hoping and even praying once the message sends, that it wasn't too forward, or worse, too late.

Good morning, Avery. You were the first thing to come to mind as I woke up this morning and I was hoping that you'd have breakfast with me.

Avery

"No, mom." I attempt to reassure her as the line continues to click with an incoming call "Of course I'm not upset that I had to stay at a hotel. I had no idea how things were going to play out, so this was the right thing to do."

From the moment I called her when I got up, she's been going back and forth with her concern over me staying at the hotel instead of at the house with Emery and her where she says I belong. No matter how many times I tried to explain that I was more than okay with the way things had played out, it never seemed to sink in. At least until now. Her resigned sigh means I finally got through.

"I suppose you're right, dear. I just don't like the thought of you being so far away. You've been away long enough."

"I agree, but I'm not that far away. Just down the road. You'll be seeing me soon enough. I'm just going to grab a shower and pack, then I'll be over."

"Really?"

The surprise in her voice bothers me more than I want to let on. I guess this is a bigger adjustment for all of us than I thought. I don't want her to be surprised that I'd want to spend time with her before my flight back home. It should be a no-brainer. I enjoyed the short time I had with her yesterday. There was no way I was going to let that be the first and last time we saw each other.

"Of course. You didn't think I would just leave town without saying goodbye did you?"

"To be honest," she pauses, and my heart aches with what I know is coming next. "I wasn't sure what your plans were."

"Well now you know. I'll be there soon and by the time I'm done, you'll be dying to kick me back to Toronto." I laugh, even though I know deep down my wording choice couldn't have been worse.

"Then plan to be here awhile young lady because I won't ever kick you back to the city."

Warmth fills my heart. A warmth I honestly never thought I'd experience given my father's inability to talk about the past and what had happened between him and my mother and then later on, his lack of a dating life. Hearing her say that she wants me there and that she'd never want me to leave, gives me something that until it happened I'd only ever wished for.

Love and want. A sense of being needed.

"Well, if you want to see me today, it means actually getting out of bed…"

"I'll let you go, sweetheart. I can't wait to see you later. I'm sure Emery will feel the same once she gets up."

Mention of my sister brings back everything I'd learned last night at the bar from Brady, bringing with it a whole new flush of guilt at not checking in with her sooner.

Some sister I am.

"Tell her I'll see her soon." I tell her softly before saying my final goodbyes and ending the call. Staring at the phone in my hands as the main screen appears and wondering again if last night with Jax had been the right decision.

Slipping my feet over the side of the bed, about to toss the phone down and head into the shower just like I'd promised my mom, a text comes through and going into the messages, I see it's from a contact I have yet to add.

Good morning, Avery. You were the first thing to come to mind as I woke up this morning and I was hoping that you'd have breakfast with me.

Jackson.

Moments from the night before spring to life inside my head and reading the text over a second time, I'm powerless to stop the grin beginning to rise on my face.

How long has it been since I got a good morning text? One that wasn't from my boss and referring to a looming deadline?

The answer is easy. It's never.

Which is why, reading it over for a third time and still grinning like an idiot, I do what I should have done when I first saw it and type a reply.

Good morning, Mr. Merrick. I'm sorry I missed your call. I was on the phone with my mother. I'd love to have breakfast with you. Just name the time and place.

His answer is immediate and taking the phone with me as I finally get out of bed, I head into the bathroom, placing the phone on the counter as I turn the water on. Turning to read it only when I'm sure the water is how I like it.

My room. Fifteen minutes?

Shooting off a quick agreement, I put the phone back down and go through the motions of stripping down and getting under the warm spray. Hearing the familiar beep of another incoming text, but putting it out of my head as I begin scrubbing myself clear.

Whatever Jax had to say, I'll answer it later in the best way possible.

In person.

Jax

"What is all of this?" Avery asks when after greeting her at the door and ushering her inside, she sees the display on the table.

"I figured we both needed to eat and since I really didn't feel like driving anywhere in town, I went with the room service option. I hope that's okay."

The smile building in the corner of her face tells me everything I need to know. Calling downstairs and having them bring up a little bit of everything was the right move.

Even if the looks I got from the guy delivering it leaned more to me being crazy.

Before I can say any more or she has the opportunity to respond, my cell begins vibrating in my pocket. Motioning with a quick wave of my hand for Avery to make herself comfortable, I pull it out and seeing the number, debate hitting ignore.

What the hell does he want now?

"Brady. What's going on?"

"Change of plans, buddy! There's some kind of storm brewing in Maryland so they're calling off the show tonight. I got the clearance from Smith to lay low here while they work out rescheduling it. Figured I'd fill you in, in case you had somewhere you wanted to be."

The hint in his voice isn't lost on me. He knows that staying here another night is like music to my ears. That it gives me time with Avery I didn't think I'd have.

Before I can even finish thanking him for the info, the calls ends and tossing it down onto the bed, I make my way over to Avery making herself at home filling her plate with food.

"When did you have time to plan this?" she asks, to which I just smile before turning my attention to my plate.

"Jax," she laughs. "Are you really just going to smile?"

"I planned on it, yeah." I admit easily, but when she pouts has me spilling my guts. "I called down after I texted you earlier. When I explained to whoever answered the phone that I wanted to treat the most beautiful woman in the world to breakfast, she fell all over herself wanting to help."

"I just bet she did." She laughs before focusing again on the array of food spread out over the table.

Not knowing what kind of food she liked apart from pizza, the hot dogs we had on the boardwalk, and macaroni and cheese, I requested a little bit of everything they had. Most of it, looking at everything here, not even breakfast food.

At least none that I've ever had.

Cornetto pastries and cappuccino the way Italians would want it, Greek Loukaniko sausage, and the American standard of scrambled eggs, bacon and hash browns, along with various different types of juice all adorned the table. I'd even gone so far as to make sure there was a Canadian staple too, in peameal bacon.

"I guess you start with whatever you like best." I shrug, reaching over for a croissant as the sound of her laughter escapes again. "What's so funny?"

"If you wanted to know what my favorite breakfast food is, all you had to do was ask. I'm pretty sure there's enough food on the table to feed the entire floor, Jax."

"Humor me, would you? Which one of these things sounds good?"

Pointing to the cornetto's she smiles, stretching her body out over the table and grabbing the glass pitcher of orange juice before leaning back and pouring some into her glass.

"For the record though, never order peameal bacon again. Even with me being Canadian and all, that stuff is gross. I'll take actual bacon over that any day."

Laughing as her nose scrunches up as her eyes flick over the peameal bacon, I file away the info for future use, though past today, I wasn't sure when I'd ever get the chance to fall back on it. Filling my plate easily with the only thing on the table that makes my mouth water, a comfortable silence falls over the table as we eat.

After polishing off the bacon and making a large dent in the eggs, I notice that Avery is finished her croissant. Waiting as she takes a quick drink of orange juice, when the glass hits the table, I end the silence and attempt to get to know her a little more.

"So I know we talked about this last night, but when exactly do you head back to Toronto?"

"My flight leaves at six a.m. tomorrow. According to my boss, I'm missed and needed back. I was kind of hoping for at least the week, but what can you do? At least I'm getting another day with my mom before I have to take off."

"Are you looking forward to getting back to work?"

"If I had your job and saw more than just the four walls of my office, I would say yes. Heading back to that and then deadlines? No. I can't really say I am."

"What have you had to report on lately?"

"Human interest pieces mostly. Things people are more likely to read about. The best example of that being the story we ran last month about the hometown boy who made it big in the music industry and came back to put on a concert that benefited a local charity. Everyone ate that one up. For me, it's the stories we write about real life heroes that means the most. Kids battling illnesses and winning, good Samaritans, that kind of thing. Though, with those, especially with the kids, they can get quite depressing."

Can't argue with her there.

"What was the hardest story you were ever a part of?"

After learning the night before just how long she's been with the magazine she works with, I expect her answer to take some time, but am met with the opposite when she leans back in her chair and the story comes out.

"There was a boy about two years ago who had been diagnosed with cancer. After going through round after round of radiation and chemotherapy, he'd been told he was in remission. My boss heard about him through a friend and sent me to cover it. Jackson, meeting this boy and seeing how someone so little could fight so damn hard and win that way, well it left a mark. We ran the piece and a few months later when we went back for a follow-up interview, he was gone."

I had a feeling that when she mentioned it being depressing, it was going to be something like this that she shared with me, but it still didn't stop me from hoping for something a little less heartbreaking.

Jesus.

Life changes in the blink of an eye.

Putting the brakes on this conversation before what she shared has a chance to hurt her anymore than it already does, I switch to a topic a little less painful.

"Did you ever write any pieces related to what Brady and I do?"

"I actually have, but not interviews with wrestlers or anything. It was more of a summary of the matches. Why do you ask? Could this breakfast be your way of buttering me up so I'll interview you?"

Snorting, I shake my head and she laughs.

"Not in this lifetime. I was just curious to see how much interaction you had with the business."

"Fair enough."

Pushing her plate off to the side, she slides her hands up onto the table, folding them together and waiting me out while I finish off the remaining scraps on my plate. The feel of her eyes watching me, pleasurable instead of awkward and reminding me again just how comfortable all of this is between us.

Our positions at the table, the way the conversation flows, and even the way we patiently took our time eating instead of attacking it the way I'm used to doing with Brady. All of it just speaking volumes to the level of comfort between us. It feeling like we've known each other a whole lot longer than a couple of days.

"There's something else I want to do if you're up for it."

"You already spoiled me with breakfast, Jax. What more could there possibly be?"

"Say yes and find out." I tease. "You know the curiosity will kill you if you don't."

"Okay. You're on. What do you have in mind?"

Pushing the chair back from the table and standing, I make my way over to the alarm clock and flipping it on, scroll through the dial until I find what I'm after.

This not exactly something I had planned when I invited her to breakfast, but now that it's here, something I'm also not going to let go of. Finding an easy listening station, wanting it to be more organic than just pulling my cell out and turning a song on, I step away and head back over to her, my hand outstretched.

The look of astonishment on her face as she comes to terms with what I have in mind is priceless and after a short break where she places her hand into mine and lets me pull her to her feet as the radio host talks, another slow tempo song begins and all of the pieces fit.

"Dance with me?"

Chapter Twenty-Four

Brady

Stretching out across the bed, the morning sun having finally made its way high enough in the sky to shed the brightest shade of orange through the room, I bring my arm up across my face with a grunt before turning over just in time to be greeted with the sound of the alarm as it begins blaring from my phone.

Sliding my hand across the screen and silencing it, I risk the glare from the sun through the parted blinds again and turn over onto my back. Now that I'm awake, my thoughts instantly floating to the auburn hair and hazel eyes that had haunted me right up until I finally gave into sleep what only feels like a couple of hours ago.

The woman that in the span of a forty-eight hour period had flipped my world completely on its axis.

The second kiss we shared here in this room, definitely not something that was the result of any bet we'd made and one that even though I still wasn't sure where it would lead, I had been powerless to step back from. With Emery having shared her reasoning about what had happened earlier in the day and me understanding better than anyone else the effect that people we care about can have on the things we do, things shifted and there was no going back.

Remembering the taste of her lips and the soft moan she'd let escape in response to my own, I can't help grinning like a fool.

There was definitely no bet needed now. Especially with everything that came pouring out when we finally came up for air and she'd made herself comfortable.

With Emery showing up and willing to share things that all things considered, I had no damn business knowing, I'd turned around and done the same. Explaining in as much detail as I could, the current status of my relationship with Kelly. Our marriage, the dissolution of it and everything that had taken place in between.

Ending with the moment I told her I understood. Her situation with Mike, what was going on with her mother, and her reasoning at the time for what she'd done. I had to make sure she knew that I got it.

What had started out as a day that was supposed to be a one off of fun and excitement had turned into something infinitely more serious the more we talked. I had learned so much about her and about me as I shared just as much with her. Both of us at the time, even though I don't think we were all that focused on it, making a connection.

One that I hoped me leaving town wouldn't break.

Because even if nothing came out this romantically speaking, I really did feel like I could open up to this woman. The first one in forever that could see and hear about the ugliest parts of me and wouldn't turn her back on me or worse...judge me.

Then there was what happened after again being told to stay put by Smith, I'd called her and we made a plan for the rest of the day.

One that after what happened, I'm sure never to forget.

*****

"You want me to do what?" I ask, completely taken off guard that despite knowing my issues when she brought it up yesterday, she was still attempting to sway me.

"Yesterday when you won the bet, I came through on what you asked for. Both things, since I'm here now. So now, I'm asking you to do the same thing for me. Spend the day doing something I love."

"Cliff diving."

She nods enthusiastically. "Mmhmm."

The no is on the tip of my tongue.

So is the need to tell Emery that it doesn't appeal to me and while I wasn't exactly scared to do it, I also wasn't comfortable with it. The eagerness on her face though, giving away just how *badly she wants to share this with me, nulling my explanation entirely.*

"Can you promise we'll be safe doing this?"

She giggles and I feel my stomach drop what feels like another ten feet. The way she's laughing means she can't promise me shit.

"I can't promise that, but I can say that since I've done it a bunch of times before today and I have no scars, we should be absolutely fine. Is that a good enough endorsement, Brady?"

As uncomfortable as I am with this, I'm powerless to fight against the innocent way she's batting her eyes at me. Even if this ends badly and the last memory I have before dying is of the jagged rocks and water, I know I have to see it through. Take the chance. Especially since come tomorrow when I leave, I'm not sure when I'll get the chance again.

"It's going to have to be. Let's get this show on the road."

Slipping her hand into mine, she starts winding her way through the hotel, pulling me along for the ride. My reluctance obviously turning my legs to stone and taking what should have been a quick jaunt through the lobby, ten times longer.

When we're finally in her car, the drive to the cliff is a quick one. No sooner am I sitting in her passenger seat than she's pulling off the main road and onto the gravel that remembering how it all looked yesterday, leads straight into our destination.

Her excitement bubbling over when after stepping from the car, she takes off at a run, forcing me to jog in order to keep up all the way down the embankment and straight over to where she stops right at the edge of the cliff.

My stomach revolting as the knot from yesterday tightens as I stop beside her.

Looking up when I feel her eyes and seeing the smile beaming up at me, I groan.

She shouldn't be this damn excited for what I'm pretty sure is a suicide mission.

"Did you wear trunks under your clothes?"

"No. You said dress comfortably, so I did."

"My mistake. So what are you sporting under the pants?" *she asks with a sly grin as she gives my body a quick perusal.*

"Is this where I say nothing?"

Two can play this game.

"Uh—no." she blushes and I resist the urge to celebrate the victory. "I just figured you wouldn't want to jump fully clothed."

"So in other words, you were wondering if I was naked under here?" I tease again, sliding my hand in and looping it in the band of my pants. Another victory when her eyes fall away from mine and her cheeks grow even darker. "I've got boxers on, so I'm pretty sure I'm good to go."

"Oh, um, yeah. That should be fine." She stammers.

She can dish it out, but can't take it.

Interesting.

Making quick work stripping off her shirt, no longer paying attention to the fact that I'm here, she throws it to the ground before doing the same to her jeans. Kicking them back from the edge before turning her attention back to me.

The vision standing unabashedly in her bra and panties leaving me at a loss for words. Frozen.

The removal of her shirt giving me a full view of a pair of tits that are bigger than I imagined them when I was alone after she left the night before and a body that seems to have just the right amount of curve in all of the right places. One that even though her ass and tits aren't exposed is still causing my dick to spring to life at the sight of it.

Damn. What I told Avery was right. Ogling Emery this way is definitely how I'm a pig.

Attempting to get control of the situation before she catches on to the way I'm objectifying her and worse, responding physically to it, I fail when her eyes meet mine and her smirk is back.

Way to act like a horny kid seeing tits and ass for the first time, Raines. *I admonish myself before shifting my eyes down to the ground below us and running a hand over my head in an attempt to alleviate my embarrassment at being caught.*

"So," I start. "If we strip down up here and jump off, how are we supposed to get our clothes when we're done?"

"Easy. There's a hidden path at the end of the rocks down there." She leans over and points, though I don't take a step toward her in order to see. "We just take it to get back up here."

Nodding, I feel her eyes on me, but it's only after a couple of minutes of just standing there silently that I see her impatience beginning to show as her foot begins tapping.

Emery is waiting for me to strip down.

Fuck. I need to shake these damn nerves. Well, nerves and the damn need I have to bring her too me that's making my blood boil over.

Catching the smile she affords me when I pull my shirt off, a heaviness present in her eyes that proves that I'm not the only one caught up in the physical response we're having to each other, I make quick work of my pants. Kicking them over the way she'd done before inching myself closer to the edge and finally looking down below.

"Since this is your first time and you look like you've seen a ghost, I'm gonna go first." When I just nod, she continues. "It's really not as hard as it looks. You just go back a few feet and take the cliff at a run, throwing yourself out as far as you can. It's a long way down, a total free fall really. You might feel a bit of pain from the impact of hitting the water, but the rush you should get is going to override that pretty quick."

Again all I can do is nod. I hear everything she's saying, but it doesn't make a damn bit of it any easier. For all my talk of not being afraid, it sure as fuck feels like it now that I'm here and we're pretty much two steps away from actually doing it.

It also doesn't help that what I really want to do is stand here and drink her in.

I've tried looking elsewhere. Even seeing the rocks and water when I looked over the cliff didn't alleviate it. She's too damn close. I can practically feel the heat permeating off her body and we're not even touching.

But fuck, do I want to touch her. Everywhere.

Following her when after a quick squeeze to my hand she jogs back the way we came, I push down the need I have to sweep her off her feet, wrap her legs around me and fuck her against one of the trees we passed on our way down here and focus instead on the real reason we're here.

Screw being scared. It's time to man up. Prove I can do this.

Pointing in front of her and making my eyes follow, she takes off running, laughing as she sails past me and in the time it takes me to blink, she's lifting off into the air. , picking up speed with each foot of space she travels until she's lifting off. Soaring off the cliff, over the edge until the only sound I can make out is the sound of her scream as she begins her descent down.

Shaking off the nerves, I lean over the edge just in time to see her hit the water, an explosion of water flying up and out as her body gets swept under.

Heart hammering in my chest at seeing her go under but not seeing her bounce back up right away, I count each ragged breath as it comes, keeping track until I finally see her break the surface and what looks like her hand moving over her hair.

Fifteen breaths or what amounts to twenty seconds with the couple that hitched as worry set in. What I know I can look forward to when I finally take the leap next.

Vaguely making out the sound of her yelling, I look over and see her arms swaying back and forth. Obviously her way of telling me that it was my turn.

Okay, Brady. Do or die time. Maybe even do *and* die if this didn't go as smoothly as it did Emery. You can take off and hitch your way back to the hotel or take the plunge and get yourself even closer to her.

The choice is obvious.

Setting myself up the way Emery had before leaping, I move back a few extra feet. Taking the cliff at a run and throwing myself off. Closing my eyes and praying as I feel the air rushing past that with all the years I spent in the gym and all of the screwing around I did in the backwoods, I'm out as far from the edge and the rocks below as possible.

Feeling the weightlessness of being in the air almost immediately after I jump, but still not having the balls to open my eyes and commit it any of it to memory. In the time it takes me to suck in a breath, I feel myself falling. The length and intensity of the drop stealing practically every ounce of breath until the panic over when I'm going to hit the water takes it place. My mind as unprepared for the pain Emery explained that my body is when after a few minutes of glorious free fall, I finally hit my mark.

Legs hitting first, the coolness of the water shoots straight up on through them, seizing me completely before the little air I did have from the fall knocks clear out of me and I begin to sink. Unable to mount any sort of defense or struggle against the beast threatening to take me under.

Closing my eyes tighter, any and all rational thought drains away as I prepare myself for what I'm positive is going to be my death. This lake, my final resting place. But what arms wrapping tightly around my midsection and pulling me upward has me pausing in my acceptance of my fate.

Hitting the surface and finally feeling the breeze against my face, I let my mouth fall open, attempting to take a breath. What quickly turns into me gasping for air as after the first breath, I go on to inhale at least another dozen or so before the reality of what I've done sets in.

I did it. I actually dived off the godforsaken cliff.

Holy fucking shit.

I did it.

"Oh my god, Brady! Are you okay?" she practically shrieks in my ear as her hands make their way to my face and she moves them frantically, checking me over.

Sucking in more air in an effort to find my voice but still unable to do much more than shiver and shake, I nod and it's impossible to miss the relieved sigh that falls from her the second I do it.

"I-I'm o-okay." I stammer through the rattling of my teeth, and with another sigh she shifts my head side to side slowly before finally releasing her hold.

One I strangely miss the second it's taken away and what has me reaching out to stop before she can make it even farther. Bringing her close enough in to get a real hold on before pulling her flush to my body.

Warning bells are going off in my brain having her this close. We're in the middle of a public body of water, one she's told me multiple times that people frequently jump from the way we just did. The water that had soaked through what little clothing we were wearing enough in any normal situation to cool me off, but didn't seem to be able to do anything to dampen the rush of heat I was now experiencing with her proximity to every exposed part of me.

"What's wrong?" she asks, wiggling her body against mine in an effort to free herself of my tightened grasp.

"Nothing, Emery. In fact, I'm pretty sure with the way it feels having you this damn close, everything is perfect."

Not overthinking it, I kiss her. Hard. All thoughts and words voided as I attempt to make her feel a little of the rush I'm experiencing. Feeding the fire that's now burning it's way straight through me into her lips. Being selfish and taking everything she's offering me when she melts into it, overcome so completely by the scent of her and the water around us that my head begins to spin.

It isn't just my head in this. It was the rest of my body too. Every damn part of me reacting in the moment to everything I can see and everything I can feel with her close proximity. My body now rigid and hard, reacting when bringing her even closer, those full fucking tits of hers brush against my chest. Setting off a chain reaction of heat straight down through me, all of it pooling in my dick as it reacts and makes my arousal known.

Fuck!

The internal pep talks, the need to be better than any other guy when placed in a situation like this, along with the bullshit I sold myself under the guise of not wanting to rush being with a woman when things were still so fucking screwed up in my head over Kelly. It all seem to fall out the window here in the water.

All I want to do is take her. Every god damned inch and make it mine.

Make her mine.

Breaking the kiss and without even thinking, I say the first thing that comes to mind the second my eyes open and meet hers.

"Let's make this even better."

Screw doing things in the right time and way. I've been doing that practically from the time I was born and look where it's gotten me.

Playing by the rules can be someone else's bag for a while. Here and now, I'm taking what I want.

"How do you suggest we do that?" she murmurs against my lips, and instead of telling her, I show her as my lips come down rough and hard on hers. Her breath halting at the surprise, but catching on quickly as she responds in kind. Pushing back against me with everything she's got.

Keeping one hand securely around her, I let the other one fall and slipping it into the band of my boxers, I yank them down before repeating the same motion on the other side, not breaking the kiss or stopping until I'm completely free of them.

Releasing her lips from mine and releasing the grip on her body, I watch as her chest bobs up and down in the water until it disappears under as her hand comes up to the straps on her shoulders and she begins sliding them down one at a time, slowly, making the need to own her worse. My dick so hard that I know if I don't bury myself inside her soon, I'm going to explode.

"Emery..." I somehow manage to choke out when after reaching around her back, the bra falls away.

"What's the matter?" she teases as she floats across the water and presses herself to me. The need to touch her, feel what she's now exposing, leaving me trembling.

"I need..."

"You need what?"

"You. I need...you."

Biting back a curse when she backs away again, my breath halts when I see the reason for it. A minute that feels like a god damned year passes until her hand comes up from the water again. This time, with her panties attached and a seductive half smile on her face.

I never thought seeing a woman holding her panties could be hot, but Emery, she's proving that it is.

It's the hottest damn thing I've ever seen.

What began as a simmering need that quickly turned into a veracious hunger is now proving almost deadly. I'm finding it hard to think. The only thing I'm capable of now that we're stripped and laid out bare, the urge to take her. Feel her.

So feel her I do.

Pulling her back, she laughs and I'm completely lost. Pressing her body against mine, I brush my lips against her neck and waste no time tasting her. Licking and sucking until I feel her go weightless in my embrace, a pleasured moan escaping as I pull back just in time to see her lips lift and her heavily lidded eyes close.

Giving herself over to me.

The first time a woman has done that since, god, what feels like forever ago.

That, how long it's been the very reason for what comes falling out of my mouth next.

"Emery, it's been a long fucking time since I've wanted to be with someone this much. An even longer time since I've had to control myself, so if this...if me fucking you isn't what you want, you need to tell me now."

Shivering under my touch, her lids slowly open and upon finding mine, show me exactly what it is she wants. The hunger present putting us on the same page.

"I want you, Brady. This, with you is exactly what I want. Please."

Her agreement all the incentive I need, I lower my hand to her waist and grip her tighter, lifting her legs and wrapping them around me, the head of my dick rubbing against what even in the coolness around us, is her hot and ready warmth.

The water acting as a natural lubricant, allows me to slip easily into her, the feel of her tight and warm around me settling the argument in my brain screaming at me to focus on her pleasure over my own. The thin thread of my self-control snapping altogether when taking the lead, she tightens her hold and grinds into me. My dick burying itself so deeply inside of her sex that I can feel it brushing against her walls.

Her moaning into my neck as she rocks back and forth my undoing. The final string in the tether of my self-control snapping as she breathlessly begs for me to move. An explosion of pleasure erupting in my brain, straight on through every cell in my body as I do as she asks, shaking me to the very core.

My hands resting on her hips and moving her up and down, burying myself with every thrust, a growl ripping from somewhere deep inside when she wraps her arms around my neck, holding on tightly, her breath releasing in heavy pants before she presses her lips down hard on mine.

Tangling my hands in her hair and gripping her head tightly as she takes control and rides me, I deepen our kiss. Sliding my tongue easily into her hot eager mouth, only to find hers and drown in her taste as they begin to dance together.

Both of our bodies coming together and moving in such a synchronized rhythm that we don't feel like two separate beings anymore, but one. Her body seemingly made for mine and the feel of it around me, the sounds that flow so easily from some carnal place inside her, bringing me to life in ways I haven't experienced in years.

With the pressure in my balls threatening to send me over the edge as she tightens and pulls me even deeper, I bite back a curse, but the second her lips leave mine and make their way down to my neck and her teeth graze the skin, the time for holding back is over.

"Fuck Emery!" I curse her name, gripping her hips as I drive myself into her, each thrust harder than the last, the release I'm needing coming and spilling into her as the sound of her telling me to let go falls like a purr from her lips.

Reality hitting the moment the fire that had been ignited when we dove off the cliff lowers from a full body born to the low simmer.

I'd been so caught up in the rush of what I'd done, the desperate need to be inside her, I hadn't even thought about protection. It doesn't matter that this is the first time I've been with someone who isn't Kelly and that I'm frequently tested by CPW. Not thinking this through, wanting to be crazy for what feels like the first time in my life, it's made me fucking careless.

"Emery..." I pause, not sure how I'm even going to bring this up after what we just shared.

"Brady..." She repeats in kind, her eyes widening as reality seems to set in.

"That was..."

"It was what?"

This is where I admit this was a mistake. That what we did was stupid. Tell her we should have waited or hell, not even done it all given the fact that I'm leaving town tomorrow. We've got to deal with the fallout of what just happened.

That's not at all what comes out.

What happened between us, while obviously careless, was also equal parts hot as hell as earth shattering. So instead of going with the logical, I go with the truth instead.

This, being with Emery this way, it wasn't a one-time thing. There's a reason she was the first person I've slept with since the split and I'll be damned if I'm going to cheapen the moment by making her think otherwise.

"Everything, Emery. It was fucking everything."

*****

Those last words I spoke before kissing her again and swimming back to shore. It's those words that are going to haunt me the most when I leave in a few hours.

Not because I didn't mean them, but because I did. Every damn one.

That moment in the water with Emery was everything and even now, a day later and with the looming threat of another cross state road trip with Jax on the horizon, it still is.

Emery did more than fuck me after we went cliff diving. She did more than just give me hope I could move on from the blast that had shaken my person life too.

She altered me.

Looking at the bags packed and waiting by the door and back over to the alarm flashing the time, and flooded by every sensation that the reminder of yesterday had awoken in me, I know what I've got to do.

I can't leave town. Not yet. Not without seeing her one last time and doing the one thing that after Kelly ripped out and stomped on my heart, I didn't think I would ever be capable of again.

Laying everything on the line and letting someone in.

Emery

"Thank you for coming. I know it's early."

I just stood silent and unmoving, watching the man in front of me as his eyes awkwardly flitted around the room to anything that wasn't me.

The very same man that just yesterday had taken the plunge and gone cliff diving with me, but more than that, the man I'd willingly had unprotected sex with right after it happened.

It's not the first time the rush of diving has sparked that reaction. Hell, it's not even the first time I've had sex, but those two things together definitely were. While I had no regrets about what happened, even after I realized that I'd let him fuck me bare, it didn't look as though he was feeling the same.

The raccoon eyes he's sporting speaking to just how much sleep he must have gotten last night. More than likely with how large they were, less than I had and at best, I could only account for two hours.

"When do you leave?"

"As soon as Jax gets his ass down here, which should be any time now."

Color me confused. He asked me here seconds before he has to leave...why?

"So why did you want me here if you're leaving now?"

Scrubbing a hand down over his face and exhaling deeply, he reaches his hand across the table and rests it on mine.

"I didn't feel right about leaving without talking to you." Cursing under his breath, he scowls. "Scratch that. I didn't *want* to leave without talking to you first."

Thankful he'd caught himself and reworded his previous statement, not wanting to give into the slight sting that had materialized after what sounded like an obligation stay, I could finally admit I felt the same way as him.

This is all new to me, what's happening with us. For as loud a supporter as I am of the wrestlers and everything they do in the ring, I've never once stepped out of line with one of them before. Let alone slept with one. Nothing at all like what's transpired between me and Brady.

What didn't feel like sleeping with a superstar at all.

When I gave myself over to Brady Raines, it wasn't the enigmatic guy in the ring I've spent years watching that I was with. It was just him. The guy, not the enigma.

There was this brief second right after he hit the water where everything changed. Seeing him go under and then the more than thirty seconds that passed with no sign of him coming up, shook things up. Put me into panic mode. Then, when I did my best to pull him out, it shifted again. This time, to desire. Need. Craving.

My body burning so intense that it overrode my rules. The part of my brain that prided itself on common sense. Not letting up in its assault until we'd done the unthinkable and given into it.

All of that culminating in the words that even now, twenty-four hours later, I can't forget.

When he said what we shared was everything.

"About yesterday," he starts. "I need you to know I don't regret it, but that what happened, well, it's never happened before."

"Do you mean in the water or in general?"

"I mean *ever* period, Emery. I have never once had a girl on the road that I've slept with. I never had a need for it. I don't have a need for it now either, but yesterday in the water when I crashed, my adrenaline was off the charts. I wasn't myself and it didn't help having you there looking like...shit. Looking like a wet fucking dream. Making me feel things I don't think I've felt in years. I couldn't help myself."

I listen to every word he says, making sure to really let them sink in. Determining quickly that I was right in what I thought when I first got here. He's been overthinking this nearly as much as I have.

We're venturing new ground together.

"Brady, I have never had an experience like ours yesterday. I've been with men, I won't ever pretend or deny that, but allowing what happened yesterday to happen at all was new. It's not something I ever thought I was capable of, much less thought about. But you should know that I don't regret it either. I just don't have a clue what it means."

"What it means?"

"You're leaving *really* soon. We've hung out together and talked. Kissed, touched, and now slept together. For people that don't have the job you do, I could easily figure all of that to be the start a relationship, but what the hell does it mean for us once you walk out the door and head to the next city?"

"Well, what do you want it to mean?"

Way to ask a loaded question, buddy.

"I want this to be more than what it looks like on the surface. More than just you needing to get laid on the road or me fulfilling some fantasy of screwing a wrestler. I want it to actually mean something, Brady. I'm not asking you to be my boyfriend. Given you being on the road, that'd be pretty damn impossible anyway. I just know that when you walk out of here today, I don't want to lose you."

There. It's out now and doesn't sound nearly as brutal as it did when I rehearsed it on the way over.

"Then when I leave, we don't let that happen."

Where I'm relieved by what he's said, as shown with the relieved sigh I let escape, when I finally meet his eyes, I see the opposite staring back at me. He looks pained.

"Brady..."

"I should have expected you to react like that. We barely know each other after all." He says, his tone clipped, only adding more confusion to the already growing pile I'm experiencing the more I watch him.

"What's that supposed to mean?"

"I know this is a lot to ask of you, Em, but do you think you can have a little bit of faith in me? People..." he pauses. "People in the past would hear what I was telling them, but didn't believe in it. It led to more shit than I can even begin to explain right now. They assumed it was bullshit and didn't focus on the real effort I was making. I don't want that happening here. When I say I don't want us to lose touch, I mean it."

Waiting a couple of beats just in case he wants to say more, I use the time to collect my thoughts. Make sense of them before I unload and with a heavy intake of breath once it's as clear as it's ever gonna get, I finally speak.

"I can, but given the way all of this started with us, can you do the same?"

There's no hiding the fact that I'm talking about my omission about Mike. Agreeing to spend time with him knowing that there was someone else, someone actually here that was in love with me, didn't exactly start us out on the right foot, especially as far as faith and trust goes.

"I can and more than that, I want to. Look, you already have my number and you can use it anytime. Day or night. If you don't get me right away, I'll get back to you as soon as I can. I've got your number so let's agree I can do the same."

Can't exactly argue with that. The idea of being able to end my day with Brady every day, even though he was nowhere near me, has me more excited than I want to admit.

"We can do this, Em. We just need to have a little faith in each other. At least that's what I've been told, though this situation definitely differs from the ones I've been in before." He admits with a chuckle.

I'm one of the most trusting people on the planet, even when in the end it brings me nothing but pain. I see myself signing up for this with Brady easily, even with all the risks to my heart I'm certain will come. There's just something about him that makes me think out of all the people I'd mistakenly put my trust in before, he'd be the one to inflict the least amount of damage.

"You really want this."

"Absolutely. I wouldn't have said it if I didn't. Honestly, this has probably been the best couple of days I've had in years. I've done things I never would have pictured myself doing and actually had fun doing them. It's strange, but for the first time in years, it feels like I'm living in the present again. You did that. You've reminded me with your bat shit cliff diving and bet making bowling trip what living is. I'd be crazy not to want to do whatever it takes to keep that feeling—that person—in my life. Are you with me?"

Slipping my hand out from under his on the table, I rest it on top, curling my fingers around and squeezing. Both our eyes falling to our hands and the hold that he expands on when with a little maneuvering, he locks out fingers together.

Hearing a voice clear behind us, the spell that had been cast over us the second I showed up falls away. Throwing us right back into the here and now. The reality of our situation. Twisting around in my seat and seeing Jackson standing there with bags in hand, I resign myself to what has to happen now.

Saying goodbye.

Brady, completely ignoring Jax's interruption, smiles softly before lifting our hands into the air until his lips are brushing against the outside of mine. Lowering them and leaning in, following it up with a delicate kiss to my lips.

One I know will linger long after he's left.

"We can do this, Emery. As soon as I get where I'm going, I'll text. Maybe even call if I've got the time. I know it might be hard to believe, but I'll do whatever it takes to prove that what I told you is the truth."

Slipping his hand from mine, but keeping his body close, he pulls me into his arms, crushing me to him in a hug that I was pretty sure the more he gripped me tighter, I never wanted to end.

A stray tear makes its way past the barrier I've wrapped myself in, sliding down my face before falling to the windbreaker he's wearing and disappearing, the only display of emotion I'm determined to have, as I steady myself as he begins to pull back from our embrace.

An ending that comes in the form of a gentle kiss to the top of my head before he turns his back to go. The nail that is his departure, hitting its mark with every step he takes as another round of tears begins to fall.

Watching him disappear into the crowd of people now mingling around the doors to the hotel, barely able to make him out anymore, I turn to go, but am held captive when I hear his voice call out again.

"Don't forget what we shared yesterday, Em! I know I never will!"

Chapter Twenty-Five

Jax

With my bags officially packed and the room cleaned out, I was ready for the next road trip in a string of them with Brady.

A trip that in the past would have made me happy because I was getting to do what I love, but after the events of the last couple of days, has me feeling a little less inspired.

Avery's fault.

Sure, I love what I do and I'm not sure what I'd do with myself if I ever had to walk away from it before I was ready, but in just three days, I'm seeing the other side.

The possibility of life after wrestling.

Leaving the ring and settling down. Hell, I can even see kids and a house with a white fucking fence.

Slow your roll, Jackson.

I hadn't even heard anything by text or call from Avery anyway. So imagining life after wrestling and worse, life with *her* after it, was definitely premature.

After a morning spent eating, then dancing, and an afternoon curled up on the bed watching movies before she'd taken off across town to be with her mom, I assumed we bonded.

Not hearing from her when I was due to leave any minute and not knowing how long it would be until I saw her again, I'd really been hoping for the chance to say goodbye.

Picking up my cell off the bedside table and going into the messages, I let hope get the better of me when I see one message unread. A hope that clearly dies when I see who it's actually from.

Brady.

Packed and ready. Meet me in the lobby.

Well that explains the missed calls earlier.

Even after all this time riding the road together, it still surprises me just how much Brady hates anything to do with technology. Always relying on calling to get the job done and not giving his cell a whole lot of thought otherwise. Case and point, the three missed calls that I hadn't heard during my shower earlier and now this message.

On my way down.

Picking my duffel off the floor and slinging it over my shoulder, I turn back one more time before stepping through. Wanting to commit the room and everything that had taken place in it over the last twenty-four hours to memory. Only turning and heading out when I'm content that not a second has been left behind.

Barreling straight into a person. Female judging by the cry that sounds out as they fall to the floor and throwing my bag to the floor and crouching in order to help her up, a female I know well.

"Avery, shit. I'm sorry. I was heading downstairs to meet Brady and wasn't paying attention."

Brushing off my apology with a wave of her hand, she slips her hand in mine and lets me help her to her feet. A hold I don't let go of until I've successfully walked us both back through the door and into the safety of the room.

"It's my fault. I got here about ten minutes ago and was working up the nerve to knock. You actually saved me by storming out the way you did."

Stepping toward her, I bring my hand to her face and run it over, looking for any sign that in our collision I'd hurt her. Seeing none, I go to remove my hand but hers comes up halting me.

"So, I guess with the way you came flying out, it means you're leaving?"

"Yeah," I agree, rattling off Brady's earlier speech. "We gotta hit the road now or we're not gonna make the next town."

Having just gotten the car and over the years developing a huge hatred for the airport, after getting Brady's agreement, we'd decided to hit most of the states on this tour driving. Which meant where most of the guys were in the sky by now, we had to do things the longer and harder way.

The way that was now affording me the chance to say goodbye the way I wanted.

"I'm really glad you're here." I admit. "I was hoping that yesterday afternoon wasn't the last I'd see of you."

Catching her blush and the way her hand immediately comes up in order to block me from it, I take my turn and stop her. Grasping her hand and bringing it down into mine before it has the chance to cast even the faintest shadow over her skin.

"I'm glad I'm here too, Jax."

Something about the quiet yet soft way she admits she feels the same, the gentle look in her eye and the way that even standing the way we are, her body seems to gravitate toward me, has me admitting thoughts that I haven't even gotten the chance to process.

What I know to be the absolute truth.

"I don't think I can do this, Ave."

"Can't do what?"

"Leave here. Leave you. I know I've got a job to do, but part of me isn't ready to do that yet. There's still so much I want to do with you. Learn about you. Hell, even find in you. I'm worried that if I walk out that door, get in the car and drive away with Brady to Maryland that I may never get the chance for it again." Focusing on the way I sound, what I'm admitting and how erratic it seems, I wonder if I'm even making sense. "Do you understand what I'm saying?"

"Yes." She admits, slipping her hands from my grip and bringing me into her arms in a tight embrace. "It's the same way I'm feeling about going back to the city. If I leave, I'm afraid the spell of the last few days, meeting you and my family, it's going to disappear and I'll wake up to find out it was all a dream."

Holding onto her as tightly as I can without hurting her, I bury my face into her hair and just breathe her in. Any attempt I might have been able to make at keeping my feelings under wraps falling away entirely the longer we hold each other.

There's no going back from this now.

I've felt a lot of different things over the years, but the intensity of what I feel standing here with Avery, it's like nothing I've ever felt before. When I was younger and just starting to notice girls, things always had this fresh new air about them, they were intense and often times explosive, but never right away. It always took some time to reach that point.

The opposite of the way things are happening with her.

Our short amount of time together putting everything in the fast lane and slamming it into me all at once. Making me hate the way it's going to feel when we're apart and things slow down and go back to normal.

Whatever normal is anymore.

"I don't want to lose this." I whisper against her ear. "I want to keep feeling the way I have for the last two days but I'm afraid to ask for more because it might not be something that you're willing to give and knowing that would change everything."

"Ask for what, Jax?"

I could easily tell her some stupid line about not wanting to lose touch, but I think we're both smarter than that. I wouldn't have admitted wanting to lose her at all if I wasn't prepared to give it all up. So, despite the lingering nervousness about how she'll respond or the fear of being shot down, I've gotta let her have it all.

All of me.

"When I leave you today, I want to do it knowing that it's not forever. That we'll see each other soon. I want to do it with the guarantee that no matter how long it takes to happen again, we won't lose each other."

Stepping back and tilting her chin up until her eyes are level with mine, I give her the rest.

"I want to find time every day to talk to you. Email, text or phone calls. I don't care as long as we do it. Shit, if I knew it wouldn't make you think I was weird, I'd break out a pen and paper and write you letters. I'm serious about this. About you. I don't want there to be a day when we're not together where you have the chance to forget about me. About us."

"Jackson…" she gasps softly.

"There's an endless list of things I want really, but most of all, I just want to leave this room today knowing that you're mine."

The confident smile she'd given when she admitted her reluctance to leave and what she was afraid would happen, along with how good those words were to hear gives me all the confidence I need to just put it all out there. Admit what I want without fear of it backfiring. Now all I need to know is if she feels the same.

"Avery, I need to know. Am I alone in this?"

Lowering her eyes down to the floor and back up again, she smiles and the second her face lights up, I know I've got my answer. This is not onesided.

"You're not. I want the same things you do, Jax."

Slipping her hand in between us and motioning to my pocket, she uses her free hand to do the same and holds out her phone for me to take.

"Pass me your phone."

"I already have your cell, so what do you want with it?"

Grinning, she taps her hand against my leg. "Give me your cell and find out."

Doing what she wants, I pull my phone out of my back pocket and hand it over. Watching as her head lowers and she gets to work entering god only knows what into it before smiling and handing it back.

"You've already got me cell, you were right about that, but I figured if what you just told me you wanted was the truth, I'd help you out and give you everything else too. I've stored my home and work numbers as well as my address...you know, for the letters you want to write."

Forgoing the use of my home address since these days, I'm not there very much, I give her a list of the numbers that matter and hand hers back. Slipping my own back into my pocket before giving her my full attention again.

"Before we walk out of here and I head down to meet Brady..." I pause, selfishly running a finger over her lips as I picture the way I want what happens next to go. "I need to know one more thing."

"Anything."

"Do you really want to do this? Or better yet, since I know it's not going to be easy...*can* you do this?"

Her answer comes before I've even finished the question.

"Yes, Jax. I wouldn't be here if I didn't. But more importantly, I want to do this."

Her absolute confidence in what she's agreeing to sends me over the edge. Her words like shockwaves to my heart. Everything I'd been wondering about before she'd shown up at my door to see me off was no longer an issue now. With just a few words and the feel of her in my arms, she's given me everything.

Bringing my lips to hers slowly, keeping it gentle, I brush against them and just like the last time we kissed, I welcome the spark and warmth that floods me. A feeling that if I had my way, I'd never have to lose.

"One more question, then I swear I'm gonna go." I whisper against her lips when we finally break apart.

"Yes?"

"You gotta promise me you're not going to laugh."

"I can't do that." She grins. "Especially if you're asking me to promise you. It means it's something worth laughing at and I refuse to make a promise and then break it."

"Okay, fine. You can laugh, but no matter how silly it sounds, just answer truthfully okay?"

"Always."

Running a nervous hand through my hair and willing myself to get over it and just ask, I let the words just fall and hope to god I don't live to regret them.

"Does this mean you're my girlfriend? No wait." I stop myself and try again. "Will you be my girlfriend?"

Bringing a hand up over her mouth, I see her cheeks rise before the softest laugh I've ever heard escapes through the cracks in her fingers and she taps my chest playfully.

"Yes, I'll be your girlfriend, Jackson. Even if you having to ask that question makes me feel like I'm back in junior high again."

The gleam in her eyes, the smile on her face and the soft way she agrees to be mine makes me feel things that I haven't felt since I asked out Greta Martin when I was ten years old. Right here in this moment, she's taken me back in time. Back to awkwardness and acne. Attitudes and what at the time felt like the worst kind of agony imaginable. Avery's right. I feel fourteen again and it's the most exhilarating feeling in the world.

Pressing my lips to hers again softly, I let her go and as she tries to be the stronger one by turning and making her way over to the door, she pauses and turns back before she can go all the way through. Her next words a line from one of the movies we watched together the day before. A line that now that she's spoken it, has made it officially ours.

"So, I guess this means I'll see you soon, then?"

Avery

Okay, you managed to say goodbye to Jax without completely breaking down. It's time to do it again. And this isn't goodbye forever, it's just for now.

This is the second pep talk I've given myself since I got here and Emery let me in. One that since I got here and Emery let me in. I should be a master at goodbyes after being the first to walk away back at the hotel, but standing outside my mom's room, I'm anything but.

Words seem to fail me, and even though we're not even standing face to face, I'm having to swallow down the emotion that any second is threatening to bubble over inside. A lump in my throat probably the size of this state and what feels like a waterfall of tears right on the edge threatening to fall the second I turn the knob and enter the room.

This is harder than I thought.

Having just got them back in my life, how the hell do I prepare to say goodbye again? Make them understand when I leave here today, what they've given me back—what my father stole from me—will be what carries me through until I can see them again?

Okay, Avery. You need to suck it up and get your butt in there before one or the both of them come out and you lose total control. I admonish myself, giving my body a good shake before bringing my still nervous hand to the knob and turn it.

Being met by the identical form of Emery as the door falls open, a smile stretching from ear to ear and a knowing look in her eye.

"I was wondering how long you were gonna stay out there." She whispers, bringing her arm around me and guiding my still numb form deeper into the room until it's not her smile greeting me but our moms.

"I really don't want to do this." I admit, bringing my hand to my head almost as soon as the words fall, hating the way they sound and immediately attempting to fix it. "I don't want to leave, let alone say goodbye."

"Then don't." Emery says to which our mother just laughs.

"I think what your sister is trying to say, since she knows you have to go back for work, is you don't need to say goodbye."

"Yeah." Emery agrees with a nod. "What she said."

This right here. The ease that comes from just being in the same room with these two is what's making this so damn hard.

I spent twenty-five years believing in a lie and now that we're all together again and things are the way they should have been, taking myself away from it, well, it just feels wrong.

Shakespeare was right.

Parting is such sweet sorrow and it's a sorrow that I know I'm going to be feeling for a very long time, no matter how close in contact we all keep.

"Since this isn't really a goodbye for me, I'm just going to let you have some time with Mom. But Avery, have a safe flight and text when you land so I don't have to make good on my threat of hunting your ass down."

Before the laugh even has a chance to escape, her arms are around me, pulling me into an embrace that with each second that passes, I fall deeper into. Committing everything about it to memory. The smell of her perfume, the darkness of her hair as it brushes against mine, and the rapid firing of her breathing that signals how close to breaking she is.

I want to remember it all.

Remember that she's real and the last few days haven't been a dream.

"I will, I promise."

"Good." She says with a smile once she's released me and with a quick mumbled goodbye, she exits the room.

Unable to move, much less turn away from the door, I remain completely still, not sure how much time has passed, but only breaking away when I hear rustling and my name being called.

"Come sit."

Willing my legs to move, I make my way over to the bed and just like she asked, I sit. My eyes trained on her as she leans forward ever so gingerly in the bed and reaches for one of my hands.

"I know this isn't easy for you. It's not easy for me either, but what your sister said is right. This isn't goodbye. We'll definitely see each other again. And when we can't, we'll talk as much or as little as we need to."

She's telling me everything I already know, but somehow, hearing it come from her instead of it just being my own wants and needs running wild, validates it. She's as invested in keeping this relationship alive as I am.

Slipping my free hand over the one she's now holding onto, I meet her eyes as I gently squeeze, hopefully letting her know without words that I feel the same. The emotional dam more than ready to burst keeping me from voicing the words.

The need to not break, at least not yet, taking everything I've got.

"Avery," she begins, the softness in her eyes carrying over into the sound of her voice as she speaks my name. "I have to be honest with you about something. When you got in touch and agreed to come here, I was positive you would be upset with us. With me."

"I don't understand. Why would you think that?"

Upset with my dad, sure. I *am* upset with him for putting us in this position. But her? Emery? Why would I be upset with either of them? They'd been victims of Richard Davis the same way I was.

"It took me twenty-five years to find you." She answers, like that statement is the answer to my question, when the reality is, it just adds to the confusion.

"I know, but why would I be mad or upset with you because of that?"

"I could have found you sooner. Had I just taken the steps earlier, we could have gotten together and done this much sooner than we did. I fear that in not doing it sooner, I've only caused more pain."

I'm still not following. I mean, I can kind of see her point, but I don't agree with it. She didn't cause me pain by taking so long. I'm happy, not sad, about this.

"I think if you'd never found me and I came across Emery or the truth later in some other way after you were gone, maybe I'd be upset with you. But that's not what happened. You did find me and we did get to meet, spend time together and get to know the people we've become. So all I feel when I look at you is happy. I'm not alone the way I thought I was. I do have family, and it's one that even with only knowing me a couple of days, seems to accept me. How could I ever be upset about that?"

"About ten years ago, I reached out to someone. A family friend that wanted to help locate you. At first, I agreed, but before she could do much work I stopped her."

Wait. What?

"You were about fifteen at the time and despite how badly I wanted to have you in my life, my need to do right by you won out. I didn't know what kind of life you were leading, but what I did know was how awkward things were for me at your age and I didn't want to put any more stress on your shoulders. Being a teenager is hard enough. Adding this to it, I couldn't do it. I couldn't be the one to cause you pain."

"Did you know I was in Toronto before the private investigator reached out?"

"No. As I said, I stopped it before my friend could get any information."

Well, there's that I guess. She didn't find me and intentionally stay away. She'd just made a choice at the time she thought was in my best interests.

"I'm sorry, Avery. I never should have stopped them from looking into it, just like when Richard left, I never should have let the investigation into your disappearance go, even knowing now that it wouldn't have made much difference with you being taken out of the country altogether. I made a mistake."

She did. She won't get any argument from me on that, but even knowing what I do now, I still can't be mad at her.

"I forgive you." I say, meaning every word. "You did what you did at the time because it's what you thought was best. I wish that it hadn't taken you getting sick in order for us to be together again, but I wouldn't change the way it all happened for anything in the world."

It's then the tears begin to fall, hers and mine. The both of us finally freeing ourselves from the struggle to keep our composure and giving into the true emotion of the moment.

Slipping my hand from hers, I move across the bed and as she leans back against the pillow, I do the one thing I've been dying to do from the moment I got here. Curling up next to her, being sure as I do to lay my head softly against her chest. Right over her heart. Doing the same as I did with Emery and committing the steady beat of it to memory, along with the soft sigh she lets escape the second my head comes to rest.

For years I wanted to have a moment like this and now I've got it. My body identifying hers as the one that gave me life and freeing me to let go of everything I'd kept bottled so tightly inside. Pain from the losses I've suffered, happiness over things I've achieved. Every instance in my life that I wanted to share with someone, good or bad, it all pours out through my eyes and down over my face.

"I never stopped loving you, Avery." She whispers against my head. "Not one second of one day for the entire time we were apart. If anything, I just seemed to love you more. Love you harder. So that even with the distance, you'd still be able to feel it. Something I'll continue to do, even when you're no longer here to hear or see it."

I know what this is, what it sounds like and I want to fight against it. This can't be her final goodbye. Not when I just got her back into my life. So pressing pause, I halt the moment and instead, tell her what I should have the very day I got here.

The truth.

"For as long as I can remember, all I ever wanted was a family. To really be a part of something. After dad died, I figured that was it for me. Then one day, as I'm sitting back and looking at my life and just how routine it's become, this letter lands on my desk and it changes everything. Going from that to hearing your voice and then landing here and meeting you, it was like all of that wishing when I was a kid finally paid off. I'd gotten what I wanted. You and Emery. You made my wish come true."

Pausing, lifting my head from its place above her heart and meeting her eyes head on, I say the only thing left to say. Words more powerful than any goodbye I would offer could ever be.

"I love you, Mom. Thank you for being my dream come true."

Chapter Twenty-Six

Jax

Having gotten the call about an hour into our four hour road trip into Morgantown, West Virginia, about the meeting scheduled to go down before the show, we booked it out of the parking lot and into the building just in time for it to begin. Throwing our body's down into the chairs in the rear of the room just as Smith's gravelly voice began barking matches from the front.

The guys, as per their usual, talking amongst themselves as their names were thrown out. Some even pondering just who was going to end up in the main event, since as Brady predicted on the ride down, Smith had flipped the script again and pulled Gavin out.

Another predictability being the grin on Brady's face when he realized that with Gavin out, it meant more match time for him.

The champion being pulled from the main event slot should be having the same effect on me, but it's not. Because while Brady sits beside me getting his hopes up, I'm doing the opposite. Not being born or bred into the business the way him and some of the others are, I've had to rely on watching it unfold in front of me. Picking up what I can along the way and basing what happens next in my own career around it. Dealing more in absolutes than in hope.

And while I did manage to put on one hell of a match in the main event with Gavin in Delaware three days prior, I know another main event spot or even a full push aren't guaranteed.

Believing in my ability and knowing what I'm capable off is one thing. Being given the ball and being told to run with it, maybe even earning the CPW title because of it is something else entirely. At the end of the day it goes down like this.

If Smith doesn't think you're ready, you're not ready.

Which is exactly what I'm expecting to hear again as my name is absent from the list of matches already called.

"Now on to what I know you're all here for." Smith barks out, causing both me and Brady to roll our eyes simultaneously. "Main event match is as follows. Jax Merrick and Brady Raines, one on one for a number one contenders spot. With Merrick to go over after interference from Ron."

Say what?

I can't have heard that right. Did he really just say I was going to go over in a number one contenders match for the title? And better yet, they were choosing me over Brady?

"What the hell is Ron interfering in my match for?" Brady calls out and pulling my head out of my own thoughts, I pay close attention to Smith's response, wanting to know almost as much as Brady what the hell is going on.

Ron may be our buddy in the locker room, but when we're in the ring, he's just as hungry as the rest of us. Having been around just as long as we have and desperate for his own shot at the title. One that both Brady and I agree probably won't ever come his way.

For all of his ability in the ring, he lacks the one thing that would take good to great.

His skills on the mic.

Without those, he's doomed to life on the mid-card. At least in Radley Smith's world anyway.

"You're working an angle together." Smith gives up before turning his attention to the men making their way over.

"Well, we're both in the main event. That's a step up, right? Means all the ass busting we've been doing is actually paying off."

I want to agree with Brady. Be excited for the opportunity I'm being given, but I can't. Not when I'm still having a hard time believing it's even real. Knowing Brady the way I do and just how intense he can get, and just how intent he's been on earning his spot in the title hunt, I just can't wrap my head around why I'm the one going over.

It also doesn't help that even knowing I'm getting a push the way I wanted, I can't seem to get excited because despite my belief to the contrary, nothings felt right since I walked out of the hotel in Delaware. The thrill of being on the road, the excitement of being in a match, all of it on a severe decline.

I'd put everything I had into the last two performances. Keeping my head in the game even when it was the last thing I wanted. I just wasn't in it and I assumed Brady felt the same way with the promise he made to Emery before we left.

Looks like I'm not the only one affected by a Davis.

Which brings me to my own promise. One that for the last couple of days has been relatively easy to keep, with me doing it whenever it was Brady's turn to drive or we'd stopped in for an overnight at a motel. Now though, with what is being handed to me, I know is only going to get harder.

A fact that did nothing for my already dwindling state of mind.

"You're thinking about her again, aren't you?" Brady asks, slugging me in the arm.

"That easy to tell, huh?"

Offering up a smirk in response, he slaps me on the back. "You've got it bad. It's written all over your face, and as much as I'd like to sit here and rip on you for being whipped, we need to get our head in the game. Otherwise, this shot we've got just might go poof."

He's right and there's no argument I can make to the contrary. We're being given the chance at the brass ring. One I've been chasing since I got here. Which means, no matter how adamant I am about not letting Avery down, I've got to spend the next few hours putting her out of my head.

"I know. I hear you loud and clear. You've got nothing to worry about. My head will be right where it needs to be."

"Good, because I don't want a repeat of the shit that went down the last time you let a girl get into your head."

Gee thanks, Brady. Like I needed the Melinda reminder.

Especially since the very man I was being slated to go against for the title is the very one she'd chosen to screw around on me with. The downward spiral I took after the shit hit the fan still so raw that I can actually feel it happening all over again instead of the months ago that it did.

I'm definitely not making the same mistake twice.

Doesn't mean that Brady and his own girl problems are off limits. Two can play his game.

"Speaking of girls, when's the last time you talked to Emery?"

"Three days ago." He offers up easily and catching my now widened eyes, he scowls. "Don't even start with me, alright? She knows what we do and where my head has to be. She knows we can't talk every day."

Something we don't agree on, but whatever.

"If you actually make the effort, you *can* talk to her every day. Especially since you're currently sitting on a top of the line cell phone. So just accept technology already and use it."

"Look, I made myself an official CPW twitter account. Isn't that a good enough attempt at accepting technology?"

"No, man. That's accepting social media, not technology."

"But you have to use a computer to do it, idiot. So your argument is invalid."

Knowing it's going to get me nowhere with the way he seems to enjoy living in the dark ages, I try coming at it from a different angle.

"If you want to share your shit with the world, Twitter is great. I'm not talking about that. I mean everything else. Texting. Email. All you ever do is call people and then send the occasional pissed off text when they don't answer, because half the time you can't get right up their face about it. It's time you realized that it's 2015 and started using the damn thing you paid out your ass for in the way it's meant to be."

"Whatever, Jax." He says, brushing me off. "I'll talk to Emery when I can, but until then, I'm gonna go out there tonight and work one hell of a match. So in the interest of business, can we just focus on that and leave the rest of this crap until later?"

As much fun as it would be making Brady see the light of day, he's got a point. We've got a match coming up and if we want to make it count, it means we've gotta buckle down and plan as many spots as we can so it's the best damn match on the card.

"You win, Raines. Let's go plan one of the best matches CPW has ever seen."

Avery

"If you want to make your article stand out more, see this paragraph second to the bottom? Cut some of it. It's up to us to report the facts with a human touch, not bore them to death."

Throwing my glasses down with a sigh when Adam, one of the reporters under my command nods his acceptance of what I've said and makes his way from the room, I attempt to take a breath before diving straight back into the thick of it.

It's been seemingly nonstop since I got back into town a few days ago and judging by the way things have been today already, was showing no signs of slowing down in the near future. All part and parcel of the promotion I'd been given when I showed up for work the day after I got home.

What I wouldn't give to be curled up on the sofa at home with a big bag of popcorn and a movie right now. The new routine quickly becoming the best damn part of my day.

Giving myself a short mental break from the next round of articles I had to go over, I pull out my phone, eager to get into the messages in order to retrieve the last one from Jax. Needing the closeness that his words bring, but before I can even pull up the messaging screen, a knock interrupts me. My assistant Karen entering the room shortly after.

"Call on line one. Says she's your sister."

"And you had to come all the way in here to tell me that why?"

Blushing, she motions back to the door. "You had a delivery and I figured since I didn't feel right being the one to move it, I'd kill two birds with one stone."

Well, if I wasn't intrigued when she blushed, I am now. What could have possibly been delivered that she would have issues moving, and better yet, why is she still blushing?

"Okay, well, I'll take the call and be right out to grab it. Unless of course you wanna give up what it is now and save me the trouble?"

"I think I'll let you see what it is for yourself." She grins before turning and heading back out, the way she's reacting making me wanna keep Emery waiting just a little longer so I can get to the bottom of my assistants strange behavior.

Since the only thing that ever gets delivered me to is usually more work, I can't imagine what it is, but instead of standing and following her out, and knowing how Emery will feel if I keep her waiting, I stick to my original plan.

"Avery Davis."

"All business, I see. Well, two can play that game, Miss Davis."

Laughing at Emery's weak attempt at changing her tone, but still preoccupied with what is waiting for me on Karen's desk, I attempt to move the conversation along.

"I'm sorry, Emery. Let me try again. I'm so happy to hear from you. Now, what do you want?"

When her laughter filters over the line, my heart warms. Thankful that just like we'd promised before I came back to the city, we'd kept in touch. Getting the chance to hear her laugh every day made the distance between us easier to take, especially since at least once a day since I came back, I've wanted to pick up and leave again.

"You haven't heard from Jackson lately, have you?"

"Not since last night, no. Why do you ask?"

Exhaling deeply, the same part of my heart that seconds before had been flying high because of her laugh, crashes back down to earth.

"I haven't heard from Brady in three days and while I know I'm probably freaking out over nothing, it's bugging the hell out of me."

Filling me in on the way they'd spent their remaining time together before he left, I knew how invested Emery is. Even more, I understand it because even though our time hadn't gotten quite that heated, I've become pretty invested with Jax too.

"You know what they do for a living, Em. You know it better than I do. Maybe he's just under a lot of pressure and hasn't had time to call or text."

It sounds weak even to my own ears, and I feel sick just saying it, but I don't know what else I can say that can help right now.

"Jax had time to call you last night, right?"

"Yeah, he did." I painfully admit. "But just because he was able to spare a few minutes to call doesn't mean Brady has the ability to do the same thing."

It had actually been about an hour we spent talking, but Emery doesn't need to know that. She's feeling bad enough as it is. I'm not about to make it worse.

"I know you're right. I just thought if he was serious about wanting to stay in touch, I would have heard something by now. I'm actually worried."

"Well if you're worried, why don't you call him? Who says you have to sit around waiting for him to pull his head out of his ass? You're better than that, Em."

"You're right again. As usual. Look, I'm sorry for calling you at work, but this was really bothering me and I didn't have anyone else I could talk to about it."

As happy as I am that I'm the first person she calls when she's got something on her mind, there's no missing the underlying meaning. Another situation she explained before I came home. Her relationship with Mike. Or rather, lack of one.

"Em, you know I love you and even though I'm working a lot, I'll always do my best to answer your calls. You're not alone. Not anymore. When it comes to Brady though, I think you might need to cut your losses. From everything you've told me, he's going through something pretty major with his divorce. Maybe take a step back and let him deal with that."

It's the opposite of what I just told her, but the more I sit here and think about everything I know about him, there's no denying he's complicated. A lot more than I thought when I spent time with him and Jackson at the bar the first night. With everything Emery has on her plate already, another complication isn't needed.

"Yeah, maybe. Thanks, Ave. I'll figure out what I'm gonna do and call you later."

Saying my goodbyes and finishing the call, making sure before I hang up that Emery is more than a little aware of just how much I love and miss her, I place the phone back down and head for the door.

Time to find out what's making my assistant act so strange.

"Where's the delivery?" I ask when I reach her desk.

"Right there, Miss Davis." She says, pointing to the right side. "I didn't have the heart to move it."

Standing on the desk is a bouquet of roses, in a variety of different colors and sizes. Running my fingers softly over the petals and enjoying the softness, I look over and spot a white card sticking out of the center.

Sliding my hand in and pulling it out, I slide it out and turn to Karen.

"You're sure these are meant for me?"

"Absolutely. The delivery man was adamant about it. Wouldn't leave until I assured him that you'd get them."

Nodding, but unable to pull my attention away from the card, and more importantly the words on it, I read it over twice more before finally looking back up at Karen and smiling.

Jackson's words not only etching themselves into my mind, but my heart as well.

He remembered.

So, I'll see you soon then?

Chapter Twenty-Seven

Brady

"Do you really think stopping the match before we gain momentum is the way to go?" I ask, sitting down on the edge of the mat, more than a little ready for the ten minute break Jax called for after running over our spots for the third time.

"You're being primed to be in a long standing feud with Ron, right? So we use that and his interference to our advantage. Once upon a time, we were a pretty strong tag team and you two are primed to be bitter rivals. It works for everyone involved. You get to keep on being the heel everyone despises and I build even more of a following going into my match with Gavin."

I have to admit, what he's saying does make a hell of a lot of sense. If one of us got serious momentum leading into the interference from Ron, it could blow the match to shit, but this way, we all come out smelling like roses.

"You're right as always. I don't even know why I bother questioning you." I admit honestly.

I've worked with a lot of guys over the years since I got here, but none of them saw as far ahead in terms of storylines the way Jax did. His ability to predict what would work would be pretty scary if I didn't know him the way I do.

Jackson Merrick really does breathe every damn aspect of this business.

"Glad you finally realized your mistake." He smirks, earning him the punch I land a second later. "You ready to go over it again?"

"Yeah, let's do it." I say, jumping back to my feet. Turning toward the middle of the ring and setting up for the initial lockup, I pause when I hear the familiar ringtone going off from it's spot in the corner of the ring.

"Is that you or me?" Jackson calls over as I head over to grab it.

"That would be me. You left your phone in your bag, remember?"

"Ahh, right. Well, grab it. I think we've got shit down, but we can always run over it again later."

Nodding as he jumps down off the ring apron, I turn my attention to the corner and where Bon Jovi continues to blast itself through my bag. Crouching down to grab it, I hit talk the second it's in my hands.

"Hello?"

"Brady?"

"Yeah. Who's this?"

"Oh, um—hey. It's Emery."

Happier than I expect that it's her on the other end of the call and not my old man, I smile and it only gets bigger when I register the stammer in her voice.

Her nervousness makes me happy. Shit. Maybe Jax isn't the only one that's whipped.

"Hey, darlin. How are ya?"

"I'm good. I'm actually about to head into work, but I hadn't heard from you in a few days and figured I'd check in before I go. I hope that's alright."

I'm pretty sure with the way my face reacted when I heard her voice that the smile I was sporting couldn't get any bigger, but man was I wrong. Having her call in check in on me, wanting to be sure I was alright, is new. Even when things were good between Kel and me, she hadn't done it. Having Emery do it is a nice change.

It makes me feel like someone out there actually gives a damn.

"It's more than okay. I've been meaning to call you, but with all the driving we've been doing and the shows and matches they're putting me in, it's been next to impossible."

I knew the second the words are out that I'd done it. Lied to her. Well, at least partially.

It was like Jax said earlier. If I wanted to talk to her badly enough, there was more than one way to do it. I just hadn't wanted to because despite the promise I made before I left

Delaware, I didn't want to drag her any further into the mess that was my marriage.

An idea that despite the best intentions being behind it, had been blown apart the second I drove my dick inside her in the water. The both of us in that moment, even being guided by need the way we were, were also being driven by something more.

Emery deserved better than some separated guy that a few days before meeting her had still been holding out hope that things would work themselves out so he didn't have to admit he was a failure. Hell, the day I met her I did that.

She deserved a guy that didn't come with baggage.

"Are you sure that's all it is, Brady? Because if there's more or you're having second thoughts about what you said before you left, you can tell me."

Even over the phone she's able to see straight through me. Shit. What the hell am I supposed to do now?

Well, genius. For starters you can stop being a total jerk and just tell her the truth.

"Emery," I start, hating the fact that again, the damn voice in my head is smarter than I am. "Before I left, we talked, and I thought that we had an understanding."

Son of a bitch! That's not what I wanted to say! Why can't my brain have a delete button?

"An understanding?" she repeats back and I'm tempted to hang up and call her back in order to have a do over of this entire conversation. This is not the way I wanted it to go, but now that it has, I don't exactly see a way out of it.

I can't exactly stop and say 'whoops, my brain just stopped working'.

"You know about my situation with Kelly, and you said you weren't looking to get too deeply involved anyway, remember? That *is* what we said, right?"

Keep going, smart guy. Since you're already on a roll, go ahead and tell the girl you have to let her go and when you're done, give yourself a huge pat on the back for being the dumbass that threw away the best thing that ever happened to him.

"You're right, we did say that." She agrees, but there's no missing the dejected sound now accompanying her words.

God damnit. Why can't I be better at this?

"What we said is still true and it really has nothing to do with why I called. I wanted to check in to make sure you were okay. It's how I am. I always worry about other people, whether they feel the same way about me or not."

Her words do exactly what I'm sure she intended them to. Effectively making me feel even worse than I did when I put my own damn foot in my mouth. A pain hitting me in the chest, from what I can only assume is my heart, since the thought of her thinking I don't feel the same way as she does physically makes me hurt.

I fucked this up so bad. I need to do some serious damage control.

"Emery, what I said the other day, I meant it. It was real. Please have faith in that alright? At least until I can stand in front of you and prove it. I just need some time."

"I get it, Brady. I'm sorry for bothering you. Have a good match tonight."

Before I can tell her she didn't bother me and I'm sorry for being the one to screw the entire call up, the sound of the dial tone is ringing in my ears.

She hung up. And the worst part?

I deserved it.

When did things become so damn complicated?

I mean, wasn't it just last week that I'd been practically begging Kelly to answer my calls? And now here I am, my heart and head tangled up in a woman that wasn't the one I was married to, but someone else entirely.

A woman that did more to make me feel wanted and appreciated in the two full days we spent together than my wife did in the last three years.

If I hadn't already realized my marriage was over, the way I feel right now would definitely do it. My thoughts consumed with Emery's wounded voice over the phone and the realization that I was the one to cause it.

Something I just can't live with. Not when I know I'm better than that.

I need to fix this and I need to do it soon.

Making my way to the back and slamming my way into the locker room, feeling all eight pairs of eyes settling on me all at once, its then I realize my next move.

Jax was right all along.

If I want things to work, I've got to make the effort. I need to go back to Delaware and when I get there, man the fuck up and end this shit once and for all.

I need to make Emery mine.

Chapter Twenty-Eight

Avery

So, I'll see you soon then?

The entire drive home, with the flowers resting delicately in the box beside me, the words on the card float around in my head. My parting line to him at the hotel in Delaware, what I was sure he would have forgotten, there in simple black and white.

Proving me wrong and in the same breath making me wish for something more.

Is it possible that was the point? Does he literally mean that he'll see me soon and the flowers were just his way of preparing me? Or is it just him proving that what we'd said to each other was important and I wasn't forgotten?

By the time I pull my car into the garage, my mind is in overdrive trying to decode what I'm sure has to be some hidden message in his words. Needing to understand it because even though I knew it was going to be hard, I hadn't been prepared at all for just how deeply I would feel the loss of him.

Caring far more than I ever expected for the short amount of time we actually spent together. Living for the last three days on memories of us curled up in his bed with movies, or sitting comfortably in the sand overlooking the water as we got to know one another. The warmth from those memories doing what I needed them to and helping me hang on and believe in something that for anyone else going through it, might seem completely hopeless.

What a few short weeks ago, I would have considered hopeless.

In a million years, I never would have thought that a trip to meet my mother and sister would have resulted in so much more, and more than that, so much more with a wrestler.

Guys that even though I don't cover it for the magazine, I've heard more than enough stories about to make me want to swear off anyone in the profession forever.

Parking the car and stepping out, I head around to the front of the house, stopping at the mailbox and grabbing the mail before making my way in. Tossing it on the table and making my way into the living room, I throw myself down onto the sofa with a contented sigh.

After allowing myself a few minutes of comfort, I sit up and start sorting through the mess. Separating the bills from the ads on autopilot, stopping only when my hands brush against an envelope with no return address.

Curiosity piqued, I turn it over and finding the back as blank as the left hand corner on the front, I rip the envelope open and slip what I can now see is a small folded notebook page out. It's crispness making a slight crinkling noise in my hand as I finally pull it free.

Unfolding it, I see the messy scrawl of my name at the top and without reading another line, feel my heart swell.

Jackson Merrick strikes again.

Avery,

Even though I'm sending this days before you'll actually get them, I hope you enjoy the flowers. It was the only thing I could come up with on short notice that would bring a smile to your face as you start your first week back at work.

I wish I could be there with you, continuing what we started in Delaware a few days ago (what feels like forever ago), but since I can't, I hope this letter and the flowers make up for my absence.

There's so much I want to share with you, yet there never seems to be enough time to do it when we're on the phone, so these letters are going to be my chance.

I want to use these letters to share every aspect of my daily life while we're apart and I'm missing you. But more than that, I want to make this letter a promise.

My promise to never give you a reason to doubt or question what I'm doing when we're apart or who I'm doing it with. Because the truth is, Avery Davis, even being all the way in Toronto, you're still the only thing I see.

And it's my hope that in making you that promise, you'll be able to make me one too.

I want you to promise to write me. Really write me, and tell me everything there is to know about you. I want the random stories and the silly laugh I know you'll do as you're telling them. Or the soft sigh when you blush the way I'm sure you are now. I want your feelings whether they're good, bad, or indifferent.

Basically, Avery, I want it all.

All of you.

The same way that each and every time I write you, I'll give you all of me.

I suppose if I want this letter to actually make it to you at the same time as the flowers will, I should probably stop writing now, but please enjoy them and know that for every minute of every day that we're apart, I'm continuously asking you...

"I'll see you soon, then?"

Yours Forever,
Jax

Leaning back on the sofa and bringing my legs up before shifting my body and lying down on my back, I place the letter to my chest. The sweetness of his words, how easily he admits that he's mine only making me want to get them as physically close to my heart as I can.

The need to be near him even stronger than it had been after the flowers.

Closing my eyes and focusing on the sound of my breathing, I let my thoughts linger on the promise he wants me to make. Writing him and telling him everything, giving him a bird's eye view into the life I'm living, while he's off doing the same. An easy one to make.

Turning over on the sofa and taking in the time on the clock above the television, remembering the start time he gave me the night before, I reach across the table and grab my phone.

If letters are what Jax wants, then I'm going to call him and tell him I accept. Letters are what he's going to get.

Finding his number, I dial and wait with baited breath as the call connects and the rings begin. After the fifth one, I finally release the nervous breath I've been holding and accept that I'm not going to get him. Resigning myself to having to wait for the sound of his voice.

Pulling the phone back from my ear, I linger over the end call button and that's when I hear it. Lower than expected, but undeniably Jackson.

"Hello?"

Now with him actually answering, I'm speechless.

Great. So much for knowing exactly what to say when he answered.

"Damn." He curses. "I missed her."

"Jackson, wait! I'm here."

"Avery? Hang on a sec. I can barely hear you in here."

After a few seconds of male voices invading the call and loud noises following as he obviously maneuvers his way out of wherever he is, he speaks again.

"There. Sorry. I was in the locker room and didn't want to talk with a bunch of the guys around."

"Thank you." I softly say after a few beats of silence, hoping he understands what I mean and of course, he doesn't disappoint.

"You got them?"

"Yes, Jax. Right when I needed them most."

"I'm glad."

"I'm confused by something, though."

"Oh yeah?"

"We've talked every day since we left Delaware and you've been extremely tired and worn out every time. How did you manage to find the time to put this together?"

Holding myself together when he laughs, the sound of his happiness making me want to melt, I wait him out and after about a minute he explains.

"Just because I've been exhausted, doesn't mean I can't dial a phone. Considering all of the long distance minutes I've been racking up the last few days, you of all people know that. Besides, I wanted to do something nice for you. Nothing was keeping me from that, not even my own body. Did you get the note too?"

"I did. I just finished reading it."

"So will you do what I asked? Will you write? Let me know everything there is to know about you?"

"Yes. I just can't figure out why what I do here day to day matters."

"That's easy. It matters because *you* matter, Avery. You matter to me." He states and before I have a chance to react, much less respond, the sound of his voice carries over the line again. "If you do write me letters by hand, though, address them to the address in your phone that I left you for CPW. It will go directly to Smith's wife, but I've already talked to her about it. It might take a bit, but I'll get them, I promise."

Pulling the phone away from my ear, I quickly go into my contacts and sure enough, listed under C is the address for CPW along with the main booking phone number.

He really did think of everything.

"I can do that."

"Good. I want all the Avery I can get."

Laughing softly, he sighs, the same contented one that I'd done not fifteen minutes before when I stepped into the house, happy to be home and off my feet.

"I know I've said this already, Jax, but thank you. What you did means the world to me."

"You're welcome." He replies and just as I make out the sound of his name being called from somewhere off in the distance, he's back on the line again. This time, his voice even softer than before. Tender even.

"So, I'll see you soon then?"

Seeing the endearment for what it is, what is quickly becoming one of my favorite things he says, I say goodbye the only way I can.

"Yes, Jax. You'll see me soon then."

Chapter Twenty-Nine

Emery

So you want space, Brady? Consider it done.

I'd practiced saying those nine words at least a hundred times since our disastrous call yesterday, and even though I was starting to believe in the words, I knew beyond a shadow of a doubt that if Brady were to show up here begging for my forgiveness, I'd forget and pick up right where we left off before he left town.

That's how strong of a hold I let him have over me.

I've tried my best to go on like it doesn't bother me. Diving back into the things I know I can count on, like going to work every day and then coming home to take care of my mom. Problem with that is, every damn word we've said to each other is still there on the fringe of my mind, refusing to let me forget.

The last words he'd said sticking out the most.

"Don't forget what we shared yesterday, Em! I know I never will!"

Why even bother telling me not to forget if a few days later that's exactly what you plan on doing? Why ask me to believe in him, trust that he meant what he said and then in the next breath, break that trust?

Having only watched these guys from the sidelines, I'm the first to admit I have no idea the kind of people they are when the curtain closes at the end of a match.

Is going back on your word a normal thing or was this just a Brady thing?

More importantly, was I really nothing more than a glorified ring rat to him? A means to an end used to make him forget about his impending divorce?

Even in a smaller place like this, there are horror stories about girls heading to shows and letting themselves be used, only to have their hopes and dreams shattered hours later when they left without so much as a fuck you later.

Is that what happened here?

"Uh-oh. I know that look."

Crap. All of this Brady shit made me forget where I was, but even worse, who I was there with.

"You wanna tell me what's got you scowling so hard it's destined to leave a permanent mark?"

"It's nothing."

"Looks like a whole lot more than nothing to me. So why don't you stop trying to lie to your mother and tell her what's on your mind?"

Do I dare?

The last time I sat here like this, a bundle of heartbroken nerves the night I lost Mike, she'd been great in doling out the advice and not judging. Can I expect the same to happen again? Better yet, can I handle it if when I did unload she did judge me?

"Does it have something to do with the young man you spent those couple of days last week with? Brady something?"

Damn her for being so intuitive. She'd seen right through it. Now I've got no other choice but spill my guts. Lying to my mom, especially now, well, it's not an option.

"It has to do with him, yes, but more with me."

"What do you mean by that?"

With my earlier thought about how well she can read me, I can't resist the pull to pick on her about it. "You mean you don't already know?"

"Contrary to popular belief, miss smart ass, I can't read your mind. Just your facial expressions. So stop stalling and tell me what's going on."

"He's married, Mom."

"Say what?" she chokes out through a cough, her hand immediately flying to her chest as she rubs it. I don't have the heart to tell her that you can't rub surprise away.

You're stuck with that bitch.

"It's not what you're thinking. He's been separated for six months or so. She filed for divorce."

"Right. So he's unhappily married and just waiting for everything to be final." She muses before locking her eyes on me and asking what she really wants to know. "Did something change? Is that why you're scowling?"

"No. I mean, I don't think it has."

"So then what has you so glum?"

Instead of letting the entire conversation with him pour out the way it wants to, I decide to ask her questions instead.

"When you and Richard were first starting out, after you first met and you acted on the attraction between you, did he ever tell you one thing and then in the blink of an eye do something else entirely?"

"Only every other day." She laughs softly, again coughing before weakly clearing her throat and leaning back in the bed. "Is that what Brady has done?"

"Yeah, kind of."

"That's all you're going to give me? Come on, Emery. I want all the juicy details."

The way she closes her eyes and sinks even deeper back into the bed proves to me that she's pushing herself, not content to give up on the conversation and take care of herself the way she should be. It's making me want to curb this conversation for another time. Give her the chance to rest. But when she opens her eyes again, leveling her stern motherly eyes at me in defiance, I keep going.

"Before he left to head back out on the road, he told me not to forget about what we shared, but when I called him yesterday, he pretty much blew me off. Made me feel like calling was bothering him."

"Did he specifically say you were bothering him?"

"No, not in so many words. I could just tell."

"Emery," she sighs softly. "You, my sweet girl, are a lot of things, but a mind reader is not one of them. My ability to see through you came with age and with how blinded you can be to what is sitting right under your nose, I do believe it skipped a generation. What you think you can tell, and what is actually happening are most likely two different things."

I want to argue the point but as evidenced with the shredded mess that is my friendship with Mike, I've become a master at keeping my head in the sand or ignoring what's clearly going on altogether. I'd also mastered the art of the misunderstanding.

Though with Brady, I wasn't entirely sure that it was me misunderstanding. Especially with how quickly he was to throw our conversation the day he left back in my face. Using my own words against me.

In this case, I believe I'm right.

"What did he say exactly?"

"He thought we had an understanding. That because I told him I wasn't looking for anything super serious that we were just playing things by ear. But it's what he didn't say that I heard clearly."

"And that was?"

"That me calling, even if it started innocently at first, was me taking things too seriously."

"But he didn't say that."

"No. Just spouted some crap about him meaning what he said before and how he needed me to have faith in him. I hung up before he could spout anymore bullshit."

"Oh, baby girl." She shakes her head slowly, lowering her eyes to the blanket in front of her. "How can you not see what's clearly staring you in the face?"

"I don't follow."

"I know it's been a long time since I've been your age, and even longer since I've been involved with anyone, so my knowledge might be a little outdated, but I do believe in this case that it's not. That young man asking you to have faith in him, was him laying himself and quite possibly his heart on the line for you."

No. Way. I call bullshit.

"I know you don't want to believe it, Emery, but mark my words. Despite the complicated situation he's found himself in, and the very real fact that he's still legally married to another woman, there is no mistaking his feelings. Even if he's not entirely aware he has them."

"What feelings do you think he has?"

"Well, Emery, I would have thought that was obvious. The boy is falling in love with you. He just doesn't realize it yet."

Unbelievable.

"You're wrong."

"If that's what you need to tell yourself. Fine. I'm wrong. But I'm telling you that whatever took place between the two of you has altered him just as much as it has you. He doesn't want to bring you into his complication. Keeping you out means keeping you safe. You know who does things like that?"

"No, but I'm sure you going to tell me."

"People, more specifically in this case, men in love. Whether you want to admit it to yourself or not, deep down in that beautiful heart of yours, you know I'm right."

Damn her. She's doing it again. Making perfect sense.

"Brady Raines is in love with you."

Brady

Tuesday.

To some, a random day of the week that doesn't really mean much because there's still another three days until the weekend. For me, it's the one day off I've got this week and all I've got to show for it is my mind spinning out of control as I attempt to put a plan in motion.

Leaving this early is a must. It's likely that a good portion of the rest of the world was still lost in slumber which means the road to the airport and the flight I booked, along with the wait once I ds reach the airport is sure to be shorter.

The first stop of two I have planned.

Tossing my duffel into the backseat, I turn at the sound of footsteps and come face to face with a dude that I know has to be wanting to kill me ten times over right now.

After filling Jackson in the night before about the plan for today and having him be surprisingly down with it, even wanting to help, I'd laid out my idea of being on the road two hours before the sun came out and watched as the guy struggled with his quick agreement.

If there is one thing Jax enjoys more than wrestling, it's his beauty sleep. Something that with us leaving this damn early, I was seriously cutting into.

With a grunt and shove into my shoulder when I smirk, he tosses his own bag into the backseat and makes an immediate beeline for the passenger side door.

"Hey, Merrick!" I call out before he can lower himself in.

"What?" he growls and its seeing the look in his eyes, the absolute murderous glare that I realize why people say that looks can kill.

They've come across Jackson Merrick on no sleep.

"You ready to go off grid for a while?"

"I get the reason for all the cloak and dagger shit. I even get leaving at the ass crack of dawn, I do. But for the love of Pete, do you really need to talk like a soldier on a mission?"

"I was not." I argue and despite his attitude there's no missing the half smirk that breaks out on his face.

"Yes, Brady, you were. Now instead of arguing with me and then going back to talking like this is some top secret mission to save the world or something, can we just shut the fuck up and get on with it?"

Even knowing how pissed he was to be up this early, his need to get out of here speaks to just how into this plan he is, and it's got nothing to do with helping me out.

This is all about her.

Avery.

The same way my plan involves ending up back in the Podunk town in Delaware and making the girl I'd acted like an ass on the phone with talk to me, among other delicious scenarios I'd worked up in my head once I got her to forgive me, Jax's involves Avery.

But hopefully without the same naughty thoughts I've had. I can imagine the guy in a lot of different ways, but that way is a definite no go.

We're not that damn close.

"You got it. Let's blow this shit hole."

The roads relatively clear, the drive to the airport is thankfully a quick one. Shoving Jax awake once I've pulled in and baring witness to the litany of curses he lets slip, I get out of the car, unloading our bags and handing his over.

Dealing with the tickets and checking our bags, we head toward our terminal. Ready to get off my feet, I spot a seat as far back from the prying eyes of the other fliers around us, but before I can take it, Jax stops me.

"How is it that you chose the one damn airport that doesn't have a Starbucks?"

Another thing my road partner can't live without.

Fucking coffee.

"I'm sorry, your highness. I can't believe I didn't factor in your caffeine addiction before making a plan for you to see your girl."

Mumbling something under his breath, he throws his body down into the seat. Yanking out a ball cap and forcing it on his head, making sure to bring it down over his face the way we've done a million times before.

The only protection we've got from those fans that follow us a little too closely.

Listening to him grumble for a few more minutes, I've finally had enough. I know I've disturbed the man's beauty sleep and he's doing this sans caffeine, but does he really need to be so damn cranky?

It's not like all of this is for nothing.

We're planning a way for him to see his girl for Christ sakes.

"Enough, Jax. Who the fuck pissed in your cereal?"

"That would be you with this bright idea to go see Marie this god damned early. But if you're talking about something more recent, no Starbucks means no scones. I really wanted a scone."

"It doesn't take much to piss you off does it?"

"Don't stand between a man and his scones. It's the one damn pleasure I'm allowed. Kind of like you and that imported fucking piss you drink."

The smirk he's sporting makes his play obvious, but it's too bad I'm not falling for it.

He's not wrong.

"So last night you said the talk with Emery didn't exactly go the way you wanted it to, but how damn bad was it if it's making you hop on a plane to see Marie and beg for extra time off?"

Marie Smith is more of a hard-ass than her husband.

At least with Smith, you understood it. He's a surly old son of a bitch, but one that earned it. At one point, a student of the very same game we're now playing. After another promoter took pity on him, he'd built himself up until he was the king of the independent scene. Owning and holding every title you could have until an injury sent him to the sidelines indefinitely.

Something that after he married Marie and she whipped his ass into shape, he didn't take lying down. Now running CPW alongside her and giving all of us miscreants a place to be what we've always been meant to be, but without the bullshit that comes with the national scene.

"Like I told you. She called. She was worried about me. I guess not hearing from me made her scared. Especially since before I left, I swore that I'd make an effort to keep in touch. Shit. None of this is news, man."

"Then tell me what is."

"Her calling me out of the blue like that, giving a shit the way she did. It meant something, Jax. But since I'm no good at this shit, I mistook her concern for something else."

"What did you do?"

Great. I tell the guy that I took something the wrong way and he automatically assumes I fucked up. I mean, I did, but still. What the hell?

"What makes you think I did anything?"

"We're going to see Marie at the ass crack of dawn. You totally did something."

He's got me there.

"I told her I needed to take a step back. Deal with my shit. The same thing we talked about before I left. I just threw it in her face without thinking."

"That doesn't sound so bad. I mean, it's the truth isn't it? You are stuck in a pretty messed up situation."

"Normally, I'd say yeah because no one knows how messed up all this shit with Kelly is better than I do, but I also made of point of calling out to her, remember? I told her not to forget what we shared and what do I do? I balk and say I don't wanna get too involved. Confusing the hell out of not only her, but me too. That bonehead move, it hurt her. I can't live with that."

"So this is your way of making it right? Hoping on a plane, pissing away the angle with Ron and possibly any future push?"

"Yeah, that's about it." I laugh, the knowledge that I'm not only one pissing my shit away funnier than it should be. "But I'm not pissing it away alone, am I?"

"No, brother, you're not. You're taking me down with you." Jax laughs, elbowing me when I scowl.

"Guess it's my turn to put you in the hot seat. Why are you doing this? Did you screw up with Avery too?"

"Nah, I didn't screw up. In fact, after my surprise yesterday, I think I may have racked up some of those bonus Avery points she joked about the first night."

"Then why are you here?"

"Because when your road partner and friend damn near takes off the locker room door after a conversation with a girl, you don't let him fix it alone."

Figuring I was at least part of the reason he agreed so easily but assuming the majority had to do with his need to see Avery, I'm surprised to hear him say otherwise. Also kind of impressed. We haven't always been friends, but there's no doubt about it, at least not for me. Jackson Merrick is becoming one of the best damn decisions I ever made.

Looks like it's possible for me to get something right after all.

"You sure about this? If you're really doing this more for me than yourself, you still have time to head back. I got this. No sense bringing you down with me."

"I'm sure. I have to do this and not because friends don't let other friends do boneheaded shit alone, but because despite it only being four days, I miss the fucking hell out of my girl and will take any opportunity I'm given to see her."

It's official. Jax is a goner.

"More to life than wrestling." I repeat my old speech back and he laughs.

"Exactly. Looks like when you stop screwing with people and really want to do right by them, your advice isn't half bad."

"Well in that case, it looks like there's nothing left to say." I admit at the exact moment the attendant's voice comes over the PA announcing the boarding call for our flight.

There's no going back now.

Delaware and Toronto here we come.

Chapter Thirty

Avery

"I've been meaning to ask. How are you finding the new position? I know it's not that different, but how are you handling the extra responsibilities?"

I'd been summoned to the office in the early morning hours for a meeting to go over the plans for the online edition of this week's release. After going over everything that was ready, and what still needed to be put together, it hadn't taken long for Markus to change the subject.

What I'm sure is the real reason he wanted a sit down this early.

"I'm getting there. It's been a bit of an adjustment, but after the first couple of days, I seem to have found my groove. Another few days and I'll be right as rain."

The truth of it is, it probably wouldn't even take that long. I've already been at it for almost a week and really had found the groove I told Markus. Sure, there was a bit more to all of this than just editing other people's work, but the extra responsibilities only meant less time to focus on what I'm missing.

Mainly Emery, my mom, and Jax.

"Good. Glad to hear it." He smiles, leaning over the table and tapping his pen against it before speaking again. "But there's something else I wanted to talk to you about."

Well this is news.

"Okay, let's have it. What's up?"

Twirling the pen around a few times before dropping it, lifting his head and meeting my eyes, he leans even farther forward and brings his hands together on the top of the desk.

"You know I'm not one to get caught up in office gossip, even when it has to do with business, but there's been a lot of it swirling around about you the last few days and in the interest of nipping it in the butt, I figure we should talk about it."

Of course there's talk swirling. Karen hadn't exactly been quiet since the flower delivery and word like that travels fast around here. By the time it made its way back to me it wasn't even about the flowers themselves anymore.

All people wanted to know was who they were from.

So many names being thrown around that I knew it was only a matter of time before it made its way back to Markus. Especially since he was one of the first names floated.

"You know how I feel about office gossip, Markus. I don't know what you've heard, but I'm pretty sure it's all nonsense."

Nodding, he picks up the pen and starts in with the incessant flicking again.

"Word around the water cooler is you received quite the delivery a couple of days ago."

I knew it. It's only a matter of time before he brings up his name being a part of it.

Unable to curb my embarrassment over this even being a thing, my cheeks begin to flush. Something that when he looks up from the table, Markus catches.

"Some are saying I was the one that sent the arrangement."

"I'm sorry about that. Karen accepted the delivery and hasn't exactly been quiet about it."

"I assumed as much, and for the record, you have nothing to be sorry for. Whether it's a paper or a magazine, we're reporters by nature, so it's only natural that the goings on of one of the top employees gets treated like news."

"Would you like me to have a talk with Karen?"

"That's not needed. I've already spoken with her about it."

Well, color me surprised. With my new position, I figured that the honors of that would have fallen to me. Apparently not.

"I just wanted to know how much truth there was to the rumors of an admirer."

Laughing awkwardly, not sure how I feel about the line of questioning but not wanting to be rude, I give him what I hope is enough to put this entire mess to bed.

"Not an admirer, per say."

"Then what would you call it?"

"Someone very important to me that isn't afraid to show the world how much I mean to him?"

"Does this important person have a name?"

Now I know we've crossed the line from work relationship to more personal and I waste no time calling him on it.

"Now, now, Markus. This sounds a lot like an inquisition. You wouldn't be doing that to one of your best employees would you?"

"You caught me." He laughs, holding his hands up in surrender. "But can you really blame me? This gossip about you is about the only exciting thing going on around here lately. So does this mystery paramour have a name or not?"

"Of course he does."

"Care to share?"

If it gets you to stop asking me questions.

"Jackson Merrick."

It happens so quickly, it takes me a minute to catch up, but the second I drop Jax's name, there's a noticeable change in Markus's demeanor. Not only does he lean back off the desk and more into the chair, but his eyes go wide and if I'm not mistaken, there's a shift in his attitude. His eyes lowering in what I can only describe as concern before shifting just as swiftly to surprise.

Strange.

Why would Jax's name cause that kind of reaction? Do they know each other or is this because he's aware of what Jax does for a living and like most, he's concerned?

"He's an independent wrestler, right?"

That answers that.

When I nod, he turns his attention from me to the laptop in front of him, typing something quickly before sliding his hand across the mouse a few times and tapping before turning it toward me.

There in bolded type is a headline with his name in the byline. A headline that based on the name used for Jax, has my cheeks overheating again.

WHY THE WRESTLING BUSINESS NEEDS THE MOJO MASTER.

"You wrote about him?" I ask, still trying to wrap my mind around what I'm seeing. Sure, he'd told me about the moniker, but seeing it there in black and white and knowing that my boss had been the one to write about him was a bit of a surprise.

What are the odds?

"That I did. He put on quite the show back then. Which I'm sure he still does now. I was a wrestling fan, what can I say? It was quite the coo to be able to write about him, much less interview him the way I did."

As interesting a tidbit as knowing my boss is a wrestling fan is, I'm struck more by the fact that Jax knew where I worked and hadn't brought up that he'd been interviewed.

Did he just not remember or was there more to it?

"I'm sure if you ask him about it, he probably won't even remember, but given that it was one of the first assignments I actually enjoyed writing, it left an impression."

Right. Surely that's all this is. Jax just didn't remember. It is possible considering that the date on the article was a little over two years ago.

No big deal.

"That's one heck of a small world." I say in lieu of anything better.

"That it is." He agrees. "From what I remember about him from back then, he had a pretty serious thing going with one of the women on the roster. Melinda something or another. Can't really recall now, though I do remember her being a part of the interview. Real spitfire that one. She kept attempting to do all of his talking for him."

Melinda.

A name I know well as Jax had brought his past with her up the first day we met.

Maybe Markus having knowledge I don't can come in handy after all.

"We've talked a little about her, but he hasn't gone too deeply into it. We're choosing to focus on the present and future seeing as things with us are still fairly new."

New being the understatement of the century.

"Avery, believe me. With what I remember about this woman, there's a real good reason why he isn't talking about her. She was a stunner in terms of looks, but that girl's attitude needed some serious adjusting. It was Jackson's interview and she took it over, making it all about her. For a time, I thought it was going to be a bust, but he held his own. I've got nothing but respect for the way he handled himself that day."

It's strange hearing your boss speak of respecting the man you're quite possibly falling in love with. It's the weirdest conversation in the world, not something I would have imagined ever happening, but there's no telling how much good it does my heart to know that at least one person here understands what it is I see in him.

During our time together and the nightly calls every day since, I don't think I can bring up one instance where Jax wasn't completely professional when it came to talking about his work and the people in his life because of it.

"The next time you speak with him, let him know that anytime he's interested in doing another piece he can give me a call. I'd gladly sit down with him again and see how the last couple of years have treated him."

"Will do, Markus."

"Before I let you get back to it, there's something else I think you should know."

"Okay."

"Jackson's patience that day during the interview, it went a long way in proving what kind of guy he is, but as you enter into this with him, I think you need to know that it also had a lot to do with something else as well."

"That being?"

"He was hopelessly devoted to her. It was easy to see at the time that it wasn't reciprocated, but it was still there in his eyes. For Jackson, Melinda held the key to everything."

Jax was hopelessly devoted to her.

She held the key to everything.

All of the other words Markus said fall away and those are the only ones I can hear. On repeat, like a bad song you can't get out of your head once it's been put there.

And none of it doing me any favors.

I knew I should have shut him down while I had the chance.

"It's a shame really. One look at that boy when I interviewed him and you could see that if he got his way there would be wedding bells in their future."

I want to stop him. Scream and yell. Something to make him shut up. Wishing that instead of continuing to tell me about them, he'd just left well enough alone. Make him see that he doesn't know anything and its best if he just quits while he's ahead, but I don't do any of it. I can't. The thought of wedding bells completely stripping away the air needed in order to breathe, let alone argue.

The earlier comments were bad enough, but the idea of them wanting to be married holds too much weight.

Picturing it happening more than enough to bring me out of the haze that has been the last week and slamming me straight back into reality.

Markus without even realizing it has ignited the very firestorm with his memories of Jax and Melinda that I'd been doing everything in my power not to think about.

My insecurities.

Is it possible Jax's intentions aren't as pure and innocent as they seem?

Is it possible I'm being used?

Chapter Thirty-One

Brady

"You want to do what?" Marie asks after listening to my request, though with the familiar scowl she wears securely in place, I couldn't tell one way or the other whether she was repeating it because she hadn't heard what I asked or couldn't believe it.

Before we even made the plan to come here, we knew it was going to be a long shot. That it could possibly be career suicide if we saw it through.

I just had hope it wouldn't play out that way.

"I know that leaving for an extended period of time is out of the question. I don't want to screw with Smith's plans for the angle with me and Ron. All we're asking for is a couple of days in order to handle personal business back home."

"Let's say I do what you're asking," she says, motioning between me and Jax. "Who is it really helping in the long term? Because the minute I grant you both the time off, there'll be more stepping forward wanting the same treatment. As I'm sure you both know with how dedicated you've been, we're running low on genuine talent as it is."

There's no way I can argue with her logic and I'm pretty sure Jax is the same way judging by the look that passes through his eyes before his shoulders begin to sag. The truth that she's speaking leaving not only him, but me feeling pretty damn dejected.

Looks like we're not gonna get what we want and my grand gesture for Emery was going to fall apart before it even got off the ground.

No way. I can't think like that.

I'm not just random wrestler on their roster. I'm Brady-fucking-Raines. When I want something, I get it. The same way my old man did in his heyday.

I'm not gonna let it play out like this, even if what Marie is saying is valid.

"I think I speak for both Jackson and myself when I say that we understand what you're saying, but with us only asking for a day or two at most, I don't foresee it causing any long term damage."

"Why is it that you want the time off, Brady?" she asks and before I can tell her the same regurgitated crap I spewed when I first asked, she holds up a hand, stopping me in my tracks. "And don't feed me that stupid personal issue line again. I heard you the first time. I want the real reason."

No way.

I can't tell her the reason I want time off is for a girl. I'll never be looked at seriously in this business again. So thinking as quickly as I can, I fire off the only thing that I've got in my arsenal that's even remotely believable.

"Kelly is looking to prolong the divorce by bringing further legal action against me. Legal action that could very well bring trouble to your front door. Trouble I know for a fact you don't want. If I don't go back to Florida and be there in court in order to defend myself, there will be ramifications for all of us. I don't want that, Marie. Not when you and Smith have been so good to me."

A little ass kissing never hurt anyone right?

I'm already going straight to hell for using my divorce as an excuse. Might as well take it all the way and sweeten the pot. Especially if it gets me what I'm after.

"Fair enough. That explains your situation, but now I'm wondering why you want the time off, Jackson."

"I need to fly to Toronto."

"For what purpose?" she pushes and Jax doesn't even hesitate with his answer, proving just how ready he was. And unlike me, he doesn't lie.

"There's a situation with my girlfriend that needs my attention. But before you say anything, since I know you're going to tell me how against relationship drama you are, let me remind you how accommodating I was after injuring my ankle."

I'm impressed. The same way he seems to see everything coming when we're putting matches and stories together, he does again here. He's using the one thing guaranteed to get him what he wants.

His ability to keep the show going on even when it means long term injury.

"If I give you both the time off, what's stopping you from extending it and screwing the show we have scheduled that night in Oregon?"

I should have known she'd have a comeback. She isn't the co-owner for nothing. If Jax has the ability to think of everything, Marie's the one writing the book. She knew what we would do even before we did it.

"Well," Jax answers smoothly, not missing a beat. "When you put it like that, there's nothing stopping us from screwing you over, but you and Smith have spent the last seven years working with me and even longer with Brady. You know us. Our word is our bond. So how about a compromise?"

"I'm listening."

I've never been much a cheerleader, but hot damn. Right now I would seriously break out some fucking pom-poms and rah-rah the shit out of Jackson. Damn guy has an answer for everything.

"If we don't show the way we're booked, terminate us on the spot. Work up the papers today, we'll sign them before we head out, and everyone's ass is covered. If we screw you, you screw us. It's a win-win."

Whoa. I take it back. What the hell is he thinking?

As badly as I want to make things right with Emery, the last thing I want to do is give up my livelihood for it. What the hell would I be able to offer her if I was out of a job?

Diddly squat is what.

But before I can speak up, tell Jax and Marie that this is something we need to discuss, she's answering and I'm shit out of luck.

"That sounds reasonable. I'll have the papers drawn up."

"We have a deal?" Jax asks in disbelief.

"That we do. Enjoy the next two days off because for the next six months after that, you're going to be worked harder than you ever have before. There will be no more opportunities for days off unless they're ones we've booked off for you." She laughs before continuing. "Your asses will be stamped Property of CPW."

Taking the extended hand into mine, still not sure how I feel about the whole thing, I shake it and step back as Jax steps forward with a smile and does the same.

What he has to smile about, I don't have a clue since he just sealed our fate if things don't work out according to plan. With the time it's going to take for her to draw up the papers though, it seems I've got ample opportunity to find out.

The way to Emery has been made clear. That's what I need to focus on. I can deal with the rest later.

Phase one is officially complete.

Jax

It probably wasn't the smartest thing to do, putting our careers on the line, but seeing this idea of his slipping away, I did what I had to do.

The more I focus on what two days uninterrupted will mean for me and Avery, the more I need to make sure it happens. It's been murder these last few days without her.

It's actually kind of crazy. I've been down this road one time before, aside from the girl I asked out in high school and who I declared love for by the end of the night and none of those experiences even remotely compared to this.

There is someone it does remind me of though.

My parents.

I just don't foresee asking Avery to marry me in two months and then taking the plunge less than a month later. While having my parents experience to go on is a good thing, I'm not sure what worked in the seventies would work here.

Yet...the idea of it doesn't scare me nearly as much as it should.

Damn, Brady was right. I've got it fucking bad.

"Earth to Merrick. Did you hear anything I just said?"

After finishing up signing the papers detailing what would happen if Brady and I even so much as thought of bailing on Oregon, we'd hightailed it out of there. Now sitting in the back of a cab on the way to the airport.

This time, going our separate ways once we got there.

"Not a bit of it." I admit honestly. "What'd I miss?"

"I asked if you wanted to stop and grab some lunch."

"Yeah, sure. Whatever you wanna do, man." I agree easily, knowing that we've got hours to burn before our flights head out, and grabbing something to eat not sounding half bad since it's been well over twelve hours since I did it last.

"Are you going to call her and let her know you're coming?"

"No. I like surprising her. Plus, if I don't tell her, I'll get to see the reaction I missed sending her the flowers."

"How do you do this shit, man?" He asks and not following, I just shrug. "You made a deal with her before you left and stuck to it. I do the same thing, but then realizing just how screwed up my shit is, try to do the right thing by the girl and end up falling flat on my ass."

"I've been Melinda free for almost three years, Brady. I've had time to adjust even though it still hits me sometimes. You were married straight out of high school and she just dropped you out of the blue for something you didn't even do. Our situations are completely different."

"Maybe." He concedes, but the scowl on his face tells me he doesn't agree.

"There's no maybe to it. Look, the way you handled it probably wasn't the way to go, but all things considered, you haven't exactly had an opportunity outside of Kelly to learn the right way. It's the same damn way with me."

"Yeah, but your girl isn't hanging up on you because you're an idiot."

"Yet, Brady. She's not doing it yet. I'll screw up. I know it. I just hope it's ten years from now after we're married and she's stuck with me."

The force and speed of his head as it swivels to me after my admission makes me laugh.

"Something I said?"

"Man, I know you're into the girl, but don't you think you're moving a little fast with the whole picturing marriage shit?"

"Nope."

"You're shitting me, right?"

"Brady, I can bullshit you all day long about a bunch of different crap and enjoy every second of it, but when it comes to something as serious as marriage, family, and settling down, I never joke."

"Damn. Well, guru of women, share your wisdom with the less fortunate."

"I can't. What works for me, what feels right, it won't be the same with you. You my friend are on your own."

"You can't give me just one thing? Come on! What good are you?"

"Talking sweet like that and you still screwed things up with the girl? Wow. Don't see how that happened at all." I say, rolling my eyes to which he just grunts and turns his attention back out the window.

"If you want to make an impression on the girl, just be yourself. Do something a little out of your comfort zone. Show her she actually matters. Whether that's just talking or showering her with presents. Do whatever works. That's all I can tell you."

"Is that what you're doing with Avery?"

"Yeah. Something tells me that if I went at her like I was the fucking Mojo Master, she'd lay me out in a second. So plain old Jackson it is."

"You forgot whipped sucker."

"Says the guy that has to go win the girl back."

"Touché." He laughs. "But seriously, two days with the girl and four days apart with just phone calls and texts to tide you over and you're already picturing marriage?"

"Weren't you the one that told me there was more to life than wrestling? Better yet, aren't you the one that did get married? So why is it so strange that I would be thinking along those lines? I'm twenty-seven for Christ sakes. I should be settling down by now."

"Honestly? It's not strange." He admits, drumming his hands off his leg a few times before continuing. "After the way you were with Melinda, I shouldn't be all that surprised. I just remember you taking your time with her and that's not what's happening with Avery. I just want to be sure that you've thought it all out."

"I know what I'm doing, Brady. I care about her. A lot. I'm not saying that we're gonna go out tomorrow and get hitched. But with everything I already know about her, what I continue to learn every day and the way it felt when we were together, she's someone I can easily see in my future."

"Tell me that when the new wears off, buddy."

"I will." I accept his challenge, determined to prove just how wrong he is about me and Avery.

"I felt the same way about Kelly when we first got together, which is why I'm telling you to tread carefully. Things got a whole lot harder after the honeymoon period wore off, and that was before we even got married. I know you probably think I'm being a buzzkill because my own shit is in the toilet, but that's not it. I actually give a shit what happens to you."

"Aww, Brady! I didn't know you cared so much. Should we kiss now or save it for the airport?" Puckering my lips and leaning over. Only shifting back to my place when the reaction I'm after happens and his entire body shakes from the force of his laughter.

"Shut up, jerk. You know what I mean. I do give a shit about you."

"Because of what it will mean having to work with me after?"

"No. It's because after Melinda, the last thing I want for you is to have a Kelly."

"I'm good, man. I won't have a Kelly. You wanna know why?"

"Sure, let me have it."

"Because I'll have something better. I'll have Avery."

Chapter Thirty-Two

Avery

I can't believe I actually agreed to this. I've obviously lost what's left of my mind.

When I agreed to the increased work load and longer hours, wanting to keep myself as busy as possible and away from the overwhelming solitude that came with being at home, it was the best idea I've ever had. I wouldn't have the time to focus on whether or not Jax would have a chance to call or on just how solitary my life had become before I flew out to Delaware to meet Emery and our mother.

I could throw myself into the work and by the time I got home, have just enough time to make it to my bed in order to crash so I could do it all over again the next day.

Sitting here in my office surrounded by the quiet—the only sound the occasional one I make while I'm shifting papers around, most of the people having already left for the day, it doesn't feel like the best idea. The loneliness that came with the quiet more alive than ever.

Reaching over and grabbing the contracts, I start going over them line by line. Bringing my hand to my forehead and rubbing at what feels like the onset of another monstrous headache. The fifth one in the last couple of days.

Maybe I should have told Markus the work load was too much.

Correcting the errors as I find them, I plead with my brain to let me make it through the next couple so I can call it a night. Something my body is obviously trying to tell me I should have done hours ago, but that I'd been way too set in my ways to listen to.

Finishing with the first, I lay it to the side before diving into the second. The process interrupted as the shrill ring of my office phone fills the quieted room.

"City Voice."

"It is a beautiful voice, but is it the one I'm looking for?"

The voice on the other end of the line is muffled, making it impossible to tell who it is, so in an effort to get it over with so I can get back to work, I attempt to speed the process along by stating my name.

"You've reached Avery Davis's office. Is there something I can help you with?"

"As a matter of fact, there is. You can help by telling me what a beautiful woman like you is doing still working at this hour."

With the line becoming clearer or the caller no longer shielding his voice and finally able to recognize it, I play along.

"No reason to go home. Are you going to give me one?"

The line goes silent, giving me pause and making me wonder whether or not I'd lost him, but before I can question it, I hear the faint trace of his breathing.

"I might be able to do that, but it would require a little something from you."

"And what pre-tell would that be?" I continue to play along. "If I can do it, you know I will."

"You can definitely do it." he laughs, the sound coinciding with a knock on my door. An interruption that now that I have him on the line, I most definitely don't want.

"You need to open the door, sweetheart."

"Very funny, Jackson."

As the person on the other side of the door knocks again, this time a little louder, I release a heavy sigh before standing. Biting back the string of curse words I want to give at whoever is waiting on the other side, I let Jax know what's up.

"Looks like they're not going away. I'll be right back."

Hearing his laughter as I place the phone down on the desk, I make my way to the door and before opening it, lean in just in time to catch the tail end of the same sound filtering its way through it.

It's not a joke.

He's here.

Throwing the door open, I come face to face with his expression, the laugh lines still evident. His lips curved up into what has to be the biggest and brightest smile I've ever seen. One that only seems to curve even higher as his arms widen just in time to catch me as I throw myself into them.

"I can't believe you're really here." I murmur when his arms come around and pull my body flush against him.

"Well believe it sweetheart. For the next two days, you're stuck with me."

"Stuck with you is not how I'd describe it." I manage to whisper before his lips catch mine. The feel of them as they softly take what they want reminding me of the night we sat out underneath the stars and we made the wish on the shooting star.

Every moment we've shared since, every kiss, a reminder of it coming true.

"How would you describe it?" He asks, his arms releasing their hold and placing me back down. Using the chance, I slip my hand through his and pull him into my office, shutting the door and giving us privacy.

"Being stuck would mean I didn't want to have something, but with us, that couldn't be further from the truth. I want these two days with you. As many days as I can get really. But…"

"But what, sweetheart?"

"There's something I need to know."

"Okay." He replies, his eyes growing serious.

"Where exactly are you planning to stay?"

"Honestly," he pauses, running a hand through his hair with a soft chuckle. "I didn't exactly plan that far ahead. All I cared about was getting the time off and standing right where I am now. Everything else could wait."

"So you planned on coming to my office?"

"Not exactly. I planned on being wherever you were at the time, and since right in this moment that's here, well, this is where I am. Where I'm happy."

Taking a page out of Emery's book, I throw caution to the wind and do what I know deep down with the way I feel about him is right.

"What if I said I had a solution to your problem?"

"I say bring it on because I'm open to anything."

Here goes nothing.

"Stay with me."

Jax

Stay with me.

Three words I'm sure countless people hear every day, but that since my life imploded three years ago, I'd resigned myself to never hearing again.

This might be moving at warp speed and because of it, I might want to take my time in other respects when it comes to what I feel with Avery, but I'm still a guy and just like any other guy in my position, the offer to stay with her is making more than just my heart rise to the occasion.

"Jax?" she calls softly. "Did you hear what I said?"

What a crazy question. With her proximity and what's literally popping up between us despite my every attempt to make it settle, I'm pretty amazed that she hasn't felt the physical response to what she's said.

Jesus. Maybe choosing to keep my dick under strict lock and key wasn't such a good idea after all. I'm no better than a dog in heat right now and it won't be long before Avery realizes it too.

Get it together, Jackson.

"Uh, yeah." I stammer. "I heard you."

"So what do you say? Will you come home with me?"

Taking a breath and swallowing hard as just like the first time she offered, my body responds before my head can, I attempt to answer before she has a chance to catch on and rescind the offer.

Something that even if I wasn't physically reacting to her, I can't have her do. Not when I want it so damn badly. The idea of two days in her space, getting to experience her in a way that my being on the road prevents me from, creates a level of excitement in me that I don't think I've had since I made the decision to be a wrestler.

"I'd love to come home with you, but only if you're sure it's what you want."

Idiot. You're not supposed to take her out of it!

"I wouldn't have suggested it if it wasn't what I wanted." She assures, but before I can speak up and solidify our plans, her cheeks begin to flush. "I've never done anything like this before."

"Asked someone to stay with you or something else?"

If there was any hope of her losing the blush, it was lost the second I asked what I did. What started out as an adorable shade of pink was now turning into a full blown red.

The red that embarrassment brings.

"I've never asked someone to stay with me before. Stay the night *or* a few days."

"Why not?"

"The relationships I had in the past, if they can even be called that, were just never that serious. I never felt comfortable asking them to stay."

There it goes again. My heart picking up on her words and soaring. Feeling like the luckiest SOB in the world with the knowledge that of all the people she could have chosen over the years, she'd waited for me.

"But it's different with me?"

Squeezing my hand, she smiles softly and stops my heart.

"Everything is different with you, Jackson."

If I wasn't sure we were on the same page before, her use of my full name and the seriousness in her eyes as they lift and never waver from mine, slams the point home now.

She's as deep in this as I am.

"Then what we are doing standing around here? Now that I'm here and we're together, let's go."

"Go where?" she asks, her eyes raising in confusion.

"Home. Let's go home, Avery."

Chapter Thirty-Three

Brady

Pulling the rental car up in front of what had to be the biggest store I've ever seen, I take a deep breath and go over everything I've done to get me here and what in a few minutes I'm about to walk in that store and make right.

It had taken a little over a day with the travel time and the stop to Marie, but I'd made it. Back to Delaware and back to Emery.

Finding out where she worked hadn't been as easy I thought, my skills in stalking with social media falling a whole lot shorter than most, but I'd done it. Coming across the only post she'd done about it six months ago and running with it. Thankful at the same time that the majority of things she posted online, she did publicly so I was able to have access without adding her.

Tipping her off was definitely not an option.

Looking down at the clock on the dash and catching the time, I realize it's now or never.

Go big or go home.

A sentiment Smith drilled into us before every show, but that was no longer just pertaining to business. It applies to personal lives as well.

Slipping out of the car, I make a mad dash across the parking lot, only slowing once I've reached the double doors that will take me into the store. To her.

Here goes nothing.

Despite how busy the store is once I stop and take it all in, it doesn't take me long to spot her. Her head angled down, but forward as she handled the cash register and the customer now paying in her line. A continuous line if the ten to fifteen people shifting back and forth on their feet waiting is any indication.

As much as I hate lines and waiting, I've never been so happy to see one in my life.

She's not going to see me coming.

Heading deeper into the store, my attention is drawn to the signs above the aisles as I attempt to find what I'm looking for. Each one bringing me no closer to what I'm after than the first.

Spotting someone in a shirt bearing the name of the store across the breast pocket, I head for him and call out when I'm a couple of feet away.

"Hey man." I say when he turns away from the shelves. "Sorry to pull you away, but I'm looking for something and don't know where to find it."

"No problem. What exactly is it you're after?"

"You guys sell flowers here?"

"Fresh cut ones or ones you plant?"

"Fresh cut would be what I'm after."

Shifting his attention up the aisle, he points before motioning to the right with his hand. "Up near register ten, there's a whole display of them. Bunch of different kinds. You should find what you want there."

The registers.

Right where Emery was working and where if I actually went up there, I'd be spotted almost immediately. Maybe the rest of the people milling around the store wouldn't know me, but Emery damn sure would.

Not wanting to be spotted before I was ready, I decide to take a chance and use the smile still planted on the guys face to my advantage. Hoping as I lean in that he goes along with what I'm after.

"Look, man, I'm gonna be honest with you. I want to grab some flowers for someone that works here, but if I do that, she's gonna see me. I can't have that yet, so do you think you could help me out?"

If it's even possible, the kids face seems to brighten even more. Either about to burst from what I've just admitted about someone he works with or in laughter at just how pathetic I sound.

"What kind you after?"

"Carnations. White ones if you've got them."

Another tidbit I picked up in my online stalking expedition. Jax's words about accepting technology ringing in my ears every second I was doing it and making me realize just how out of touch I was.

"Yeah, we got those. They don't sell much though. People seem to go for the roses." The guy admits and I just nod. "Though there is one girl that works cash that buys a few bouquets a week."

Emery.

I don't even have to ask him to confirm. I just know it's true.

"Grab me every white carnation you've got and while you're at it, take all of the other colors too."

"You're shitting me right?"

"Nope. I'm dead serious. I'm gonna buy them all now, but the other colors, if you're interested in making some extra cash after work, I want delivered."

"You want to pay me to deliver flowers? Damn. This girl must be pretty special."

"Man, you have no idea. So will you do it?" I ask, hoping the pull of extra cash will draw him into the plan, sweetening the pot of what I was already planning to do face to face once I saw her again.

"You got a deal. Give me a sec."

Taking off out of the aisle, he heads in the direction of the flowers and I take the chance to peek out around the aisle and watch Emery as just like she'd been doing when I got here, she's handling the line of customers. This time, the line shorter than before as there's another woman working in the lane beside her.

"Alright man, here you go."

Handing over two bouquets of white carnations, he grins before turning in the direction I've been watching and smirks when he catches just who I'm looking at.

"Figured it was for Em. She's the only person here that loves carnations." Turning back to me, smirk still in place, he motions to the register. "You wanna pay for them through her or you want me to take you back to the meat counter and let you settle up there?

This kid right now. God. The best thing I ever did was reach out to him. He knows what's up without me even having to tell him.

"Definitely at the meat counter. Don't want her seeing these babies until I'm ready."

"I get it. Come on."

Tearing my eyes away from Emery and hating the emptiness I feel once she's out of sight, I begrudgingly follow behind the kid, stopping at the counter and letting him explain to the guy behind it what we're doing before he motions to me to put them up on the glass.

"All yours, Max." the kid says but before he can walk away, I call out.

"What time do you get off?"

"About an hour, why?"

Pulling out my wallet, I slip the hundred out and hand it over. "That should be enough to cover the delivery of the other flowers."

"Holy shit, man. You sure?" he laughs, keeping his hands at his sides despite the urgency I see in his eyes wanting to grab the money I'm offering and run.

"Positive. I'll make it two hundred if you can grab a different bouquet and deliver them to her mother."

This, how far I'm taking it, wasn't part of the plan, but knowing what I do about Emery and what she's dealing with at home, there's no way I'm backing down. Both of these women deserve this, whether one of them forgives me for being a colossal jackass or not.

"You got yourself a deal."

"What's your name?" I ask, handing over the other hundred before turning toward Max and doing the same with the carnations.

"Tim."

"Pleasure doing business with you, Tim." I grin and when he returns it, I motion back to the aisle I stole him away from. "You better get back to it before you get in shit, but thanks."

"No, thank you. You just made my night."

After watching Tim head back to work and waving off the change from Max, I pick up the flowers as gently as I can from the counter and head up the nearest aisle. One that I see the closer I get to the end of it, brings me even closer to Emery than where I'd been standing around with Tim. Jumping into the lane, keeping the flowers low and around my back for fear of her catching them before I'm ready, I attempt to settle the nerves that are now bubbling back up the surface now that there's only two people standing between me and what, or rather who, I'm really here for.

Seeing the **Please Use Next Available Lane** sign resting at the end of the conveyor belt, I pluck it out from its spot and lay it down flat making sure as I do that Emery's attention is still on the people in front of me. Wishing as I see her engrossed with the older man she's talking with that I could do the same with the light above her head.

I don't want any interruptions.

Watching the man accepts his change with a smile and grabbing his bags, the sound of her voice hits me and something about the happiness I hear in it, the genuine sweetness that I'd seen shades of during our time together, melts away the remaining nervousness I feel.

As the woman in front of me moves closer and her attention snaps away from the man, I pull the cap I've got on down as far as it can go over my face and observe.

Struck stupid by the ease she has with people. Something that while we're trained to be able to do it when we've got to interact with fans, I've just never been the best with. Able to paint a smile on like the rest of the roster, but never able to maintain it for long. Another thing about Emery that I like, and further proof that I'd made the right decision coming back.

I don't just like this girl. I admire her.

An admission that makes the smile I'm wearing as the woman grabs her bags with a wave, the most genuine one I've ever worn.

One that's only for her.

The same way I am.

Emery

Seeing the guy grab the sign that we use to close off our registers when we're going on break but not wanting to say anything while there were other customers around, I hold my tongue until his tall frame lands directly across from me and I'm able to meet his eyes.

Eyes that I also caught him blocking from my view after I'd said goodbye to Mr. Jamieson, but that for some reason I can't explain, I need to see.

It's only when he finally looks up and adjusts his cap that the reason for the pull becomes obvious.

Brady.

Shit.

"Before you get pissed and tell me to fuck off, I need you to hear me out." He pleads, his eyes growing softer yet more insistent while I can feel mine hardening.

"What else is there to say? I think you said it all the last time we spoke, Brady. There's nothing you could possibly have to tell me now that I would need or want to hear."

Take that, asshole. There's my understanding.

"I deserve that. I deserve a lot worse than that, really, but if you'd just give me a chance, I swear I'll explain everything."

"Did you not hear what I just said? I don't want to hear anything you have to say because you said it all two days ago. Now if you don't mind, I need to close for the night and get home. My mom's waiting."

Turning my attention back to the register and closing my eyes, I will him to take the hint and leave before I end up caving and give in to the way my heart had damn near jumped out of my chest when I realized it was him.

Unable to let him go despite the way we left things along with my mom's words playing on a continuous loop.

I can't react, not to any of it. He hurt me on the phone that day, no matter what pretty concoction of words he puts together now. It won't change it. Not even a love declaration would. Not that I'd get that anyway.

I'm not even sure we like each other much, let alone love.

"I won't keep you long, I promise. Please, Emery. I came all this way."

Oh please. Like trying to guilt me into talking to him is gonna work. He needs to try another tactic. I see right through this one.

"If you're here now to say you screwed up, you were wrong, and you suddenly realize how much you care, spare me. It's bullshit and I'm not falling for it."

"That's not what I was going to say, Em." He pauses. "Well, not like that anyway. I'd be lying if I said it like that and I won't do that."

"Will wonders never cease?!" I laugh, fighting the urge I have to hear him out by letting the anger I still feel run the show. "Someone needs to get over here and give you a medal!"

"Emery, please." I plead quietly, looking around to make sure no one else is paying attention to her boisterous declaration. "I know you're done for the night and you've got to get home. I won't keep you from that. I'm just asking for a couple minutes to talk before you go."

If the pitiful look in his eyes and the droop to his face wasn't enough to break down my defenses, the reminder of what my mother said does it.

"He doesn't want to bring you into his complication. Keeping you out means keeping you safe. And you know who does things like that? Men in love."

Damn it. I'm gonna crack.

"Who are those for? I ask instead, motioning to the flowers I can see hiding behind his back. Wanting to put the focus on anything but those sad as shit puppy dog eyes.

"For you. They're for you."

Rolling my eyes in an attempt to deflect off the way the last of the coolness I've been maintaining is breaking down, he sighs and that's all it takes. As upset as I've been, I can't do it anymore. It's not me.

I want to hear him out because against my better judgment, I've missed him since he left. I didn't want to, but I just didn't have it in me to hate him.

Sometimes I really hate being my mother's daughter.

Taking the flowers from his now outstretched hand, I bring them up and inhale deeply. Moved as always by the familiar aroma.

"How did you know?"

"Know what?"

"That white carnations are my favorite?"

If I wasn't seeing it with my own eyes I'd think I was dreaming it, but sure enough, the big bad wrestler that throws people around for enjoyment, is actually blushing.

"You really don't want to know."

"I asked, didn't I?"

"Facebook." He gives up, the coloring in his cheeks deepening. "I checked you out and saw you talking about them. Posting pictures and stuff."

Brady Raines actually used social media?

Now I know I've gotta be dreaming.

"Facebook." I repeat, the word in relation to *mister can't stand anything to do with the internet,* foreign even to my own ears.

"Yes Facebook. Crazy, I know." He admits before filling me in on the rest. "One of the guys you work with helped me grab them when I got here."

One of the guys I work with?

Now he's got my attention. Just how many people did he bring in on this drop in visit?

"Who?"

"Tim."

Well, that makes sense.

With as many nights as we end up working together, we've gotten to know each other pretty well and he knows better than anyone just what flowers are my favorite.

Brady lucked out.

I don't want to admit it, but the flowers, along with the lengths he went to in order to find that tidbit out, is making my heart soften.

"Brady..." I sigh softly, feeling what's left of the residual anger fading away. "What the hell is going on with us? What is this?"

Shifting his eyes from me and looking around us, he pauses on Jane. Scowling as he turns his attention back, he leans across the counter, his next words low and obviously for my ears only.

"Is there someplace we can talk privately?"

Understanding the need for privacy now that we've got an audience, I nod and turning my light off, motion for him to follow me, which once he catches on, he does easily.

Pausing at Jane's cash, I point to the door.

"I'm gonna be right back. Five minutes tops. Cover for me?"

"No problem, Em."

Slipping my hand into Brady's and catching the slight raise to his lips when we touch, my own reaction torn between enjoying it and hating myself for giving in so easily, I pull him along until we're heading out the employee exit.

"Okay, look. You asked what's going on with us and I want to answer, but before I do, I think there's some other stuff you need to know first."

Nodding instead of answering, not entirely trusting that he'll tell me the truth, he huffs out a breath, rubbing his hand over his hair and starts.

"Kelly and I were together for a long ass time. High school sweethearts and married straight out. Until a week ago, I was still willing to do just about anything to prove I wasn't the man she thought I was, even though deep down, I knew it was over a long time ago and the separation was just a technicality. I wasn't ready to admit it to myself though. Couldn't admit that like with most of the things in my life that have nothing to do with wrestling, I screwed up. Then in walks you, or at the very least, Avery, and something flipped. A switch went off. Nothing made sense anymore."

Taking a deep breath, obviously having more to say, I take his hand and wrap it in mine, walking him over to the bench a few feet away.

"Those two days we had together before I had to head out, they were eye opening. I was finally learning how to be myself again. Not Brady, the husband that fails at everything, even though he's as loyal as a Saint Bernard. Not the one that lives in his father's shadow. I was the Brady that loved life and everything in it. The guy that wasn't afraid to take chances or risks. I was happy. You helped with that, Em. You're the reason for it."

"The day you took me cliff diving and what happened after, well, it threw me into this tailspin. I knew that going back on the road, I was going to have to shut those two days off and let the business take over again. The only area of my life that no matter how badly I screw up in my personal life, I always succeed at."

Again he stops, only this time, instead of just taking a breath and beginning again, he reaches across the bench, his hand brushing against the side of my face. Stroking it until I finally give him the payoff he must be after and look up and meet his eyes.

"But I also knew that I didn't want to lose what we shared, so I said what I needed to in order to keep it. I meant every word, but after the first few hours of driving and really thinking about what I was capable of giving, I realized you deserved better than me."

I want to stop him. Inform him that he has no right deciding what I deserve, but with the pained expression he's wearing, I hold back. There's time for me to say my piece, but right now I really do have to let him have his.

"You deserve better than some guy that is still married to someone else. A guy that by his own admission has been hanging onto something that he should have let go of a long time ago. I couldn't bring you into my mess. I couldn't make you the other woman or whatever label you wanna put on it. Something that you aren't, but that I'm sure you probably would have thought you were until I was actually free and clear of Kelly for good."

"When you called that day, it was like you were reading my mind, but at the same time, weren't. I wanted to reach out and call you the way Jackson does every day with your sister but every time I thought about it, I kept seeing me screwing it all up again. So I didn't. I swallowed down the urge until it damn near drove me out of my mind."

"Why didn't you let me decide what I deserved?" I ask softly and he sighs, again scrubbing a hand over his hair and down over his face.

"Because I'm an idiot?" he says and taking it as a joke, I laugh, but he holds up his hand and stops me. "It's not a joke, Emery. I'm an idiot. I'm no good with this kind of thing. I made the decision for you because I'm a moron. That call, the things I said to you. God, the way I know I made you feel because I swear even over the phone I could feel the knife going in as I did it, it was me stupidly talking before I was done thinking."

"Your attempt at protecting me." I whisper under my breath and he inhales sharply.

"How do you..." he starts, pausing in surprise. "Yeah."

"I'm a big girl, Brady. I can take care of myself. I don't need you or anyone else doing it for me. I get it, why you did what you did and why even now, you still seem to want to do it, but you don't need to."

"Truth is, you scare the shit out of me, Emery."

From the second he started talking, I knew he was being honest, but this admission just be the most real and telling part of everything that he's said.

"If you're so scared of me and the out on control feeling you seem to have with me, why are you here?"

He doesn't answer right away, but watching him, seeing the focus of his eyes, and the way his forehead seems to crunch and groove in, I know that when he does speak again, it will be more of the same. The way he's been since he begged me to hear him out.

After releasing another breath he brings his hand out again, cupping my face and bringing me into him and rests his forehead against mine.

"This is going to sound insane, I know it, but I know it's true. I'm here because I fucked up and I want the chance to make it right, but I'm also here because..."

"Because why, Brady?"

"Because I'm falling for you. And Emery?

"Yes?"

"I don't want to fall alone."

Chapter Thirty-Four

Avery

"Brady did what?"

Practically diving out of the car the second he pulled into my driveway and making his way around to the passenger side in order to hold open the door for me, I slip my hand into his as he pulls me out and into his arms, repeating what he told me again.

Filling me in on everything I'd missed since the last time we spoke and ending with the stunt Brady had pulled in order for him to get to my sister and for Jackson to end up here.

"I honestly never though he had it in him to do something like it, but he used his divorce to secure time off to be with her."

I have to admit hearing it for a second time that I hadn't been expecting to hear it myself. Screwing with other people and their lives in the name of fun, sure. But this? No way.

"He's not going to have an easy time with her." I admit, remembering the sound of Emery's tears over the phone the day after she'd made the call and knowing that if she was anything like me, she might forgive, but the wound will still remain long after.

"Good. Brady operates better when shit is hard."

Walking hand in hand to the door, I slip the keys out of my pocket and unlock it, but before I have the chance to step in, I lose my footing. My legs coming out from under me as I'm lifted and being swung in the air.

"Jackson! Put me down!" I cry out.

Smacking his arms when my plea goes unanswered, I laugh as he makes his way through the door and crosses the room quickly, only putting me down once he's made his way into the living room and my sofa.

"What was that about?" I ask the second I'm comfortably down and he's resting on his knees on the floor.

"Always wanted to do that." He grins. "Now let's get those shoes off your feet and get you comfortable."

"Excuse me?"

"You heard me." he answers and pulling my boots off, he repeats the same action with my socks and lifting me up just slightly, lays me out flat across the sofa. Doing what he said and making sure I'm comfortable. The attention he's paying me only seeming to make me want him more.

Is this normal? Where something as small as him pulling off my boots and socks has me wanting to pull him in as close as possible until I'm not the only one whose clothing is being removed?

With as long as it's been since I've been intimate with anyone and when it did happen, it not being anything like this, I have no idea if this is right.

Despite finding the way he carried me over the threshold and placed me down on the sofa incredibly sweet, it's also making me needier than I've ever been. Even now with him smiling the way he is, my thoughts drift to what he'll look like wearing only that smile. My breath catching in my throat as the vision of the man I've done nothing but dream about all week naked comes vividly to life in my head.

Wow. I need to stop this before I end up making a fool of myself.

"Now, I'm going to need you to point me in the direction of the kitchen. It's been a long day for both of us. I haven't had anything since before the flight and I'm pretty sure given the way I found you earlier, you haven't either."

I'm dreaming, right? He didn't just ask me to point him to my kitchen so he could go cook dinner for us. No way.

"Jax, you don't have to do that."

Shifting his weight on the floor, he moves in close, smiling as he rests his face against mine. "I know I don't have to. I want to. So be a good girlfriend and just point me in the right direction."

"I can't. You're supposed to be *my* guest." I say, attempting to sit up and losing the battle as his hands gently push me back down.

Chucking to himself, obviously pleased with the way things are playing out and my lack of fight against his hands, he leans forward and kisses my nose before lifting his lips to my forehead. Shaking his head and lowering me down when again I attempt to get up.

"Jackson." I attempt to admonish him and placing a finger against my lips, affectively silencing me, he smirks.

"Humor me, sweetheart. I want to do this for you."

When I finally relax into the sofa, giving up the fight, he lifts himself up off the floor.

"Good girl."

Leaning over and brushing his lips against my head again, he follows here I'm pointing and heads toward the kitchen. Watching him go, still slightly amazed at how adamant he's been since he got here to get me off my feet, I smile. Closing my eyes only when he heads around the corner and out of sight.

After what only feels like minutes, but when my eyes open and adjust I can see has been almost an hour, I sit up on the sofa, about to call out when he walks into the room. Making his way over and holding his hand out, he waits until I take it before lifting me off my feet.

"Come with me, milady. Dinner is served."

As we make our way through the living room and into the kitchen, I see the sink filled with dirty dishes but no plates or food of any kind in sight.

"Where exactly is dinner being served, Jax?"

"When I came back into the room and realized you fell asleep, I took a look around. I came across the door that leads out to your veranda and since it's a relatively cool night, I thought we could enjoy dinner outside. In a way, recreating our first night together."

After saving for what seems like forever and looking at so many places it would make your eyes bleed in an effort to find the right one, I ended up here and had quickly fallen in love. But having spent the majority of my time since moving in a little over a year ago stuck at work, I hadn't gotten as many chances as I wanted to actually enjoy it.

Being able to stand out here and see the water a few short feet away, well, there was no better view in the world. Especially having him here to enjoy it with me.

Maybe that's why I didn't spend more time out here enjoying what basically had been the deciding factor on me buying the house.

I was waiting for the right person to share it with.

Pulling out my chair and waiting while I seat myself, he pushes me in and makes his way around to the other side, taking my hand in his the second he's seated comfortably.

"You must love having a place this close to the beach."

"To be honest, since I moved here, I've only been out here one or two times. One of them when I had to chase a raccoon away." I share, blushing in embarrassment at the lack of time I've spent here now that I know just how taken by it he is.

"Well, now that I'm here, I'm going to make it my job to change that. I haven't had a view like this since I left my condo in LA."

"I'm sure Toronto doesn't even begin to compare to LA, Jax."

"You're right. It doesn't." He agrees. "It's better."

Forcing the heat rising in my cheeks to slow, I focus my attention on the plate and bring the fork to my mouth, swirling the spaghetti tightly around it before slipping it in and moaning when the warmth and taste hits my tongue.

After taking another couple of bites once I feel his eyes lower away to start eating himself, positive now that the blush I felt creeping up on me before has passed, I ask the question I'm most curious to hear the answer to.

"What's better about Toronto?"

Placing his own fork down on the plate and reaching across the table until his hand is resting over mine, the smile playing on his lips transforming his entire face, he answers.

"I'm looking at her."

Jax

After I managed to make Avery go speechless for what feels like the tenth time since we left her office, we fall into a comfortable silence as we eat the dinner I prepared, the only sound around us the sound of our laughter when we catch each other stealing glances.

"Thank you for this, Jax." She says after putting her fork down and pushing the plate away. "It's been a really long time since I've had a home cooked meal. Let alone one that someone else prepared."

That makes two of us.

"It was my pleasure, honestly. Being on the road so much, I'm sure it's been just as long for me."

"You don't get home often?"

Isn't that the understatement of the century?

"When I first started out, I was staying pretty close to home so I'd just head back there after every show. When I signed with Smith and we started travelling, I was going back less and less. In the end, I decided to sell my condo and basically live like a nomad."

"Oh, Jax." She sighs. "That doesn't sound like any way to live."

"It wasn't." I agree easily. "But it wasn't like I had anyone to go home to. My parents and sisters are scattered all over the state and after everything with Melinda happened, the condo was the last place I wanted to be."

Reaching across the table and running her fingers in spirals over the top of my hand, she smiles, but it's weak. What I've admitted is obviously causing the one thing I didn't want to happen. Pity. It won't be long now before its shining back at me in her eyes.

The smile she's wearing just a precursor.

"Enough about all of that." I attempt to brush it off. "Are you done?"

"I am. I don't think I've ever eaten so quickly in my life."

Standing from the table and holding my hand out as I make my way around to her side, I motion to the plate and taking it, brush my lips over her hair in an effort to silence the argument I know is coming.

Avery needs to realize that making her dinner and then cleaning up after it, I want to do it. Not because I think she needs a break or I'm trying to woo her by making a good impression, but just because doing something as simple and dinner and cleanup gives me back a feeling I never thought I'd feel again.

A sense of home. A feeling of belonging. Stability in a world that due to my choices is anything but.

Rinsing the pots and placing them on the counter after filling the dishwasher with as much as it could handle, I head back to the sliding door leading outside. Pausing when as my hand goes to the handle, she stands from the table and makes her way over to the edge, looking out over the water.

Capitalizing on her being blissfully unaware of my return, I just stand and watch. Let the peacefulness of the moment really wash over me as I come to terms with just what being here with her right now means.

What I'm starting to feel for her or based on the visceral reaction I have whenever I so much as think of her—let alone get close—I already feel, and what it all means moving forward.

The truth is, what I'm sharing with her tonight, what we've shared in the week since we met, is something that even during the years with Melinda and in the three years that followed, I've never truly felt before.

The rush and intensity that comes when you first meet someone you're attracted to is there, the same way it was when Melinda and I got together, but with Avery, there's also something more.

Every beat of my heart, breath that I breathe, they all come easy, whether we're in the same room or not. Meeting her and connecting the way we did, it's causing that.

She's making me believe again.

Changing my view of what love is. Maybe even showing me the way it's supposed to be. What I'd been too blinded by what I thought was love with Melinda to be able to see.

It's such a powerful thing. When I'm not touching, holding or kissing her, I'm thinking about doing it and if that wasn't enough to prove to me that things are different given the way Melinda and I used to be, the electricity that seems to spark when she's near and the fire that rages just beneath the surface whenever we're together would.

The physical pull to her almost as strong as the emotional one we're building, and making me want things I told myself I never would again.

What I'm positive I'm in with her now.

Love.

Maybe I'm no better than a lovesick teenager, but everything I've been shown so far during our brief time together and our calls and texts—how easy it is to talk and open up—I love it all.

From her mind to her heart, straight to her soul and then her body, I want to love every part for as long as she'll allow.

Stepping onto the deck and moving toward her, I stop when she laughs, bringing her fingers up into her hair and attempting to brush it away just in time for the wind to knock it back down. Taken hostage by the stillness I find in what is such a simple act.

If for some reason I had to leave and could never come back, this is the vision I'd want to take with me when I go. Avery at her most natural. Not realizing anyone else is watching. The way she looks under the moonlight, the most beautiful vision I've ever seen.

Stepping forward, careful not to startle her, I wrap my arms around her and the way her body leans back easily into mine, like she read my mind, steadies me.

"It's a beautiful night." I whisper, breaking the silence.

"It is."

"I'm so glad I did this." I confess. "When I left last week, I honestly wasn't sure when or even if I'd see you again. As much as the calls and texts helped with that, they didn't quite fill the void of other things I needed."

"The need for human contact?" she asks softly.

"No, Avery. Not human contact. *Your* contact."

"And how are you finding the contact now, Mr. Merrick?" she taps my chest playfully.

Leaning my forehead down onto hers, our eyes locked and lost in each other, neither of us so much as blinking to break the connection, I continue the game.

"The contact is almost perfect."

"Almost, huh?"

"Yes, almost."

"Don't keep me in suspense. What would it take to make this perfect?"

"Something we shared before, but I've missed almost as much as the person I did it with."

Knowing I'm being purposely evasive, I'm ready for the frown and furrowed brow that quickly follow what I've said.

"We've shared a lot of different things in such a short amount of time. All of them things I've missed over the last few days. I'm going to need you to be more specific."

"It's something that you owe me since we didn't get to do it for nearly as long as I wanted. As I recall, you ending it far too soon so we could watch movies."

Shoving her hands into my chest playfully as she laughs, I take the opportunity and spin us both around when she shifts, only stopping when we're facing the inside of the house again.

"Jax, what are you doing?"

Pointing through the glass to where her stereo rests against the side of the staircase, I wait as the light bulb seems to go off and nuzzles into my chest with a soft laugh.

I've been thinking about that dance in my hotel room for days. The way she felt in my arms, pressed so closely to me that it felt like we'd become one instead of the two we were. Every move of our bodies weightless as we danced to the song on the radio and continuing it when the song ended and we just moved to music of our own design.

The music I'm positive our hearts created.

I want that again and this time, I want to make it last forever.

"Dance with me, Avery."

Chapter Thirty-Five

Emery

"Because I'm falling for you. And Emery? I don't want to fall alone."

Even a little over twelve hours later, I'm still having a hard time believing those words were actually spoken to me. Little old average Emery Davis. Don't even get me started on the fact that it was Brady Raines saying them.

I would chalk it up to being the most imaginative dream except I've been awake for the last two hours and the warmth that was born from those words alone, let alone everything that was said afterward, is still just as alive as the moment they were said.

He was right the first time he came to town. He really isn't like the others and all one has to do is look at the way he followed me home just to get a goodnight kiss at my door before driving away to see it. Let alone what happened thirty minutes later when Tim from work showed up at my door, trucking in about ten different bouquets of carnations, along with the lone bunch of lilies he said he was under strict instruction to deliver upstairs to my mom.

Brady is unlike anyone I've ever known.

He deserved the chance. I owed him that much after everything he's said and done since he got back into town and standing here in my kitchen, the milk I pulled out going warm with as long as I've been glued to the spot by the fridge door reliving the night, I'm determined to be different for him too.

Be unlike everyone in his life that came before me. Accept him for the man he is and not the larger than life wrestler he was before.

It's time for me to live in the moment.

The first step in doing that, accepting what despite how unreal it sounds, after the way the conversation went after he told me he was falling for me, ended with me as his girlfriend.

*****

"Emery, did you hear me?"

Unable to think straight, much less formulate a response, I sit frozen on the bench.

I was expecting him to say a lot, but declaring that he was falling for me definitely wasn't part of it. Especially since until we'd come out here and he started unloading, I wasn't even sure he liked me.

"Is your silence a good thing or a bad thing?"

"I heard you." I say, finally finding my voice. "I just...I think I'm in shock."

"Hmm..." he hums. "Shock isn't good."

"In this case it might be." I admit even though right now I'm not entirely sure myself. "But just to be sure, I think I'm going to need you to say it again."

"What part?"

"You're falling for me? As in love?"

He nods almost the second I answer the question and just like the first time he said it, everything just seems to stop. Time seems to freeze, the noises around us fading until I can't hear them at all, and even the wind, which until that moment had been moving swiftly, stopping altogether.

Yep. This is definitely shock.

"I know it sounds trite and that if it were happening to me, I would think it was some kind of ploy, but I'm telling you, Emery. There's no other explanation I can come up with for the level of stupidity I've been displaying. The feelings I have that I have absolutely no control over."

"I have some ownership in this too, Brady. After what happened on the phone that day, I basically deleted you from my life, at least in any way I could at the time. I didn't understand and *honestly, I didn't want to understand what your position was. I'm sorry."*

"You don't owe me a thing. Least of all an apology. This is all on me, Em."

"I know that's what you think, but I think we're both guilty. I knew where you stood with Kelly, you were upfront with me about that from the start. I should have given you the benefit of the doubt and known that what you were saying on the phone stemmed from that."

Running his fingers through his hair, he reaches out to touch me but stopping himself before his hand can make contact.

Uncertainty at its finest.

"I want to start over, and this time I really mean start over. I want the chance to do this right. I mean, I can't be openly affectionate in public until the divorce is final, but if you'll have me, I would really like to be able to call you my girlfriend."

Breathe Emery.

"And if I say no?"

"Then I would leave. Head back out on the road and back to whatever life I've got left waiting for me in Florida. I would respect your decision."

Mulling over his words, remembering what the last couple of days have felt like with me pretending not to be affected by what had most definitely felt like a knife being plunged straight into my heart, I focus on what trusting him would mean.

The risk I would be taking if I let him in again and what I would feel like if I didn't.

"Emery, please say something. Scream at me if you have to, yell even, but please end the silence. I can't take much more. It's already been two days too much already."

"You want me to be your girlfriend?" I repeat, paying close attention to the way my heart seems to soften with the use of the word. "But we can't be public about it until after the divorce is final. Do I have that right?"

"Yes. Even though keeping you a secret makes me sound like an even bigger jerk than the way I treated you on the phone. I want a real shot to prove I'm not the asshole I was the last time we

spoke. The first step to getting that is admitting what I really want."

"Which is to date me even though we both know you're going to be spending the better of the year on the road?"

"Yes, but using every day off I have to be with you. I know it's asking a lot and I don't really have the right, but can you do it?"

Looking at everything he'd done in order to make things right. Showing up here when he didn't have to, giving me the flowers, and baring his soul the way he has since we walked out here, the answer is obvious.

Of course I want to be his girlfriend.

Our time in the water, no matter how short, bonded me to him. That one intimate moment meaning more than just some random screw in the lake to me.

Brady Raines has left a mark on my soul and he doesn't even know it.

"If I agree to be with you, you have to do something for me and this time follow through so that what happened before never happens again."

"When I told you I was falling for you, it wasn't just words, Emery. I'll do whatever you need me to. Whatever it takes to keep you in my life."

"As appealing as it is thinking of ways to make you jump through hoops, what I have in mind is much simpler."

"And that is?"

"If this is going to work, you need to find more ways than just calling to stay in touch. You need to put in the effort, something I know we both agree we didn't before. When I said I was worried about you, I meant it. If I'm going to be your girlfriend, public or not, I need it to be all the way. You need to be all in. Can you do that?"

Not wasting a second, he answers me in the way I crave, but am the least prepared for. Crashing his lips down on mine and letting all the passion and need that had built up since our time in the water pour out into it, his lips hard and unforgiving against mine.

Just the way I want them to be.

Pulling away a few seconds later, he bites my lip before reaching into his pocket and pulling out his phone. Confused, I just watch in silence as his fingers glide across the screen, a minute or two of just the sound of the clicking keyboard as he types before sliding it back into his pocket.

Leaning his forehead against mine, he smiles when my own phone begins to vibrate.

"You going to get that? He asks, the grin never once wavering. "It might be important."

Pulling it out and looking down at the screen, I see the result of what he was doing on his phone.

I missed you so much, girlfriend. <3

Five words and a heart that repeat the promise his lips made when they took mine.

"I missed you too...boyfriend." I whisper and proving it, I kiss him, this time softer, the desire taking a backseat to the only feeling in the moment even more powerful.

Love.

*****

"Emery?"

Looking up and seeing April, my mom's day nurse standing at the entranceway of the kitchen with her lips drawn tight, I swallow down the lingering effect of Brady and focus on what I should have been when I woke up this morning.

My mother.

"What's up?" I ask and when her eyes lower to the ground my mood plummets. "April, did something happen?"

"No, at least not the way you're thinking. I was just wondering if you had a couple of minutes to talk."

Motioning to the chair across from me, I wait as she crosses the room and takes it, lifting her hands and bringing them together tightly on the tabletop.

"I know that it's not something you want to hear, but with each day that passes, I think it's something we really need to discuss."

"What is?"

"Emery, your mother, despite appearing in the best possible spirits whenever you're around, is getting worse."

I've known she's been getting worse since before Avery came to visit and with her daughter now gone and across the border again with only daily calls to tide her over, she's struggling to keep going.

"I know she is. I've tried my best to ignore it and believe she'll bounce back in a couple of days. But when those couple of days turn into a couple of more and nothing changes, it's hard to ignore."

"Can I offer some advice?"

"Of course. You're practically family, April. You can say whatever you want."

"I know how she feels about going back into the hospital, wanting her final days to be here surrounded by the people that love her, but with her condition deteriorating more rapidly every day, I think you might want to talk to her about going back."

"Is there something they can do that could turn this around?"

Shaking her head before again lowering her eyes to the table, I get my answer. The entire reason she ended up back here to begin with wasn't because it was her dying wish the way we've all let her think. It's because along with her wish, the doctors said all they could do at this point was make her comfortable.

Something I know she won't be if I talk her into going back. There's no comfort at all to be had at the hospital. Not for anyone.

"How much longer do you think she has?"

Everything is a guess at this point, but I want to know just how bad April thinks it is. I already know it has to be pretty bad if she's coming to me, but whether its days, weeks or even hours, I need to know where we stand.

"I can't say for certain, but if I were to hazard a guess, I would say a couple of days, maybe a week at most. In saying that,

I also think it couldn't hurt to call your sister and fill her in. I'm sure she'll want to be here to say goodbye."

Avery. Shit.

In the midst of this conversation, not once did I factor her in. The events of the last week still so new that my default setting is to go it alone.

April is right. I need to reach out to Avery and let her know what's really going on.

If I don't and Mom somehow slips away before I have the chance to, I'll never be able to live with myself and something tells me Avery wouldn't be able to live with it either.

"I'll call her when I head upstairs later."

"That sounds like a good idea."

"Thank you for coming to me, April. I know it wasn't easy and I appreciate it. So much has happened in such a short period of time that I needed the wakeup call."

"Anytime." She responds, but where I expect her to turn and head back upstairs, she lingers. "For what it's worth, she's been a lot happier since Avery came home and you all reconnected. It's done her heart a world of good."

"That makes two of us."

"Emery, there's one more thing."

"What's that?"

"Whoever the man is that filled the living room and her room with flowers, hold onto him. She probably won't tell you, but the first thing she said when she woke up this morning, were those words."

Of course she did.

She's always just going to know what's best.

"I plan on it." I tell April and when she smiles, I know that the answer I've given is not only the right one, but it's also going to be the one she heads up now and shares with my mom.

Giving my hand a little squeeze, she turns and heads out, leaving me alone with my thoughts.

One in particular. Sweet to think about it, but also true.

Brady is my one.

Brady

Flipping channels and coming across yet another hockey game in what seems like an endless stream of them, I push the power button on the remote and toss it on the table beside the bed as the screen goes black.

The silence in the room giving me ample time to think about the last couple of days, especially the night before and exactly what it all means moving forward. One truth in an endless stream of them standing out more than the others.

Being here with Emery is where I belong.

Everyone for months had been telling me to move on. Not missing an opportunity to remind me that I deserved more than the hand I was being dealt with Kelly and that if I just let go, I'd find it.

Now that I'm actually doing it though, there's a nagging voice in the back of my mind telling me that I need to slow down. Not take what I know I want with Emery out into the light where anyone can see because in doing it, I could ruin it before it even begins.

The very real threat of my soon to be ex-wife and the endless ways she could use the knowledge to her advantage in our divorce, too strong to ignore. Emery being dragged into what I know would be one hell of a mess if Kelly got wind of it, making me doubt everything I just spent the night trying to rectify.

No matter how much I care and how badly I want to experience this, I can't let her get dragged down with me.

I don't much care what Kelly does to me, having already lived through enough with her over the last nine years to see anything she might throw at me coming, but the same can't be said for the girl I just brought home.

These doubts now, I know where they're coming from and it's got nothing to do with what I know is looming on the horizon when I do head back to Florida in order to see the divorce through to its end in court.

It's because what we shared at her store and the kiss I'd given her before letting her slip out of the car when I followed her home was too damn right.

When things are this right, it usually means it's only a matter of time before the shit hits the fan and something, or someone, comes along to fuck with it.

Having already lied to Marie and Smith, it was already happening. Which just made the need to keep what I was doing here and what I'm doing with Emery a secret. Keeping my mouth shut so that when I do head out in two days, I do so having the girl and my job.

When what I really want to do is climb to the top of this hotel and scream to the entire world that I'm falling for the raven haired beauty with the adoration for carnations and boneheaded wrestlers.

The way she deserves.

Twisting over in bed as my phone starts ringing, I slip it off the end table and bring it to my ear.

"Raines."

"Good evening to you too, Brady."

Pulling the phone away and staring at the lit up screen, I groan.

I should have known it was too good to be true.

"What do you want, Kel?"

As her laughter filters over the line, I do my best to block it out. A sound that for years I'd been so familiar with and adored, but that now just sent shivers down my spine.

It can't mean anything good.

"I just had the most interesting phone call."

"And this has to do with me, how?" I demand, wishing now that I'd signed the papers sooner so I didn't have to sit here and attempt to be civil.

"It was about you."

"Alright, I'll bite. Who called and what did they say?"

"Marie called, Brady. She said you told her that you had to fly home to deal with issues surrounding our divorce." Swallowing the lump in my throat at being caught in the lie, I wait with baited breath for her to continue. "Issues she specifically asked that I cease causing as it was affecting your ability to do your job. Isn't that the funniest thing? I mean where would she come up with a crazy idea like that?"

Knowing by the smug sound of her voice that she knew it was me, but still wanting to hold onto the lie a little longer, I play dumb.

"I have no idea where she got it. What did you tell her?"

"I told her I would go easier on you and that I was sorry for any issues I caused. Don't worry, Brady. Your secrets still safe."

"That all? Because I've got somewhere to be and it's not on the phone with you."

"No, Brady, that's not all." She says, her voice noticeably lower. It was almost like in the moment she wasn't the cold hearted bitch she'd turned into when she took her mother's word over mine, but the girl I met when we were teens.

"I was hoping that if you weren't too busy, you might be able to come home. I've been doing some thinking. I think it's time we talk."

Where was her need to talk six months ago? For that matter where was it a few short weeks ago when like the stupid chump I am, I still attempted to reach out in order to save us?

Something's up. Her change in demeanor is just too damn convenient and I'm not buying into it. Especially not now. There's no way with everything I just set right with Emery that I'm gonna do a damn thing to risk it. Even if in not doing it, it would probably do more harm than good.

"I don't get you, Kelly. Didn't you tell me just last week that you moved on and wanted me to do the same? Now all of a sudden because of some call from Marie, I'm supposed to believe you've been thinking and want me to come home? Sorry, but if you want me to believe anything you've got to say, you're gonna have to try a little harder than that."

"No, Brady, this isn't all of a sudden. I've been doing a lot of thinking since the last time we talked and I even had a long talk with my mom. She admitted that what she told me was a lie, baby. You were telling the truth all along."

No shit.

I'm a lot of things, but a cheater isn't one of them. Considering the way I felt about her, the attention I showered her with when I was home for extended periods, attempting to make up for lost time, I would have thought she knew that. Turns out I'm a bigger idiot than I originally thought.

Just not stupid enough to fall for this.

"So your mom coming clean is supposed to be enough to get me to hop on a plane and come back? Are you delusional?"

"Brady," she whispers sighs. "I love you. I've always loved you. I'm sorry I took her word over yours. I should have trusted you."

Well, ain't that some shit? The words I spent the last six months praying to hear from her are being handed over on a silver platter. Too bad they're six months too late.

Not one week. Not a couple of hours. Not the amount of time Emery's been in my life and made me change my perception. None of it. It's exactly like I thought.

Six months too late.

"I've heard enough. Spare me your apologies and your sudden need to remember that you love me. I don't wanna hear it. I'll come home when I need to for court. That's when you'll see me. Now do us both a favor and don't call again."

Hanging up before she has a chance to attempt another lie in an effort to make me stay, I power down my cell before slipping it in my pocket, putting the call and Kelly out of my mind altogether.

The only thing that needs to matter now, the next stage in my plan to keep Emery.

Kelly and her ploy be damned. I was going to make this a night to remember and not even the threat of my soon to be ex-wife and all of the trouble I know she can cause if she really wants to, is going to stop me.

I'm going to give Emery what I promised last night before I left. What I've spent the last week running from instead of embracing it the way I should have.

I'm going to give her me.

Be the man she deserves.

Chapter Thirty-Six

Avery

"Do you remember the day we met?"

What a silly question. It was the day my life was forever altered. Something as simple as stepping out of my car to get gas starting what has become one of the most meaningful experiences of my life.

"How could I forget?"

Resting his hand under my chin, he guides it up until our eyes meet.

"I knew that day, Avery."

"Knew what?"

The sea of feeling I see flooding his eyes as he continues to lead our bodies in time with the tempo of the music tells me so much. The longer our gazes linger, the heavier the buildup of emotion in his eyes grows until it begins to spill over as a solitary tear falls.

Whatever it is he has to say so powerful it has him completely surrendering control.

"I knew you were the answer."

Affected by his words and the sight of his feelings on full display as another tear slips out and begins its descent down his face, I lift my hand and reach out, catching it. The warm dampness on my skin filling my heart and making it swell and spill over until he's not the only surrendering control.

"I don't understand, Jax."

"I've spent the better part of three years searching for my place. I lost it and things had gotten so heavy, I wasn't even sure I *had* a place anymore. I was a bystander in my own life. Watching powerless as I became more jaded and withdrawn with no way stop it. Finding solace or happiness in absolutely nothing. I gave up. Accepting that the way things were, was the way they were meant to be."

Hearing him speak this way about the way he felt before we met pains me because I was a lot like Jax. A bystander in my own life and completely unable to call out or wake myself up in order to change it.

Until him.

"The second we pulled in and saw your hair blowing in the wind, everything shifted."

"How?" I ask softly as he slows our bodies to a crawl, changing the dance, but still keeping it uniquely ours.

"The haze I'd been living in, going from one show to the next, never really paying attention to anything going on around me, determined to just do my job and move onto the next one, it lifted when I saw you, Avery. You, even with your eyes all wide and frightened, were the first person since everything fell apart that I could actually see."

Before I can respond, he brings his face closer to mine. His next words whispered against my skin and leaving their mark on me. Making me feel them everywhere until they wrap themselves securely around my heart where they belong.

"I saw you then, the same way I'm seeing you now. Clearly. You're the only thing that is."

His earlier question, I understand it now. Even more, I understand why I'm the answer.

The same way I understand that he's mine.

Why, even after every attempt I made, I could never make it work with anyone. Why my work always took precedence and why even though I felt the loneliness in every single pore of my being, I never did anything to change it.

It's because of him. This moment.

Nothing could work before because it was always meant to be Jackson.

Fate. Destiny. Soul mates. An instant connection made that while unable to explain, only becomes stronger and more potent the more time and attention given to it.

I just couldn't believe in its validity before now.

Before him.

Right here, I recognize this for what it is. Why even though common sense wants me to believe otherwise, my heart doesn't let me.

I know what I feel. What I've been feeling nearly as long, if not longer, than he has.

What I can't waste any more time trying to deny.

"Jax..."

"Hmmm?" he murmurs softly against the edge of my lips as he gently takes them with his. Lingering for just a breath of time before moving and doing the same to the other corner. The sweetness of the tender gesture only solidifying what I know to be the truth.

"I-I," I fumble over my words as he moves and fully captures my lips. "I love you. I'm in love with you."

Jax

"I'm in love with you."

Not *I'm falling for you* or even *falling in love with me*.

No, this beautiful woman with the soulful hazel eyes, soft as silk hair and larger than life heart, is *in love* with me already.

The same way I am with her.

It all makes sense now.

Why I could never shake feeling like I was only half a man. It wasn't because of what had been done to me. It's because until Avery had driven her way into my heart, I wasn't complete.

She's the missing piece.

Her love the only answer I'm ever going to need.

"You don't have to say it—"

Cutting her off before she has the chance to regret what she's spoken, I press another kiss to her lips, pulling away only long enough to whisper what I hope she sees is my attempt at telling her I feel the same way.

"Say it again."

"But—" she attempts again and just like before, I shut her down. Not wanting to say the words back until I hear her say it again. Needing to experience her own reaction to it almost as badly as my own.

"Avery, say it again."

"I'm in love with you, Jackson."

There it is. The musical lilt to her voice as she uses my full name and the buildup of water that any second is about to force its way out of her eyes.

She means every word.

They're not words spoken for affect, or to get something from me. No. Avery, right here in this moment, her body a perfect fit pressing so delicately into me, has her heart open and is letting it do the talking for her. Her feelings real. Pure.

A reflection of my own staring back at me.

With the words on the tip of my tongue, but driven by a need stronger than my own to tell her guiding me, I lower my hand from her face and slip it around her back. Smiling when I see the look of surprise cross her face, I bend and slipping my other hand around her legs, lift her off the floor. Quickly stealing her breath with a kiss before she has the chance to question what I'm doing.

The words she wants to hear coming, but not until I get her upstairs behind closed doors where not only can I repeat them as often as I want for the remainder of the night, but where I fully intend on showing her how deeply I mean them for just as long.

"Jax?" She questions when turning sideways once I've reached the top of the stairs and the door to her room, I break the connection and allow us both to come up for air.

Placing her down at the foot of the bed once we're in, she takes a step back and reaching out before she has a chance to lose her balance, I bring her flush to me again, only this time, her hand coming out across my chest halting me as she tries to get a read on just what's gotten into me.

Not realizing that it's her.

"I'm hopelessly in love with you, Avery. I have been right from the start. For some reason I can't explain, you got me. Here." Taking her hand, I place it over my heart. "You captured me, sweetheart. Every damn part of me. It's all yours."

Bringing her hand away from its place over my heart, my breath catches and my head fills with doubt. *Did I read this wrong?*

"Avery..." I start, but just like I'd done with her downstairs, she silences me with a kiss before lowering her head to my chest and repeating the same tender motion in the very spot where her hand had rested seconds before.

"Show me."

"Show you what?"

"How much you love me." She says with a smile. "Not answering me downstairs, kissing me quiet after you swept me off my feet; even asking me to repeat what I said. It all makes sense now, Jax. It's because what you feel, is more to you than words. So take all of the need, desire and passion I know you're trying to keep buried and use it to tell me in the only way you can."

Show her.

Her ability to see everything so clearly without me so much as saying a word only making me want her more. Pulling me even deeper into her spell and demanding that I show her how true my own declaration is.

Love her the way she loves me.

Heart and soul.

Completely.

And after undressing her, while attempting to maintain what's left of my self-control when her hands fall to my chest as she returns the favor, I lift her off her feet and place her down gently on the bed. Sliding in beside her and bringing my body over hers, I lock our fingers together above her head, never once taking my eyes off hers, that's exactly what I do.

I make her feel my love.

Chapter Thirty-Seven

Brady

"Yes, I got them. They were right where you said they'd be. Thank you."

For every time I damned my father for his popularity and the way he used his name and connections to open doors that would normally be closed otherwise, I was seriously eating my words now with as fast as the old man's connections had come through.

Since I got here, I've been looking for a way to make this visit count and while Emery was across town working, I focused every bit of energy I had into setting this plan, what could very well be one of the biggest surprises she's ever had, in motion.

Reaching over into the passenger seat and picking up my phone, immediately laying it down between the seats and hitting speaker so my attention wouldn't be pulled away from the road, I listen as the rings go in and pray with everything I've got that she picks up.

"Brady, didn't we already agree I would call you when my shift was over?"

"Hello to you too, Sunshine."

"What do you want, Raines? I'm sitting here trying to cash out for the night. I have a date with this super cocky—I mean, filthy rich guy to get ready for. You calling and keeping me from it is going to make me late."

"Wouldn't want to do that darlin'. I hear he gets real upset when people screw with his time."

"Right! And since I fully plan on getting laid tonight, I'm hanging up now."

"Laid, huh? You really think you two are ready for that?"

Snorting and attempting to cover it up by pretending to cough, she laughs and it doesn't take long for me to follow suit.

"Okay, enough joking. I'm actually calling for a reason."

"You're going to be seeing me in less than thirty minutes, Brady. What reason could you possibly have?"

"I'm gonna need you to stay there a little while longer. You think you can handle that?"

"It's after seven!" she groans. "The store is going to close and if I stick around, I'm going to end up being here alone since most everyone is starting to clear out already."

Shit. I don't want her there by herself. *Damn.*

"What's this about, Brady? Why do I need to stay here?"

"I had to head into Philly to handle some business and I'm on my way back, but I'm still a little ways away. I wanted to warn you so you didn't worry if I wasn't there when you got out."

"I can wait, but if you're gonna come here and pick me up, what am I going to do with my car?"

"We can pop back around and grab it after your hot date." I joke and when she laughs, my worry over leaving her alone, even if it was only going to be a few extra minutes, starts to dissipate.

"Fine. I'll see you when you get here, but don't make me wait too long. I have it on good authority that Matthias Kemper is doing a signing about fifteen minutes away from here. I'm sure he'd have no problem coming out with me."

Over my dead body Kemper is getting anywhere near my girl. I'll rip his head off before he can even take a step.

"Thirty minutes, Emery. I'll be there in thirty. Don't make me kill anyone tonight."

Ending the call, I focus on the way her doing something as innocent as joking with me about going to see another man has my blood ready to sear straight through my skin.

No one, and I do mean no one, is going to get within a foot of my girl. Her body, her attitude, every smile, laugh and blush she does, are for me only.

Pushing the car as much as I can without getting nailed, I pull up in front of her store, three minutes over the thirty minute deadline. Meeting her scowl and smiling my way through it when I pull to a stop directly in front of her and roll down the window.

"You're," she pauses, looking down at her watch. "Four minutes late."

"Very funny. You gonna get in the car or make me get out and put you in?"

Giving her the finger when she sticks her tongue out, she laughs before running around to the passenger side door and doing what I ask by sliding in.

"So, you wanna tell me why you had to spend the first half of our date night doing business?"

"The business was about us."

"Say what?"

"What I had to do, why I wanted to be the one to pick you up tonight and was late doing it. It's because I have a surprise for you."

"Why did you have to go all the way to Philly for a surprise?"

"What if I said it had to do with tickets to a hockey game?"

"I'd say, what the hell are we still doing here?" she laughs, reaching over and smacking me lightly on the arm, obviously thinking I'm joking, when the reality is I couldn't be more serious.

Something that once I reach over, hit the glove compartment door and grab the tickets, changes things real fast.

"Wait a second!" she exclaims and just as I start to pull out, I'm slamming on the brakes.

"Do we need to go back? Did you forget something?"

Shaking her head, she grins and looking down at the tickets, it all becomes crystal clear.

"Are these what I think they are?"

"If you think they're playoff tickets for the Flyers-Blackhawks game tonight, then yes. They're exactly what you think they are."

"What? How? When?"

"You're forgetting who and why, babe." I joke and again she reaches over smacking me.

"How did you pull this off?"

"Well you see, after spending the majority of my night watching nothing but hockey on TV after we got off the phone when you went to bed, I knew I wanted to take you to a game. I also knew that some random peewee league game wasn't gonna cut it. So I went one better."

"No kidding."

The grin on her face inescapable along with the shriek that's felt through the entire car when the reality of what awaits her finally sets in.

She's definitely getting her wish of getting laid tonight if she keeps this up.

"So I take it with you freaking out like that, this is okay?"

"Of course it's okay!" she screams again, fidgeting in her seat, reminding me of the way my brothers and I used to be on Christmas morning when we finally pulled our parents out of bed in order to open presents.

"Then sit back, close your eyes and relax. I'll wake you when we get there."

Unable to stop the smile that appears when she does what I say, I turn my attention back to the road. The response to the tickets reminding me of the thank you that is owed when I'm finally back home in Mississippi again.

Bill Raines, for the first time in years, earning it with the connections he's maintained.

Emery's reaction demands it.

Emery

"Holy shit! Did you see that save by Neuvirth?" I elbow Brady and when he side eyes me, point toward the Flyers goalie. "Damn! He's on fire tonight! Completely cock blocking the Hawks."

"Cock blocking?" Brady laughs. "I think you got the wrong sport, darlin'."

"Whatever. It's still true."

Turning my attention back to the game, not wanting to focus on the fact that again, much like the last two periods that have already passed, Brady is spending more time watching me and not nearly enough paying attention to the game he scored us tickets to.

I figured when he sprung the tickets on me in the car that he would be as into this game as I am, but he's not.

Don't get me wrong. I'm glad that he's not like the guy a few rows back who is passed out cold, but if this isn't his idea of a good time, why'd he bother getting the tickets in the first place?

Deciding not to wait to find out, I slip my arm through his and lean in close, making sure to get my lips as close to his ear as possible given how loud everyone is around us.

"You're not a hockey fan, are you?"

"Not really, but when I stalked you online a few days ago, I learned you were."

"So you got tickets even though you knew you'd be bored?"

"No."

"Then why?"

"I did it because I was hoping you would enjoy it, and considering you're on your feet more than in your seat, I'd say I nailed it. And Emery," he pauses, angling his head to the side before moving in and placing his lips directly to my ear, sending a shiver through me. "I'm not bored."

"You're n-not?" I stammer when he runs his tongue over my ear before nipping it with his teeth.

"Not at all. I've found something to watch that's way more entertaining than the game. Something that responds better too."

Attempting to keep my breathing in check, but powerless against the sensory overload that floods through me when his lips travel from my ear and down over my jaw, I suck in a breath, releasing it right when he presses his lips to mine. A soft moan escaping when parting my lips he slips his tongue deep into my mouth.

"See what I mean?" he whispers when he pulls away. "Definitely not bored."

For the first time since my mom sprung for tickets when I was six, I don't want to focus on the game. Brady effectively taking all of the pent up excitement and turning it into something else. Something only for him.

Desire. Need. A release from the very real aching awareness pumping through my veins and turning my insides to lava.

We need to get out of here.

"Emery..."

"Mmhmm?" I moan, the warmth from his breath against my ear sending waves of heat straight through my body and lingering in the one place that right now, he can't do a damn thing to help alleviate. My lady parts coming to life, more than a little ready for his attention.

"Your man scored." He growls into my ear before taking it with his teeth, my mind focused on the feel of his mouth on my body and not even taking into account what he's talking about. The game long since tuned out. The only man I want scoring being him.

"Not yet he hasn't."

"Fuck, Emery. Keep talking like that and I'm not going to be responsible for what happens."

Who knew a hockey game could be this hot?

I sure as hell didn't and I've been coming to games for nineteen years. Not once in that time had I ever thought about tuning out the players, the game, and the fans around us in favor of climbing into the seat next to me and doing the real scoring.

The fire Brady brought to life now ignited into a full blown burn as his hands begin their descent down my arm and over my thigh, grabbing it and massaging, making sure as he moves to moan his own pleasure in my ear.

Pleasure I desperately want to feel as the more his hand moves inward, I feel my panties beginning to dampen.

"We need to go."

Before he can answer, the crowd is on their feet and his hand is pulling away. A blast of cool air washing over me at the loss of his touch. Freezing me in place when I realize just close we'd come to taking things a little too far in public.

Hearing the sound of his chair flipping back as he follows the crowd and jumps to his feet, I turn and looking up, am met with my own need staring back at me in his heavy dilated eyes.

Offering me his hand, I slip mine into it and pulling me to my feet, he gives me the answer I've been craving since before the crowd rudely interrupted our moment.

"Let's get out of here."

Chapter Thirty-Eight

Jax

Feeling the warmth from the sun streaming through the curtains before cracking open an eye and being hit head on by the brightness, I twist around in the bed, turning completely away from the violation. Bringing my arm out and stretching it, brushing against the smoothest and softest skin I'd ever felt. Bringing my arms around her midsection and smiling when her body shifts closer to mine, the events of the night before come back in a flourish.

This isn't a dream.

I'm not imagining waking up in bed with Avery. I'm really here and living it.

Propping myself up on one arm, I sneak a peek over her shoulder and am surprised at what I find. Expecting her to be asleep the way I had just been, that's not at all what I get. Instead she's curled up close to the edge of the bed, a book resting in front of her with her hands moving delicately over the page before turning it, completely oblivious to the fact that I'm watching her.

The way she is right now another first for me.

While I'm sure that in my past there has been a time where a woman woke before me, never before have they woken up and not slipped out of bed. Content instead to stay as close as possible or like Avery now, be near and comfortable enough to read.

I could definitely get used to spending my days waking up like this if she's the one I get to wake up to.

Not wanting to disturb her by moving, but just like the night before, needing to lose myself in the feel of her, I lower my head to her shoulder and place a soft kiss before turning over onto my back.

"Good morning, sleepyhead."

Smiling at the soft sound of her voice, I watch as she closes the book and slides it over onto her nightstand before turning her body and her attention to me. Lowering her body down onto mine and resting her head in the crook of my arm, her hair falling in waves across my chest. The brief contact bringing back the warmth that I first woke up and pulling her even tighter into me, I place a delicate kiss to the top of her head.

"How long have you been awake?" I ask, the sound of my voice rough to my own ears.

"About an hour or so."

"Why didn't you wake me up?"

"Honestly, with everything you told me about the last two days, I figured I'd let you get as much sleep as possible. You looked so peaceful. The last thing I wanted to do was wake you."

This, another way Avery is different than the people I've been with before. Her actually hearing what I told her on the way back from her office, filing it away and caring enough about me to give me what she remembered my body needed.

Well, what it needed second to her.

I could definitely get used to this.

"Hey," she murmurs, stroking my face with her hand. "Where did you go just now?"

Bringing my hand up and resting it on hers, stopping her as she goes to pull it away by wrapping my fingers around, I give her the answer she's after.

"Nowhere, sweetheart. I'm right here with you."

"Then what you were thinking about? You looked so far away."

"I was just remembering last night and honestly, enjoying this morning."

Snuggling closer and almost as though she can see straight into my head and read my mind, kissing my chest. One kiss turning into two until her lips are trailing a gentle line all the way across before beginning their descent down.

"Do you really want to start that again?"

My words having no effect whatsoever as she continues to press her lips over every part of my exposed chest she can reach, I try again. "Don't you have to get to work?"

Pausing in her movement and meeting my eyes, I know with the pout developing on her lips that I'm killing whatever playful mood she was in.

"Mood wrecker. Speed Demon. Fun ruiner." She smirks, pulling away and moving to the end of the bed while I do the same, rolling over and finally sitting up. Hit again by the chill that seems to appear whenever there's distance between us.

"You can call me all the names you want, beautiful. It doesn't change the fact that I'm right."

Standing from the bed and grumbling under her breath, I jump up before she has the chance to get away, grabbing ahold of her and spinning her around quickly, bringing her close. Running my hand softly over her face before bringing my lips down on hers.

Her arms wrapping around me as she presses back, deepening the kiss and making me want to take back my earlier words in favor of tossing her back down onto the bed and recreating the magic we made the night before.

"I love you, Avery." I tell her when after a few seconds of enjoying her taste, she breaks the moment and pulls back.

"I love you too, Jax. Even when you're being a complete buzz kill." She smiles, pressing her lips to mine again and giving me a quick kiss. "But if you want to me to actually go to work today the way you claim, you're going to have to let me get ready."

Letting her go the way she wants, I kiss the tip of her nose softly before motioning with my hand to the bathroom door. Smacking her on the butt playfully when following my pointed finger she turns and makes her way toward it.

Finally looking away when she disappears into the bathroom and closes the door behind her, I turn my attention to the clothes strewn over the floor surrounding the bed. Collecting everything that we'd kicked off when I'd carried her up the stairs last night, I throw my shirt on and sit down on the bed, slipping my legs into my pants, met with the vibration of my phone as I'm pulling them up around my waist. The generic ringtone given to anyone that isn't family beginning to repeat a third time when by the time I've slipped on my socks, I pull it out and look at the screen.

Three missed calls and two incoming texts there to greet me.

Wanting to deal with the more pressing of the two first, I open up the call log and seeing the numbers, two of which I can see have left voicemails, I call in to pick them up.

The first from my sister Denise asking when I'm making my way home again. The second, the familiar grown of Smith, with Marie's voice going off in the background, shooting off questions while her husband tries to get a word in edgewise. From what I can make out, the call not even being about me, but Brady and his whereabouts, and ending with a request for a callback at my earliest convenience.

What I hadn't been expecting as I hit delete was for there to be another message waiting. This one different than the previous two as it was just a hang-up, but a callback number attached at the end that as I played it over in my head a few times, I still couldn't place as one I knew.

Pulling up the texts, figuring they're more of the same since Marie isn't against texting, I read over the one from my sister before finally landing on the one from the same number that hung up on the machine. One that as I read it over immediately makes my heart freeze and chills radiate down my spine. The reason for not recognizing the number making all the sense in the world now as I'd gone to impossible lengths to delete the sender from my life a year before.

Been thinking about you a lot today. Wanted to touch base. Miss you babe. XOXO

Melinda.

Not sure what to do with this newest development, especially with Avery only a few feet away, I closed out of it, bringing the phone back to the main screen before slipping it into the back pocket of my jeans.

Out of sight, out of mind.

Pushing the message out of my head, I head out and down the stairs to the kitchen, even more determined now to make sure the rest of the morning went off without a hitch.

The first step in doing that? Making breakfast.

Melinda Richardson and her drama be damned.

Avery

I can't put my finger on exactly what it is, but things have been weird since I left Jax alone to take a shower.

Sure, we had an enjoyable breakfast together. The both of us stealing glances across the table at each other before being caught by the other, laughing, and going back to eating.

The drive to work, with Jax taking me in his rental after leaving mine at the office the night before was more of the same. There wasn't anything super overt that someone looking at our interactions from the outside would assume was off, but I knew different.

Maybe it was the distant look I'd seen in his eyes the few times I did manage to steal looks at him without him noticing. How he didn't seem to be there in the kitchen with me but a million miles away. Or maybe it's the chaste way he kissed me goodbye before telling me he'd see me at home after work. The kiss after the other ones we've shared, tamer, with less feeling. Something that up until we slept together, had been the only setting Jax operated on.

Everything he was feeling he threw into every touch, every kiss.

Except for the one in the car.

Was he having regrets about last night? Had we taken things too fast too soon, even though our hearts seemed to have already decided during our time in Delaware that it was what we wanted?

Could I have gotten too swept away and made a mistake?

After attempting to call Emery to get her advice and failing, her phone ringing off about ten times before going to voicemail and the second call not even ringing at all, I was running out of options. I needed to focus on work but with the night, morning and every moment since taking over my mind, focus was the last thing I had. The only way I could see this working out being to sit down and explain it to someone that wasn't involved.

Which left me with two options.

My mom or Markus.

Neither option more appealing than the other, but my mom fairing slightly better than my boss.

Tapping my nails against the phone, I finally let my need to talk this out win and picking it up, dial the number that has now become almost as familiar as my own. Silently hoping as the rings go in that she's having a better day today than she had the last time I called.

A hope that's answered when I hear her voice over the line, her tone light, but obviously happy to hear from me.

"Good morning, Avery."

"Morning, Mom."

"I don't think I'll ever get tired of hearing you call me that." She sighs softly, the sound of it making my heart swell and fill with warmth.

"Good, because I've got twenty-five years to make up for, so you'll be hearing it a lot. Wouldn't want you to get tired of it."

"Never, baby girl." She whispers softly over the line before her voice picks up and she nails me for calling. "Now since I know you're at work and usually don't have the time for calls, why don't you tell me prompted this one."

"I need some advice."

"Well, I'm all ears. Let's have it."

"I've been seeing someone." I admit, immediately feeling guilty for not bringing that to her sooner.

"The same man that you spent time with when you were here? The friend of the young man Emery has been involved with?"

"One and the same."

"Are you happy?" she asks and the pressure that was lifting slams down on me again full force. It should be an easy question to answer because with the way we spent the night and then the earlier part of the morning, I am most definitely happy, but there is still that niggling doubt in the back of my mind that makes it impossible to answer yes honestly.

"That's actually what I'm calling to get your advice about."

"You don't know if you're happy?"

"No, I do." I shake my head before remembering that we're on the phone and stopping myself. "He makes me happy, Mom. It's just..."

"It's just what, honey? Tell me what happened to make you doubt what you feel."

"He spent the night." I admit, even over the phone feeling my cheeks heat with the admission. "Things were great when we woke up this morning, perfect really."

"So what's the problem?"

"I went to take a shower while he went downstairs to make us breakfast and I don't know what happened, but it was like something shifted and no matter what I do to try and not focus on it, I can't seem to shake it. It feels like something's changed and not in a good way."

"What happened between you to make you think things changed?"

"He was quiet, more subdued. Like he had a lot on his mind. I didn't want to push it so I just kept making random conversation, but there was this look in his eyes, Mom. It was like he wasn't there with me and it didn't get any better when he dropped me off at work."

"Okay, well what happened when he dropped you off?"

"He kissed me."

"That's good, right?"

"Yeah, of course it is. Kissing Jax is always a good thing. It's just the kiss was different than the others."

"Could it have been that because he was dropping you at a place of business that he held back a bit? Wanted to keep a respectable distance?"

Of course it's possible and I want to slap myself for not being the one to think of it first. He had no issue sending me flowers because he was doing it all from a distance and wouldn't have had to worry about anyone from the magazine seeing it. Dropping me off at the front of the building where anyone could have come up on us, well that was an entirely different thing.

Leave it to my mom to get it easily.

"That's probably all that was. You're right. I guess I was reading too much into after all. But what about the other stuff.

The morning and the weird awkward silences and his zoning out? How do I explain that and the feeling I have that something is wrong?"

"I'm not sure, sweetheart. There could be a lot of different reasons for the way he acted before you left the house this morning. He could be feeling nervous after what you shared the same way that you are. He could have a lot on his mind and just not have the words to explain it, or maybe he got a call or something happened and he just needs time to process it. There's really no way of telling."

All of her reasons make sense but it's the last one that my mind lingers on most. Could that have been what happened? Did he get a call or a message that changed him in some way and he just hadn't brought it up because he hadn't had time to process it? Or is it more?

The same tightness I experienced when Markus talked to me about Jax and Melinda rises to the surface now, my insecurities over just how fast I allowed this to move and exactly what it is and where it was going taking over and making it impossible to see or hear much else.

How many times had I heard horror stories about wrestlers and the way they did things on the road? Marriages falling apart, relationships breaking up and even careers being ruined by the combination of drugs, alcohol and women?

Enough times to know that I wanted more for myself than that.

Yet here I sit on the phone with my mom, in a relationship with one of those very same men and doubting not only him but myself.

"Where are you going in that pretty head of yours, little one?" she speaks again, pulling me away from the manic road my mind was about to take, bringing me back to her just the way I need her to.

"Nowhere, Mom. Just thinking about everything you said."

"Can I offer some of that advice that you called me for?"

"Of course. Please."

"The reason for Jax acting different could be just about anything, but the worst thing you can do for yourself and your relationship is to try and figure it out on your own. If you want to know why things are different, there's only one thing you can do."

Go to the source.

She doesn't even have to say the words. Given what I do for a living and how my personal situation pertains to it, the advice is simple. I need to talk to him. It's the only way this feeling is going to cease.

"You think I should ask him, right?"

"I do think you should talk to him, yes, but there's more. When you question him, don't forget to listen. As hard as it might be to hear, whatever it is that changed the way he's acting with you, just listen."

Just listen.

I can do that no problem.

But before I can tell her the same, she speaks again and what I had thought was going to be easy, suddenly becomes that much harder.

"Don't just listen with your ears, Avery. Anything worth hearing won't just be coming from his head. Make sure that when you hear him out, that you do it with your heart too."

Listen with my heart. Right.

"That's where you'll get the answers you want. In the words spoken from his heart to yours. The same way that for the past twenty-five years, ours have."

Chapter Thirty-Nine

Brady

"I still can't believe you took me to a hockey game when you can't even stand the sport." Emery jokes before forking another bite of her breakfast into her mouth.

After leaving the game early and stopping by her work to pick up her car, with the desire that had fueled us almost screwing at the arena sufficiently tamed when she brought up wanting to head home to be there for her mom, she mentioned wanting to take the party back to her place, and I hadn't had any complaints.

Leading us to a night spent in her bed with me devouring her. Needing to get a fill of her I didn't think would ever come and her meeting me with an insatiable need of her own. One that even when we passed out sated a few hours later, didn't seem to be satisfied even in the morning light.

My dick wanting her again almost as much as my heart seemed to.

"And a playoff game no less." I tease, laughing when not paying any attention, she opens her mouth to say something and some of the lingering milk she'd just taken dribbles back out over her chin and down onto her shirt.

Always the gentleman or forever a perv, I lean across the table, curbing my laughter before running my tongue over her chin, licking it off. Lowering my eyes to the very real stain now setting in on her chest, tempted by the lace trim of her bra peeking out at her neckline.

"You're insatiable, you know that?" she asks, when my lips follow the trail my eyes had taken and I taste the exposed area of flesh.

"Mmhmm." I moan in agreement, kissing a trail from her chest back up her neck.

Fueled by memories of our kissing in the past and what it led to, I continue tasting her, until her sharp intake of breath when I bite down and begin to suck, pauses me.

"It's your fault. You taste so damn sweet. I can't help myself."

Moving from her neck, over her chin and up to her lips, where I take the biggest taste as she moans softly, I feel her body begin to melt into mine.

"I somehow doubt that." She argues, taking the control back and leaning her body back into the seat, her lips curved up in a grin. Obviously enjoying the tease she'd just given me. One that when I follow her lead and move back to the seat across from her has he eyes going wide.

"This is all the proof I need about your sweetness, darlin'. All your doing." I look down and point to the beast she's successfully awakened in my jeans.

"Oh, that reminds me." She says, pulling her eyes away from my crotch and putting it back on her food as she moves it around on the plate. "In your animalistic state last night, you missed a call."

"I did?" I ask, shifting uncomfortably in the chair, righting myself with the mood effectively killed.

"Yeah. I heard it somewhere between round two and three, but put it out of my head until it happened again this morning during your shower."

"Did you see who it was?" my breath halting, hoping to god that whatever it was that prompted Kelly to call yesterday had been worked out and it wasn't a message from her waiting.

"No. I mean, I probably could have looked, but I didn't feel right about it. All I saw was that you missed two calls."

Thank fucking Christ.

"But I have been doing some thinking about them, Brady."

"What are you thinking?"

"I was thinking, what if one of them was from Smith or Marie? I know you told me that you lied to her about why you wanted time off, but I'm thinking that in doing it, you might have caused more problems. Like, what if she found out and that's what the call is that you missed?"

She has a point. It was even more possible with the strange call I'd gotten from Kelly when I got here. If Marie was reaching out to her after the lie I told and she'd said anything to make Marie suspect that I wasn't telling the truth, the call could very well be about work.

More importantly, my termination.

"I did what I had to do to see you, Em. If I hadn't lied to get here, I never would have gotten the chance to make up for being a bonehead and we wouldn't have been able to share what we have since. You get that right?"

Reaching a hand over the table and placing it delicately on top of mine, she smiles. "Of course I do and I'm glad you did it. I just don't want you jeopardizing your career over something as small as seeing me. We can figure out another way around that where no one has to lie."

Before I can answer and tell her there's nothing small about my desire to see her, my phone starts vibrating across the table, effectively ending the discussion and taking what had been a pretty playful mood and driving it straight into the toilet.

Bringing her hand to my lips, I kiss it, placing it gently back down onto the table top and picking up my cell.

"We're not done." I whisper before pressing talk. "Raines."

"Son! Glad I caught you." The raspy voice of the man himself, Bill Raines, bellows over the line.

"Actually, I was just about to—"

"You're about to shut your mouth and listen."

Here we go.

"You want to explain why I'm fielding calls from Radley Smith and his bitch of a wife?"

"Yeah, about that..."

"Don't even bother lying, Brady. I already had someone fill in the blanks."

Someone already told him? Considering the only people that even knew I was here were Jax, Smith and his wife, and by his own admission it's not them, I don't have the first clue where he got his information. But just like always, he doesn't keep me in suspense for two long.

Meeting Emery's eyes when again, her hand comes across the table attempting to rub away the tension by running her fingers over my now fisted knuckles, I roll my eyes and covering her mouth she chuckles softly.

"Despite your every attempt at distancing yourself, it appears as though Kelly is doing what any good wife would do. Even doing it in her devastated and heartbroken state."

Devastated my ass.

"Imagine my surprise finding out that not only are you not with her where you should be, but that you're off in Delaware dipping your dick in a hot piece of pussy that's not hers."

That vulgar piece of shit. No way am I letting him talk about Emery like that.

"That's enough, Dad. There's no reason to talk like that, unless you want me to hang up. Whether I'm in Delaware dipping my dick or not, it's none of your business. The same way my marriage is."

There's no missing the rise to Emery's eyes, the knowledge that she's being talked about doing the complete opposite of what I wanted today. Filling them with defeat instead of passion and love the way I want.

"As for Kelly, you're the one that told me she was full of shit back when I told you I was going to marry her. So spare me that support shit. I see right through it."

"What happened to you? When did you start lying and throwing everything under the bus for a piece of ass? Start biting the hand that feeds you?"

The hand he means isn't CPW. It's him. Of course he's gonna turn it around until the entire thing is about him. Bill Raines at his finest. I've been through this so many times I almost know the script by heart.

"I needed a couple of personal days, Dad. Stop making this into something more than it is."

"Two days that you had to lie in order to get?"

"Yes!" I growl, tempted to throw the phone across the room and about to do it too until Emery's hand slides off mine and she backs away, my anger obviously scaring the shit out of her.

Scaring the shit out of me too considering I don't usually have an audience for this bullshit.

I need to end this fucking call before I do something stupid.

"Look, it's been real, but I've got someplace I need to be. Can you wait until later to berate the shit out of me?"

"Listen closely boy, because I'm only going to say this once. There is a one way ticket to Vegas waiting with your name on it at the airport. To the show you're bailing on to get your dick wet. If you give a shit about your career, about your future in this business, and being able to settle down before you're sixty, you'll be on that flight."

"And if I'm not?"

"Then consider yourself cut off. From the family, from the money, and after the conversation I had with Smith before calling you, CPW. Consider yourself done."

Fuck! What the hell is happening right now? Since when did two days off turn into me losing everything?

Towing the company line, following every damn piece of advice my old man has ever given me and making him proud in every damn thing I did has been completely thrown out the window all because I made the choice to come here and chase after what could possibly be the best damn thing to ever happen to me.

The one aspect of my life that didn't center solely on what I did for a living.

Where most people can have the love and respect of their family *and* the girl of their dreams, it looks like I'm being given a choice and god damnit, it's not one I want to make.

I don't want to have to choose between Emery and wrestling.

"Dad, just stop and think for a second here. Don't you think you're being a little overdramatic?" I appeal to him. An appeal that falls on deaf ears.

"Get your ass to the airport and on that flight, Brady. I won't tell you again."

With the sound of him slamming the phone down reverberating in my ears, I end the call and just as I'm about to throw it down on the table and attempt to fix what just happened with Emery, it rings again.

"Dad?" I answer quickly.

"Brady, baby. I didn't wake you, did I?"

Hearing her voice, my blood runs cold. What are the odds? First my father and now her.

"What the fuck do you want, Kel?"

"I was just wondering if you'd given any more thought to coming home. We really do need to talk." She replies sweetly, the sugar just dripping off her words and turning my stomach inside out.

I don't even have to look across to see what this is doing to Emery. I already know. The way it's turning me inside out, my mind still trying to process everything that had gone on with my father, had to be happening twice as hard to her.

The conversation, my anger since I stupidly picked up the phone, and now the very person that stands between me and a happy future with her on the line trying to act like the devoted wife she's not, definitely more than she signed on for.

There's no way I'm gonna be able to make this right. There's just too much shit to sift through. I was right. I'm too damn complicated and Emery deserves a hell of a lot better.

"We have absolutely nothing to talk about. You made all the decisions for us six months ago."

"Baby, don't be like that. I told you, I made a mistake and I want the chance to make it right. Please just come home so we can talk."

Pulling the phone away from my ear, and covering it with my hand, I attempt to do some kind of damage control with the girl sitting across from me with what I can already see is a combination of fire and hurt in her eyes.

"It's Kelly. She wants me to come home so we can talk. I guess she's finally sick of making me talk through her lawyer."

The lie sounds awful even to my own ears, but I can't let her know the truth. I can't let her know that my father has my balls in a sling and is making me choose between her and wrestling. And I damn sure can't let her know that Kelly is attempting to get me home so she can win me back. I've already hurt her enough.

This will break her and the only one of us allowed to break right now is me.

I've got to keep her as far away from this as possible. Which means I've got to give into their demands.

I've gotta go home.

I'm sorry. I mouth before pulling my hand away from the phone and ending this once and for all. Letting them win, just the way they wanted.

"I'll see you later tonight."

Ending the call and tossing the phone back down hard onto the table, no longer caring if the damn thing breaks or not, I slam my fist off the table and sigh heavily before finally lifting my head and meeting the eyes of the girl whose heart I know I just broke.

Looking away quickly, she pushes her seat back and stands, grabbing our plates from the table and making a beeline for the sink. Turning her back to me completely as she focuses all her attention on turning on the water and attempting to scrub them clean.

What feels a lot like her trying to scrub the effect of me clean off her at the same time.

Sitting and waiting for her to say something, or even just turn around and curse me out, nothing comes. She just continues to scrub away at the dishes and leaving me at a complete loss of what to say or do next.

It's only when a few minutes later, as the water splashes up and over the countertop that she finally reacts as a garbled sounding sob escapes and her body gives out as she sinks against the counter, gripping the edges to hold her up.

The words that follow taking the knife that had already been plunged six feet deep into my heart seeing her break and not being able to do a damn thing to fix it and slamming it straight into my soul.

"So much for making things right, Brady. I should have known falling for you...giving you my heart, would only end with you breaking it. Go. Do whatever you need to do. Just do it far, far away from me. I'm done. I can't do this anymore."

Emery

Giving my last customer of the day their change and watching them walk away before turning back and slamming my register shut, I'm met with a gasp followed by a throat clearing.

"What?" I spin around and curse under my breath when I realize it's my boss.

Shit.

"Not sure who pissed you off today, but taking it out on the register is probably not the way to go."

Twenty-four hours.

Twenty-four long and torturous hours since one of the best dates I've ever been on had been blown to shit by not one, but two phone calls.

"Sorry Laney. It's just been a long day."

"You've been having a few of those lately."

Of course I have. They've all been long since I let Brady into my life and handed over my heart without doing a proper screening to see if he even deserved it.

"I know." I embarrassingly admit, hating the fact that despite my every attempt otherwise, I managed to take my personal crap to work again. "I just need to go home, soak in a bubble bath for a while and I'll be good as new. This won't happen again."

Giving me clearance to go with a bob of her head before turning and walking toward the back, I make quick work of pulling my tray and heading to the cash room to count it.

The faster I can get this over with, the better. No one else needs to be made a part of my emotional breakdown.

How could I have been so stupid?

I knew nothing was resolved when he got to town. He was still married, still not mine for the taking even though for a short time, I'd forgotten that in favor of just enjoying the moment. Nothing had changed on that front, so why did I just let him back in so easily?

Because when he got here, he was honest with you.

Right. How could I forget?

He was honest, even though at the end of the day, he still chose her over me. Agreeing to go home when I thought for sure after the time we shared together, he knew his place was with me.

Brady belonged with me.

At least, that's what I so stupidly, maybe even blindly, believed.

The truth is, what my mom said is wrong. Brady isn't going to end up being my one, and our relationship—whatever it is, isn't the kind of epic that real love stories are made of.

We're not meant to be anything.

Depositing the money into the cash bag, I zip it up tight and slip it into the padlocked container, unlocking my cash locker and sliding it in before slamming it closed, the same bitter way I did out on the floor. Enjoying the way the metal clanging sounds with as angry as I am. A metal locker door slamming, closing the door on us the very real way I did yesterday when I asked him to leave.

I wish I could go back in time. Back to when things were easy and Brady was just a wrestler I paid good money to watch whenever him and the rest of the CPW roster came to town.

Getting involved with him, letting feelings develop as quickly as they did, especially when I knew better, it ruined all of that.

Waving goodnight to the night shift girls, I make my way out through the store's automatic doors and make a beeline for my car. My phone, which had been eerily silent all day, beginning to vibrate against my side.

Jogging across the parking lot, I stop once I'm safely across and out of the path of incoming cars and slip it out to see what I missed.

Five Missed Calls.

Going into my call log, I see that four of them are all from the same number and the other one, a number for one of my mom's nurses.

Slipping around and through the cars in the parking lot, I reach my car and after throwing my purse across the seat, slide in, shoving the key in the ignition and starting it up, using the minute or two before I put it in gear and pull out to head home, to go over the numbers again.

Staring at his name with the bracketed four beside it, I debate the pros and cons to calling him. Telling him I overreacted and that I understand how awkward this situation is. That if he's willing to forgive me and give me another shot, I won't send him away again.

My head and my heart doing battle and in the end, my head winning out. Avery's voice fighting through the haze and putting me back in my place.

His life is complicated and it's only going to hurt more the longer I stay in it. What I did sending him away, is what's best. Until he can figure out what he wants one way or the other, it's safer this way.

I have to be strong. Resist the urge to back down and give into Brady just because of who he is and what he makes me feel. I'm not some stupid naïve little girl. I'm Emery freaking Davis. I deserve better than to be someone's side piece or even rebound.

Two things that no matter how badly my heart aches over what happened twenty-four hours ago and all that we shared before it, I can't deny being.

Screw you, Brady Raines.

Looking down at the log again, it's then I'm reminded of the fifth call. The one from my mom's nurse. Noticing the little cassette tape symbol to the left of it, signaling a message left, I dial into my voicemail and hit the speaker button once I've entered in my passcode.

The shaking in her normally soft voice as she asks me to come home, sucks all the air from the car and my lungs. Making my heart freeze before it drops, leaving me with a sick feeling in my stomach and a spinning sensation in my head.

Her final words confirming what I've been trying to deny since Avery came home, but I can't anymore.

It's happening.

While I've been wasting the day at work and then here in the car bitching and moaning over what's going on with Brady, making everything about myself, the unthinkable has happened.

Her struggle is over.

She's gone.

Chapter Forty

Jax

Watching intently as Avery put the finishing touches on the breakfast she made, I'm struck again by just how easy things are with her.

How something as simple as the way her fingers run delicately over the utensils, can get the same rise out of me that putting together a match does.

Taking her time, careful not to touch any of the food directly, yet placing it so perfectly on the plate that I can almost forget I'm in someone's kitchen and not some fancy restaurant where things like food placement and setup actually matter, completely captivating me.

The smile she wears the entire time, and the way it never once lets up, no matter how busy she seems to get is a look I know all too well. One that I've worn myself whenever I get time off and can spend it surfing or anything remotely having to do with the mechanics of a match when I'm on the road.

Just further proof that she's perfect for me.

Taking a seat at the table while she moves from the fridge back to the counter putting the finishing touches on the meal, I use the time to let my mind wander to the message I still hadn't gotten around to deleting.

Surprise as even getting it, along with attempting to figure out why she's sending it to begin with, my reason behind keeping it, despite the way I know it would appear if anyone else caught it.

Contrary to what people think, there's no residual feelings lingering for Melinda or what for two years we had. The three years since has done a pretty good job at erasing that, along with what Avery's doing now. Showing me things that in all of the time I was with her, I never knew.

I can't seem to delete it or let it go because despite not wanting to care at all, I'm curious.

Has she found out I've moved on with Avery? Or is this more game playing and things have finally turned sour for her and Fortune and this is her way of reeling him back in?

I just need to delete that text and rid myself of it once and for all.

I'm sitting and watching the woman I love make us breakfast and instead of basking in that, enjoying the fact that out of all the people she could have chosen, I'm her choice, I'm sitting here because of a text with my head jammed up in the past.

Letting my obsession with understanding what the hell the text means take me away from the very real thing I have here.

Flicking my eyes up when I hear the sound of plate hitting the table, I return her soft smile before picking up the fork and diving straight in. My attention so drawn to it, I don't feel her eyes on me or her attempt at getting my attention until she clears her throat and taps the table with her own fork.

"Can I ask you something, Jax?"

Nodding and waiting for her follow-up question, I place the fork back down onto the plate and give her my full attention. Something that I have a feeling with the way I've been acting since I got the text, I haven't been doing enough of.

"You haven't said more than two words since you came downstairs. I guess I'm just wondering if you're okay or if there's something you wanna talk about."

Here's your chance. Tell her. My mind screams at me, but swallowing it down, I go a different route.

"There's nothing wrong, Ave. Just thinking about tomorrow."

"What about it?"

"Leaving you. Same as the last time. It wasn't easy then, but after everything..." I felt my voice trail off, letting her come up with the rest.

"It's going to be impossible to let you go." She answers, understanding what I'm getting at just like I knew she would.

Unsure what to say, I just nod in agreement and focus my attention back on my breakfast, polishing it off when after a few minutes of just watching her in silence, she picks up her fork and does the same. A reprieve from the awkward silence coming a few minutes later when she pushes her chair back from the table and picks up her plate, squeezing my shoulder as she passes and heads into the kitchen.

Following suit, I shove the last bite of food into my mouth and stand from the table, heading into the kitchen and placing a soft kiss to the side of her head as I pass by on my way to the dishwasher.

"There's more, isn't there?" she asks softly, when after slipping the plate in, I shut the door and lean back against the counter.

"More what?"

"More going on than just leaving tomorrow."

"Of course not. Why would you think that?" I ask, looking away before the guilt I know just has to be staring back at her in my eyes can give me away.

"You're lying." She accuses and reaching out and running her hand along my face, she uses my own feelings against me when as I start to turn into her touch, she grips me and pull my face the rest of the way, staring me down.

"I'm not lying to you, Ave. I wouldn't do that."

Says the guy that while not exactly lying, isn't exactly telling the truth either.

With a shake of her head and a dejected sigh, she pulls her hand back and starting to walk away, thinks better of it, turning back to face me again but making no move to come closer.

"Then you won't mind telling me again, but this time, looking me in the eyes when you do."

Determined not to screw this up, I meet her gaze and do what she asks. Telling her again and praying that as I do, she'll take it at face value the way she has with everything else I've ever told her and drop it.

"I'm not lying to you, Avery. There's nothing going on past the dread I feel knowing that in less than twenty-four hours, I'm going to have to leave you for god only knows how long."

The agreement I signed and Marie's own promise of not having another set of days off in the near future driving me now that I'm actually focusing on it. A twist in my gut over not being able to tell Avery when we'll see each other again, making what was already a painfully awkward situation that much worse.

Stepping toward her and bridging the gap she's put between us when she turned to leave, I pull her into my arms. Wrapping her up so tight and kissing her forehead before following it up with another one to her nose and then her cheeks before finally ending with one gentle kiss to her lips.

"What you're seeing is just me not wanting to leave you. That's all. I swear."

Avery

"I'm going to head up and take a shower so we can head out."

Brushing his lips against my forehead softly and releasing me from his embrace, he turns and heads out before I have a chance to respond. Again, the way he disappears from the room making me question what's going on between us.

I'm pretty sure he thinks I didn't catch it, but I know he lied to me when he looked me in the eye. What, even though we don't know each other all that well, I didn't think given our earlier interactions and how honest he was, that he had in him.

Pulling my attention away from the sound of his socked feet on the floor above, I turn my attention on putting the rest of last night's dishes away.

Back and forth from the counter to the various cabinets, I place everything away, turning my attention to the table and the mugs we left behind after finishing breakfast. Slipping my fingers through both mugs, I go to head back to the dishwasher and that's when I see it.

Jax's phone.

The first real look I've gotten at it since he tossed it down onto the nightstand the night before, and even though I've tried my best not to read into it, what hasn't seem to leave his side not once since we woke this morning.

Ignoring the pull inside to head back to the table in order to grab it and get answers to his strange behavior, I focus my attention on rinsing the cups before sliding them down onto the prongs at the top of the dishwasher. Sorting through the rest of the dishes, I take my time slowly going through the motions of setting it up and turning it on. Anything to distract me from the very real siren flashing in front of my eyes and blaring in the back of my mind at the answers I could possibly get if I just grabbed the phone.

Call it old reporter instincts or being concerned about the man I know I've fallen head over heels in love with, but despite my every attempt at ignoring the way things have changed, I can't fight the belief that all of the answers I'm after are somehow hidden in the device.

Tapping my fingers on the counter and attempting to push out the sound of Markus's voice as he explains the way things were years ago when he interviewed Jackson, along with my own fears and insecurities that won't seem to leave me be, I scan the room, looking for anything that can hold my attention.

Prevent me from doing the one thing that just like I believed Jackson was incapable of lying, I've also never been capable of.

Snooping.

Hearing the pull of the pipes before the sound of the water starting filters its way downstairs, I look to the stairs before flicking back over to the phone on the table and digging my teeth into my bottom lip, the sting of pain supposed to be enough to stop me from making what I know will be a big mistake, I give up the fight.

He never has to know. I'll just take a little peek and put it down where I found it.

It's not that big of a deal. Couples do this all the time. If he had anything to hide, surely he wouldn't have left it on the table, right?

All of the excuses I give myself all the motivation I need to cross the room to the table and pick up the phone.

My face the first thing I see when I power it up, and a picture of the both of us, looking happier than ever set as his home screen once I've slid my finger across the screen and unlocked it.

Finding the messaging app, I close my eyes and take a deep breath, giving myself the chance to abort what I'm about to do, but what I also don't do as I finally open my eyes and take in the conversations listed on the screen.

Four conversations, the one he started with me third from the bottom, with only one that he had with Brady below me. The two above the ones catching my attention most.

One from Denise, who I know to be his sister and then a conversation that bares no name. Only a number. The unknown one sitting at the very top. Like a beacon in the dark, calling to me until I can't so much as blink as I stare at the first couple of words that I see.

Read it. You've come this far.

Swallowing down the lump of guilt that's building, I tap the screen and open the conversation. One single chat bubble waiting, with what looks to be no response from his end.

Only when I've processed the fact that he hasn't responded, do I finally read what the person has written. The time stamp when I'm done reading along with the words, telling me everything I need to know about the way the last twenty-four hours have gone.

Been thinking about you a lot today. Wanted to touch base. Miss you babe. XOXO

Seeing the words, I don't need to have a name at the top of the screen to know who sent it. The only person I can imagine sending him words like these and what she ended the message with being Melinda.

Closing out of the app and tossing the phone back down on the table, I turn away. Almost as if in doing it, I can make my eyes unsee what they've read, when the reality is, I don't think now that I've seen them, felt them, I'll ever forget.

Jax pulling away, his flippant answers when I ask if there's something going on and the way he can't wait to leave the room to get away from me. It's never been clearer what's going on.

I was right all along. I was being used. Lied to. Made a fool of.

Way to go, Avery. You're an idiot.

Not wanting to give into the hurt at seeing the message on his phone, but unable to stand here with it just a foot away still calling to me the same way I did before, I slip my way around the table and head out into the living room. Moving as quickly as I can until I've escaped the stifling air of the kitchen altogether.

Throwing myself down onto the sofa, I lean back right at the exact moment that my phone, which I had left on the end table when I'd come down earlier, begins to ring. Swallowing down the sinking feeling that floods me, I lean forward and grab it, seeing Emery's name flashing across the screen.

Is this some kind of twin ESP? Did she sense I needed her?

Knowing the only way I'm going to get the answers I want is to answer, I hit talk as I lean back into the softness of the cushions.

"Emery, I'm so glad you called. I—"

Calling my name, her voice hitching and then shaking, she cuts me off.

"Ave...you need to come home."

"Why? What's going on? Emery, why do you sound like you've been crying?"

"Avery," she starts again and just like before her voice chokes on the sob I can hear her trying to hold back. One that as she takes a breath and starts to say my name again, she loses her fight with as it falls out. The sound of her crying so openly causing my own eyes to well up.

"What is it, Emery?"

"It's Mom. You need to come home. Ave, she—she's..."

"She's what?" I practically yell into the phone, which judging by the sound of the sniffles I hear only makes things worse. "What's wrong with her?"

"Avery, you need to come home." She repeats before finally dropping the bomb that makes the tears I've already been trying to keep down, finally fall.

"She's gone. Mom's gone."

Chapter Forty-One

Jax

I don't know how much more of this I can take before I snap.

Avery's been mute since I begged her to let me take her to the airport and with only a couple of minutes remaining before the turn off, I need to do something to change it. Fast.

With everything that happened before we left the house, I can't let it all end this way.

"Will you talk to me, please?"

Refusing to look at me, but not even trying to hide her obvious disdain, she rolls her eyes, while continuing to keep her attention trained out the window. The sight of it what finally has me losing what's left of my patience as I slam my hand off the wheel with a defeated and depressed sigh.

"I can't fucking win." I whisper under my breath and that's when she finally does it.

"What's there to talk about, Jax? Before Emery called, you spent the majority of the morning completely zoned out. After being shut down every time I tried to get you to open up, I finally stopped. I gave you the quiet you obviously wanted and now suddenly, that's a problem?"

I deserve that. All of it. How cold she's being, I earned it.

"I'm sorry, alright? I really am. I've had a lot on my mind and I didn't want to burden you with it. Especially not now. Not after Emery's call."

Grunting with what I could have sworn was a curse muttered under her breath, hating that because of my reaction to one stupid text message, I caused her to feel like this, especially now, I do the only thing I can to rectify it.

Seeing the opening in traffic leading toward the airport, I flip the blinker and merge over three lanes of traffic until we're as far away from it as we can get. Not stopping until I've pulled us over to the shoulder of the road.

I've got maybe thirty minutes to get to the airport and I'll be damned if I spend them completely drenched in silence. If Avery isn't going to talk on her own, I'm going to force it.

Never let her walk away angry, Jackson. No matter what situation you find yourself in or the reason for it, always find a way to talk through it. Never give yourself a reason to have regrets.

It's been a long time since I've had to use my mother's advice, but right now, with the situation I find myself in, it's almost as though her words were designed for it. Like somehow she knew I was going to need them.

Running my hand nervously over my face while stealing glances at the woman I love, catching the pain etched into her tired eyes, along with the rigid stance of her body, I swallow down any residual feelings I have about what me pulling over like this is going to cause and go to speak. But before I can, she beats me to it.

"What are you doing, Jax?"

"What does it look like? We need to talk."

"About what exactly?"

"This. Us. What's really going on."

Avery laughs, but not the way I've heard her do in the past. It's the kind of laugh that you do when you're uncomfortable, or like she is right now, upset. As beautiful as she can make any noise she makes sound, in this instance it's all kinds of wrong. There's nothing beautiful or sweet about it.

It's fake. The one thing I know she isn't.

"You really are hilarious, Jackson."

Despite my need not to feed into this, or worse, upset her even more, I can't seem to help it. I need to know what the hell she means.

"You wanna fill me in on what you think is funny?"

"Well gee, Jackson, I don't know. How about the fact that you spent the morning ignoring me. Then, when I ask you what's going on, you shut me out and shut yourself down even more. You expect me to believe you're not having second thoughts about what happened, and that you don't regret the last couple of weeks, but even now with that pitiful look you're wearing, you're telling me otherwise."

"Ave—" I attempt to stop her, but freeze when her hand flies up between us.

"And if that wasn't enough, I get a call from my sister telling me that the time I thought I was going to have with our mom, the years I still hoped I would have so we could make up for all this lost time, well, that's been taken away too. She's been taken away."

Having spent time with Avery, hearing her out as she explained what she wanted now that she'd found her sister and mother again, I know she wanted more time. That even though they lived in two different parts of the world, she was determined to come up with a way to make it all work so they'd be a real family again. Even knowing her mom was sick, she held out hope that the reunion between the three would make things better.

With Rebecca passing though, all it did was take an already fragile situation and make it worse. So with no other words coming, I go with the ones I hope will be able to break through until I can come up with ones that can.

"I love you."

Please, God. Let this work.

"Jackson," she sighs. "Just take me to the airport."

Well, so much for that. Looks like forcing her hand it is.

"How many times am I going to have to tell you I don't regret our time together for it to sink in, Ave?"

"At least once more." She snaps angrily.

"Is this really how you want to leave things? Get on a plane and go back to Delaware alone? Because you know, if that's the way you want it, I do have places to be where I'm actually needed."

I don't know if it's her upset tangling with my own that's causing me to speak before I've thought everything out, but now that I've gone and put my foot in my mouth, Avery flinching at my words, there's no going back.

I've stepped in a pile of shit and now I've gotta deal with the fallout.

"Well, don't let me stop you. Do us both a favor and just go. I was handling things just fine on my own. I can do it again."

Holy shit. I need to slam on the brakes. Stop this before she says something I know she's going to regret later. Something we both will.

When I said I loved her, I meant it. I can't let the emotional rollercoaster we're on right now make us lose sight of that.

"You don't mean that."

"Yeah, Jax. I do. I need to be at the airport and on a plane in order to console my sister and make plans to bury my mother. And you, well, you've got shows and other obligations you need to fulfill. Coming to Delaware with me isn't one of them. So maybe," she pauses, wiping at her eyes with the back of her sleeve. "Maybe it's time we call yesterday, this past couple of weeks, what it really is and move on."

"And what exactly was it to you?"

"A distraction, albeit a fun one. A use of poor judgment on both our parts. Nothing more than a fun mistake."

Hell-fucking-no. I'm not going to sit here and let her belittle what we have. What we are. Not when I know for a fact that she doesn't mean it.

There's more going on here. Something she's not saying that has nothing to do with my silence this morning and the call from Emery.

"That's bullshit, Ave. So why don't you stop trying to turn what's going on between us into something insignificant and tell me what the hell is really going on!"

There it is. The anger that served me well years ago, but that after having my heart put through the grinder had faded away with the rest of me. The backbone needed to fight for something I believe in, something I want, draining away until only an emptier version of myself remained.

It's back in full force now, which only stands to prove my earlier point.

I am *in love* with this woman. She did more than just melt and warm the ice block my heart had become. Avery brought me back to life.

"Fine!" she raises her voice in retaliation. "When were you going to tell me that you and Melinda were talking again? Better yet, when were you going to stop pretending you actually give a shit? Before or after you came home to Delaware?"

The way she seems to fall back into her seat when she's said her piece tells me so much. It wasn't Emery's call, the loss of her mom, or even my silence this morning that had her wound so tight. It was the fact that she'd seen the text and had been letting my silence about it eat away at her ever since.

Son of a bitch.

I haven't had contact with the woman since we ended things and she left CPW, yet she was still managing to screw with me and everyone I cared about.

The worst part of it all being that while Avery has it all wrong, there is one part of all of this that she's got right and I can't talk my way out of.

I let Melinda do it by keeping my stupid mouth shut.

I could love Avery every second of every day for the rest of our lives and it wouldn't mean shit because when the chips were down, instead of telling her the truth, I stayed silent.

This is all my fault.

Avery

Damnit. This is not the way things were supposed to go.

Ever since I got the call from Emery, I've been doing everything in my power to keep it together. Not lose myself in the overwhelming sadness I can already feel making itself at home in my chest. The hole that's starting to grow knowing that the time I thought I had, I didn't anymore.

I lost and cancer won.

Taking my mother away from me for the second time.

My need to stay calm and remain in control, meaning that I couldn't get into this Melinda thing even if deep down I was looking for any excuse to go off on him even before we left the house.

"How do you know about Melinda?"

"You left your phone on the table. You were so far gone from me at that point that I figured it might have something to do with work. Especially with the way you couldn't seem to let your phone out of your sight. So even knowing it was wrong, I checked your messages."

"You read my messages?"

"Yes. I know it was wrong, but I wanted answers. Considering what I ended up finding, I can't really say I regret doing it. If I hadn't then I would still be clueless to what is really going on here. What you're really doing with me."

I can tell by the scowl creeping across his face that he doesn't like what I did, so I prepare myself for the venom that's sure to follow, but that's not at all what I get once he finally meets my eyes.

He looks sad. "What I'm doing with you?"

"Yes, Jackson. What you wanted with me. What I figure you've gotten the last two nights when I mistakenly thought we were making love and connecting. Or is this where you tell me it wasn't even memorable enough to remember?"

"Avery, you're wrong. About all of it. Holy shit. You really think that everything I did over the last week was just so I could get into your pants?"

When I don't answer or give him as much as a hint to go on through my body language and facial expression, he curses under his breath.

"If I wanted sex that fucking badly, I most certainly wouldn't have wasted a week of my life chasing someone in order to get it. Do you forget what I do for a living? If all I wanted was a fuck, I could have gotten it from the ring rats. What we did was more than that. So much fucking more."

"Just tell me the truth, Jax. Was it like Brady in the beginning, when he wanted to double with twins and you just wanted to see if you could nail one of us? Have bragging rights in the locker room? A story to tell on the road? Something for you and Melinda to laugh about when you finally went back to work?"

"I can't fucking believe you're asking me this." He mumbles, shoving a hand through his hair and pushing it back from his face, allowing me to further see the hurt now lingering in his eyes.

"I can't believe you don't already know. What I said to you the day I got here and we made love, I meant. What I've been saying every damn minute since. I love you. I can't explain why or how that's even possible this soon, but it happened and you know how I know? Because my first thought this morning after you let me sleep in was how I could wake up this way for the rest of my life and never get tired of it. Dancing with you, kissing you, and then carrying you upstairs and making love to you, it was as close to perfect as I'm ever going to get. It was everything to me. You're everything to me. How do you not know that? How can you not see?"

As hard as I want to keep fighting this, him, and everything he's just said, I can't because I believe him. I feel the same. It's just not enough to erase the real reason I'm upset.

"What about Melinda?"

As soon as I ask the question, the softness in his eyes grows hard and turns darker, effectively taking what little progress he made in getting me to lower my guard and putting my defenses on high alert again.

He can try and make me believe that there's nothing going on here and that he's in love with me all he wants, but the look on his face now tells a completely different story.

"Take me to the airport. I say, finally breaking the silence. "And when we get there, change your flight. Go to work. Find Melinda and do whatever it is you two do because no matter how much you want what you said to be true, after seeing your reaction to that question, your place isn't here anymore. Not with me. I'm starting to think it never was."

With my decision final, he does what I ask and pulls back out into traffic, merging back into the lane that will take us straight to the airport and the flight back to Emery that awaits. Readying myself when he pulls the car to a stop when we finally arrive at my terminal, I unbuckle the seatbelt and shift my body as close to the door as I can get. Taking it a step further when he puts it in park and opening the door to step out, pausing only when his hand comes flying out and around my wrist to stop me.

"Don't leave."

Turning toward him but shaking my hand free of his grip, I take a minute and really study him, committing as much of him as I can to memory, knowing it's going to be the last time I see him.

Not understanding the need for it, but not having enough fight in me to stop, I reach across the seat and placing a hand to his face, a move he readily leans into as his eyes close and a soft sigh escapes, I lean in even more until my lips lightly brush against his. Letting them linger just a second before pulling away and saying the two words that this morning when I woke up, I never in a million years thought I would ever have to say.

"Goodbye, Jackson."

Epilogue

Avery

"She was waiting for you, dear. Your mother didn't want to move on until she found you."

"Your mother can finally be at peace now."

"With the way Rebecca felt about Richard, I have no doubt they are together now."

Condolences are a tricky thing. Like, what's the proper reaction when someone comes up, slips their hand over yours and repeats one of the twenty or so sentiments they probably picked up from Consoling for Dummies? Are you supposed to return their small smile with one of your own? Are you even supposed to smile or should you just dab at your eyes with a handkerchief and cry until you've got nothing left?

The way I normally am, if I'm not feeling something, I won't do it. I'll distance myself as far from it as I can get and deal in what way works for me. Something that standing here surrounded by all of these people that were friends with my mother, knew her better than I did, I can't seem to do.

So I fake it. All of it.

The smiles, the whispered words of thanks and appreciation. I look them in the eye and I just fake it all.

One week.

That's all I was afforded with my mother. Well, one week if you don't count the short period of time I had with her as a baby before my dad snatched me.

One week that wasn't nearly long enough since for a few of those days we weren't even together. Not the way I would have wanted anyway. A connection maintained through the phone nearly as impersonal as one that would have carried on through email or text.

I should have been with her. Been here.

She died and I was in Toronto. As far as you can get from where I truly belong.

"Hey…" Emery interrupts my pondering, wrapping her arms over my shoulders and hugging me close. "You doing alright?"

What kind of question is that? I mean, really.

"I want to get out of here. I've had enough."

Squeezing me a final time, she pulls her arms back and makes her way around to face me, a look somewhere between pity and sadness marring her normally brightened features.

"I'm sorry about this." She motions to the people taking up space around us. "Mom lived here all her life so she had a lot of people that wanted to pay their respects."

"It's alright, Em. It's just…if I have to hear another person tell me she's in a better place and that the better place is with our father, I don't think I'm going to be able to maintain what little composure I do have."

"I know you hate hearing it. I mean, I hate hearing it, but she loved him, Ave. She never stopped. Most of the people here know that."

The remains of the finger sandwich I'd eaten in order to acquiesce one of my mother's friends when she dropped it off earlier, swirls as my stomach tightens. I hadn't been around her all that long before she passed, but I do know Emery is right about her. She loved my father to the bitter end.

The same way that even now, with as much loathing as I have in my heart for what he did and everything he kept from me, I still do.

"Ave, can I ask you something?" She asks, moving into me as people pass, lowering her voice to an octave barely above a whisper.

"Sure."

"Have you heard from Jax?"

No. Way. I'm not doing this.

Of all days to get into this, I would have assumed this one would be Jackson Merrick free. Shows what I know.

It's been a week since Emery's call and my hightailing it out of Toronto to get here so my sister wouldn't be alone. Also a week since the text I found on Jax's phone.

I really wish I could go another week not having to talk about it. Especially since not thinking about it has been a total failure.

"No, I haven't. Even if I did, I don't think I'd have much to say."

"He called me, you know."

"Who did?"

"Jax."

Well, there it is. Knowing Jax called my sister all the ammunition my stomach needs to twist just enough for the acidic burn of the unsettled food to rise in my throat.

I'm going to be sick.

"Good for him." I say, looking around Emery and taking in every conceivable escape route I can use if she's going to continue with this conversation I'm in no shape to have.

"Don't you even want to know what he wanted?"

"Not really. What Jackson Merrick wants is no longer any of my business." I spit out bitterly, causing Emery to flinch and take a step back.

I know this isn't her fault and I'm directing all of my pain over what's transpired on the wrong person. I also know that this isn't me right now. I haven't been myself for a week. I just don't know how to rewind the tape and reset myself. Make it so that I'm not taking everything out on the one person in the world that doesn't deserve it.

I'm out my element here. Surrounded by a house full of people who knew my mother better than I did. Being expected to play this part that requires me to wear a mask, while at the same time nursing a broken heart from more than one reason. I've never been through something quite this debilitating before.

I'm sad. Heartbroken. Destroyed. Completely at a loss. I've not only lost the man I love, but my mom too, and the loss of them just continues churning around inside me until the only response I have is one filled with anger.

"I'm sorry, Em. This isn't your fault." I weakly apologize before compromising and getting back into what she wanted to tell me. "What did he want?"

"To talk about what went down with me and Brady mostly, but he also told me how sorry he was to hear about our mom."

Sure he's sorry. More like guilty.

"Oh."

"Yeah, oh." Emery repeats, turning to accept a hug from yet another person I don't know before turning back and flashing me the same fake smile that the rest of the room has been giving me since we made our way back here after the service.

God help me. I love her, I do, but I want to knock that smile off her face so bad I can taste it. Emery is supposed to be the one person here that stays real. Wearing that smile just makes her appear as fake as the rest of the people here.

The ones that when they leave here, get to go back to their happy lives while Emery and I have to learn how to breathe again without our mother, much less live.

"How can you do it?" I ask, explaining when her eyebrow raises. "How can you smile at these people when I'm pretty sure you're feeling even worse than I am?"

"I do it because even though we lost her, it's not their fault. They loved and respected her. So even though you're right, I want them to know that I'm appreciative."

"I'd appreciate them so much more if they left."

"Were you the same way when our dad—Richard," she catches herself. "Died?"

Remembering the day of my father's funeral and all of the industry people that turned out for it, an entire church full of people that didn't know shit about him outside of business, and just how alone I felt there, I nod slowly.

"Yeah, I guess I was, but his funeral was different than this."

"Different how?"

I almost forgot she doesn't know. I mean, I knew she wasn't a part of our lives, but for just a split second, I let myself believe that things hadn't gone down the way they had and we've been together all along.

"The only people that came to see my father were the clients he represented. They came, stood there while the pastor said his piece, and bolted the second it was over. No thought to who or even what he left behind when he died. No thought to me at all."

"Different." Emery surmises and I mumble a quiet agreement.

"I'm sorry you had to go through all of that alone, Avery. I wish I could have been there for you."

"Same."

"I can't go back and time and change that, but I'm here now. And I know you don't wanna hear this, but so is Jax. You just need to let him in."

Since when did Emery become team Jax? She's my sister, damnit. You don't see me going at her about Brady. In fact, I've been respecting whatever happened between them so much, I haven't so much as thought about him since she brought it up.

"Since you seem to be so pro Jackson, maybe you should let him be there for you. He probably wouldn't even notice the difference."

It's catty and childish, but I don't wanna hear about Jackson, what happened between us, or how much he cares anymore. It's not the time or place for it.

This is supposed to be a day to honor our mother and damnit, honor her is exactly what I'm going to do. In the one place I know for a fact I'll be able to.

"I'm going upstairs." I announce, leaning in and giving Emery a tight squeeze before turning my attention to the stairs and the room upstairs waiting for me.

Her room.

"I need some time alone. I need to breathe, and I can't do that down here."

"I'll come with you." Emery says, reaching out in an effort to take my hand. One I immediately pull away and separate myself from. "I don't think you being alone is what's right."

"Well, since this is your first go round losing a parent and my second, I think I'm a better judge of what needs to happen here. I'm going upstairs. I'll be back down in a bit, but please, just let me have this."

Turning quickly on my heel, maneuvering my way around the people still milling about, I break free of them and run as fast as I can. Breathing becoming easier the higher I go. The closer I get to her room and what I know will be my safe haven.

Reaching the top of the stairs and leaning against the wall, I catch my breath before pulling myself back up and heading across the hall to her door.

Twisting the knob and pushing it open, I let it fall all the way back as I take in all the changes since I was here last.

Gone are the machines that monitored her, the wheelchair no longer sitting in the corner of the room where she kept it, but gone as well. Charts, medical supplies that had filled buckets before, all stripped away until all that was left was the bed, the dresser, and the carpet that had absorbed all of my tears.

A carpet that as I make my way across it, I know will absorb another set today. Only this time, the tears different than the last.

Tears of sadness instead of joy and happiness. A sadness that will rip the hole that opened when Emery called last week apart until it's gaping. The loss of her, the lack of her scent on the air and the missing jubilancy in her voice all shoving it as wide as it can go.

My life changed the day I met her, and no matter how much I wish it didn't have to change again, as the first tear begins to fall as I look around the room, I just know it will.

Changing me until I've turned back into the person I was before love altered me.

Before I'd been given it all and had it stripped away.

More lost than found.

I suppose it's true after all.

I really *am* my mother's daughter.

Emery

To someone looking at this from the outside, I seem to be unaffected by what's happening here today. That even though it was my mom that was lost, same as Avery's, I'm not as broken by it.

It's not right in the slightest. I am just as affected by the loss of my mother and my heart is definitely breaking. I feel every bit of the loss. I was just better prepared. I knew deep down that one day it would happen.

Even if I still think it happened way too soon.

Rebecca Davis was the type of mother you wish all kids could have.

Her giving nature, big heart, and the way she would sacrifice her own well-being and happiness to ensure I didn't want or need for anything, are all attributes I think any good mother should and probably does have.

I knew, even from a young age, I wasn't always going to have that. Nothing lasts forever, no matter how much you wish that it would. So I knew one day, especially after she was diagnosed, that I was on borrowed time with her.

I'd lucked out enough to get to have her as my mother for the first twenty-five years, seeing me through everything from the first day of school, to the first crush I ever had on a boy. My first date, first kiss, first real heartbreak. She'd been there through it all.

The same way I tried to repay later when after sensing something and not feeling or acting like herself, she'd gone to the doctor and the diagnosis had been handed down.

I saw this coming.

Not that I wanted to believe it. No one ever wants to settle for what some guy in a lab coat tells you. But the more time that passed, the changes that seemed to take place, there came a point where I couldn't deny it anymore and I had to start preparing for the inevitable.

It's just too bad my mother didn't feel the same.

Rebecca didn't prepare. She didn't settle. Something tells me that until she saw Avery again, she wasn't planning on going anywhere. It was only after the two of them had been brought back together that she could finally stop, take a breath, and come to terms with the war that had been raging inside her body.

Once she brought Avery home, she could go home.

Knowing about it, living with it for the time that I did, is making today slightly more bearable. I can make it through this because like so many people have already said today, my mother is in a better place now. A place where the pain she'd been dealing with no longer exists and her soul, along with her body is finally able to be at peace again.

What might be hocus pocus nonsense to most, is truth to me.

I just wish I had some way, a magic spell I could use, or the right combination of words to make Avery see it the same way. To lessen the loss I know she's feeling. Not only because like me, she'd lost her mother, but because she'd lived through the loss of our father, and now the loss of what I know was something truly beautiful with Jax.

Standing in the doorway of our mother's room, unable to leave her alone the way she requested, I know it's only a matter of time before she sees the letter resting on the pillow where she's sitting, head in her hands, as her body is racked with sobs.

Not long until she reads it, learning exactly what our mom was thinking about—what she was feeling—in her final moments.

I've read the letter. In fact, before she died, she asked me to read it aloud so she could be sure everything she wanted to say was there. That it sounded right and captured her feelings, both before Avery was taken away and the reunion almost three weeks ago.

I know the letter off by heart, so when I hear the ruffling of the sheets, followed by the shredding sound of the envelope and the rustling of the paper that quickly follows it, as my sister's voice fills the room, my lips part and I read them with her.

My Beautiful Avery,

If you're reading this, it means I'm gone.

Now before you find yourself overcome by what that truly means, I want you to do something for me. Close your eyes, take a deep breath and pay close attention to what comes next.

When people tell you that they're sorry for your loss—and they will—I want you to do what Davis women have been doing for generations. I want you to hold your head high, look them straight in the eye, and tell them that you didn't lose a thing.

Because, sweet girl, the truth is we didn't lose anything.

In our short time together, we gained everything.

What at one point in my life seemed forever lost to me, I found again and that's what I'm going to take with me when I go.

I found you, Avery Marie Davis.

I got to look into my beautiful baby girls eyes and see that even with all of the time we spent apart that she did as I always hoped and became the woman I always knew she was meant to be.

Richard and I, we made our share of mistakes in life. Often times taking roads that maybe weren't the most favorable, but the one thing that we did do right was you and Emery.

So beautiful girl, I want you to celebrate that. Not drown in what I know will come after.

Focus on the fact that even now as you sit alone reading my words, you're not alone. I'm with you. I'm just with you where it matters most. I'm resting comfortably in the biggest and brightest part of you. The part that no matter what happens in your life from here on out, will always guide you back to where you truly belong.

I'm in your heart.

Avery, stand strong. Keep fighting. Never give up.

Losing Richard and now me, can't be easy, but I'm going to need you to dig in your heels and stand tall despite the pain.

I want you to live your life hard, but allow your heart to love even harder.

Which I suppose, brings me to what I want you to hear most.

When you find the one whose heart beats for yours; the person that makes your life brighter just being a part of it, and the one that

*when pushed away, doesn't take it sitting down and pushes back
even harder, hold on to it.*

Hold onto them and let them do what they're meant to.

Transform you.

*The same way that your father and you girls have in the short
time I had with all of you, did for me.*

*Now sweet girl, open your eyes, wipe those tears, and prove to
the world just how amazing Davis women can be.*

And remember,

*Until we see each other again, I'm with you every step of the
way.*

With all my love,
Mom.

When she curls up onto the bed, pulling her legs in and
burying her face in her arms as the tears continue to fall, I know
I've stood on the sidelines long enough.

Avery has spent the better part of her life alone, and with
her loss today and the ones she's already suffered, I'm sure she
feels like she doesn't have anyone or anything left. It's time to let
her know that while she's lost a lot, even more than I have really,
she's not alone.

She hasn't lost me.

Pushing the door open just enough to be able to slide
through undetected, I make my way over to the bed, lowering
myself down to the mattress and situating my body until it's
wrapped around hers. Holding on tighter as the tears she's
crying seems to come even more powerfully than before.

"W-why?" she sobs. "Why did she have to go? W-why
couldn't I have m-more time?"

I wish I had the answers, but considering how quickly it all
happened, I was having a hard time answering that one myself.

Even if she'd given me another ten years, I don't think it would have been enough.

There just isn't enough time. Not when it comes to the people you love.

"I don't k-know." I choke up, finally letting emotion get the better of me. "I wish I did, Avery, but I don't."

"I n-never even got to say g-goodbye."

"Yes you did. You said it before you went to the city and every time you answered when she called. She knew how much you loved her and she heard your goodbye."

"I never should have left." She states evenly, lowering her hands from her face and beginning to pull away as she stretches her body away from mine. Not stopping until she's distanced herself completely and is sitting on the edge in the corner.

"Avery…"

"No, Em. I know what you're gonna say, but you're wrong. If I had just stayed here and been with her, maybe I could have stopped this."

"She had cancer, Ave. She had it for a long time. There was nothing that could be done, otherwise I would have. *She would have.* The whole reason she was at home was because she knew there was nothing else that could be done. She was readying herself. Readying me."

It's hard to admit to myself, let alone admit to Avery, because I know the words are going to hurt, but I can't and won't lie. Our mother knew the end was near and as hard as this is to accept, she did get her wish. Along with a whole slew of others once Avery came home.

She died happy.

"I miss her already and I barely even knew her."

"I miss her too."

This gets her attention as her head swivels back toward my place on the bed as the tears continue to slip out and slide down her face.

"I'm so sorry, Emery."

"For what?"

"For making this all about me. I'm not the only one that lost someone today, yet here I am pushing you away when all you're trying to do is help." She lowers her eyes, tears dripping down over the bridge of her nose and into the comforter. "She predicted it, you know."

Confused by what she means, I wait her out and when she points to the letter before reaching over and grabbing it again, I take it from her hands, looking exactly where her hand is pointing as I do and reading.

"What does finding the love of your life have to do with me?"

"It's not about the love of your life. It's about finding the person that doesn't give up. Emery, you're that person. When I'm pushing you away, leaving you alone to deal with mourners downstairs, you're not having it. You're pushing back. You're it."

Having been a part of that letter and understanding our mothers real meaning, I want to argue the point. Tell her that I filled our mother in on everything Avery wouldn't tell her about Jackson and that just like she had in her letter to me, she'd done here too.

There's no denying the person she's speaking of is Jax.

I just wish Avery could see it. Wanted to see it.

"Yeah, I guess I am." I begrudgingly agree, handing the letter over before scooting across the bed and wrapping my arms around her. "But I think she also meant someone else. Someone who could do for you what dad did for her."

"Pretend to love her, you mean?" She asks bitterly and all I can do is shake my head. That's not what I wanted her to pull from that at all.

Shit. I don't know how to do this.

I can barely keep myself afloat. All the energy I've got going into keeping me upright. There's no way I can do what my mom asked and set things right for Avery too.

"If that's what she wants, maybe I never should have come back at all."

"Avery, don't say that. If you didn't come back we wouldn't be here now. I know this is hard for a lot of different reasons, but I wouldn't give up having you in my life for the world."

Turning her body around and into mine, I prepare for the feel of her arms as they come around me in a hug. One that tightens when she's curved herself entirely around to face me.

Another round of tears flowing freely from her eyes as the reality of what I've said seems to set in.

"And that's not what she meant even though it is what he did."

"Then what does she mean?"

My mother's words from the last time we spoke come alive in my head and despite not wanting to get into it with her, knowing that it's only going to add insult to injury, they tumble out anyway. Guided by a force more powerful than my own.

Our mother.

"Make her see, Emery. Make Avery see that the love she so desperately wants in her life is already there. It's always been there. It's just buried in the blue."

To Be Continued...

Acknowledgements

It takes a village.

That's been true in the past with my other books and it most definitely is with these as well. This book, and its follow-up in *Into the Blue*, wouldn't even exist if it wasn't for some very important people. So here's where I pull a Brady (you'll see) and thank the real people that deserve it.

My mini Winchesters.

Goes without saying. There is no greater acknowledgement I can give than the one to you four. Thank you for inspiring me, pushing me and teaching me while I'm attempting to do the same with you. There is no me (at least not one worth knowing) without you. I love you. All of you. Forever and for always. You can believe that ;)

My beta-readers.

You're invaluable and none of my books would exist without you and your advice, expertise and support. You're a gigantic piece of that village I mentioned before and for as long as I'm doing this, you always will be. Thank you.

Wrestling.

I'm pretty sure this one should go in every book I write based on the fact that wrestling saved my life more times than I can count and even these days, still has the ability to do so. Without this sport (yes, it's a sport), I'm not entirely sure I'd be the person standing here today. So thank you. Whether it's the Indies, the WWE, TNA or ROH, you all impacted my life and for that and everything else you do in the world apart from the sport, thank you.

Cheryl

Let's face it. This story wouldn't have existed without you. What it was and then what it became (which in my estimation, is something even better than before), it all centers on you. Your support, your love and your undying adoration for all things wrestling and the written word. So, sweetheart, these are for you. Mordiase forever.

Joey
"But every Bonnie got a Clyde with her. Every woman needs somebody that's gonna ride with her." Thank you for being my Clyde. For being everything really. There's no better ball busting, ass kicking guard dog than you. You and me, it's an always and forever kinda thing. Love you like madness.

Reader, Bloggers & Reviewers
Now in a sense, I saved the best part of this village for last, because quite honestly, without all of you there is no me. There is no author at all. You play such a huge part in our lives—in my life, and I thank each and every one of you. Whether you like something I've written, hate it or are indifferent one way or the other; for taking the chance, you'll have my unwavering love and thanks forever. We appreciate everything you are, everything you've done and will continue to do in the future. Much love for all your faces.

About the Author

Melyssa is a mother of four from Toronto, Ontario, Canada.

She's currently working on Luke Grayson's story from *Remembering Sunday*, **Ready When You Are** and the third book in the *Black & Blue* series, **Heroine**.

When she's not writing, you can find her buried under the covers with her portable DVD player, watching marathons of Supernatural and Veronica Mars. When those aren't available, she can be found curled up in a corner with her e-reader and a plethora of books, falling in love with characters written so well she deems them her book boyfriends and girlfriends.

If you want to find her, check Facebook or Twitter (@WinchesterBooks) as she may just have an addiction to both. If those don't work you can always keep up with her progress on her personal site.

Other Works by the Author

Count On Me Series
Count On Me
Hear Me Now
Take Me With You
All My Heart
Here & Now (w/Joey Winchester)
Unbroken
What Lies Beneath

Love United Series
Holding On To Heaven
No Surrender
Wanted
Stairway to Heaven
A Light in the Dark
My Heaven (Alternate ending to Holding On To Heaven)

Before The Light Series
Hold On To Me (Michael's Story)
Absence of Light (Ryan's Story)

Standalone Titles
The Space in Between
Remembering Sunday

Coming Soon
Heroine (Black & Blue #3)
Ready When You Are (Luke Grayson's story)
Infinity (Standalone Second Chance Adult Romance)